# SPLINTER

Bronzeville Books, LLC
269 S. Beverly Drive, #202
Beverly Hills, CA 90212
www.bronzevillebooks.com

Copyright © 2023 Paul McHugh

Support copyright, support author's authentic works, and maintain
a platform for the arts.

Library of Congress Control Number: 2021949269

ISBN 978-1-952427-43-5 (hardcover)
ISBN 978-1-952427-44-2 (paperback)
ISBN 978-1-952427-45-9 (ebook)

First Edition

Cover Painting: Jim Gleeson
Book Design: Reggie Pulliam

# SPLINTER

## Paul McHugh

BRONZEVILLE™
— BOOKS —

*To the miraculous Erin Mitchell, guardian angel of*
*many a mysterious character*

# PROLOGUE

Paul Nikolaus von Falkenhorst strode out of a stationery store in central Berlin and onto an icy sidewalk. An adjutant who scurried along behind him popped open an umbrella to hold above his general's head. Before he could thrust it into place, a sprinkle of wet snow swirled down from the sky to spatter the general's peaked cap and the shoulders of his black leather trench coat.

"*Verdammt,*" Falkenhorst growled. "I tell you, this town in February..."

"*Ja,*" the adjutant, Jürgen Bosch, agreed.

Falkenhorst jammed the book he'd just bought into a side pocket of his trench, used both hands to turn up his coat collar. They stomped together through the slush to a Mercedes 770 limo that idled at the curb. Bosch opened a back door. The general slid onto the seat and wrenched the book back out. As the car pulled away, he thumbed through its pages.

At the front doors of the Kaiserhof—a hotel of sufficient quality, and conveniently close to the new Reich Chancellery—Bosch jumped out, swung the rear door wide and spread the umbrella again. They entered the building, took a lift up to the general's suite.

"What else might you require, sir?" Bosch asked, as he tugged Falkenhorst's coat off his broad shoulders, draped it over an arm, then used his free hand to accept the general's hat.

"Coffee," Falkenhorst said. "A great, big, hot pot of it. *Kaffee mit Milch.*"

Bosch hung the coat, shelved the hat, turned and saw the general sink his vast bulk into an armchair over by the window. The adjutant moved quickly to slide a hassock up toward his feet.

"Remove your boots, sir?"

Falkenhorst waved a hand as he swung his legs up. "*Nein.*"

"Anything else?"

"Do we have cigarettes?"

"A fresh pack, sir. *Nordland Schwarze Zigaretten.*"

He sighed. "*Ach.* That *Sturm* shit. Very well. Put them in my little silver case, bring that."

"Very good, sir."

The book his general had picked at the store now lay face-down on an end table. Taking a swift glance at its back cover, Bosch discovered the volume was a Baedeker travel guide. *Unusual choice,* he thought. *Are we heading out on vacation? Well, it would be a delight to have some relaxation… after the crap we had to wade through in Poland!*

"How did it go with the *Führer,* sir? I mean, if you don't mind me asking."

The general's grim visage shifted briefly to a mirthless smile. He turned his head to the window and gazed for a long moment at the flurries of sleet now relentlessly plastering Germany's capital. He swung his head back toward his assistant.

"A conversation with that military genius is always an amazing, amazing thing," he said. "But I can say, this particular chat almost turned my knees to jelly."

"Sir?"

"Apparently, the Sudetenland, all of Austria and half of Poland aren't quite enough," he said. "The Reich's horizons must now quickly widen, to the South, the West and to the North. The latter course is to be my responsibility. However, I was given no intelligence, no maps, no actual plan. I *have* been blessed with a strong infusion of our dear *Führer's* opinions. These are, in no particular order: that England now endangers our flank by preparing to occupy Scandinavia and we need to hustle and beat them to it; that on no account must I allow our iron ore shipments from the North to be threatened; and that we need U-boat bases located all the way up to the fucking Arctic Circle to keep the Bolshys and the Brits from ever linking up with each other. Oh, and I'll be given command of a mere five divisions to accomplish all this. Our innate superiority as Aryan warriors indicates I shouldn't require more. And sheer surprise is a force multiplier, you know. That, plus daring, as well as my creative initiatives, shall soon make up for any lack. Plug any holes in his genius scheme, as it were."

Bosch nodded gravely. He didn't know what to say.

"I'm supposed to appear back at the Chancellery at 1700 hours today to present my ideas for an effective overall strategy," Falkenhorst said.

He picked up the book, turned it over, pulled it onto his lap and flipped it open.

Bosch saw that it was Baedeker's guide to vacationing in Norway.

Falkenhorst turned to its map section, then scowled as he studied a page.

"Would you care for a light snack, to accompany your coffee, sir?" Bosch offered tentatively. "The Kaiserhof does serve an excellent *Zitronenkuchen*."

*"In war, what you don't dislike is not usually what the enemy does."*
—Winston Churchill, *Their Finest Hour*

# CHAPTER 1

Ice crackled like thin glass as Kristian stepped onto the deck of the *Snekka*. He glanced down, saw a maze of fault lines radiating outward from the soles of his boots. The previous night a sleety thunderstorm had raged, chased by a frost that had glazed white every plank, spar and rope on Ragnar's fishing smack.

Kristian's father had named his boat *Snekka*, to honor Norse work boats of old—*snekker*—while also making a joke. In Icelandic, *Snekka* now meant, "yacht."

*Might another rough storm hit us today?* Kristian wondered.

He glanced at the dawn sky, assessing a swollen belly of clouds that hung above Oslo Fjord, drooping far enough to blur nearby hilltops. On the east side, just one beam of quicksilver light managed to spear through the leaden horizon.

*April weather can always swing in any direction*, he thought.

He made his way astern past the deckhouse, heard the *phut* of an alcohol burner being lit in the fishing boat's tiny galley, a clatter from a metal coffee pot. Lars—the only crewman left on board—must be up. Five others had lumbered ashore at their home port of Stavanger, then the *Snekka* sailed on, aiming to deliver her load of fresh cod to Oslo, at the head of an estuary a hundred kilometers long.

Kristian climbed the ladder to the wheelhouse, pricking his ears for a sign his father was up and out of his favored bunk in the chartroom. Brittle ice kept crunching under his feet like eggshells. Then ice made a sound when he didn't step. Because someone else just had. Kristian glanced over his shoulder to see the wool-clad bulk of his dad loom up behind him.

They looked similar, this father and son, with blocky, open faces and eyes of a faint blue rendered a bit odd by a much darker limbal ring that circled each iris. Kristian, at age seventeen, hadn't yet attained Ragnar's height or his girth. It would be a while before the blond fuzz on his cheeks became anything like his father's tangled beard.

"Breakfast ready?" his father asked.

"Soon," Kristian said. "Sounds like Lars is on it. But not for me! I've got to run off to meet Helene and Uncle Otto. Remember?"

"Of course."

Ragnar kicked his heel at the deck ice to send a host of shards flying. "Not so bad," he said. "Should melt off fast." His blue eyes peered out from shaggy brows. "You feel sure about your talk with Otto?"

"Yes! If Uncle helps me to attend University, and I score a degree in biology, or business, or something, well, that's my path to a good future, right?"

Ragnar's grunt revealed some doubt. "Maybe," he said. "If you don't end up feeling high and mighty. Get some idea you're superior to a working man."

The fundamental equality of all people was one of Ragnar's bedrock axioms. Another was the supreme value of physical labor. Norway's slog through the shell-shocked economy of the 1930s had confirmed his belief that any real job had to be done with one's hands. Trustable harvests were things a person could touch and hold. All else, all too often, stood revealed as a hoax riddled with blandishments and balderdash.

"Don't worry, even while I'm at University, I'll come back and fish with you. When I can."

"We'll see."

"Can't let Helene get all of Uncle Otto's help. She's merely his ward. But I am blood."

Ragnar clawed at his curly beard and peered at him. "Aha! So, you must be a match for Helene. Is that girl the true reason you wish to go to all this trouble?"

Kristian flushed and turned his face away.

"Too shy gets nowhere ahead," his dad said, readily plucking an adage from his repertoire of folk sayings.

His son's cheeks reddened further.

Ragnar's grin widened.

A sound of distant thunder rumbled up the fjord from the sea. Ragnar turned to the southwest, studying both the dark clouds massed above the fjord and a mist that hovered low on the water. There was no need to shield his eyes at such an early hour, but from sheer habit he raised the edge of a callused palm to his forehead.

"All right then," he said. "Off with you! But come back soon. If our cargo doesn't get to market fast, we'll have to dump it off at an oil-rendering plant. Or would you prefer to spend the morning helping us shovel chips of storm ice into the fish hold? Because that's what Lars and I will be doing."

∾

Kristian jogged away from the dock where they'd gained permission to tie up overnight.

On its broad and winding southward course to the Skagerrak Sea, the Oslo Fjord narrowed like the neck of a funnel right here at Drøbak, a rural village that amounted to not much more than a single street lined by two-story houses, a few shops and a single church, before the fjord broadened again to debouch into the strait.

As he ran up Drøbak's main street, Kristian's nose and mouth puffed gray breath into the cold air like gouts from a steam locomotive's stack. He'd made it perhaps a hundred meters along the Husvikveien road when he saw them: Uncle Otto in a long black coat and knitted cap, a muffler knotted around his throat, and the shapely Helene Berg, clad in a blue wool dress with a white *lusekofte* sweater over it, and a shawl draped on her bronze hair.

"Hello Uncle. And a good morning to you, Helene, as well… "

A smooth oval face with olive skin, bowed lips and eyes of a color so tawny and pale they seemed to glow, turned to regard him from the shadow of her mantle. She awarded Kristian a cool nod.

"You only arrive now, you laggard!" Otto scolded. "Has no one told you—a man who hopes to get anything of significance done, each day he must arise with the sun?" Otto had aphorisms, too. The big difference between him and Ragnar was that Otto made up his own. They were usually lines written into his sermons.

"It's perhaps a minute after sunrise, uncle."

"*Umph.* Nevertheless, a wondrous day in history has begun! An event is about to occur that I aim for you to witness. You'll be able to boast about having seen it to your grandchildren."

"Truly?" That word of response held a dose of teen sarcasm. Kristian grinned. He dared not utter the rest of his thought aloud. *May I start on those grandchildren today, as well?* He didn't tempt fate by stealing a glance at Helene while he thought this.

"What?" Otto said, cupping a hand around one ear. His hearing wasn't the best. "Is it true, you ask? And you are what, eh, a doubting Thomas?" He shook a finger. "'Be thou not unbelieving, but believing,'" he proclaimed, a quote from the Gospel of John. Otto, a long-time deacon for Drøbak's tiny Lutheran church, loved to remind people of his high calling, his devotion to the cross and collar.

"Oh, I'm sure we'll find that you are correct," Kristian said. "As usual, Uncle," he added.

"Before this promised event, I wish to say a prayer for our nation from this enduring rock where our forebears worshiped, even back as far as the days of King Christian. Who was your namesake, you understand! So, pardon me," Otto said. He turned and stepped up onto a bare outcrop shaped like a low pulpit that poked out from the shore. He stood there with both of his leather-sheathed hands spread to the heavens.

Behind him, Kristian mimicked his uncle's devout posture. Then he squinted at his palms, as if to check on whether the heavens had sent rain or hail—or perhaps nuggets of bird droppings—to fall into them.

"Do not mock that man, not in front of me!" Helene hissed. "You're being an idiot. Deacon Thorsen has done a great deal of good. Not just for me, but for all in Drøbak. Show more respect for your uncle."

"Imitation is flattery, right?" Kristian grinned at her. "In which case, I praise him."

"You scorn a man of the cloth, and dare to make fun of prayer as well? God is not mocked! Are you so proud, so vain, that you'd risk divine wrath?"

"Interesting. How should God display his wrath today? Hurl a bolt of lightning? If it hits the trees to spark a fire, might not be so bad. Warm us all up a little."

Helene tossed the rim of her shawl back off her head to glare at him. She felt infuriated by his daring to tease her in such a way.

For his part Kristian marveled at Helene's loveliness, just as he'd done for three years. Her oval face had nearly perfect proportions, but its symmetry was disrupted and underscored by a round chin that seemed to have a stubborn jut to it. He also admired the unusual, golden tone of her skin. And that thick mane of dark honey hair that could tumble in waves down past her shoulders, whenever she let her tresses fall loose and unbound—a revelation that didn't occur often. Mostly she kept her hair tucked under a hat or bound in braids.

*Was she Dutch? Hungarian? Something else?*

Helene had been raised in an Oslo orphanage from the age of one week until she reached age sixteen. The missing tale of how her parents had delivered Helene in Norway, the reasons they put her into the hands of strangers just days after she'd entered this world—such accounts were not available. The lost intelligence was perhaps due to a missing document, a lapse in institutional memory, or most likely a fulsome indifference.

The Lutheran deacon Otto Thorsen was newly widowed. He fought to cope with an avalanche of grief, sought to transmute his pain into generosity by doing what his own pastor suggested: giving from a wounded heart to others in need. He'd selected Helene to be his ward out of a corps of potential foster children because she'd been the one that held her head up to confront him with the most level gaze.

He'd taken it as a sign of an impressive measure of spirit and self-possession. This girl excited him in a manner that he could never satisfactorily explain. He did succeed at channeling his desire for much more of her company into a formal, legal, and socially acceptable relationship.

When Kristian won his own chance to meet Uncle Otto's new ward, he felt even more impressed than Otto had been. No female, old or young, had ever aroused Kristian's interest to such a pitch. It wasn't merely her exotic, non-Nordic look that intrigued, he also sensed a fabulous depth in Helene. Beyond the lure of her appearance lay a dimension of cool control. Beneath which he detected a feral wariness. Finally, deeper, he sensed a vitality that was nearly volcanic.

Kristian felt sure that from Helene one day might burst a rare and marvelous spirit, if only she'd ever loosen up enough to release it. Whenever he saw her, a yearning to be a prime instrument of its unveiling took hold of him.

Yet on this morning, Kristian sensed that he was nearing a line that he shouldn't cross. If he did, he'd receive a blast of something unpleasant. And even less of her regard in the near future.

"All right. I'll stop." Kristian said. "Ragnar says the best way to deal with Uncle Otto is to take him lightly. So, I do."

"No! Deacon Thorsen must be taken most seriously. He's a man of principle."

"You know him better than his brother? Dad says Otto's lust for purity is foolish. Our world shall be unruly for all time. I happen to agree."

"Your father and you might be the fools. Have you considered that?"

Helene's amber eyes sparkled. Kristian always enjoyed provoking her reaction. It made him feel visible, like he could have an effect. But perhaps he should rein himself in, just now.

"We should try to be much friendlier, you and I," he said. "You know, we could wind up being roommates."

"What?!" Those pretty eyes bulged.

He smiled. "Housemates, I meant. Want to ask Uncle if I can move into your apartment in Oslo next year, so that I can attend university. After I pass the exams."

Otto had leased a flat in downtown Oslo after winning his appointment as a high school's vice-principal in Norway's capital. A sinecure that Otto saw as an achievement. However, Kristian's father Ragnar saw dwelling in any city as a peril akin to getting your leg crushed in a vise. He knew his son loved the sea, and nature, and the great outdoors as much as he did. Hence his lingering doubts about how well his son might do in Oslo.

Otto and Ragnar Thorsen grew up in rural Drøbak—then chose lives that caromed off in opposite directions. Otto, the eldest, chased success on land in urban centers, working first in civil service, then in the country's school bureaucracy.

Ragnar yielded early to the call of the sea.

The brothers retained their ancestral house in Drøbak, using it as a meeting place and a vacation home, as well as a sometime rental. Otto had made it his main domicile recently, before moving further north.

"How can you be so sure that you'll even get through university admissions?"

"Think I can't? Maybe you should help. Tutor me. A favor you can easily offer, since you're trained to teach. We could pass many lovely evenings together. Bet I could learn a lot from you."

"Now, listen! Don't want to have to repeat it. Ever." Glowing eyes fixed him in a baleful stare. "Kristian. I'm older than you. By two whole years. Sorry to say this—really, you should've already seen it. Every message I send has zero effect. So now I must be blunt. Aim your yearning at girls your own age."

"Why?"

"Had I an interest in romance—and I don't—it would be with a man I meant to wed. No boy."

"I might seem young," Kristian conceded. "But due to my harsh circumstances, I'm much older on the inside."

A corner of her mouth quirked. "*What* harsh circumstances?" she demanded.

"Well, being teased by you. That's one."

"I am not teasing, I'm rejecting. Is that not clear? Learn the difference!"

"You see? Harsh."

Uncle Otto clomped back down from his sacred rock. He tugged out a gold pocket watch by its chain to glance at the Roman numerals on its face and smiled. "In a minute or two, you shall see how our nation's security shall be mightily girded up, by the grace of God!"

"Uncle, please. What on earth is this about?" Kristian said. "May I just take a second to raise a more practical matter?"

Otto peered past his nephew's shoulder and his eyes widened. Kristian and Helene turned around to see what had impressed Otto. They too were startled by the sight of a gray-whiskered gent lurching toward them as he fumbled at buttons on an artillery officer's uniform. His tunic was completely out-of-date, almost from the previous century. And the man had evidently donned the outfit in a hurry, since legs of pajama bottoms drooped below the cuffs of his trousers, bunching above the tops of his boots.

"Hello, Stein Hansen!" Otto said. "Where are you heading, all dolled up in your antique uniform, so early on a day of glory?"

The old man didn't slow his lurching stride. "Let the idiocy drool out of your mouth once and for all, Otto Thorsen," Stein said. "After today, no patriot in Norway will ever speak with you again!"

He stumped vigorously on by. Kristian gazed after the irascible vet with an avid curiosity.

*What in thunder was that all about?*

Stein Hansen was a town character, a retired artilleryman who never tired of relating bawdy tales and scurrilous jokes harvested from his extended tenure in Norway's military.

*But Stein doesn't sound like he's joking now...*

From his dress and his direction of travel, Kristian deduced that Stein could only be heading to the Fiktiv gun battery, located a few score meters down the road, right along the Oslo Fjord's very edge.

Otto shook his head. "Anything that rickety warhorse or anyone else does to interfere with us today shall prove useless. Just asinine," he said. Then he shouted out as he pointed to the southwest, past the narrows of Drøbak, where the estuary began to widen again on its final lunge to the sea. "Look! Our salvation comes. Is she not magnificent?"

From a bank of cold mist that yet hovered low upon the water, a gray shape with a scarlet pennant on its bow rammed into sight. The massive vessel was a German battle cruiser with no good reason to be so far up a Norwegian fjord. A flapping red flag emblazoned with a stark black swastika was followed into the faint dawn light by this warship's giant turrets and long-barreled guns, its towering bridge, a pair of green reconnaissance seaplanes perched upon catapults, fuming smokestacks, then another array of large gun turrets.

Kristian gaped at it, astonished.

"She's the *Mehrlicht!*" Otto exclaimed. "Brand new. Pride of Herr Hitler's *Kriegsmarine*. Leading one of many task forces Germany sent to the ports of Norway this morning to guarantee our neutrality. Isn't she splendid?"

As Kristian stared at the battleship, his mind raced. *Protect our neutrality? By invading us? That doesn't make a lick of sense!*

He recalled the far-off booms of lightning strikes that he'd heard earlier, rumbling up from the mouth of the fjord. Now he realized that might've been the sound of a fight between naval guns and shore batteries. He thought of Stein Hansen buttoning his coat as he hurried for the Fiktiv Battery. It suddenly did make sense. A throb of primitive, tribal fervor prompted him to abruptly sprint away in the same direction. *I really like*

*Stein. If he must join a fight, I know which side I'd choose to be on!*

"Kristian! Stop! Kristian!" Otto and his ward screamed in unison.

He ignored them.

As soon as he reached the Fiktiv Battery he spotted two soldiers in far more current Norwegian uniforms. They looked nearly as young as Kristian himself, like cadets. One was untying the weather cover from a 57-millimiter gun while another struggled to heap a steel cart with shells from a newly unlocked ammunition chamber. Kristian spotted Hansen inside a half-shell pillbox, looking out through its observation slit as he spoke into a telephone handset. He slammed it down onto its hook and turned.

"*Oberst* Birger Eriksen says he might win a King's Medal, or he might get court-martialed, but as soon as that bastard is in range he shall order, 'Open fire!'"

Oscarsborg Fortress stood on a high island that clogged the narrows of the fjord like a bone lodged in a throat. Its massive Krupp cannons took 11-inch shells. Birger Eriksen, the fort's commander, was an active-duty military man. But his gun crews were an impromptu mix of veterans and recruits, hastily summoned to duty. As news of the *Mehrlicht's* arrival spread, even the fort's cooks and clerks had to pitch in to service the great cannons, now being readied to dispute the warship's passage.

Down at the Fiktiv Battery, one young artilleryman whooped in glee at Stein's defiant pronouncement, while the other froze and became pale. The one who yelled then spotted Kristian standing on the escarpment. "Who the hell are you?" he demanded.

"Just a citizen," Kristian said. "I wish to help."

"Get out of here!"

"Wait!" Hansen shouted. "Our gun requires two to work it properly. We need a man on supply."

"I'll do it." Kristian came down the steps. "Show me," he told the pale one.

"Kristian! What on earth are you thinking?! Come up out of there!"

Uncle Otto stood on the parapet steps, beckoning to him. Helene peered worriedly around his shoulder.

Stein Hansen saw Otto and scowled. "Get lost, you damnable Nazi! Or I'll blast you to scraps where you stand!" he roared. "Death to traitors!"

"But who's the real traitor?" Otto yelled back. "Maybe you!"

Hansen snapped open a holster on his belt and hauled out a horse pistol with a barrel that looked as long as a tire iron. He waved it in Otto's direction.

Otto merely put his hands on his hips and puffed out his chest. "My rank in the NS party is higher than yours in the army," he scoffed. "Do you still have a rank? Do you even know who shall be the true boss around here? From now on?"

In addition to membership in his church, Otto was also a proud member of Nasjonal Samling or NS, the "National Unity" party. Vidkun Quisling had formed NS to be a Norwegian clone of Adolf Hitler's NSDAP, or National Socialist German Workers' Party in Germany.

Quisling had once served as Norway's defense minister, and Otto's friendship with him dated back to the 1930s, when he'd clerked in Quisling's office. Quisling constantly lectured his staff about a swelling threat from the Soviet revolution. He felt certain that Stalin planned to export communism by any means, fair or foul, until he dominated all of Europe.

Even after leaving the government, Quisling had searched for an ally to help shield Norway from Stalin. He picked Germany. Under the sway of its bold new chancellor Adolf Hitler, Germany was certainly becoming a power to be reckoned with. Unlike decadent France or feckless England!

Quisling urged Hitler to take robust measures to support an independent Norway. Hitler had sent him back with a king's ransom in *Reichsmarks* to nurture development of the NS party and added a vague promise of grand measures to come.

Hitler liked to play all high cards near his vest. Now *Der Führer's* hint of partnership was coming to fruition. Based on the morning's revelations, the dictator had more than an alliance in mind.

Thanks to links at an upper level of Nasjonal Samling, Otto had been privy to secrets of the impending invasion. On this April morning, with the arrival of Nazi battleships in the major Norwegian ports of Kristiansand, Stavanger, Bergen, Trøndheim and Narvik as well as Oslo—Hitler's scheme for a swift take-over of the country became obvious.

Otto felt that peace and prosperity could rest upon Norway's fresh status as a German protectorate. It meant Quisling's stature would soar; he'd soon be the nation's top man. And of course, the status of esteemed colleagues such as Deacon Otto Thorsen would rise right alongside that of his boss.

Helene remonstrated with her guardian, frantically tugged on his coat sleeve. Otto might feel confident about the future, yet his safety in the present was by no means assured. In fact, as Stein Hansen peered at Otto through the sights of his cocked pistol, it seemed rather in doubt. Finally perceiving this, Otto permitted Helene to drag him away from the battery parapet.

That pair's departure was followed by noises of astonishing vigor—one large *boom-shriek-BLAM!* that was quickly trailed by a second. The Oscarsborg's cannons had opened fire. Waves of concussion rolled across the fjord. The air had not ceased to tremble from the passage of the huge shells when *Mehrlicht's* decks erupted in dark smoke and billowing flame. Both rounds scored direct hits, one on the ship's bridge, the other on the aircraft hangar and its fuel and ammunition supplies.

"Aaron and Moses have spoken!" Stein yelled, citing the nicknames the soldiers used for the Oscarsborg cannons. "Now it's our battery's turn. Aim high, for that superstructure. Our popgun can't inflict harm on her anywhere else."

~

Otto and Helene, guardian and ward, clutched at each other as they stood rooted upon the street, near the natural pulpit where Otto had invoked the power of the Almighty just minutes before. As he watched the *Mehrlicht* explode in flames, Otto gripped the gray hair that hung off his skull and yanked at it distractedly.

"This is a calamity!" he exclaimed. "Such an insult. Norway dares to spurn its savior… "

They could see the dark flyspecks of sailors being flung or leaping into the water from the battleship, a few of their bodies trailing wisps of smoke.

"Can we do nothing to help? To stop it, change it?" Helene said. Her voice sounded ragged and despairing.

"No, no… all wolves of war run free," Otto responded. "But we must leave! *Mehrlicht* will fire back. We can stop nothing. Our only task can be just to report what we see. Come!"

*Mehrlicht's* big guns, the ones jutting from deck turrets, remained silent. Their hydraulic systems had been wrecked by the Oscarsborg's early and accurate rounds, as well as by flames which raged through the crates of invasion materiel stacked on her decks. But the warship's medium caliber weapons, her anti-aircraft cannon remained capable. They launched an answering fire, hosing down the Oscarsborg's sprawling redoubt and peppering the Fiktiv Battery with HE shells. *Mehrlicht's* sailors had the range, their aim was perfect and their fury total.

Rounds from the *Mehrlicht* soon whacked into Fiktiv's main gun and sent scraps of shrapnel and chunks of concrete whirling about the battery like deathly scimitars. Kristian found himself on his back, with a warm and sticky substance trickling into his eyes. He wiped it away, felt the sting of torn skin across his forehead and sat up. He saw both the young soldiers had already recovered from the blast and knelt by Stein Hansen, who lay on his side with a sleeve of his tunic ripped and darkly soaked in blood. Kristian jumped up and ran to them.

"Fight on! Fight on!" the old artillery officer ordered. His message was firm, but his voice was faint.

"How?" a soldier demanded. "Our gun's out. You want us to throw rocks?"

"Yes!"

They cut away the torn sleeve and saw a gash that steadily welled with blood on the old man's thin arm. They slit the cloth of his uniform tunic into ribbons then wrapped Hansen's arm and tied it up tightly.

"Need to evacuate him before they blast us again," one soldier said.

"Is a medic team somewhere about?" Kristian asked.

The soldiers glanced at each other, seemed to mutely agree there might not be one. "Don't know," a soldier said. "We got sent here barely an hour ago."

"My father's not far away, on our boat. Let's get Stein down there. On it is a first aid box. Then we can go for help."

"All right."

They hoisted him onto his feet. Kristian tugged Hansen's good arm across his shoulders. Aided by the soldiers, he got him up to the parapet and out into the street.

Above them, another Norwegian battery higher on the ridge sent five-inch shells screaming toward the *Mehrlicht*. The warship continued steaming up the fjord at flank speed—a gray giantess who swam on with her long and tumbling locks of smoky hair interwoven with crimson ribbons of fire.

The young soldiers glanced at each other, still appearing to communicate by some form of telepathy.

"Looks like you've got him?" one asked.

"Yes," Kristian answered.

"Good. We'll join our guys up there, pitch back in." He pointed at the higher battery. "Since Hansen's last order was, we must still fight."

"Okay."

The soldier whipped off a salute, then the pair of them turned to jog away side-by-side, heading uphill.

*Did the soldier salute Stein Hansen,* Kristian thought, *or... us both? Am I a volunteer fighter now? Is my father still tied up down there, is our boat all right? Can we get back to it without being all shot up? The only thing I know is, if this is what war's like, can't say I like it. Poor Stein... that wound of his looks ugly.*

The old man sagged against Kristian's ribs and mumbled incoherently. But he lifted his head and managed to revive as they continued down the road toward the pier. They reached a gap in the shoreline groves and won a clear view of the open waters of the fjord.

"Where is she?" Hansen rasped, "That rabid Nazi bitch?"

Kristian understood. "There," he said, pointing.

"Aha! Right across from our torpedo battery!" Hansen said.

"What?"

"Look!"

Northeast of the Oscarsborg lay a smaller, lower island with an oblong gap chiseled into its shore. Kristian saw a white streak begin to arrow from the gap across blue waters of the fjord toward the *Mehrlicht's* bow, followed by another white streak aimed much more precisely at her amidships.

Both submarine missiles struck with a bass *whomp!* that sent cascades of spray high into the air.

"She's done for!" Stein Hansen exulted. "They hit the parrot!"

Kristian turned to look at him. "Sir, are you from Bergen? I mean, originally?"

Hansen's accent had indicated Bergen as his hometown. And his parrot idiom was a bit of historic lore that referenced an old shooting range on the outskirts of that city. That range had used a wooden parrot as a traditional target. Kristian had been told about it by one of his teachers who'd come from Bergen.

Hansen gave a hoarse chuckle. "You know of that? Right!"

Hansen looked about, assessed the situation, and became far more alert and cheerful now that he saw the *Mehrlicht's* doom was sealed.

"Where are you taking me?" he demanded.

"Down to my father's boat. You were wounded by a shell fragment. Your men ran away uphill to help at Drøbak's other battery."

"Quite correct," he said. Hansen looked over, saw blood on Kristian's face. "You got hurt, too."

"Only a scratch."

"That's the talk of a proper soldier!"

Guns of the battery on the ridge above Drøbak continued to boom. More shells shrieked over the fjord to the southwest, aimed for yet another German warship, one following at a distance in the wake of the *Mehrlicht*. That gray shape seemed about ready to charge from the mist also, then thought better of it and hung back to hurl its shells toward the Oscarsborg from a more secure remove.

Then came an eerie pause, as guns both afloat and ashore simultaneously ceased to fire. As the raucous din faded, a shift in wind bore a faint human sound back down the fjord to them. German sailors had finally been ordered to abandon the *Mehrlicht* before she turned turtle and sank. As men gathered on the deck of their listing vessel, they joined to sing a Nazi anthem, *Deutschland Über Alles*.

"Now, even I must admit it," Hansen said. "That is brave!"

*"Our organizational brilliance and racial selectivity shall make world domination fall to us, automatically."*
—Josef Goebbels, from *The Goebbels Diaries*

# CHAPTER 2

Among the final clumps of soldiers and sailors on the *Mehrlicht*, most sought to flee the conflagration by jumping down to a tiny flotilla of lifeboats and rafts. Then a bass *THUD* reverberated across the fjord as the warship's main ammunition magazine detonated. In an instant the ship became a steel-rimmed volcano that lofted a gout of burning fuel laced with streaks of exploding ordnance high into the clouds. Fatally ruptured, *Mehrlicht's* hull began a slow and relentless roll… and the singing of those still alive yet trapped on board became a joint howl of terror.

After the ship capsized, the scene went eerily silent.

Rigid with horror at the sight, Otto stood at a dormer window, high up in the Thorsen family home. He held a set of high-powered Zeiss binoculars in a white-knuckled grip. He lowered the field glasses. Tears tracked down his lean cheeks. His Adam's apple jerked in his neck as he blinked and swallowed.

He emitted a heavy sigh when he recalled that, even in this contingency, he'd been assigned a chore by the NS that he had to keep doing. He reached for the phone equipped with a long cord that he'd placed atop a nearby bookcase. *If there is tragedy, also there is also duty*, Otto thought. *And the one can heighten the other.*

He dialed up the suite of offices in Oslo where Vidkun Quisling's senior NS staff gathered updates on Operation *Weserübung*, the code name for the blitz of Norway by Germany's armed forces. On this April day, the *Kriegsmarine, Wehrmacht and Luftwaffe*—the navy, army and air force— had demonstrated an ability to operate at full throttle with an exacting synchronization.

Thus, the NS staffers in general spent a joyous morning as they collected, then disseminated, reports of triumphs all up and down the coast of Norway. But to their dismay, the wreck of the *Mehrlicht* could not be shoehorned into any narrative of splendid victory.

"Terrible! A grotesque development," a grainy voice at the other end of Otto's line said. "A huge setback to our cause."

"Believe you me," Otto said, "it's far more horrid to watch it happen than for someone like you to just hear about it. I can barely pry words out of my mouth to describe it. Thank God you have good news of smooth victories at other ports. The fewer casualties Norway suffers, the easier our next phase of joining hands with Germany shall be."

"True, as far as it goes. Yet this calamity in Oslo Fjord is worse than you know, Otto! Aboard the *Mehrlicht* were specially trained and equipped army commandos, Gestapo police, and SS squads. Their job was to sprint through Oslo at the landing ceremony, see to the security of the king and the parliament, also the safekeeping of Norway's gold. That mission is now in the shit-pot. Or at best, it shall be delayed. Badly!"

"Well, no one told me *that* part of the plan. Glad to finally get informed. Even by you. But… with the *Mehrlicht* gone… Hmmm… Can't other ships in the convoy land a few squads south of Drøbak, then march them up along the shore? Or… why don't they order German paratroops to fly into Oslo, then have them drop into the park, right by the palace? It's very open there, they might land easily."

"Don't trouble yourself, Otto, inventing tactics for our German friends." The voice sounded amused. "Military brains far better than yours are in charge. Any recommendation to Berlin shall be generated here at the NS office. Focus on your assignment, please. Just report on what you see going on in Drøbak."

"Which is what I *am* doing." Otto huffed. "It's not clear?"

This intel operator must not be very senior. Most likely, a deskbound lout with no notion at all about the lofty status of Otto Thorsen in the NS. A stooge incapable of grasping how wrenching it was to bear witness to a violent military action—at some risk to one's own person. Had this uppity clerk ever seen a huge pistol pointed at him by a deranged old soldier? Probably not!

"Continue to perform your duty, then," the voice said calmly. "I'll pass along your Oslo Fjord info, put it into the mix. Sorry, Otto, now I go. Other calls are piling up. Heil Hitler."

The line went dead.

Otto glared at the telephone receiver, slapped it back in its cradle. *Continue to do MY duty?* he thought. *Oh, certainly! And I'll soon ask around to find out how well you do your job, insolent pup…*

~

Helene suddenly was right at Otto's elbow.

When they'd entered the house, he'd directed Helene to stay on the first floor for safety's sake. Or, if artillery shells began to hit anywhere nearby, to open a trapdoor and take the stairs from the kitchen down into the potato cellar.

But after he saw she'd come up to join him in the attic dormer, he neither upbraided her nor sent her away. Instead, he found his resolve oddly bolstered by her presence.

"Gaze out at that terrible sight, dear girl," Otto said, pointing. "Fuel is leaking from the ship, it may ignite. Lifeboats can pull away. But those poor men swimming in the water? They can't escape. I fear so much for them."

"I'm sorry, sir," she said. "I grieve to see so many people hurt. Yet I also fail to understand. Why did such an ugly fight need to happen?"

"It did *not*! But Norway has always failed to heed the wisdom of Minister Quisling." Otto glanced at Helene, patted her on the shoulder as if to console her. "I said this day would be wondrous, my child, yet I spoke far too soon.

In other places, things have gone well. Yet, even in nightmares, I never thought entry of our friends into Oslo Fjord could take such an ugly turn."

Otto could not resist raising his field glasses again. Yet he also could not stomach looking at the sheets of oil, now finally erupting into red flames that encompassed the area where the *Mehrlicht* was sinking. He swept his gaze along the Drøbak shoreline. He noted human figures shuffling along the road from the Narvik battery to the harbor. He soon grasped that he was looking down at his nephew Kristian and that nasty old army gunner Stein Hansen.

With the focus knob on his optics, Otto adjusted his view more precisely. Two more men in Norwegian army uniforms stumbled up to join Kristian. Leaning on one another, the whole clump of four walked out on a pier to go on board Ragnar's boat.

Otto sucked a breath in through his teeth. "Now, that's a bad idea," he muttered.

He lowered the glasses. Except for blazing chaos around the wreck of the *Mehrlicht*, the scene seemed oddly tranquil.

Otto felt sure it wouldn't stay that way for long.

"Helene," he said, "I'm no longer vigorous, or I'd do this. Also, I must stay here to report from my post. But you, your legs are young. Here's a chore I'd ask of you. Feel free to tell me 'no.' Shooting seems to have quit, for the moment. Can you run down to my brother's boat? Tell Ragnar he should *not* sail off with those soldiers on board. He'll never reach Stavanger. The mouth of Oslo Fjord is crammed with German warships and planes. Norwegian boats interfering with any of their action have already been sunk. The smart thing is for him to stay where he is. He needn't worry. After this is settled, every cooperating citizen in Norway shall be treated with mercy and with respect by our German friends."

Helene drew herself up. She nodded. "I've hoped to help out. I'll do as you ask. Happily."

"Tell him, if Ragnar wishes to gather some good will for himself, he can just motor for a kilometer or two, and pull some of those poor *Mehrlicht* sailors out of the fjord."

She nodded.

"You're a most loyal young lady. I thank you. But if you hear cannon fire resume, turn yourself about and run straight back here. All right?"

****

Ragnar and Lars assisted Kristian in boosting Stein Hansen and the two other wounded soldiers over the gangplank, through the rail gate, and onto the deck of the *Snekka*. The fishing boat's massive, one-cylinder diesel was already warmed up enough to squirt puffs of smoke and pulses of noise up a vibrating pipe that ran from the engine room through a corner of the wheelhouse—where its muffler could function as an ersatz heater—before exiting the roof.

Ragnar noted bloodstains on all the men's uniforms, even saw a red smear on the forehead of his son. He promptly sent Lars down into the aft hold to grab the boat's medical kit.

"This day has knocked our world onto its ear," Ragnar growled to Kristian. "When shooting started, for the life of me, I couldn't imagine what kept you from galloping straight back to our boat. When I saw you come just now, I felt ready to give you a proper chewing out! But now that I see who you've brought along, I see you might actually be doing something right... "

"But first, I helped Stein's gun battery fire on the German ship!" Kristian boasted.

"He did," Hansen confirmed.

Astonished, Ragnar switched his gaze back and forth, not sure if he believed either of them. Then his attention shifted. He stared past them, at the dock. A dark figure struggled up a ladder from the water, rolled over onto the planks and stood up. The man's clothes were filthy and torn, his face sooty enough to make the whites of his eyes pop by contrast as he glared at the *Snekka*. This newcomer tugged an object from his belt. It was a Luger PO8 pistol—an officer's sidearm. He slapped it with his free hand, knocking water out of the action, and snapped the toggle link on top to load a round. He jumped over the rail and onto the *Snekka's* deck.

*"Ich übernehme das schiff!"* he snarled. *"Wir werden überlebende aufnehmen!"*

None of them spoke German, but it seemed clear this angry intruder wished to take command of their boat. No one consented to that, and so no one moved. Stein, Ragnar, Kristian and the soldiers remained stock-still, grouped in a mute, resentful knot.

*"Schnell!"* he roared. *"Binde sie los!"*

Kristian observed Lars emerge from the aft hatch. A savvy sailor and a veteran of many a waterfront brawl, Lars absorbed the situation at a glance. He set his medical box down quietly on the deck and snatched a boat hook out of a holder.

Kristian saw someone else come onto the scene. A young woman, holding her fluttering skirts up with both hands as she ran along the road out of town. To his considerable chagrin, he recognized this running woman as Helene.

Lars wound up his torso in order to deliver a blow with the boat hook.

"No!" Helene shouted. She had gotten near enough to be heard.

The German turned his head just in time to get whipped on the temple by the end of the pole. The Luger fired a shot as it flew out of his hand. The German crumpled onto the deck.

"Anyone hit?" Ragnar yelled. "No? By the devil's forked tongue! Such luck. A true blessing. Okay, let's throw this bastard back in the drink where he belongs, and get underway."

"Stop!" Helene stood on the dock, panting, her chest heaving. "Don't leave. Otto says there are German warships in the lower fjord. It's best and it's safest for you to stay right here. He'll make sure everyone gets treated properly."

Ragnar stepped over to the boat's rail and glared at her. "Silly girl, you run back and tell my Nazi fool of a brother... " he paused, then shook a clenched fist in her face. "That he is a reeking bag of shit!"

Helene stiffened and blanched. She turned beseeching eyes to Kristian, who frowned at her and shook his head.

"Cast off," Ragnar ordered.

He stomped up to the wheelhouse.

Kristian leaped past Helene to free the *Snekka's* lines from dock cleats. He heaved the gangplank onto the dock, let it fall with a hard *clang*, then put a hand on the rail and vaulted himself back aboard. Meanwhile, Lars and two soldiers hauled the stunned German officer up onto the boat's gunwale, then dumped him over into the fjord.

A slab of dark water where the German's body bobbed, low and face-down, began to widen as the boat pulled away.

Kristian and Helene found each other's eyes. They stared, faces shocked and blank, across the spreading gap.

Ragnar spun the wheel of *Snekka* and shoved her throttle forward. The exhaust stack began to cough—*tonk-a-tonk-a-tonk!*—with more urgency as the vessel pulled off from the pier.

～

Up in his dormer window, Otto Thorsen reached for the phone, set it back down, frowned, and picked it up again. He rang the NS office.

"I wish to report the murder of a German officer," he said.

"An officer, eh?" the grainy voice inquired. "Of what rank? Where and when?"

"That's all I know. Hold on just a moment… "

Otto had glimpsed other movement at the docks. He raised the binoculars. He saw Helene, wielding a pole of some kind, moving along the dock as she struggled to poke the floating body of the fallen officer nearer to the shore.

"Wait," he said into the phone. He watched Helene jump off the dock and wade into the shallows, grab the floating man by his shoulders, turn him over, and struggle to draw his upper body onto land. The man looked quite heavy. He was large, and all his clothing waterlogged. Obviously, she could not complete a rescue without some help.

"Hallo? Hallo? Are you there?"

"Got to go!" Otto said. "I will call back later and give you a full report." He hung up.

*"The overrunning of Norway proved the deadly power of the German initiative."*
—Winston Churchill, *Their Finest Hour*

## CHAPTER 3

*Snekka* rode out from the mouth of the Oslo Fjord on an ebb tide, assisted by a shove from a night breeze. Ragnar had hidden their boat in a narrow cove, then waited for hours after sundown before launching his stealth maneuver.

Big red canvas sails raised on Snekka's cargo hoist masts snared the wind, while her engine remained still and silent. As they crept along over inky waters, Kristian watched distant beams of the searchlights on German patrol boats scissor through the night. At one point he spotted signal lamps blink from the bridges of larger warships as they transmitted Morse Code dispatches to one another.

Ragnar steered as near the black land mass of the western shore as he dared. His boat remained a spectral presence. Even the whispers of chatter on board had ceased.

The boat slid out into the Skagerrak Sea, a triangular strait that linked the North Sea and the Baltic. Ragnar used a speaking tube to the engine room to tell Lars to poke an iron bar in the flywheel, give a heave, and crank up *Snekka's* diesel. They had to cruise about 140 nautical miles to pass the port of Kristiansand, and it would take another 140 to reach Stavanger—a voyage requiring some 37 hours at the vessel's modest top speed.

Unfortunately, even maintaining this pace demanded that they lighten their boat. Which meant throwing a valuable cargo of cod over the side.

Couldn't be helped. The fish would begin to spoil in another day, anyhow.

Amid their day-long layover at the hidden cove, Lars and Kristian had gotten the Norwegian soldiers all fed and doctored up as best they could. Now, under cover of darkness, they set to work shoveling fish into a woven steel wire basket, yarding it from the hold with the winch and dumping it into the sea.

When done, the pair switched between drinking coffee and relieving Ragnar at the vessel's wheel or going for naps in the bunks forward. They also talked with the wounded men about what they had experienced, discussing such orders as they'd been able to receive and act on, and what that meant about the condition of their command structure. In this manner, all on board finally began to grasp the scale of Germany's insult to Norway's sovereignty.

"A call from Oslo Command startled me out of my snoring around 0400," Stein Hansen related. "Said I had been un-retired and assigned to duty. Next, to stand by. And then one more call said I should get my butt into uniform and scurry off to our shore battery.

"Alarms had gone off up and down the coast! Our brass either shivered with their heads crammed under their pillows or ran around like chickens with wrung necks, trying to consult any politicos they could find, gather troops, dream up some general orders… "

"That's what happens when you wait too long," Ragnar said. "Norway should have mobilized months ago. But we did not wish to annoy Herr Hitler. Now, his boot comes down on our necks. And we're far from seeing the end of it." He shook his shaggy head, grimaced. "'Nothing's so bad that it cannot be worse," he said, plucking one more Scandinavian proverb from his hefty stash.

"Yes, we should've taken action years ago!" Hansen yelped. "When that paint-dauber Hitler was a loony street troll, and the whole German economy was a staggering drunk. Should've thrown a pile of *Kroner* into the most modern defenses. Sad it never seemed to occur to anyone."

"You said alarms went up. In which places, please?" Ragnar asked.

"What did they say was happening?"

"All our major ports got hit at the same time, every single one. Warships, then cargo ships. They poured crowds of armed men onto shore."

"Cargo ships?" Ragnar looked skeptical.

"Freighters that tote metal ore from Narvik and the Baltic to forges down in Germany. Usually, they dead-head back to get more ore. But this time, they weren't empty. Crammed full of troops and weapons, they were."

"Oh. Clever."

"Satanic!"

"We're closing in on Kristiansand," Ragnar observed. "You said that the Krauts invaded there, too. Maybe I ought to steer us further out to sea."

"Also, Stavanger is a port," Kristian interjected. "Our home. Where we must steer a course in from the sea. Tell me, will we go home, yes or no? Would it be smart?"

"I do own a speck of awareness of the problem," Ragnar grumped.

They looked into each other's eyes, as if at a mirror. Each knew the other's thoughts. Kari was Kristian's mother and Ragnar's wife. She partly owned and partly lived on a farm in Sola, a rural zone south of Stavanger. But the Thorsen family resided mainly at an apartment near wharves at the port. On days when her men were off fishing, Kari stayed down on the farm where she'd been born and raised. If she expected them back in port soon, she'd ride the train or a bus north to town, and so be poised to welcome them home as soon as they tied up.

But where had Kari put herself yesterday, during the tumult of the German invasion? Her farm, or the city? And what had happened to her then?

"We have more than your *Mamma* to consider," Ragnar said. "She'll always be number one for us, of course. But now we have others on our list. Stavanger has doctors. Maybe we can persuade one to come aboard to stitch up these lads. And Stein too. Then we have to figure out where to take them."

～

Three thousand meters off the ragged peninsula that held both the northern port of Stavanger and the southern farm region of Sola, lay a small, nondescript island named Ukjent Øy.

A large lump of wind-blasted rock, Ukjent Øy's distinguishing feature was a long, narrow inlet, at the end of which stood a primitive boathouse. Local fishermen knew of it, but almost nobody else. The structure was a long, low chamber of stacked and mortared native stone, barely above the max high tide line. It had a door of rugged oaken staves secured by a padlock and chain.

When Ragnar purchased the *Snekka*, rights to use that boathouse came with it. He couldn't claim to own the patch of land that it stood— or lurched—upon. But the fisher folk understood this boathouse was now Ragnar's to do with as he pleased. If he wished to knock it down and take its flat rocks to erect a chimney somewhere over on the mainland, he could. But instead he left it standing. Within this venerable pile of stones and mortar he stored drums of diesel fuel and other durable goods—a spare anchor, kegs of fresh water, ropes and hooks and glass float globes and extra lobster pots and sails and basic engine parts—so he wouldn't have to sail around the whole blasted peninsula and return to port any time he needed such an item.

Ragnar, Kristian and the crew moored the *Snekka* at this primitive outpost, unlashed a dinghy from the roof of the wheelhouse and hand-lined it down into the inlet's smooth waters. Lars and Kristian installed its brass oarlocks and pair of ash sweeps. They rowed a narrow strait strewn with white peaks of wind chop over to the mainland.

～

A day later they rowed back. A pair of Norwegian military men huddled together on the skiff's aft thwart. One, badly wounded, sat sullen and uncommunicative. Both were officers who had commanded a bare-bones and too-brief opposition to the German landing at Stavanger. When that onslaught proved irreversible, they told their soldiers to shed their uniforms and disperse through the countryside and wait out in the woods for further orders instead of surrendering to the invaders.

The Gestapo sought to hunt down the Norwegian officers who'd given that particular order. They planned to force them to rescind it.

Kristian's news was of a more personal nature.

"Sola got hit by German paratroops who landed on the airfield," Kristian told his father. "They came to the farmhouse and told Mother to give it to them. They admired its stout timbers and brick walls, and they wanted it for a command post. She argued, but they threw her out and told her to stay away. Neighbors say she left soon after for our apartment in the city. And that means, I hope, she should be now safe. I wrote Mother a note and gave it to her cousins to deliver. But I didn't know what to say, other than that we're all right. I mean, have you decided where we ought to go next?"

"Norway's ability to resist is shriveling," the senior officer put in. "Any unit still in action is beating a retreat northward. We do know Germans chased King Haakon from Oslo up to Hamar, and they're still trying to kill him with paratroopers, even with bombs and planes! We can't know that he'll escape. We do know the fighting continues from Narvik to Trøndheim, and the British and even the French are trying to help, by sending in expeditionary forces. But if our resistance is to last, we'll probably need to base ourselves far outside of Scandinavia. In our last radio contact with the Tommies, they said they'd be willing to help. Granted, England is a long trip. Maybe a risky one, captain. But can you take us over there?"

Ragnar gnawed on a large, rough knuckle as he thought it over.

"That's not a small request, and it's far from an easy voyage," he said. "Let's sleep on it, all right?"

∽

The next morning, after breakfast, most of those on board crammed into the wheelhouse and chartroom. Ragnar stood in the doorway that connected these spaces.

"The British might be still be putting up a fight in Trøndheim," he said, "but that's an even longer trip," he said. "I laid my calipers on the chart last night. Scotland to the west would be 350 kilometers or so, Trøndheim to the north much more, about 560."

"Balance that against conditions, though," Lars said. "The sea can get much rougher between here and Scotland. And on a course north to Trøndheim, we'd have islands to shelter behind if bad weather occurs."

"Possibly, that is true," the senior Norwegian officer countered. "But if the weather is good, Nazi warplanes will be aloft and patrolling along the coast. Those, you won't be able to hide from."

"So what?" Ragnar said. "We're just a fishing boat. Must be a hundred just like us that cleave through coastal waters on any given day."

Kristian held up a hand. "*Pappa*, we might not be anonymous any longer. When we took the officers away from Sola on our skiff yesterday, people on the beach stood there just staring at us. They might know our boat, and who you and I are."

"All right. But if they're good Norwegians, they won't say anything."

"But what if they're not? Quisling's supporters live mostly in rural spots like Sola," Lars offered. He was an activist and leftist, who felt driven to track both local and national politics. He even read up on world politics, whenever he could make it to a library in town. "They'd be more than willing to turn us in to the Krauts."

"Just a second ago, you sounded like you wanted us to sail to Trøndheim!" Ragnar groused.

"Everyone ought to keep an open mind," Lars responded. "I only wish to make a point."

"Well, here's one major consideration. We've got enough fuel, on board and in the boathouse, to get us to Scotland. But not enough to bring us back from there. Let's assume the Brits are thrilled to see you guys. It makes them feel so happy, in fact, that they refuel us. On the other hand, we *won't* have enough fuel right now to go from here to Trøndheim. And I can't imagine what refueling between here and there might look like. Will people on the coast share what they have, or be so upset by the Nazi invasion that they seek to hoard all of their supply?"

"*Pappa*, does it need to be either Scotland or Trøndheim? Wouldn't a third choice be sailing around Tungenes to go straight into Stavanger? Remember, you wanted to try and find a doctor."

"Yes. And that would be fantastic for you and me, since we'd end up all snug and cozy at home. But what about these men?" Ragnar swept his hand, indicating the men wearing army uniforms, including Stein Larsen in his venerable tunic. "If the Nazis have taken over the city, they'd be subject to arrest and detainment, right? And what might happen to them next? It's a bigger question than finding them a sawbones, now."

"Speaking for myself," the senior officer said, "I'm not eager to find out."

"In Britain, on the other hand, we can gather and regroup, with other Norwegian refugees," Stein Larsen said. "Make common cause with the Tommies. Then eventually join in some kind of counterattack on the Germans. That would be best for Norway and her patriots."

"But what about *Mamma*?"

Ragnar nodded solemnly. "Our Kari is strong and smart, Kristian. A woman with a true bone in her nose." This Scandinavian idiom described a person deemed to be both capable and determined. "It's why I married her. Kari can be bold, or she can be patient, whatever might fit best. She'll do the wisest possible thing. But what that is, we might have to wait to find out. It pleases me that you sent a note to her, to say that we're safe. Good work! That shall ease her mind. And I want to aim in general at safety, for all our sakes. Right now, my assessment is that we'll be safer by a huge margin if we head for Scotland. Get these men to a refuge, and let Stavanger settle down before we return. Now you know my judgment. But let's handle this in the old-fashioned way, by a vote in council. Who agrees crossing to Scotland is our best option?"

The ayes had it.

Ragnar clenched his fist and thumped the lintel of the doorway. "Done," he proclaimed. "Let's get you across the North Sea so you can begin to mix it up again, but this time, hand-in-hand with the Brits!"

~

The *Snekka* rose and plunged over meter-high swells as they sailed out from the coast and into the open ocean, steering a course for Scotland. They made a good number of sea miles, and all aboard were nearly lulled to sleep by gentle rolling of the seas and the metronomic *tonk* of the engine exhaust.

But then their boat was spotted by a German seaplane on patrol, a tri-motor BV 138 Sea Dragon.

The men on *Snekka's* deck heard the buzz of the plane's engines first. The ungainly shape of the forked-tail aircraft—resembling a Moroccan slipper with an upturned toe and two trailing laces—dropped straight down out of the sun to circle slowly around the fishing boat. It flew low over the crests of the rolling waves. They could see a co-pilot with a set of black binoculars held up to his face, staring at them out of the side of the cockpit.

"We've got wounded on board," Lars said. "Maybe I should go paint a big red cross on top of our wheelhouse."

Ragnar grunted. "How about a bullseye?"

"He has to see that we're only a fishing boat," Kristian said. "We should be safe."

"Then why aren't we fishing?"

"Good point. Want me to throw some troll lines out?"

"No. Looks suspicious if we start now. Let's say, we happen to be heading to a place where we plan to fish. Offer them a friendly wave, if you want."

"I don't."

"Should we cover up our registration? *Snekka's* name?"

"No. Won't have any meaning for them. Anyway, by now they've got our number and name jotted down, more than likely. We can change all that later. Maybe, even repaint in Britain."

The Sea Dragon lofted back into the sky. Engine noise faded.

It startled them when they next heard that sound increase again. Their surprise became shock and alarm as they saw the German aircraft dive on them from astern, a white light flashing ominously on its nose. They heard a bass stutter of automatic cannon fire. A line of geysers chased up their wake. Ragnar threw the wheel hard to port, and the splashing rounds passed a mere meter to the right. Then the plane roared overhead.

"Shit! He's after us!"

"What should we do? We can't outrun him!"

"Shoot back? What do we have?"

Snatching up their pathetic arsenal of weapons, all the able-bodied men aboard armed themselves. They resolutely took up a position on the aft deck. Stein Hansen staggered as he tried to cope with the wave motion while gripping his horse pistol in both hands. Ragnar held a breach-loading shotgun he'd seized from a locker in the chartroom. Kristian cradled a box of corroded 12-gauge shells, ready to pass reloads on to his dad. The senior Norwegian officer jacked a round into the chamber of his sidearm.

Lars stayed in the wheelhouse, with instructions to veer to starboard this time as soon as the Sea Dragon was locked on its run.

Here it came. Lars turned the boat. But the seaplane had anticipated this maneuver and tweaked its own rudder. White geysers chased them with greater precision and persistence. The men on the stern of the *Snekka* unleashed their ragged and useless volley. Before a first 20 mm round slapped into *Snekka's* fantail, Ragnar punched Kristian in the shoulder to knock him prone to the deck. Instead, his powerful and unexpected blow made Kristian stumble against the side of the boat, and he tripped over the gunwale then fell into the sea.

Kristian gasped out a great bubble of breath as his head dropped under icy water. It felt as if sharp tips of icicles poked through his clothing to rake at his skin. His mind for a second was numbed by the realization that his own father could make a mistake so ridiculous and so huge. Then his willpower surged to life and he thrashed his way back to the surface.

*Snekka* was already turning in a circle, preparing to pick him up.

The seaplane also carved a circle in the sky. A larger circuit, but a much faster one.

The aircraft drilled a fresh blast of 20mm rounds into its target, sending up dusty gouts of debris. As the plane thundered overhead, a rear-facing machine gun between the twin booms of the plane's tail also flashed and cackled.

Ragnar stood on the vessel's stern, holding a life ring, ready to toss it to his son.

Kristian saw him tumble down onto the deck.

He swam desperately, trying to get back up onto the boat. He kicked off his gumboots, thought of removing wool sweater and trousers too—but realized that would take too long, and he could still swim with them on.

*Snekka*, slowed, faltered, wandered off course. Kristian saw that puffs of exhaust smoke had ceased to come out of her stack. Every window on the wheelhouse poked up in glittering shards from shattered frames. The plane spun around in the sky to carve the boat up anew with cannon and machine gun fire.

*Snekka* began to list heavily at the bow. Kristian's whirl of inchoate thoughts narrowed to one cold calculation—her sinking bow would now be the easiest spot for him to climb back on board.

The plane circled low, not firing, as its crew assessed the damage done. Perhaps it had become time for them to conserve ammo.

Kristian clambered aboard *Snekka* by jamming one foot into the hawsehole and reaching up to grasp the carved serpent's head that Ragnar had bolted onto his boat's stem as a good-luck charm. Panting from his bout of severe exposure plus the exertion, Kristian ran up the steeply canted foredeck. Without bothering to generate an emotion about it, his brain recorded a vision of Lars slumped over the boat's steering wheel, his arms tangled in its spokes.

Kristian found his father. The aft deck was slicked by blood, pocked with holes, heaped by drifts of wood slivers. The Norwegian officer and Stein Hansen lay in limp mounds, their uniforms sliced to tatters. Ragnar was on his back. Broad crimson bands painted his chest. Pink saliva dribbled from his mouth into his beard. He gasped for air, but his eyes already were rolling back in his head. When Kristian seized the lapels of his coat and shouted Ragnar's name, the remarkable eyes came briefly back to life. They even managed to focus on him.

"Glad you got back on the boat," his father mumbled. "Sorry about all this." He emitted a wet, hacking cough. "Here's what you do. *Vær sterk. Vær nordisk*," he said. "Be strong. Be Norse." Then his eyes turned flat and vacant, his body quivered and slumped. Ragnar was gone.

Kristian threw his head back to emit a howl that mingled rage and pain and grief.

He saw the plane circling back. He fell silent. A stinking cloud of diesel fuel, burnt and unburnt, belched out of the *Snekka* and her bow lurched down to a steeper tilt. Kristian leapt to his feet. He searched quickly through the still-dry portions of the wheelhouse and cabins. He saw no sign of the other men—they had to be in the submerged portions of the vessel, and from that part emerged no sound or noise of struggle. Kristian had to be the last one left alive. Perhaps in knocking him overboard, his father hadn't made such a bad mistake after all.

Survival instinct demanded Kristian focus upon the next thing that needed to be done. He went to the dinghy and unlashed it. Just before he slid it over the rail into the water, he saw that a bullet had punched straight through the transom, beneath the skiff's waterline. He pulled off his jacket and thick woolen sweater, removed his flannel shirt, tore off a sleeve, tied a figure-eight knot in it, then pulled the fabric in back through the bullet hole until the knot stuck fast.

He redressed, went to Ragnar, patted him on the forehead as if to say a final farewell, then curled his fingers around a button off his father's coat, yanked it free and slipped it into his own pocket. He ducked into the galley, to see if any provisions were close to hand. He saw a square tin box that Lars used to store leftover pieces of bread and grabbed it.

He launched the dinghy and got into it, then shoved himself away from the *Snekka*.

The seaplane next flew a pass that was amazingly low to the water and remarkably close—its wingtip only about twenty meters off from the foundering vessel. As its propellers clattered and engines thundered on by, Kristian could see the white face of a pilot wearing a brown leather helmet, looking out at him through a side window of the cockpit. This pilot threw his head back in a laugh, and he awarded Kristian a mocking thumbs-up.

Then the plane soared on high and winged away to the east.

*"The young students in university towns are becoming impudent. We must take tough measures against them."*
—Josef Goebbels, from *The Goebbels Diaries*

# CHAPTER 4

The day after German paratroopers secured downtown Oslo, top NS party officials informed Otto Thorsen they deemed the city secure enough for him to travel up to town with Helene and move into their new apartment in the Frogner District.

Otto and his ward lugged their bulging suitcases down a narrow street to Drøbak's main commute stop on the Torggata thoroughfare, then boarded an old bus with a faulty muffler for a noisy ride up the east side of Oslo Fjord.

They found a pair of empty seats side-by-side and settled in, Helene at the window. As their bus labored up the steep ridge to the east of town, she gazed across the fjord's calm and blue waters at the hulk of a shattered Oscarsborg. Smoke twirled up from the fort's battlements, residue of the pounding the German bombers had awarded the place just after the *Mehrlich* sank. Helene recalled the roar of wave after wave of twin-engine planes, and a relentless, deafening thunder that had made the sky above Drøbak shudder for hours.

It didn't seem likely that any soldiers would have been able to survive such a vindictive reprisal. Before leaving town, however, she'd heard gossip that all the Norwegian soldiers had been able to find shelter in tunnels beneath the fort.

German aircraft still flew on missions up the fjord, but now kept their bomb bay doors shut and their guns quiet. Meanwhile, convoys of German vessels sailed peacefully on those blue waters, delivering yet more troops, arms and materiel for the Nazis' ongoing assault up through the valleys of Norway. Rumor also had it that scattered units of the Norwegian army, bolstered by volunteers, resisted valiantly at a few chokepoints to the north. But everywhere they strove to make a stand, they soon found themselves overrun.

Helene considered what Otto had told her about King Haakon. Incredibly—Haakon still evaded the advancing German forces. And he adamantly still refused to salute Quisling as premier of any replacement government. She wished Haakon would change his mind and return the nation to a semblance of normalcy. Yet, she had to admire the king's determination and resilience. She didn't wish to see him captured or coerced into submission. She *did* hope to see him accept reality, embrace the inevitable, and return to Oslo voluntarily. If he did so, he'd likely be allowed to keep his throne and help lead the nation into a peaceful alliance with Germany—as his royal sibling had done just to the south in Denmark.

Helene glanced over at Otto. His eyes were half-shut. Each of his exhaled breaths sounded like a sigh. The man was either napping or lost in thought. Even so, she felt she had to rouse him and raise a concern that had troubled her over the last two days.

"Sir?"

The lids went up on eyes that appeared poached and bloodshot. The lean face turned to her.

"I know you have much to consider. And I've hoped not to bother you. But I wonder if you've heard anything you can tell me about the *Snekka*, or about Ragnar and Kristian. Are they all right?"

Otto blinked. He scratched at his chin, then he wound his fingers together in his lap.

"It's my belief that they must've sailed safely out of the fjord." He paused. "Beyond that, there's not much I'm able to tell you."

"Oh. Well, when we get up to Oslo, could we try to telephone Mrs.

Thorsen? Kari over in Stavanger? By now, she must've heard something. From them, I mean. That's the first place they'd head for, right?"

"Um. Good. Excellent thought. We might very well attempt to see if Kari can be reached."

"Since we were able to pull that German officer from the water... We saved his life. They can't be in *that* much trouble for harming him. Can they?"

Otto worked his interlaced hands and grimaced. "It's not for me to say," he said.

"Now, Minister Quisling and the Nasjonal Samling will be in charge of things. Due to that, you probably enjoy a great influence, sir. Perhaps you could see to it that they're not arrested or treated harshly."

Otto cleared his throat, and his Adam's apple bobbed. He unwound his fingers and patted Helene on her knee.

"My child, I'll do what I can to ensure the best possible outcome for all parties. You're right, I've much to consider. And if you don't mind, now I'd like to enjoy a measure of rest. Our first days in the city are bound to be taxing."

He patted her knee again, leaned back in his seat and shut his eyes entirely.

Helene bit her lip. There was another, less important matter, but she thought they still ought to deal with it. It had begun to seriously annoy her, the way Otto always seemed to refer to her as, "my child."

It was as though the passage of years had made no difference. She was all of nineteen now, and would qualify as a trained, professional woman as soon as she could graduate. Otto should call her Helene most of the time, not just upon occasion. Either that, or his use of 'Miss Berg' might suit—that being the random last name her orphanage had picked for her. Continuing to refer to her as a child, well, that had begun to sound demeaning. It seemed like he didn't want her to grow up, or acknowledge that she, in fact, had.

~

The bus rumbled into Oslo's central transit station, then parked just north of the train tracks to disgorge its passengers. Disembarkation went slowly. Everyone who clumped down those bus steps instantly had their IDs pawed over and scrutinized by a squad that included a member of the Oslo local police force, a Gestapo officer dressed in a leather trench coat, and two green-clad German paratroops who clutched submachine guns across their chests with fingers poised on the trigger guards—as if ready to perforate any troublemakers on the spot.

Otto pulled rank and managed to hire the only waiting taxi, taking it away from an elderly couple by waving his NS membership card. They stuffed their four suitcases in its trunk, and Otto gave the cabbie the address.

"Where is everybody?" Otto asked, amazed. They drove along city streets that seemed almost deserted, except for military vehicles with black crosses on their doors and occasional squads of marching troops in steel helmets and *feldgrau*—field gray—*Wehrmacht* uniforms.

"Oh, hiding indoors, all those who stayed," their cabbie said. "We had a giant panic, due to rumors the Germans would flatten our whole city! Made for one hell of a stampede out into the woods." He chuckled. "But as you can see, it's not all that bad. In fact, with people trying to hide all their vehicles so the Germans won't seize them, my business has been soaring."

Otto laughed. "Good. But your own steadiness and calmness on this day hints to me you might be an NS comrade yourself. Is my guess correct?"

The cab driver nodded and smiled.

"Well, then, I should mention you might score very well in real estate. Ask the new authorities about the shops of the cowards who fled. Particularly, the properties owned by Jews. Seizures like that have made the fortunes of quite a few quick and clever folks in Germany!"

"An excellent idea. Shall we go halves on it?"

The men chuckled together.

Helene stared mutely out the window, a furrow between her eyebrows.

Absorbed in her own thoughts, she barely listened to the men. It seemed surreal, how much youth and brightness and vigor had drained so abruptly from the city. Where were the high school students, laughing and shouting and teasing on the sidewalks? And where her college mates, waving to one another as they pedaled their bikes to classes? The city had turned grim and still, its quiet buildings now tall, silent tombs of stone and brick. When and how could the place ever come back to life?

The cabbie dropped them off at the urban intersection of Torsgata and Odinsgata, where they discovered they had a personal welcoming party. Of a sort. Two uniformed members of *Rikshirden*—a Norwegian paramilitary group that Quisling had modeled after Hitler's brownshirts—lounged by the entrance to the apartment building. Their tunics were blue, their pants were black, and they wore the red-and-gold patches of swords laid over St. Olav's cross. They were young and muscular, with flinty eyes and joyless expressions. They looked like men prepared to conduct political discussion solely by means of blows from their truncheons.

"Good you're here, finally," one told Otto. "We have orders to bring you to Prime Minister Quisling. Our government is taking power, and the Prime Minister wishes to inform you of your new role."

The *Hird* men were civil enough to help carry their bags inside—where they piled them in a heap in the spacious entry—then hustled them into the back seat of a Mercedes sedan parked nearby.

To Otto's surprise, they were not driven to the NS office suites, but to the Handelsgymnasium on Parkveien—a recently built Trades High School where Otto had been appointed the new vice-principal. It was the post he'd come here to take. But in front of this building they found a remarkable group assembled. They saw jut-jawed General Nikolaus von Falkenhorst, commander of the German invasion force, standing next to the tall and fleshy bulk of Quisling himself. They saw a squad of gray-clad *Wehrmacht* soldiers drawn up in ranks, a bunch of *Hirden*, and a cluster of SS men in peaked caps emblazoned with their death's head insignia, looking as sleek and dangerous as a pack of wolves.

"Ah, Otto," Quisling said. "Welcome to the birth in Norway of our Great European Order! Let me introduce you to…"

But Falkenhorst had wandered away from Quisling and was now engaged in vigorous chat with the SS. Men in that group began to gesture and point up to various floors of the school building.

"Greetings, Prime Minister!" Otto beamed at his boss. "I congratulate you heartily on your victory."

"Our victory, Otto, ours!" Quisling bellowed, as he pivoted back to him. He delivered a clap on the shoulders that nearly knocked Otto down. "It's not quite over yet, but immense change is in the wind."

"I can imagine. And may I inquire, what's going on right here? Are these SS men planning to enroll in my school? Heh-heh. I should think, they earned some sort of worthy diploma when they gave their oaths to the *Reich*."

"No, no!" Quisling said. "Your school's been closed. General Falkenhorst picked this building to hold offices for German staffers. Because it's all nice and fresh and new, y'see. Not sure which branch shall work out of the place yet. He and his brass will occupy suites in the Royal Norwegian, the Grand and the International hotels. And… Don't give me that look, Otto! We're not picking on you! *All* schools in the city are shuttered, as of yesterday. Be grateful that yours will be used for offices. Many other schools, ordinary soldiers will use for barracks. Such places will take quite a beating, whereas yours should remain in good shape. And someday it might even be a school again."

"But… but… "

"Do not worry, old friend. For you, other important work shall be found. How does the role of Minister of Education and Propaganda sound? Such a minister could accomplish in Norway what Goebbels has achieved in Germany. I'd certainly consider you for that job. Either you, or Gulbrand Lunde. But you ought to make a case for me to award that post to *you*."

"All our schools? Closed?" Helene echoed. Annoyance and disbelief were mingled on her face.

"Ah, lovely Helene! I bet you have no idea how famous you've become." Quisling enthused. "Nickolaus, my dear general, look who we have here." He shouted and beckoned to Falkenhorst again, who continued to pay him no mind. Quisling turned back to Helene, lifted her chin with a forefinger and smiled down upon her as if he were the sun itself, bestowing his rays upon a blossom. "The story of you saving the life of *Oberfähnrich* Schultz from the *Mehrlicht* has made all the rounds. It's repeated in every corner. A splendid example of how the good people of Norway and of Germany can join and cooperate and solve problems. You displayed heroism of a most inspirational kind!"

"Excellent thought, prime minister," Otto agreed. "Efforts should be made to spread the tale far and wide. Of course, you know that I myself was fortunate to assist in the rescue…"

"You've even won yourself a lovely nickname by this deed, *Engel Rettungsschwimmer*," Quisling told Helene. "A bit long-winded. Germans like to hook words together like boxcars on a freight train, don't they? But it means Angel Lifeguard. Altogether charming, don't you think?"

Helene blushed. She pushed Quisling's hand down with both her own and lowered her eyes. "I know what that means, I speak German," she murmured. "But I protest, anyone facing that situation might've done as I did. Nobody should ever wish to just stand by and watch someone die."

"That victory wasn't won without difficulty," Otto interjected. "Schultz is a bulky person, and his clothes were utterly soaked. My goodness, he was heavy! But working together, I and Helene managed to drag him up onto shore in the nick of time. Then our struggle to resuscitate him succeeded, thank God."

Falkenhorst remained engaged with the SS men. But another officer, one in a gray camel overcoat, stood quite near the interaction between Helene, Otto and Quisling, quietly smoking as he observed it. He now plucked the butt of a dark tobacco cigarette loose from his ivory holder, dropped it and ground it out with the toe of his boot. He pocketed the holder and stepped over to them.

"*Engel Rettungsschwimmer*," he repeated. His voice was low and suave. "A fitting accolade. But then I think, madam, beauty such as yours could bolster the life of any man who happens to get a good look at you." He picked up Helene's right hand, inclined his head, brushed his pursed lips over her fingertips. "I am *Oberleutnant* Hans Ziegler of the *Abwehr*, at your service." Heels of his polished boots clicked together. "Our agency gathers and shares information, among other tasks. Discovering useful stories is our calling, one might say. I can help ensure your fame spreads in a way that does us all the most good."

A rattling noise, a series of harsh shouts intruded. The sounds grew steadily louder in the street below the school. All the soldiers stiffened and gripped their weapons while craning their necks as they looked about to identify the cause.

The disturbance soon was revealed to be a pair of nervy Oslo students who were marching up to the shuttered school. One beat a tin drum and the other held a placard with dripping red letters that read, *"Norge for Nordmenn! Tyskerne går hjem!"*—"Norway for the Norwegians! Germans go home!"

Lieutenant Ziegler emitted a chuckle. But Quisling's cheeks burned pink with embarrassment. Next his doughy face knotted into a snarl of revulsion. He glanced at a cluster of *Hird* men who stood nearby and jerked his chin toward the demonstrators. His mute command was, *Run down there right now and shut those idiots up!*

Smiling in glee at their brutal fun to come, Quisling's cadre of jackbooted henchmen jerked clubs and blackjacks from belts and pockets, then leapt down the steps that led to the street.

*"You may have to fight when there is no hope of victory, because it is better to perish than live as slaves."*
—Winston Churchill, *The Gathering Storm*

# CHAPTER 5

Through a frigid and interminable night, Kristian forced himself to keep rowing the *Snekka's* dinghy westward. He kept Ursa Minor, a constellation that held the bright spark of the pole star, positioned over his left oar as he raised it to make every blade plant and sweep. Each stroke would advance the boat on its long crawl toward Britain, he reminded himself. Even so, the apparently endless and incremental process provoked more despair in Kristian than hope.

Still, he persisted. Exertion kept him warm at first, even while nighttime temperatures plummeted. A bank of damp fog drifted in to hide the stars. He tried to keep his bow pointed at the same angle to the low swell in order to maintain his course.

The knotted sleeve he'd used to plug the bullet hole in the dinghy's transom had slowed the leak yet failed to stop it. Whenever the dark water rose to form an icy puddle about his feet—now protected solely by Kari's thick, hand-knitted wool socks—he had to quit rowing and use the emptied-out bread tin to fling it back out over the side. Repeated immersion began to seriously chill his hands.

He quit reaching into his pocket to touch his all-important talisman—that single button he'd torn away from Ragnar's coat—when he discovered he could no longer even feel the thing with his numb fingers.

Cold steadily accumulated in his limbs, crawled up into his body's core, and began to defeat all the heat generated by his physical efforts. Finally, its unrelenting assault blew frost deep into his chest and thrust an icy spike into his brain.

The previous afternoon, as he'd begun this solo voyage, his mind spun with dreadful images and thoughts—visions from *Snekka's* tragic sinking, the unfathomable loss of Ragnar, a recurring indictment of himself for being too dumb to grab spare boots or dry clothing or fresh water, his livid rage at all Germans everywhere. Most of all, he felt choked by fury when he thought of that sneering, laughing seaplane pilot.

He also struggled to push all such daunting visions out of his awareness, no matter how often they surged back. Instead he fought to recall and cherish the words of Ragnar's valediction—*Vær sterk. Vær nordisk!*

Eventually all of Kristian's conscious activity grew slow, then turgid, then ceased. By sunup of the following day his gelid brain had grown as silent as the unruffled surface of the sea.

He sat slumped and unmoving, leaning upon the oars, back bent, head down, his eyelids closed and their lashes frosted together, his heartbeats infrequent and his breathing shallow.

A rising sun torched away the last scraps of mist, and the ocean around the pale sliver of the boat again turned a vivid blue. By then, the cold water collecting around Kristian's feet had risen up as far as his ankles.

Then another aircraft flew over him.

It was a Hawker Hurricane fighter, with the RAF's rondel insignia marking the bottom of its wings. Or what was left of its wings—the end of the starboard one looked as though it had been gnawed away by rats, and the aircraft's entire tail and fuselage had been stippled and slashed by machinegun fire. The Hurricane flew low to the sea as it went by, its Merlin engine still twirling out a vigorous hum. The plane did not slow or circle or waggle its wings. It gave no sign that Kristian's derelict skiff had been spotted.

An hour later, seawater had nearly reached Kristian's knees. Small waves had just begun to slop in over dinghy's gunwales, threatening to finish the job of sinking it.

And then a gray vessel with colorful dazzle camouflage streaking its sides and a thick plume of black vapor shooting from its stack glided to a halt some fifty meters off from the drifting skiff. Davits swung out and rope creaked through block-and-tackle pulleys as a launch with four sailors aboard was lowered to the water.

As the launch drew near to the *Snekka's* dinghy, one sailor used a megaphone to hail the unmoving lump that sat alone on a central thwart but received no answer. They came alongside, grabbed Kristian by the shoulder to give him a good shake and to shout into his face. The young castaway looked dead. No matter how deeply they probed his cold flesh the sailors could not locate a pulse in his wrists or throat.

Despite this early phase of the war, the Royal Navy men who crewed the corvette's launch had already dealt with too many hypothermia victims to conclude that Kristian was truly deceased. Finger by finger, they pried his hands free from the oars then dragged his stiffened body over the rail and into their launch.

≈

"Can hardly credit seein' you up 'n' about just one day after we plucked you out of the sea, mate!" said the helmsman.

Kristian Thorsen stood on the tiny bridge of the Royal Navy corvette *Bramble*, a rough wool blanket draped around his shoulders, both hands cradling a mug of hot, thick cocoa. The skin on his face and hands was raw and red and his blue eyes thoroughly bloodshot, yet their gaze remained steady and hard.

"You looked pale as a marble statue when we hoisted you on deck, my friend. Absolutely knackered! Thought we'd have to berth you on our galley stove and crank up the burners to have any chance of bringin' you back."

"That might have felt good…" Kristian said slowly.

"Good to see you up, walkin' and talkin' now. Ain't quite the King's, but your English ain't half bad, y'know. Better than my Norwegian—which I have not got."

"Our school teaches it to us. We had to pick that, or German."

"By my lights, you took a flutter the proper way. Picked the champ! But still looks like hit'll take a bloody long while to sort our match out."

Kristian puzzled out the man's meaning, gave a nod of response and gulped a swallow from his mug. He'd lost count of how much hot cocoa he'd consumed since his rescue. All he knew was, although he must've consumed several liters, he didn't feel at all ready to quit swilling it.

*Bramble's* OOW or Officer of the Watch was a short man with huge set of gunnery optics that dangled from his neck and swung so low that the objective lenses nearly touched his belt. The OOW strode in off a wing of the bridge, shot them a quick glance, spent a few more seconds checking a chart spread on the table, then went back out.

"When we make port," the helmsman continued, "I want you to buy me a couple of lottery tickets, mate. How 'bout it? Be a pal! I've never seen anyone with better luck than yours. There's you, floatin' out in the bleedin' middle of sod-all, and you get spotted by one of ours. And us, if we'd not had to stop dead in the water to fix a buggered main bearin', we'd still be guidin' our convoy out instead of comin' 'bout and cruisin' your way on in. Whatever you've got, man, bottle and label it, and you'll make a fortune!"

It took Kristian a bit longer to make sense of this. "My luck was very bad, then good," he answered. "I cannot say that I make any. But if yes, I now wish to make bad luck for Germans."

"Spot on!" The helmsman grinned.

The OOW came back indoors. "Cox," he said, "Port ten."

"Port ten, aye, sir." The helmsmen spun the ship's wheel.

"Steer two-one-five."

"Steer two-one-five, sir." The helmsman confirmed.

"Look sharp for a red groaner. It's where we take on a pilot for Banff harbor."

"Aye, sir."

The *Bramble's* signalman entered the bridge to hand the OOW a paper, which he quickly scanned.

"Make, 'Received and understood,'" he said.

The signalman nodded, saluted, and left.

"It appears the Secret Intelligence Service has taken quite an interest in our guest," the officer said. He looked at Kristian. "You'll be met on the quay by some redcaps from our military police and taken in tow," he said. "You're heading to London by train. Since we've got you kitted out with spare Navy odds and ends, you may as well keep 'em. Your trousers, sweater and pullover have been washed, dried and packed. You can tote the duffle off with you. But we'll need to keep that woolen blanket. We're a bit short of them at the moment. Any questions?"

Kristian considered this, then waved his mug. "More *sjokolade*, if you please?"

*"Some say that a Jew cannot be expelled simply because he is a Jew.
But this type of reasoning couldn't be more superficial."*
—Vidkun Quisling

# CHAPTER 6

Helene and Otto struggled to not have an argument as they sat face-to-face in the new apartment. They didn't succeed. This fraught encounter offered unexplored terrain to both.

"Of course, a new prime minister should be given a chance to prove himself," Helene said carefully. "He does have a right to be treated with respect. But then, the same must be said for the youth of Norway."

"Quisling already has been quite generous to them. He's offered uniforms, training, direction, opportunity, and status. What more could he do?"

"For God's sake, I'm not talking about the *Hird!* I'm talking about those poor students. Vidkun had those *Hirden* thugs of his beat them senseless."

"They might've over-acted to a certain degree, I won't say they didn't. But they were forced to answer a provocation. Surely, as you must've seen, Prime Minister Quisling showed mercy. He brought that whole incident to a halt with a single wave of his hand."

"After those boys had been stomped to a bloody pulp, yes."

"Social change seldom occurs without a struggle. Action provokes reaction, just as Newton would have it," Otto intoned, using his preaching voice. "And, well, one simply can't make an omelet without cracking a few eggs," he added.

"Eggs? Eggs? Sir! We are speaking about human heads." Helene herself assumed a stern and professional tone, sounding indeed like someone who one day might be a schoolmarm. "Of what use is a human being if you whip him into an omelet, may I ask?"

"It's a mere figure of speech," Otto protested.

"All right. But under these circumstances? A damned poor choice."

Otto sought to reclaim the high ground. "Don't lower yourself to profanity," he sniffed.

"I'd prefer not to, sir. But if any situation rightly demanded the use a swearword, it would be this one."

"Your sympathy is wasted. They were likely only Jews, anyhow. Those snotty troublemakers."

Helene's round chin lifted. "And what if they were?"

"Jews are West Asian, you see. Not true, actual Norwegians. They simply don't belong here. Some might claim, with considerable justification, that they do not belong anywhere in Europe."

"Your policy, then, is that true Norwegians should join Quisling's *Hird*, where they can learn to bash everyone else? Club the Jews first, and next who—Catholics, I suppose? But what if those who protest are Lutherans? Loyal Norwegians and true people of faith who hate watching a flock of Germans swoop in and take over?"

"Oh, you exaggerate. Don't put words in my mouth."

"I'm not! My purpose right now is to put questions in your head. They've certainly begun to pop up inside of mine lately."

"'Simply pray, then let God worry,'" Otto said, parrying with a popular epigram from Martin Luther.

"'You're not only responsible for what you say, but also for what you do *not* say,'" Helene retorted. It was her own favorite bit from Luther. "Would Jesus stand idly by as people were wantonly abused? I think not! But today, I watched you, the Lord's ordained deacon, do absolutely nothing."

"Prime Minister Quisling knows what he's about."

"Maybe, maybe not. But do you?"

"You shouldn't have confronted our prime minister and dared to criticize him to his face. That was highly presumptuous."

"But at least I got him to stop them."

Otto shook his head. "My child…"

"And I'm *not* your child!" she snapped. "In point of fact, I am nobody's child."

Otto's face whitened. "Of course not," he said slowly. "Forgive me, however, if I tend to think of you that way. You will forever be precious to me, Helene. It bothers me more than I can say that we seem to suffer a disagreement here. If only I could persuade you to see this whole affair in the proper light…"

Helene's eyes rolled upward as though she sought divine guidance. Then she leveled her gaze at Otto and vented a sigh. She stepped to his side, patted his arm and gave him a wan smile.

"I am sorry we disagree too, sir," she said. "And all I find myself able to say to you right now is, we shall probably have to leave it at that."

She went over to a coatrack by the apartment's front door and pulled a beret, a scarf and a jacket off the ornate bronze hooks.

"Where are you going?" Otto asked.

"Out."

His Adam's apple bobbed vigorously in his throat. "Will you…"

"I'll go to the harbor and see if I can buy a fish. I'll be back to make dinner for us at the usual hour. All right?"

"Be…"

"Safe. Yes, I know."

She shut the front door quickly and firmly behind her, not quite slamming it.

～

The outside air felt crisp and cool, yet something in it held a promise that spring might finally be *en route*. Helene tilted her head back, closed her eyes and drew a deep breath in through her nose, while pretending to herself she could detect a hint of the many flowers to come. Then she adjusted the angle of her beret, stuffed her hands into her coat pockets and set off down the street.

She decided not to head straight for the harbor. A long walk might be a better remedy for her feelings. She needed to burn off steam. Otherwise, it felt like either her head or her heart or both might explode. She strode vigorously up to the rise where the National Palace dominated the west end of Karl Johan Boulevard.

The grand old palace gradually rose up before her, and the sight of it made her think about the status of the king. Current rumor had it that King Haakon refused now to even contact the Germans, much less negotiate. It was said he might try to link up with British expeditionary forces at the ports of Narvik or Trøndheim, where they had made insertions in an effort to stem the mighty German tide as it swept up the Norwegian peninsula.

Helene shook her head. German forces had romped through Poland and Czechoslovakia, which shocked France, Belgium, and the Netherlands out of their boots. Germans had secured the dominance of fascist forces in Spain and thus made an ally of that country, had annexed Austria and also united with fascist Italy. Clearly, they could not be beaten now, not in this war. Norway's only smart move would be to work out a deal, just as Denmark had. Limited cooperation, perhaps, in return for some measure of autonomy. Perhaps a compromised "neutrality," such as Sweden enjoyed.

She saw men in paratrooper green moving around the walls of Oslo's national palace. She realized then that the Nazis had possessed the nerve, the raw gall, to put machine gun nests all about this revered landmark of sovereignty and independence, blighting its carefully landscaped grounds.

*How disgusting! Rude! Why on earth were such ugly tools of death even needed in such a sacred place? All right, they'd won. But why do they need to rub our faces in it?*

Soldiers who manned the sandbagged gun pits saw a lovely Norwegian girl stride past them all by her lonesome. They waved and called out. Helene scowled, put her head down and quickened her pace.

She drew abreast of the stately colonnades of the university buildings.

Every one of them stood closed and shuttered. When would they reopen? She felt desperate to return to her classes. For her world to return to the way it had been barely a week before. She sadly had to acknowledge the prospect looked dim.

A squad of *Wehrmacht* soldiers in field gray marched down Karl Johan Boulevard, heading straight at her. Helene made a sharp right turn, went a block south. She could still hear the rhythmic clash and grind of their boots on the paving behind her. The noise made her clench her teeth. More even than the roar of a Messerschmitt overhead, that marching sound formed a theme music for the Nazi occupation.

Then she heard something new and rather odd. *Is that an accordion, for goodness sake?!*

Well yes, right over there on the entry plaza of Stortinget—the parliament building. A German soldier, four of them actually, with their helmets off and not a single firearm in view. One squeezed and fingered the accordion while the others sang Bavarian folksongs. A circle of citizens stood around, listening. *Attempting a charm offensive, are we? Well, good luck with that!* To her shock, Helene saw that one of the bystanders was a girl from her university classes. She noticed Helene, grinned, and beckoned for her to join them. Helene frowned, wagged an index finger back at her and strode on.

Now she neared the Oslo Central station. Probably high time to make another turn, go past the old Akershus fortress and head down to the harbor. Get her fresh-caught fish there at the docks, as she had planned, maybe even score a fresh-caught salmon if she was lucky, then go home.

She saw a skinny boy at the opening of a blind alley, making some scrawled marks on the corner of a building. He had a piece of white chalk in his hand and had just formed a giant V. In legs of that V he drew a large H, then put a number 7 so that it pierced the horizontal line of the H. Helene needed only a second to realize what his symbol meant. V was for victory. The rest stood for King Haakon the Seventh.

Well, if this youth hoped to provide a dose of encouragement to the city's resisters, he was certainly not going about it in any sort of brilliant manner. He was sticking up that rune in broad daylight! Also, a red watch cap adorned his head as if—boastfully or perversely—he hoped to draw attention to himself.

Helene glanced around to see if anyone else on the street had spotted this subversive act. *Well, not yet, I guess... Then* to her shock, she noticed a swaggering patrol of blue-clad *Hirden*.

The boy then dared to cross the alley, apparently to repeat his provocative graphic on its far corner.

*Got to warn him, she thought. Stop that, right now! Boy, you only make a target of yourself.*

As she tried to make a fast but unobtrusive cut across the street, she saw this lad toss a calculating look back over his shoulder. Then he smiled, turned, folded his arms, and casually leaned back against the building.

The *Hirden* patrol finally took note of him and his artwork. The four young men began to jog forward as a unit. The youth thumbed his nose at them, flung his bit of chalk at them too, then wheeled and darted into the blind alley. The *Hird* men broke into a run. Two laughed outright, feeling they had their prey cornered.

Helene froze. *Oh no, I don't want to see this again. I cannot bear it!*

Her heart felt like it had leapt to her mouth and lodged behind her teeth like a molten rock. She raised her clenched hands to her breast, overwhelmed by panic and revulsion for what was about to happen. Even so, she could not make herself look away.

Something astounding occurred instead. Other figures appeared, popping out from heaps of pallets, stacks of debris and refuse cans that lined the alley. They were a half-dozen men in dark-colored trousers and jackets, with caps tugged down low over their eyes. They fell as one upon the smaller group of *Hirden*, smashing at them with ax handles and barrel staves. In seconds, the startled NS thugs found themselves beaten flat to the ground.

Mission accomplished, the pack of ambushers exploded back out of the mouth of the alley and began to scatter. Helene saw the thin boy with the red hat yank it off his head and stuff it in his back pocket while scampering away to the right. A tall youth slanted his route to go right past her. She saw a physical confidence, a daring, in the way he moved that made her imagine he must be the ringleader. As he dashed by, she saw black hair, a quick flash of white teeth, observed him touch a pair of fingers to the visor of his cap in a salute to her.

Meanwhile, behind him, groaning *Hirden* lay sprawled all over the alley's dank cobbles.

*I should find a way to summon help for these poor injured men,* Helene thought.

Yet that idea lacked any urgency. It seemed dull and reflexive, and she immediately realized that she was not about to act on it to the slightest degree. Helene grimaced. *This feels odd. Damned odd, even!* she thought. To do nothing to help just wasn't like her. Not in the least.

*"Enterprises must be prepared, with trained troops of the hunter class, to develop a reign of terror down these coasts."*
—Winston Churchill, *memo to Gen. Ismay*

# CHAPTER 7

Kristian sat jammed next to two men in the rear seat of a sedan with metal shades covering its headlamps. Pale beams shone through slits, providing barely enough light to drive as the car swerved on a tangled course through London's blacked-out streets.

Not that Kristian could get much of a glimpse of the route he was on, anyway. Prior to placing him on the car's back seat, his escorts swathed his head in multiple windings of a blindfold. Had he not grown up on a fishing boat, such a long and swaying automobile ride without a single visual cue might've made him violently seasick. As it was, the experience only rendered him nauseous.

The big men on each side of him wore musty-smelling khakis that bore no insignia. He'd noted that detail when the military police escorted him off the train from Scotland, then these two new men had taken Kristian into their charge. Unlike those redcap military police or the sailors on the *RMS Bramble*, these guys seemed brusque and purposeful. Any sort of convivial chit-chat was out of the question.

*Like saying who they were. Or naming the place where they were taking him.*

The car ground to a halt, whereupon his blindfold was removed. Kristian blinked, and saw their driver leaning out from the window, speaking to dark-clad men with guns who stood beside a gate set in a tall wooden fence. The top of this fence was decorated with two coils of barbed wire, stretched across a long row of crude lumber 'Y's'.

The gunmen waved them through, and the sedan parked in front of a large, three-story manor house. A stonework façade distinguished some of its walls, and thick mats of green ivy draped down on others. The soldiers hustled him past an entry and down a set of stairs to a basement, where he saw plank benches on a bare floor… plus a line of barred cell doors that receded into the shadows.

"You bring me to a jail now"? Kristian asked, dumbfounded. "This is arrest?! And for what, please?"

"Naw," one soldier said. "It's your hotel, guv'nor. A cozy sort of inn, as y'might say. Special place where we get to know our visitors."

"Obey every order, do 'zackly as they say, and all should work out just peachy for ya," the other said.

Three more men appeared and took over Kristian's custody. The soldiers left. A dapper man wearing a banker's bowler hat, with a gentleman's well-trimmed mustache hovering above his thin lips, appeared in a doorway for a few seconds, gave Kristian a keen-eyed once-over, then vanished.

He decided that his wisest course would be to comply, though the things this new set of guards told him to do, Kristian found insulting in the extreme. Such as: strip and get subjected to a full medical exam, including a search of oral and anal cavities. Putting on humiliating prison garb with a white diamond sewn to its back. Having photos snapped as if he were a common criminal, in both profile and frontal views.

Perhaps it was all meant as a test of his patience. If so, he found it a severe one.

He finally was confined in a narrow cell, where he brooded about his unwarm welcome to Merry Olde England.

After hours in isolation he was escorted to a spartan interrogation room, forced to sit on a tippy, three-legged stool beneath a bare light bulb, and face a balding man dressed in full Gurkha uniform, right down to the puttees swathing his lower legs. The only non-regulation—and odd—part of his outfit was he wore no boots, but dark tennis shoes instead.

A monocle was clenched in the man's right eye socket, where it gleamed like a polished coin. The unshielded eye, with a blank gray iris, resembled a hard-boiled egg with a splotch of mold on it. Kristian thought that eye might be blind—an impression heightened by the jagged shrapnel scar that rippled over his left cheek. He found it hard to decide which eye he should look at. Both were baleful.

The man glanced down at some papers, shuffled them, and put his bleak gaze back on Kristian.

"Now see here, lad," the man huffed. "You're up to the tip of that blond quiff of yours in a quite serious matter, right? You have to be held for an indefinite period in this special unit of His Majesty's Prison Service."

"A crummy hotel," Kristian told him. "Unpleasant, to a large degree. I wish to make to you a complaint."

The man didn't smile. "I demand your actual story right now, this instant. Damn you, make it true! We know things about you that even you don't know. Try to pass a lie off, and the consequences will be quite severe. When we find a spy we hang him, you know."

"I have told all of you English a true story already. Your sailors found me adrift on the sea."

"Do you claim, then, Germans are incapable of sticking a secret agent on a lifeboat? And then observing us by aircraft or U-boat periscope while we pick him up? Do you take us for fools? What if I told you that we've managed to determine that your yarn about being a dead fisherman's son is total codswallop?"

Kristian stared back at him, unsure if he could make his own gaze as hard and unyielding.

"We had no cod," he said stiffly. "None. We had to pitch it all over the side before we sailed to Stavanger."

~

A key ground in a lock. Kristian's door creaked open. He rolled over, tugged a blanket off his face. He drowsily observed a new warder, a short, plump, cheery-looking man with sandy blond hair, shaved close on both sides but foppishily long on the top. He stood by his lonesome, nary a goon at his side for back-up. He wore neither a billy club thrust through a belt ring nor any "darbies"—Kristian had learned this nickname for handcuffs—tucked into his belt.

And below the man's khaki uniform, another one that lacked all insignia, he wore those same black tennis shoes.

This round man grinned and gestured at Kristian, his palm up, fingers curled. "Look alive, onto your feet then, lad! Rising up in the world now, y'are. Done quite splendidly for yourself. And by-the-bye, our many apologies for any inconvenience."

He beckoned for him to get up, then amiably stood aside as Kristian exited his cell. The man followed tightly behind him as Kristian plodded up the stairs from the basement. When Kristian came out into a hallway, he stood stock-still for a moment, bewildered. In a wide room before him was a row of desks staffed by tidy men and women, conversing with one another as they shoved files and stacks of paper about. He heard the ubiquitous clack of typewriters. A telephone rang. A young woman at a desk, sipping tea from a china cup, raised her eyes to him, saw him staring at her and smiled. She toasted him with her cup.

The fat man behind Kristian touched him on the shoulder and pointed to the next staircase. "Two more flights up, right? Here we go," he said.

"To a desk of your big boss?" Kristian asked. "We walk to him now, is that correct?"

"Y'mean, our man who's been your interrogator?"

"A jackass with a spectacle on one eye, yes," Kristian said.

"Oh sure, Cyclops!" the round man chuckled. Climbing the stairs made his wide cheeks turn pink. "Robbie does seek to put himself over as a thorough-going hard-case. Fancies that he's quite the finder and breaker of spies, y'know." These short sentences burst out between puffs of heavy breathing as he continued to mount the steps. "Well, we'll see about that. Haven't nabbed us a one of 'em yet, now have we. Oh well. Perhaps on some auspicious day to come, we'll turn lucky. 'Callooh, callay,' right?"

He tapped Kristian on the shoulder again, and when he turned, the round man thrust out his hand. "You can call me Tom, by the way."

~

Tom swung open a door to the mansion's top floor parlor and beckoned him inside. Kristian saw a round buffet table draped in a white cloth, set with a crystal wine carafe and goblets, a basket full of bread, a bowl of figs and apricots, assorted nuts, a platter of cheese, dried fish and sliced sausages. Every saliva gland he owned jetted a geyser in his mouth. They'd fed him nothing but vapid porridge or watery soup since the day he'd arrived. *And just how many days had that been?* He had no good idea. *But it felt like, oh, three or five or thereabouts.*

The parlor's blackout curtains had been drawn back from a large central window, and Kristian looked out upon a lush lawn, a hedge of topiary bushes growing shaggy and ragged due to neglect—as if each animal shape were receding back into its personal jungle—and beyond that he saw the perimeter fence topped with barbed wire.

A movement caught his eye. A spiraling wisp of blue smoke. A wingback chair had been set to a side of the window. Someone sitting there next to the drapes was holding a lit cigarette.

"Come on, let me introduce you to Greta," Tom said. "A guest, just like you. And also much like you, she's a graduate. Passed every one of our tests, with all her pennants flying."

As they approached, a slim blond woman leaned around a wing of the chair and smiled.

They stood before her. She had a round face, hazel eyes, straight champagne-blond hair cut in a sassy bob with long bangs that she now pushed out of her eyes with her fingers and tucked back over her ears. She wore black pumps with thin straps crossed above the ankle, dark nylons, a pleated black skirt, and a wonderfully sheer and clingy blouse of cream-colored silk which—Kristian couldn't help but notice—showed no sign at all of anything like a brassiere being worn underneath it.

"Greta, please say hello to Kris, from Norway. Kris, let me introduce this guest of ours from Belgium."

A few minutes later, following an exchange of pleasantries, Tom told the pair to get acquainted and enjoy their lunch. He'd rejoin them in a bit if he could, he said.

∼

She leaned back against the parlor's flocked wallpaper, her arms crossed. At intervals she tapped ash from her Pall Mall into an ebony ashtray at one end of the mantelpiece. She watched Kristian fill a plate, rapidly empty it, and fill it again.

She crushed out her smoke, went to the table, tipped the carafe above a wine glass and held the glass out to him.

"Something to wash it down?" she said.

Kristian eyed the glass. "*Ja,*" he said.

He sipped, nodded his head, threw the rest of the red all the way down his throat and set his glass on the table.

"Do you want more?" Her gaze was inviting.

"Maybe later."

She poured a half-glass for herself, then raised it up as if toasting him. "To you," she said. "*Du bist ein extrem attraktiver junger mann. Aber das weibt du schon, oder?*"

"Sorry," Kristian said. "I have Norwegian and high school English only. What did you say?" And he thought, *Sounded like German. Didn't know they spoke that in Belgium. But they need to speak something, I guess.*

Greta's gaze seemed a bit predatory as she studied his response. She was after something.

"Oh, I only ask if you find this place as boring as I do!"

"I did hope for better treatment from the Brits," Kristian conceded.

She came toward him, draped her left wrist sensuously over his shoulder. Took a small sip of her wine, then her mouth relaxed into a full-lipped smile.

"Not very nice, are they?" she said.

"No. Except for that man who said he was Tom. But he's only an actor. And you… Well, you seem nice enough."

"Surely you don't think I'm with them?"

Kristian was expressionless.

She shook her head.

"Degrading someone, humiliating him, that's no way to bring him over to your side, true? Look, they've still got you wearing prison clothes! So stupid." She leaned closer, put her lips next to his ear. He now detected her scent, something floral with a citrus note. It hovered like a tropic butterfly within a more general aura of strong tobacco. There was also a faint layer of hormonal sweat. Her cocktail of aromas made his head swim. He'd heard about the charms of sophisticated, urbane women. He'd even glimpsed them from time to time, strolling through Oslo. And now here was one not only within reach, but almost in his arms.

"These English are complete idiots, actually," she whispered, her voice husky. "I can teach you to outwit them. Get yourself skilled at it, and excellent rewards might come from certain other parties. These Brits haven't got the only game going, you know."

He snatched her by the wrist and squeezed hard.

After the wine glass dropped from her hand he booted it across the room and it shattered into fragments against the fireplace.

"You're hurting me!"

"So?"

She kicked him on his right shin with an edge of her shoe. He smiled, gripped her elbow with his free hand and bent her forearm backward. She kicked him viciously in the other shin, right below the kneecap. He let her go, she jumped away from him, and they stood facing each other. She rubbed her wrist then her elbow as she glared at him, then her wrist again.

"You shit," she said.

"Sorry," Kristian said.

His eyes were watering from the bolts of pain that shot up his calves, but he refused to award Greta a more obvious reaction—such as yelling, hopping about, and clutching at his legs. Instead, he stepped to the table, refilled his wine glass and tried to take a casual sip. All of his focus was required to keep his hand from shaking.

"I am so tired of it," he told her. "I wish for your attention to me when I say all these bad uses of me have to stop. Sorry," he repeated. "Can we go and talk to Cyclops now? Have all of this tomfoolery over and done? We have more important matters to get to, yes?"

"Tomfoolery." Greta arched a slim eyebrow. "*Really?*"

"My English teacher, she was indeed English," he explained. "Did I say that wrong?"

"No… No, not hardly." She shook her head, gave him a crooked smile. "Kris, you just sailed past your final test. Now, I think, you'll find that they'll treat you far better."

≈

Hours later, Robbie—otherwise known as Cyclops—drew shut curtains on the same window in that exact same parlor. Wing chairs had been shoved up into a cluster and three men sat on them: Rob, Tom, and the gentleman with the bowler who took off his hat and laid it aside. He was Stewart Menzies, the head of the Secret Intelligence Service.

"He's solid," Rob said.

"Brilliant," Menzies replied, while Tom upheld one of his own thumbs in agreement.

"Cognac?" Rob inquired.

"Capital idea," Tom responded.

Rob went to a sideboard opened it and plucked out a crystal decanter, lifted snifters off a rack, then poured each of them a few fingers and passed the globes around. Tom lit a cheroot, puffed gray fumes from it down into his snifter, inhaled them back in through his nose along with the alcohol vapors, whereupon he took on the look of a cat who had just lapped from a saucer of cream.

Menzies sipped once from his snifter and set it down by his hat.

"Here it is," Menzies said. "The Admiralty thought ship movement in early April was a German effort to break out into the North Atlantic. We now see that guess was dead wrong; those maneuvers only set up their Norway invasion. To its credit, the Royal Navy adjusted quickly, did manage to sink or damage *Kreigsmarine* vessels from Narvik to Trøndheim, destroyers to cruisers and even a U-boat. Yet the overall Hun success in Scandinavia has won them strategic ports for such battle groups and U-boats as remain. Soon they'll be able to sally forth at will to attack our northern convoys."

"Exactly as feared," Tom said. "But y'see, the Huns have also gotten 'emselves vulnerable there, in a way, at the same time. Now, that fat peninsula of Norway's usually calculated as about a thousand miles long. However, once you factor in all of its long coast, indents included, you end up with a shoreline of twelve thousand miles. That's a huge lot of estuaries, coves and promontories to guard. No way the Germans shall ever be able to cover it all."

"You're talking about insertion points, for agents."

"Indeed I am."

"Such as our lad."

"Exactly," Menzies said. "The crying need of our Sea Lords now is for accurate briefs on German shipping movements. No margin for any more errors in that quadrant. We *do* own a pianist in Stavanger with sources of fresh intel that filter in from major ports. Basically, we borrow a bit of that man's time from another entity. A nation of ruddy troublemakers to the east." He laid a finger along his nose and winked. "A fine double agent is what he is, one of our best ever. But what he lacks, which thus we lack too, is a steady and reliable W/T radio signal. We've needed to put that pianist's fist on a fifteen-watt wireless transmitter key since the day before yesterday."

"I'd guess this to be the nub of the question," Cyclops said. "Can Kristian Thorsen sneak a radio into Stavanger for us?"

"Indeed. He's a local fishing lad who knows the landscape, town and country, inside and out. He's a square peg for a square hole."

"Bloke *is* bleeding damn clever. Precocious. And rather hardened for one of such tender years. His youthfulness alone can help allay suspicion. He's motivated in full, no question about it. All our lad needs is means and opportunity."

"Add a dose of training and offer him a shot, I'd say."

"With the Section D boys?"

"Right. And should young Thorsen *not* pull it off? In that case, we just try, try again."

"*Au contraire.* I say, don't waste this opportunity. Do everything to make this first attempt work. Commit resources. Call in favors. I should think you'd want a good, quick, solid win to brag on here, old chap."

"Why's that?"

"Because of Winston."

"Aha. The grizzled cherub!"

"Who bids fair to be our new PM."

"Far better him, than Halifax."

"Better either, than Chamberlain."

"Indeed. But y'see, Churchill's begun to make noises that Britain should overhaul our Service, *en masse*, to deal with the weighty chores that confront the Realm. Perhaps even give birth to a new agency. A new and competing one."

"And sporting what sort of parentage, I ask you? Hatching what offspring? Recruit amateurs? Mere tyros? Nonsense! We're the only capable entity to hand. Effective clandestine groups can't be formed overnight, man."

"Well, I'd say we ought to demonstrate that to all parties involved. And convincingly, to boot. To preserve our bailiwick, if you catch my drift. Not permit funding or influence or personnel to dribble off elsewhere."

"Hear, hear!" The Cyclops raised his snifter.

"One can talk to Hitler. He's reasonable. Sees your point of view, if you point it out properly."
—Adm. Wilhelm Canaris, chief of the *Abwehr*

# CHAPTER 8

Helene carried a neat stack of folders up the stairs of the Handelsgymnasium to the office of Norway's freshly appointed *Reichskommissar*, the former Gauleiter from Essen, Josef Terboven. Her immediate boss, Frau Heinlein, an office manager who'd been imported from that same German district along with Terboven, had told Helene in no uncertain terms that properly performing a secretarial role here meant she should at all times remain disciplined, quiet and demure. So she dressed to fit that role, wearing a long skirt, a high-collared blouse, and pulling her bright chestnut hair back into a tight braid. Grow it out a few centimeters longer, and she'd be able to wrap that braid around her head like a proper *fraulein*.

At Terboven's office door, a uniformed adjutant thrust out gray-gloved hands to receive the paperwork from her. Through the open portal, she scored a brief peek at a German officer sitting behind an oaken desk, a thin, bespectacled man with dark, slicked-back hair and a severe expression. This was Terboven, now the Third Reich's *de facto* ruler of her country.

"*Danke, fraulein,*" the adjutant said.

"*Bitte.*" She bobbed her head.

She descended the stairs to find someone in the lobby waiting for her. Hans Ziegler, the *Abwehr* lieutenant, stood there in his gray camel topcoat, holding both hands clasped behind his back.

*"Guten Morgen,"* he said.

"Hello, *Oberleutnant* Ziegler. What brings you here?"

"You," he said, smiling. He swept a hand around to his front. It held a single red rose of bewitching perfection. "And this."

Helene couldn't help herself, she was astonished and entranced by the bloom. Such a phenomenon should be next to impossible, even late in the month of May.

"Where on earth did you find that?"

He waved his free hand. "Where it comes from is less important than where it goes, and whom it is for. I bestow it upon you to brighten your desk and our day."

She accepted his gift with a mock curtsey, then quickly detected an unnatural stiffness in the stem. It was made of wire wrapped in green paper. The bloom itself then must also be artificial. A rather intricate and convincing piece of artwork, though. It even had an appropriate scent wafting from it.

"Thank you," she murmured. "But I don't know if Frau Heinlein would let me put it on my desk."

"Oh, she will. I just mentioned it to her. She'll also permit you to go out with me to lunch."

"Really?"

"To foster good relations between our tribes of Aryan *volk*, you see." Ziegler held up a pair of fingers pressed together, to suggest near kinship. *"Deutsche und Norwegisch,"* he said.

"Is that right?"

"Absolutely." He winked. "I also told her I needed to conduct an interview with you on an intelligence matter. A more thorough background check. Best done in a casual setting. Frau Heinlein was completely in favor of that. One can't be too careful these days, you know."

∼

"How about the Grand Café?"

"What about someplace quieter? Max's, on the Solli Plass?"

"Excellent. Make it your choice, madam. Of course."

She would have preferred to walk by his side without touching. But when he picked up her hand and tucked it in the crook of his arm, she didn't pull away.

"You've done well, finding a job for yourself in the *Reichskommissar's* office," he said. "Of course, while the sparkling legend of our Angel Lifeguard endures, she can pretty well go where she wants and do whatever she pleases."

Helene blushed. "I wish everybody would forget about that."

"Oh, as indeed one day they shall. But not soon."

"As far as working for Terboven? What I truly wanted was to finish my studies at university, then start to teach," she said. "But that path leads nowhere now. You invaders have turned most of our schools into your barracks. I guess the only job to do in them now is try to teach German soldiers. Something."

"You should! And you may start with me."

"And so, farewell to that job," she continued, ignoring his remark. "And my uncle didn't get his post, either. Quisling just tossed the public information minister job to Lunde. Otto doesn't much like Lunde. I don't know how long he'll work for him. But we need a paycheck from somewhere. That's why I applied at the gymnasium. Why do you smile at me?"

"Oh, it's not you. Any mention of Quisling amuses me. That barrage balloon of a man didn't fly very high for very long. He spewed gas and lost altitude quickly. Had to resign in less than a week. He could sell Hitler and Himmler on his ability to lead. But he's not sold your people on it."

"Not yet," Helene agreed. "Perhaps, not ever."

"Looks like we need to keep him on anyway. Propped up. As a sort of figurehead."

"Or lightning-rod?"

Ziegler grinned wolfishly. "Or that," he said. "But your man Quisling lacks a degree of spine that's required in a true leader."

"He's not my man."

"A top boss needs an aura of command," Ziegler continued, "an ability to compel and direct order. For that, Terboven's the real deal. He was a Nazi gauleiter—party boss for a whole region—in western Germany. Tough customer. Won't take any guff. I predict that your protesters and resisters shall soon be astonished at how much luck they've run out of."

Helene pursed her lips, said nothing.

They passed a street roadblock formed by sawhorses painted in black and yellow stripes. Here a group of soldiers and Norwegian national police halted pedestrians, cyclists and vehicles to check papers and perform inspections. As soon as they noted Ziegler's rank, they saluted and let both of them pass.

They reached the Solli Plass, a plaza where the tram lines joined at multiple Y's and cars clattered ceaselessly past on their rails.

Outside of Max's, a short, gray-haired woman, plump and round as a dumpling, was carrying a heap of small bread loaves in a wicker basket. She gave them a hard stare, spat in the gutter and turned her back. Helene gave an involuntary start. The woman's disgust at seeing a German officer with a Norwegian girl on his arm had been made clear.

"Do you wish me to have her arrested?" Ziegler asked, amused.

"No."

"I'm joking. We can put up with a measure of disrespect, for a time. But it must end. Did you see what happened with all those resisters who ran around wearing red caps? Nabbed and detained. You don't see anyone wearing red hats now, do you? Your resisters then adopted a subtler symbol—paper clips! Meaning, they'll stick together, I guess. But we've grown wise to that, too. Just as we will learn any other signal. Terboven's hounds shall have all the ringleaders rounded up shortly, I expect."

At Max's, they were shown to a table by a waiter and their orders were taken for bowls of savory fish stew, rye bread and coffee.

Helene studied her companion. Ziegler had short, dark blonde hair, chocolate eyes, an aristocratic, aquiline profile; he was not an unhandsome man. She guessed his age to be in the early thirties. He aimed to broadcast a mood of sangfroid, but beneath that, she detected a jittery, unsure quality. She wondered if the man fully bought into all the Nazi Party views that he spouted. Not that he seemed dishonest, she thought. But it was as though he sought to convince himself of what he ought to believe via rote repetition. It gave him a superficial air of cohesion and confidence, but it seemed to conceal a more turbulent mentality.

Their coffee arrived. Ziegler took out his ivory holder and plugged a cigarette into it. He probed a coat pocket for matches.

"Please, don't," Helene said.

"Have you somewhere acquired a prejudice against fine tobacco?"

"I am allergic to any tobacco."

"How unfortunate for you. And me."

He sighed and laid his smoke and holder aside. From a different pocket, he drew out a small blue and orange tube, unscrewed the cap and tapped a pair of small tablets into his palm. He tossed them into his mouth and swallowed them with a sip of coffee.

"Are you ill?"

"No. These are health boosting pills. Most of us carry them. Pervitin! Recent invention, quite scientific. I began to use them while keeping long hours in Poland. A true energy enhancer. Remarkably effective. Our SS panzer divisions swear by them. Would you care for one?"

"No thank you."

Their lunch arrived. They quietly ate for a while, then Ziegler wiped his lips with a napkin and leaned back in his chair.

"All right, miss," he said. "That last time we happened to meet each other on the street, you made a request of me. I hereby announce to you that I have done my level best to fulfill it."

"Yes?" Helene fought to keep from sounding too eager.

"You asked me about Kari Thorsen, the wife of your guardian's brother."

"Thank you. Because I and Otto did try to call her, but her number had been disconnected. Then an NS party member went there to visit, but the family apartment in Stavanger was locked and empty, with no one residing there."

"I remember. Sorry that I can't add much now to the basics you already told me. I do believe that Thorsen woman is alive and well. However, she's no longer in Stavanger. Those are the main things I was able to find out."

"Where is she, then?"

"That part is lost in a bit of the murk, I'm afraid. You see, your Mrs. Kari Thorsen was denounced, then after that, arrested by the Gestapo. They can be damned secretive when they wish to be. And they happen to be very much so in this case."

Helene's eyes widened. "Who denounced her?"

Ziegler drummed his fingers on the table. "These were separate events. A denunciation came first. Appears to have been anonymous. But then she interfered with a local police matter, and was taken directly into custody."

"So, Kari's being held? Can I go visit her?"

Ziegler turned the palms of both hands up and shrugged. "Unknown, also," he said. "But if you like, I shall continue to inquire."

"Also, any news about the vessel *Snekka*, or the whereabouts of Ragnar Thorsen? Or his son Kristian?"

"Nothing to say there," Ziegler said. He shifted in his seat. "Fog of war again, you know. Sometimes, impenetrable. That's why it's best to focus on those whom you find near you in the present." He smiled raffishly. "Gather ye rosebuds while ye may," he added.

*"If a main artery is cleanly severed, the wounded man will quickly lose consciousness and die."*
—Maj. W. E. Fairbairn, instructor,
British Special Operations Executive (SOE)

# CHAPTER 9

"Right then, gents. Are you comfy? If yes, I advise you to stock up! As training proceeds, much less comfort shall be on tap. And after you deploy? Your comfort zone will be smaller than a sporran on a clegg, as these local boyos might say.

"By-the-bye, a 'clegg' is one of those horseflies who sting big welts on you out here in the moors. Cleggs and I are on the same team. We both aim to toughen you up, y'see. Maybe you consider yourselves tough already. But I assure you, you'll soon make many fresh and important findings in this area."

Kristian sat cross-legged with two other men under a huge ash tree on the lawn of a remote estate in the west of Scotland. He now wore some of the wool khakis fully shorn of all insignia, as well as those black tennis shoes. Clad similarly were his companions, known to him as Tomás from Poland and Václav from Czechoslovakia. But those were not their real names. Exchange of any accurate, detailed personal data was forbidden. And they only knew Kristian as "Fiske"—a code name assigned to him as he became a brand new agent for Section D of the Secret Intelligence Service, or MI6.

"I am Colour Sergeant Ted Barnes of His Majesty's Royal Marine Commandos. You may call me either Colour Sergeant, or Sir. You may also call me Scotty, but only if you come across me at a pub in town. Not that

I'm the least bit Scottish, mind you, but I seek to blend in. Advise you to do the same! I hope to acquire a burr. I've heard that single malt can help with that, and I'm eager to put it to the test. You're welcome to join me, but only after you graduate from the course. *If* you do.

"Now gentlemen, I'm grieved to inform you that this training is more than a bit of a rush job. Can't be helped. Missions you've been assigned have been judged by all our brass to be of the highest priority and time is a-wasting.

"Should you by some miracle survive your missions, we'll happily welcome you back to take additional classes. Please think o' this covert base as your new home-away-from-home. But on this first go-round, we've been given barely enough time to focus on a woefully castrated syllabus. The basics. To wit, skills with pistol, blade, hand-to-hand, camouflage, and deft covert techniques. Otherwise known as stealth.

"We'll start with the ideal stealth tool, a blade. Mankind's primitive yet eternally effective weapon, whether made of chipped flint or modern steel."

Colour Sergeant Barnes was a tall, spare man with square shoulders and a pugnacious glint in his eye. In contrast to his loquacity—which suggested he'd foreswear any short way to craft a monologue if a longer way might be found—his physical motions were deft, speedy and efficient.

And thus it came to pass that they suddenly saw him hold a long knife upright in his hand without ever having seen him reach for it.

"The quartermaster will equip each of you with a Hunter's Dagger in pattern number 784. Our weapon here boasts a blade seven and three-quarter inches in length, and it measures twelve and three-eighths inches overall. It's sold in a black leather sheath with a spring retainer, and is of course produced by our illustrious armorer, Wilkinson Sword.

"I call your attention to the 784 model's many excellent features, which include a rather sharp tip, keen edges on both sides, guard, then a hilt of checked ebony, including a prominent boss at its end. Now, would any of you ladies—pardon me, I meant to say 'laddies'—care to guess how such a weapon ought to be used?"

Kristian raised his hand. "We try to stick that pointy end into an enemy?"

"Correct, Fiske! Tad obvious, though. Y'see, much more to a knife than its lethal tip, hey? Any part of it may be used as a weapon. Stabbing can be effective, certainly but a commando might not always be in position to deliver such a blow. Your typical knife fight is nasty, brutish and short. Just as life was for poor Piltdown Man. And his girlfriends. Thus, a blade fighter should maximize aggression while bearing in mind his many striking options.

"For example, regard these edges. They can be used to slash the arteries in your target's neck, elbows, wrists and groin. Also, either end of this guard can rake across a human face to good effect, particularly if one manages to catch a prong on an eyeball or up a nose or a corner of the mouth. This hardwood boss at the end of the hilt can deliver an incapacitating blow, even a fatal one, if you can ram it into a skull's thinnest part. Right here, at the temple." Barnes tapped a finger by an eyebrow.

"Are all of you understanding me here. Do those blank stares I see happen to suggest a dim level of comprehension? Ah, two nods from my available three. Thanks, gentlemen. And you, Tomás? Please see me after. And do tote along a notebook and pen. You Poles can write and read I hope, hmm? If not, I'll endeavor to scrawl you a picture.

"Following our lesson and throughout this course, you will be required to practice upon one another with rubber knives until these moves turn instant and instinctual. During practice, you'll both please me and score a higher grade if you can gobsmack your fellow students by leaping on them from a closet door, or out from behind a bush.

"You need to stay on your toes, gentlemen. Even when sleeping. I can't emphasize this enough. If you're lucky enough to be engaged in pursuits of a romantic nature—something I regard as highly unlikely with you lot, but admittedly, still, remotely possible—commando protocols demand that you simultaneously hold a knife in your hand, and keep at least one foot on the floor. With practice, you shall become adept at it. However, I do *not* recommend that you try out this combat situation upon one another. If any of you feel drawn that way, I'd prefer not to hear about it. Bottom line? Don't scare the horses, as per dear Missus Pat. But all bets are off if you can terrorize the German nags. Especially when they're hauling field artillery.

"Now then, Fiske, by answering first, you showed initiative. That makes me want to select you as our 'test dummy.' Step up here, please. Then face away from me."

Kristian complied, feeling a bit apprehensive about what might occur next. Appropriately, as it turned out.

"The blade is an up-close and personal weapon," Barnes said. "Your key word here is 'close.' Subtract distance between yourself and a target via deft use of surprise.

"We'll start by learning a sentry attack. A commando's normal job is to sneak past a sentry and go blow things up, not raise a general alarm. But if your sentry happens to be lounging in the wrong spot or seems unfortunately alert, well, slaying one can prove crucial to your mission.

"Here's how you go about it. Study the man's moves. Set up your ambush point. Make a silent rush from behind—and the shorter this route is, the better. First move, you wrap your left hand around his face and clap your left palm over his mouth while pinching his nostrils shut with thumb and forefinger. You jerk his head back while kicking the toe of your right boot into the rear of his calf then drag it down to paralyze the muscle and throw him off-balance. Third move, with your right hand you drive your blade into the side of his neck and shove it forward with a burst of strength to sever the carotid artery. The swifter and more accurate all these moves are, the far better.

"Your man goes limp, he drops and he starts to die. Finally, you award him a lovely send-off with a good, hearty kick in his balls. Got it?"

Kristian absolutely had gotten it. The Sergeant's lightning-quick moves had tweaked his neck, stunned his lower leg and flung him violently to the ground. But luckily, Barnes had jabbed him in the neck with the hilt of the knife instead of its blade. And in another bolt of good fortune, Barnes' statement about finishing up by crushing a man's testicles with a boot to his crotch had just been one last flourish of rhetoric. He left that move out entirely.

⌇

The sound of an aircraft approaching made Kristian flinch. He wondered if his adverse reaction to hearing the drone of any plane's single engine as it drew closer would ever cease.

He looked up through the trees to see a bulky monoplane with long, gull-like wings circle over the estate—a Westland Lysander, an aircraft of a specialized design that SIS Section D had begun to use on nocturnal insertions and extractions.

Kristian, Tomás and Václav paused in their run through the woods. They were heading back "home" after receiving a final lesson in camouflage and sylvan stalking from an old Highlands gillie, or gameskeeper.

"They deliver to us a new instructor now?" Tomás hazarded. "Don't they know we've had plenty?"

"Or a new 'guest,' joining us, maybe," Václav said. The SIS still referred to agents recruited from among the savviest and fittest European refugees who'd fled to England as the outfits "guests." But these days they were first brought to an evaluation facility called The Royal Victoria Patriotic Building before being shunted to Latchmere House for a deeper grilling, as Kristian had been from the get-go. In other words, they were softened up first. If they managed to wriggle through the Cyclops' final sieve, only then could they pass onward to a commando school like this one in Scotland to prepare for assignment.

Kristian swept an appraising eye over his pair of companions. Their training had lasted nearly three months. Each day of that period had been crammed with unrelenting demands on their comprehension, will-power and endurance. Yet their youth and resilience meant that all these physical, mental and emotional challenges had only resulted in harder muscles, more focused minds, and a grim resolve to succeed at their missions.

Details of those individual missions, they were also forbidden to share. Yet some hints were obvious. For instance, Kristian had been given special lessons in the assembly and use of the new MK-1 folding kayak on waters of a nearby loch. Václav was their only class member to undertake a parachute course. And Tomás now was expert at the assembly, maintenance and use of Sten automatic carbines.

They'd been ordered to reveal nothing of their pasts, and not to speculate about each other's future. Nevertheless, the trio had bonded in their intensively shared present. They'd groused about their suffering, gloried in their developing prowess, and been proud to claim a victory in brotherly tussles as they drilled at close-quarters combat.

And so they'd become pals. They didn't know many personal facts about one another, other than who had a mole or a tattoo and where, but they had a full grasp of each other's essential nature. And Kristian knew that he'd badly miss them both.

With full packs on their backs, they jogged out from the fringe of forest, and watched the Lysander float down from the sky and bounce to a halt on its balloon tires. It stopped near the same tree where Colour Sergeant Barnes had first greeted them, then offered that initial class in knife-fighting.

They watched the pilot exit the side door and tug off a leather helmet, revealing a pale bell of flaxen hair. The pilot was a woman. It was Greta.

Barnes strode up. "Fiske!" he said. "Duffle your kit. I hereby declare you mission ready. You've got twenty minutes to pack up for your escape from this hellhole and my gentle guidance."

Kris stared at him. Transition to active duty was what he'd labored and hoped for. Yet when it came, the shift seemed harsh and abrupt. He realized, as rigorous as their training had been, it still had offered him a kind of rest. He'd enjoyed weeks of exercise in fresh air, entertaining course work, stimulating companionship, ample food and deep sleep. But no real danger. Not of the sort he'd soon face, at any rate.

"What, you were hoping for some sort of graduation ceremony? Well, here." Barnes thrust out his right hand, gave Kristian's own a brief, iron-fingered grip. "My fatherly bit of encouragement is that you've learned well, and you show especial talent at the close-quarters wet-work. Of course, I'd wager you've filleted a fair number fish in your day, Fiske."

"More than a few."

"That's my boy. Jump over the drink to gut a few Nazis for me. There's a good lad. Now, away with you, my prodigious prodigal!"

~

Greta flew him off to His Majesty's Naval Base Clyde in Scotland, sheltered from the sea at the end of the Gare Loch, near Faslane.

"The very long blue water down there. From the sky, it looks much like a fjord," Kristian observed, using the intercom link between the aircraft's two cockpits.

"You feel lonesome for Norway?" she asked.

"As it was, probably. Not as it is now, perhaps."

After a radio exchange with the base's control tower, Greta landed the plane smoothly at the base's airstrip. She taxied it up to a hangar, where they were presented with the keys to a small, nondescript sedan.

"Come on," she told him. "You've earned a day of total liberty before you set sail on the *HMS Beluga*."

"I did? And what about you?"

"I'm your minder." She peered at him through the parted strands of her blond bangs. "Which means, you're under orders to mind me. At all times." She pointed at the car. "Get in."

"Where are we going?"

"I know of a lovely country inn, less than an hour away, where they serve you meals out on the balcony of your room. It boasts a vista of a tumbling burn, or creek. Medallions of red deer is the chef's specialty. Before this gruesome war hit its stride, the sommelier filled his cellar with quality French wines. Or if you like, you're welcome to sample the output of a local distillery."

Kristian grinned, opened the car door and flung his duffle bag onto the rear seat.

"Lead on, Macduff," he said.

"Where the hell did you pick that up?"

"From our instructor. With a few other things. I feel my English has improved. Many people tell me now that I'm a fast learner."

Greta smirked. "We'll see about that," she said. "But the line actually is, 'Lay on, Macduff,' mister. That is, if you truly wish to quote from Shakespeare, and not some lesser bugger."

Kristian twirled his glass by its stem and admired the ruby rays of a setting sun as they filtered through the red bulb of wine. He sighed. It wasn't that he felt happy, exactly, he reflected. It was more as though he enjoyed an abrupt absence of physical pain or emotional stress. The rigors of Section D training had distracted him from the tragedy on the North Sea, and now Greta was distracting him from the rigors of Section D. Plus, he'd been put on his heels by the splendidly crafted alcoholic beverages he'd swilled. But that intestinal deluge had also granted him a surreal—albeit shallow— brand of peace. He felt entirely within himself, yet detached and afloat above this rural setting at the same moment.

He watched Greta regard him through her bangs and half-lowered eyelashes as she puffed lazily on a Pall Mall.

"Are you really a Belgian?" he asked. He'd been curious.

"Just half," she said. "Dad was an Etonian. Worked for the British Foreign Service in Belgium, where he met Mum. She's from Malmédy."

He instantly sat up straight in his chair.

"What?"

"You answered my question!"

She shrugged, smiled. "Our general ban on sharing personal info applies mainly to agents who need to go over into the mess. They have to use false and concealed identities. And if captured, must know as little about each other as possible," she said. "Me? I stay here. On the auld sod. Merely shuttling planes and personnel about." She tapped a cone of gray ash off the end of her smoke and into an empty saucer. "Besides, obeying every order they can give you to a fare-thee-well is an utter bore. Mark my words, young man."

She took a sip of her wine.

"Also, your other work is to charm men into revealing truths about who they are."

"At times. A game I'm willing to play. When it seems useful."

"To the Cyclops?"

"And a few other bosses." She shrugged. "Think of it as my sideline."

"Yet you're very good at it."

She gazed at him through half-lidded eyes. "Thanks," she said.

"Plus, you're a pilot! That's no small thing."

"I fly, because my husband did. It's my way to feel a bit closer to him, still."

"*Did?*"

"I am a widow."

"Oh. That makes me sad. What happened?"

"William flew Hurricanes. Sent to France, right after Hitler took Poland."

"What was he…"

"I have no wish to discuss it further."

"Sorry."

"Don't be. We're at war. He's gone. You and I, we're both still alive." She crushed her cigarette out in the saucer. "For now," she added softly.

She stood up. He saw both of her hazel eyes brim with a crescent of extra moisture. "It's grown chilly. Let's go back indoors, Kris."

"Must you not call me Fiske, now?"

"We already know each other better than that."

He set down his wine glass, but she spread her fingers and snatched up both of their glasses with a single hand and grasped the bottle of Chateau Pétrus by its neck with her other. As he followed Greta into the room, he felt as though the floor might be tilting, about to make him slide into her. He stopped the moment of vertigo by turning around to carefully shut the balcony door. When he turned back, he found that she had set the wine down on an end table and now stood right in front of him.

"Where will you stay?" His speech was slow, his tongue felt balky and thick.

She laughed. "My bag is already in this room."

Her eyes glistened. She stepped to him and flung a slim arm around his neck. She tilted her head. Her lips pressed his, and the tip of her tongue flickered against his mouth. Kristian felt as though he might fall over backwards. Yet soon he was kissing her too, and a shudder of utter excitement was ricocheting from the soles of his feet to the top of his head and making all his limbs quiver.

Kristian had managed to kiss girls before. More than a few times. Yet he'd never experienced this level of revelation. A sensual wisdom was awake within Greta. Her power revealed itself and retreated, teased and veered away but then generously gave. A shred of tobacco was borne into his mouth when her tongue thrust in once, briefly, deeply, and he could feel that savory particle combust within his mouth. He found he strangely enjoyed its mild chemical burn. It was the taste of an unusual, rapidly widening, extremely worldly dimension. He even liked the tobacco-scented breath that drifted out of her nostrils.

He felt certain he was now en route to finding out all that a man might be able to know about being with a woman. This time, a fretful girl wouldn't stop him. And he already knew that he'd never halt on his own. There'd be no turning back, no shamed half-apologies between a pair of clumsy innocents. He saw he could simply hurl himself into this quickening dance with Greta and let her lead him on into sensation, into discovery, and into a far deeper awareness.

Their bodies slowly found a way in which their curves, their soft parts and those particular ones that were rapidly growing stiff, fit together in the most delectable manner. Synchronizing a rhythm for more intimate contact took more time. It was as if a pair of touring orchestras from quite separate continents attempted to tune up together prior to a concert, and they sought to find each other's symphonic heart.

He was from a virgin continent. She, a far more urbane one.

Kristian felt a spectacular hardening of his loins. It seemed as if a fencepost had been stuffed down the front of his trousers. Suddenly that impossibly large object had been drenched in petrol and set ablaze. Flames on its tip jetted upward, became like lava and turned into a burst of scalding fluid.

"Oh… Oh… Oh. *Helvete!*"

He broke their clinch and pushed her out to arm's length, then swayed on his feet, his face hot with embarrassment. He could sense the globs of hot ejaculate trickling down his groin, across a thigh.

"I…" He said, then stopped. "Don't know what to do," he confessed.

Greta's smile was both delighted and sympathetic. "Oh, quit your worry!" she scolded. "I know enough for both of us."

She wrapped a fist around Kristian's belt and tugged him toward the bed.

"Let's lay odds you've got much more than one geyser in you," she said. "So, I'd say, my assignment is to find all the others."

*"Terboven reports on Norway. Quisling gains more support. Old political parties are in ruins. Our cultural forays into plays, films, have a nice effect on the local feeling."*
—Josef Goebbels, from *The Goebbels Diaries*

# CHAPTER 10

Helene stood at Frau Heinlein's tidy desk and bowed her head as she accepted a thick folder crammed with files.

The folder's cover was stamped 'Geheim'—'Secret'—and its flap had been sealed by a paper medallion rendered in black and gold. On the front, this seal presented a gold eagle with outstretched wings perched upon a swastika, the words "Polizei Division," plus the sig-rune lightning bolts of the SS. And on the folder's back, the seal medallion displayed a sonnenrad—a black sun with more sig runes thrust outward to form a wheel of dark sun rays.

Frau Heinlein peered at Helene over the rims of her half-circle reading glasses, gave a curt nod, and turned her attention to the next item on her work agenda.

Helene spun on her heel and exited. On the lower floor of the Reichskommissar's headquarters, a women's rest room was located just around a corner in the main hall, and Helene walked there briskly. She pushed open its door, bustled inside, and began at that instant to count.

One second... two seconds...

Then she occupied a stall and seated herself on a toilet.

Four seconds... five...

She took a round cork from her left blouse pocket and pulled out of it a keen shard of broken razor blade. Helene took a deep breath and sliced open the center band of the seal. Then sucked in another breath as she opened the folder.

*Seven… eight…* These were moves that she'd rehearsed more than a dozen times in a bathroom of the downtown apartment she shared with Otto. At home, she'd sat on a toilet and flipped through a stack of files, rapidly scanning their contents. She concentrated on not skipping a page or wrinkling paper or smearing ink or dropping anything. Amid these practice sessions, it had appealed to her sense of irony that she'd soon be alone in a high school girls' bathroom, taking the test of a lifetime. And failure was no option! She didn't know precisely what might happen to her if she was caught snooping on secret documents in the nerve center of the German occupation. But all the consequences would likely be unpleasant in the extreme.

Helene set her jaw and continued to riffle through the files, scanning each page at maximum speed. At length, in the second-to-last set of papers the folder contained, she found a name she'd been searching for: Frau Kari Thorsen.

*Nineteen seconds…*

Hurriedly now, her brain ablaze, she focused on that page, translating on-the-fly every bullet point of the Gestapo's charges against the wife of Ragnar and the mother of Kristian. Kari had first been denounced as a known and vocal critic of Quisling and the NS. Kari had been named as the wife of the brother of Otto Thorsen, and because of that link, she was considered a potential security risk. Kari had been arrested when she appeared on the night of April 21 at a large rest home for the elderly on Wesselsgata road in Stavanger where the Gestapo sought to commandeer the facility in order to use it as a station house. Kari had been an eyewitness to deployment of an *Aktion Gnadentod*—a covert "mercy-killing" program— any observation of which was strictly forbidden. In fact, she'd been bold enough to intervene, physically attacking police officers and disrupting their operation. She'd been instantly arrested for this rebellious offense. Transferred to Oslo, she was now being held in the jail at Møllergata 19, awaiting determination of her case. The SS recommended: either Frau Kari Thorsen's outright elimination; or a long imprisonment, perhaps at Sachsenhausen concentration camp, just north of Berlin.

*Fifty-one…*

The door to the restroom opened and shut. Marooned atop her toilet seat, Helene froze. Water splashed in a nearby sink. A woman hummed, apparently as she gazed in a mirror. More water splashed. Despite the terror of discovery that gripped her, Helene knew she had to force herself to finish reading Kari's file. She heard paper towels get ripped from a dispenser. The main door opened and shut again.

*Seventy-two…*

With trembling fingers, Helene drew a fresh seal out of her other blouse pocket, licked it to moisten the glue and began to carefully apply it to the folder. First, she needed to get the severed band pieces together where it went across the opening and stick them to the new one. Then put each medallion on the front and back, so perfectly aligned that the folder did not appear to have been sealed for a second time.

The restroom door opened and closed.

And one last thing. She'd reasoned this out. Planned it. Helene dragged a thumbnail viciously up the back of one calf, feeling it tear one of the silk stockings Lieutenant Ziegler had given her.

Then she left the restroom, went out in the hall, and ascended the stairs to the conference chamber.

An adjutant met her at the door.

"Where have you been?" he hissed. "They're waiting to start!"

She held up the folder. "Here it is."

She looked past him, saw *Reichskommissar* Terboven sitting at the head of a cluster of long tables covered in black cloth, with other uniformed officers flanking him. The men sipped coffee and chatted amiably with one another. None looked particularly bothered or impatient.

"Sorry," she said. "I got a run in my stocking, and I just had to go into the little girls' room to find out how bad it was. You know how precious silk is now to a woman. Terribly hard to find." She turned and hoisted her skirt to her knees with a free hand to show him her leg. "See?"

When she turned back to him, she saw the tip of the lieutenant's tongue sliding across his lips. Then his expression went blank. He snatched the folder away, then shoved the conference room door closed with a loud snick.

Helene leaned back against the wall and tried to subdue her thumping heart by laying a hand on her breast.

She thought she'd been able to keep any expression on her own face from betraying her. But now color bloomed on her cheeks as emotions she'd held in check surged up. The stimulus for this final wave of feeling was the last footnote she had read in Kari Thorsen's file.

It said the motor vessel *Snekka, N-306-92,* owned and operated by Herr Ragnar Thorsen, Kari's husband, had been spotted by a *Kriegsmarine* patrol plane trying to flee across the North Sea to Britain from Norway on April 13. Authorities had been informed that aboard this vessel were renegade Norwegian army officers, as well as criminals who had tried to murder a *Wehrmacht* officer after the wreck of the *Mehrlicht* back in Oslo Fjord. This vessel, appropriately, had been sunk. The footnote added: the crew of the plane had observed no possible survivors of the vessel's destruction.

*"And now, go and set Europe ablaze."*
—Winston Churchill to Hugh Dalton,
Minister of Economic Warfare, at launch of SOE

# CHAPTER 11

Kristian Thorsen, not just alive but feeling quite lively, fought to keep his balance atop a ponderously rolling, slowly plunging hull of the British mine-laying sub *HMS Beluga*. Sailors shuffled around him in pitch darkness, finding their way and performing duties aided only by the rays from red-filtered flashlights that were clipped to their life-vests.

The sailors assembled a new type of folding kayak, one with a hinged hickory frame and a rubberized canvas shell.

After its final joints clicked into place and stiffened its fabric, they lowered this kayak to the awash surface of one of the submarine's diving planes at the bow—left rigged out for them to use as a kind of improvised launch deck.

Next came the kayak's cargo. First, a fifty-pound wrapped and taped object that was the W/T radio, to be stuffed into its stern, then a waterproofed bundle of a smaller, reception-only radio, and finally bags of weapons and explosives to be slid into the kayak's bow. Topping the load off were packets of clothing, incidentals and rations.

"Time, lad," a sailor muttered.

Kristian stepped over a rope, brought it up and over his right shoulder and pulled it down by his hip, kicked off and rappelled down the curve of *Beluga's* massive hull, landing by the kayak.

Two other sailors held the kayak steady in the water as Kristian slid into its cockpit. One handed him the black-painted, double-bladed paddle. "*Bon voyage*, mate," he said.

"Happy hunting, too," the other said.

"And to you gentlemen, the same," Kristian replied.

He shoved away and paddled off from the submarine, feeling the kayak's hull flex beneath him as it adapted to the black sea's rolling surface. Weight of the cargo, wedged down against the small boat's keel by the lighter items on top, gave it a remarkable feel of stability. He looked back over his shoulder once to see the bulbous bow and conning tower of the *Beluga*, decorated by the red sparks of the lights her sailors carried as they returned to the submarine's hatches and prepared to dive their vessel once again beneath the sea.

Kristian did not bother to switch on his own red flash to check course on the brass compass securely lashed before his spray deck. He simply paddled past the dark bulk of the north shore of Ukjent Øy until he could see the bright beam of the Flatholmen Fyr—the Flat Islet Lighthouse—then turned south. He found the entrance of the inlet and slid through its suddenly calm waters until he reached Ragnar's stone boathouse at the end.

He found the spare key in its usual spot, underneath a slab of slate up on the roof. The oak door groaned open. He stood for a moment, inhaling the mingled odors of cordage, diesel, grease, moss and mildew. Last time he'd been inside this low structure, he'd been with his father. Some four months later, he was entirely alone. That difference did not go unremarked. But in a way, Ragnar still was with him, yet only as a negative presence, a shape cut out of reality. He could not see its outline, even speak to it. And as of yet, he'd not received any sort of signal. Nor did he expect to.

He unloaded and stacked supplies: a Sten gun, one of the Webley pistols, ammunition for both, a sealed tin of white phosphorous fuses for making incendiary grenades, ration packages. Then he locked up and relaunched.

He had thirteen more kilometers left that he had to paddle through the darkness, making a covert cruise northward to a bare outcrop called

Alstein. It lay close to the Tungenes Fyr—a lighthouse built to guide ocean-going vessels into safe harbor at Stavanger.

~

Alstein, a wave-scoured rock an acre or so in size, was shaped like a low, heavily fissured dome. That made it easy for Kristian to find a notch where he could hide the kayak. For good measure, he unrolled a camouflage net over it. Then he heeded the advice of his Section D briefers, to make no movements in daylight hours, to keep from being spotted by a German patrol plane or vessel. Instead he dozed next to the kayak and under the camo net, keeping comfortably warm in his own woolen fisherman's sweater and the wool long johns and matte-black oilskin coverall and mac provided by Brits. In periods of wakefulness, Kristian would pop his head out of the crevice to recon the Tungenes lighthouse through a collapsible telescope. The light and its outbuildings were too far off for him to absorb much detail, yet he could spot movement around it, German army vehicles coming and going.

Which was how an inspiration sparked and began to burn within him. The presence of German soldiers at Tungenes Fyr would offer a fine chance for him to deploy his commando training and test some newfound skills. Plus, make a payment on his bill of vengeance for the destruction of *Snekka*. He felt more than ready to expend some of his too-long banked rage over the deaths of Ragnar, Lars, Stein and the other Norwegians aboard.

~

Since the latitude of the port of Stavanger was similar to that of Juneau, Alaska, this mid-summer night would consist of only about six hours of shadowy twilight. That time constraint meant that he'd need to be extremely swift and efficient if he was going to add an impromptu raid to his schedule. The bosses at SIS would certainly condemn him for attempting anything that might imperil success of the sole mission they'd assigned. But now he was out beyond their control. He relished the opportunity to act on impulse.

Kristian secured another small cache of weapons and other supplies in the topmost crevice of Alstein just as the sun floated near the western horizon, then launched his kayak.

Tungenes Fyr sat atop a stony peninsula that thrust out into the sea. The name Tungenes meant Tongue Point. The low peninsula that hosted the lighthouse was a barren slab eroded into long ridges separated by rivulets of sand and grass. Kristian knew he could not risk having even a low wave hurl him up onto the ocean side. That could hole his boat—which would cost him everything. He opted to glide around the tip of the peninsula to the estuary side.

While making this passage, he spotted a sentry walking on a route around the lighthouse's outbuildings—a dark shape wearing a steel helmet and greatcoat while carrying a slung rifle. The man appeared only briefly in silhouette, illuminated by the radiance of the rotating lighthouse beam.

Kristian made landfall on the northeast shore, in a shallow cove. He exchanged his paddler's gumboots for a commando's black tennis shoes. He draped the camo net over his boat, then scattered more clumps of seaweed and grass over and around it.

He crouched down as he moved up from the cove. He waited for the lighthouse beam to sweep by again, saw it strobe past the sentry as he plodded dully along on his circuit.

*Absolutely correct, Kristian thought. Right now you're stuck in the Third Reich's most boring job, Siegfried—or whatever the hell your name is. You can barely keep from falling asleep in your boots as you stumble along here, isn't that right?*

But he saw no easy way to sneak up on this man. Other than its outbuildings, the site provided no significant cover. And if he hid behind any building's corner, he wouldn't be able to determine exactly when the guy was approaching.

Kristian fingered the hilt of his dagger. He wore it sheathed in a leather harness he'd stitched himself in order to carry it between his shoulder blades. Then he could snatch it out swiftly by dropping either hand behind his neck. He also tapped the butt of the Webley Mk VI revolver he'd holstered on his right hip. This weighty handgun boasted a six-inch barrel and was chambered for huge .455 cartridges. He could probably sneak up within ten yards and then fire accurately. Just one of those giant bullets center-punching the man's torso would knock him dead. But he dare not risk the *boom* of a gunshot; he didn't know how many other German guards had been billeted here, or how quickly they might respond.

The only effective stealth option he could conjure up required him to lie down and wriggle up one of those seams of grass that lay between the low ridges of rock. Then he'd need to leap quietly to his feet just after the sentry marched by.

*Ah, but will he take the same path on every circuit?* Kristian settled down to watch. *Thank God for methodical Germans.* The man turned out to be wearing a rut by repeating each of his circuits almost exactly atop his own boot prints.

Kristian laid his body down in the grass and began to writhe toward the light. He took care to remain still as the soldier completed his next round. By the time his man passed again, Kristian had moved up into position to strike. He lay face-down in the grass, dagger gripped in his fist, listening to the scuff of those hobnail boots going by.

Then he rose silently to his feet and took two leaping strides.

He never knew if it was the scrape of a shoe or some other unfortunate sound he'd made that alerted the sentry. Perhaps the guy was simply preternaturally aware? But instead of getting his right arm around the muzzle of the slung rifle and driving his blade into the soldier's neck, Kristian found his attack thwarted as the soldier yanked the rifle off his shoulder and spun in his tracks. The man was preternaturally quick too, because without even lowering his Mauser to use its fixed bayonet, he was able to smash Kristian across the face with the steel gun barrel itself, clubbing him to the ground.

The only saving grace was that, for some odd reason, this soldier decided he ought to fire a bullet at his assailant instead of simply using his bayonet.

Given a second of confusion that reigned after Kristian's abrupt attack, this error might've been understandable. But it still was an unforgiving choice—since the sentry didn't have a round chambered in his rifle. He dropped his hands to work the bolt and at that instant Kristian sprang up from the ground, his right fist wrapped around his dagger and his left palm shoving against the base of its hilt.

Kristian later marveled, wondering where *that* move had come from. Certainly, it was no technique Colour Sergeant Barnes had ever taught. But he flew over the soldier's outstretched arms, buried the tip of his dagger under the man's jaw and continued to drive ahead as the soldier dropped his rifle and fell over backwards.

The dagger drove into his neck and up through the soft palate, the base of his skull and deep into his lower brain, only stopping as the cross guard caught on his throat. Kristian wound up on top of his victim, lying belly to belly, and he absorbed the tremendous convulsion that wracked the sentry's body as he died.

When the final tremor subsided, Kristian scrambled up onto his feet and stood there, panting.

*I've just killed somebody!* This thought vibrated around in his head. *And with not a single word spoken between us... But wait... Why should that even matter?*

He warily glanced about. Didn't seem as if anyone else had grown aware of their brief struggle. Grounds around the lighthouse were still deserted. He looked down again. The soldier's eyes were wide open and staring, his taut face frozen into a near-parody of shock.

*Not much blood. Less than one might expect. Must not have hit any major vein.*

Kristian bent to retrieve his knife. Considering how easily the thing had gone in, it seemed astonishingly difficult to pull out. Kristian planted one of his black tennis shoes on the dead soldier's forehead and gave the handle several hearty yanks. The blade finally came free. He wiped the knife clean on the inside of the man's coat and stood over him again, looking down.

He'd expected to feel anger or contempt or hatred, but he felt none of these. No glee, or pride. No sadness, no grief. Nor relief, no sense of sated revenge or gloating triumph. But such an utter lack of sensation was fascinating, in and of itself. Kristian groped around inside himself, trying to understand it. So how *did* he feel?

Numb. Calm. Maybe a bit tired.

It was as though he'd just spent an hour fighting off boredom while calmly gutting cod on his father's fishing boat. Kristian wasn't sure he liked the comparison. He thought he ought to experience realizations or emotions that were somehow grander or more profound. Even if, you know, the feelings happened to seem a bit diabolical, he'd still welcome them.

*Why can't I even hate the bastard?*

Then another, far more practical thought struck.

Surely, this sentry hadn't been scheduled to remain on patrol throughout the night. At some point, another soldier had to come along to replace him. Which did not necessarily mean that Kristian should now flee. Play his cards right, and he could end up nailing another German soldier. One more step toward settling the tab.

～

Killing the second sentry proved easier.

Kristian had prepared for his next attack by posing the corpse of his first kill to make it look like the man was taking a nap, wrapped in his greatcoat and curled up on the stiff grass. The new sentry arrived in search of the dead man, even cupped his hands to his mouth to shout a loud "Halloo!" a couple times. When he finally located that apparently slumbering body, he kicked at its boots and cursed.

"*Wach auf, du Schwein!*"

That was when Kristian launched his ambush. It proceeded in more classic fashion, indeed, just as he'd been trained. He got his left hand over the target's mouth and pinched his nose, he drove the blade into the side of his neck, he raked his foot down the man's calf to make him stumble and then shoved his right hand forward to sever the artery. The sentry wheeled and dropped, spraying black fluid into the night.

*Two down!*

This time he experienced a tiny burst of gladness. It was a relief finally to feel something. If Sergeant Barnes could only see this! But now it was time for him to run back to his kayak. With eleven more kilometers to paddle, he had to reach Stavanger well before the horizon brightened any further.

Then another thought came, a dark impulse that amused him.

Dragging and tugging at the limp and heavy bodies, he arranged them in such a way that at first glance it looked as though this pair of sentries had dueled to the death. The wound in the neck of the first, he filled with the bayonet on the second sentry's rifle. Then he got a knife off the belt of the first, and wrapped the dead man's fingers around the hilt, and prepared to thrust it into the neck wound of the second man.

As he did, the lighthouse beam swept around, and in its brief radiance he could see the words etched into the blade. *"Blut und Ehre,"* it said— Blood and Honor, a German slogan simple enough for him to read.

"Well, now you've won some of that first stuff," Kristian told the dead sentries. "Can't say if you'll ever see the other. Depends on your destination. Which shall it be, you think? Valhalla, or Hell?"

*"Germans can never be qualified to rule other people. They lack the gift of understanding the mentality of other nations. The way the Germans have acted in Norway is the best proof of this."*
—King Haakon, *speech on the BBC*

# CHAPTER 12

Sunup pushed a band of bright indigo above the horizon as Kristian finally paddled into the port of Stavanger, much later than scheduled.

It was exactly the sort of moment briefers at SIS Section D had dreaded.

After a debate, they'd said that if "viz"—i.e. visibility—happened to improve as Kristian arrived, he'd draw more attention from shore if he tried to sneak in. They said he should cruise on in boldly, acting unconcerned, as if he were just one more fisherman making an early start on his day. As if his commando kayak was simply some sort of strange Norwegian rowboat.

So, that's what he did. He paddled past the port's commercial zone—including a gigantic wharf where several *Kriegsmarine* destroyers were now moored—and on to fish docks that occupied an older, more dilapidated stretch of the Stavanger waterfront.

*If Germans see me, they won't know what I am. But they'll scoff that any boat this tiny and flimsy could pose any sort of threat,* Kristian thought. *When Norwegians see me, they also won't know what I am, but by their very nature they won't want to admit that. Above all, Norwegians don't wish to appear giddy or excitable. And over what? Seeing some poor* slask *on the water in his dinghy? Så hva er nytt? So, what else is new?*

As Kristian mulled this over, he chuckled. *Is that what I think shall happen, or merely the things that I hope?*

The reality seemed to be that few people were even up or alert at such a dim and chilly hour. None bothered to look out into the band of open water off Stavanger for a small vessel that made no noise and left no wake. Sentries on duty were occupied with keeping their hands warm and trying to make sure a crumpled pack of smokes would last past the end of their watches.

Kristian's dark clothing, dark paddle, and small, dark vessel glided by offshore, completely undetected.

He came to the third fishing dock. He used to play underneath this very pier back when he'd been a kid. But that was then, and this was now. The morning's big question was if everything below the pier had been arranged in a manner that showed Kristian's covert arrival was being welcomed. And by the proper individuals—by certain local resisters, or co-workers, one might say. Certainly not the Gestapo!

The worn and splintered edge of the dock loomed above his head. Then his kayak slid in beneath it, slipping between pilings as it entered a lingering zone of night, a deeper darkness than the half-light of dawn that had spread over the channel. Kristian heard the scrape of a piling's barnacles against the hull and veered sharply off. Ripping open his boat's fabric now, so close to his goal, would be idiocy on an epic scale.

He looked up. Overhead he saw the ghostly white line of the insulated water pipe that he knew connected a series of faucets that ran all the way out to the end of the pier—in order that visiting skippers might hose down their gear and flush out their fish holds while securely moored in each slip.

*Good. Smack in the middle of this pier. Exactly where I need to be.*

Moving slowly, barely sinking the ends of his paddle into the black water, he followed that white line to a point where it vanished. Then he halted and risked switching on his red-filtered flash. He immediately saw two ropes, dangling from pulleys that had been bolted to the underside of the dock. Ahead of him was a small and slimy-looking beach clogged with algae, and up high, a couple of boards nailed across under the pier joists to make a shelf.

Kristian caught the ropes by the snap-hooks tied to their ends and tugged them along to the beach. As soon as he got out of the cockpit, he snapped those hooks to grab-loops on his kayak's bow and stern. Then he unloaded the boat. The heavy, oblong bundles of the W/T and the receiving radio went up onto the board shelf. The last bundle of ammo and pyrotechnics and one Webley revolver went into a rucksack he would take with him, along with a hand spade.

He pulled off the rubberized weather shell garments and the thick woolens and the gumboots he'd worn for the voyage, replacing them with worn civilian work clothes he took from a sealed bag. He felt for the wallet with forged ID cards; it still lay securely buttoned inside an upper pocket of the shirt. His cast-off clothing and the bag he rolled up together and tossed into the kayak's cockpit. He next used the pulleys to haul his boat far up between the joists, then tied the hoist lines off, using cleats screwed next to the board shelf. He shrugged on the rucksack and began a slippery climb out from under the dock.

Old stones of the bulkhead and seawall still had the same chinks and rough seams that had made for such great handholds, back when he'd been a boy. He was glad he'd told Section D of it, during a planning session. Hard to imagine that the port of Stavanger could offer any kind of hiding place that would be superior to this.

He peered around the waterfront as soon as his eyes attained a street level view, then hauled himself up the rest of the way. Brushed his clothes off with his hands and shook out his trousers. Almost involuntarily he turned to gaze up the Verksgata to a building that held the Thorsen family apartment.

"*Sov godt, Mor. Hvis du er der!*" he whispered. "*Jeg kommer og besøker deg om et par timer.*" Meaning, sleep on, Mother. If you are there. I will come visit you in a day. Or less!"

Then he set off uphill, hiking to the head of the green valley that held Lagård Gravlund—an urban cemetery to the west of Birklandsgata boulevard.

At Birklandsgata, he descended a stone staircase to reach the upper end of the graveyard. Just above its grass scraps of mist hovered, as if spirits were beginning to slink back to their graves after a night on the town.

With the sky steadily growing brighter, Kristian could spot a big flake of rock, jabbed into the earth amid a tangle of greenery near the valley's headwall. This stone was flecked with lichen and had a ragged but somehow symmetrical shape. Looked at the right way, it resembled a large piece of knapped flint, a large arrow or spearhead driven into the soil.

"'A *menhir*,' that's what some people call it," Ragnar had told him, the first time they had come to see it. That had been six years ago, when Kristian was twelve. "Basically, it's a *stående steiner*, a standing stone. Grave marker for some ancient chieftain. Which should prove to you that this place was a gateway to Valhalla, long before any pious Christians got ahold of it."

Other than his surfeit of Norwegian folk sayings, Viking history had been one of Ragnar's areas of supposed expertise. But in school, Kristian had found that many of Ragnar's theories were founded on his affection for legend, not on actual history. Myth made better stories.

Kristian walked over and clawed a path up through tangles of ivy to position himself on the standing stone's uphill side. He dropped the rucksack, took out the hand spade and began to dig.

He cut out a square of vegetation, laid it aside, then dug a hole that went a half-meter deep. He looked down into the patch of dark, exposed soil, inhaling its reek of wet loam and rotting duff. He hesitated for a second, then reached inside his shirt to grab the button from his father's coat, where he had it dangling around his neck on a string. He snapped the string, brought the button out, dropped it into the hole. Leaned on it with a finger to push it deeper.

"Goodbye, *Pappa*," he whispered. "You can sail off, now. Go and drink mead with the chief."

He was then seized by an illusion that the black earth had grabbed his finger, his hand, his arm, his whole body and was hauling on him, had begun to drag him down into the black soil along with his father's button. Now he and it—the button grown impossibly large, as big as a tram, as

big as a house, with a gravity all its own that drew and drew on him—
they had broken through the solid earth and were tumbling freely together
down into a realm of shadow, an underworld that was flooded by sadness
and agony, one haunted by a grief so universal and so overwhelming it
surpassed all of humankind's other emotions welded together.

*NO!*

Kristian soared back up and into himself, found his body squatting
down with his hands braced on either side of the hole, his breaths shallow
and fast. It felt as if he might vomit. Ribbons of thick saliva already were
drooling from his mouth, he felt his stomach convulse, and a sting of bile
jetted into the back of his throat.

*No!* he yelled silently at himself. *You will NOT be puking into your father's
grave, like a mewling landlubber on his first trip to sea. Get a grip on yourself,
man!*

Kristian sought to comprehend what had happened, to grapple with it.
A chasm of feeling had opened up. A gorge with no bottom.

*And it damn near gulped me down! I can't let it do that. I need something
else. And I know what. I need that utter coldness, the numbed emptiness I felt
as I looked down at the first German that I killed. I need that cool emptiness
to last for much longer. In fact, I might need it to take me over entirely. It's the
only way I can survive all of this. And if I don't survive, I won't be able to get
a single damn thing of any importance done. Nothing to affect the real fight.
Letting myself go the other way? Paralysis!*

But how could anyone engineer such a shift?

*I must acknowledge that I have feelings. Everyone does. But there must be
a way to have them, without tumbling deeply into them. Just see them, only
name them, and that's all. You must choose to put any and all such sensations
off, to defer them. Even be rid of them! Some of them. Most. Keep maybe a
few, to help you remember the person you used to be. But mainly, focus on
something else. Go for cold control. Like, when you just saw our flat, but you
didn't let yourself immediately run over there to see if Mamma was home.
Yeah, like that, but with it all, and much more so, and every time.*

Kristian came up out of his crouch.

He took the packet of ammunition and explosives from the rucksack and stuffed it in the hole. He added the Webley revolver and the red-filtered flash, both wrapped in an oiled cloth and tucked into a rubber pouch. He scraped soil back across the top, then put back the square of vegetation. In late summer, this patch should flourish and render his cache undetectable.

He stood, then made his way back down to the cobblestone lane that threaded past the clumps of more modern tombstones. The ivy on the hillside looked somewhat disturbed. So he went back and churned up more of it in a few different places, so it did not look as if any particular path led anywhere.

"*Ha det, Pappa*," he said. "Our score has improved. Now a pair of them are laid low. Five more to go, before we reach even. At the very least! And I promise, I'll keep you informed on how the accounting goes."

He turned and walked down a path that led south.

～

Where the Kirkegårdsveien crossed through the valley, he took a set of stairs back up out of Lagård Gravlund. A man sat on a park bench outside a tiny funerary chapel, smoking a pipe. When he noticed Kristian, he took his pipe out, tapped it against the side of his knee, and thrust it back in his mouth.

Kristian sat down beside him.

"I have not seen many black storks return this year," Kristian said.

"Not many are left," the man replied.

"I miss hearing the clatter of their bills at night," Kristian said.

"A black stork would be lucky to nest near Stavanger now."

The man turned his head slightly and looked Kristian up and down. Kristian looked back. He saw salt-and-pepper hair curling out under the rim of a dark green Tyrolean hat. The man had a prominent nose, a deeply lined and somewhat saggy face, rheumy brown eyes that seemed thoughtful and a bit remote. He was clad in a tailored gray tweed jacket with leather trim, and a waistcoat draped with a gold watch-chain and fobs. The tobacco he was smoking had a rich and exotic fragrance.

He took the pipe out and pointed its stem at Kristian's feet.

"Those shoes," he said sternly. He frowned and shook his head.

"What about them?"

"Don't look much like civilian kit now, do they, lad?"

The man startled him by uttering this last sentence in perfectly accented English.

Just before, he'd spoken Norwegian like a native, in fact, someone from a central city, most likely Trøndheim. Yet now he sounded like a working bloke straight out of London.

Kristian looked down at his black tennis shoes and had to concede the point. Section D should also have supplied him with workman's brogans. Instead, his only choices had been these or gumboots.

"What should I do?"

The man sighed. He poked a forefinger into the bowl of the pipe to crush the coal and extinguish it. He stood up and dropped the pipe into his coat pocket.

"Let's go along the waterfront. Maybe we'll find a passed-out drunk. You can yank off his boots."

Kristian, frowning, stood up too. "I don't…"

"Relax," the man said. "It's a joke." He held out his hand. "I'm Rolf."

"And I am Fiske," Kristian said. They shook. Rolf's hand was smooth and well-manicured, its grip light.

"I'm curious," Rolf asked. "Did your bosses teach you how to follow people, Fiske?"

Kristian shook his head. "But I think I have an idea how it works."

"Really? So how, then?" Rolf shoved his hands into his coat pockets and rocked back on his heels. He was tall, lanky, bemused.

"Be inconspicuous."

Rolf smiled. "Correct. To a degree where you seem indifferent to me, and most other things on the street. All right? I want you to dawdle as you follow me. Keep way back. Don't worry about losing me, though, because *I'm* the one in charge of keeping *you* in sight. Just barely. And I'd like you to try to see if somebody else is following me, from a point a bit closer."

"When do we start?"

"Right now."

"Where are you taking me?"

"To our apartment. If you do spot a tail, he'll probably drop off as soon as he sees where I'm going. He already knows where I live."

"Then what?"

"Go around the block once, then come in the door you saw me enter."

"Won't that give me away?"

"All sorts of people go in and out of my door, at all hours."

"Why?"

"It's a bar."

"You live in a bar?"

"Man's got to live somewhere. Why not in a bar? Or above one! Cuts down on said man's travel time, should he require a snifter of cognac." Rolf leaned closer, peered at him. He drew a line with a finger, down from his own forehead to a cheekbone. "Say, what happened to you there?"

That was the spot where the German sentry had clubbed Kristian with his gun barrel. Kristian already knew the area felt tender; it likely also looked bruised.

"I got reprimanded by a German," Kristian said.

"Why?"

"Ahhh-h." Kristian paused. "I guess, for annoying him during his evening stroll."

*"We will not submit voluntarily. The struggle is already under way."*
—Norway's foreign minister, Halvdan Koht

# CHAPTER 13

Rolf had named his bar *Scrimshaw Puben*. Above its door hung a sign that displayed a painting of a huge sperm whale tooth. This pale tooth itself bore a maze of black scrimshaw lines that depicted a Viking ship riding the billows of a stormy sea.

Kristian halted to admire the sign for a second.

That whale tooth looked realistic, the image of the ship carved on it far more abstract. It made him think of some off-watch sailor, whiling away rare free time, crouched in a forecastle on a becalmed vessel, gouging a vision into a hunk of ivory with his sailor's awls and sail needles. Then rubbing in soot and tobacco juice, to make lines of his etching stand out. Kristian was able to visualize this easily, because scrimshaw had been Lars' hobby, and he'd gotten after it whenever he had an idle hour.

*Lars, you are now avenged*, Kristian thought. *Well, in part, maybe.*

Kristian recalled something a teacher had told him in class. *The prime function of good art is that it sparks your imagination.* This sign certainly did that. If the Stavanger waterfront had not already been flooded with bayside and ocean smells, tar and seaweed and salt, this sign could stimulate an onlooker to imagine them—and a vista of rolling swells and a yar ship too.

He tried to remember what the building had been before Rolf turned into the *Scrimshaw Puben*. A shop? A small warehouse? Probably just another bar. He looked down from the sign and saw that the tavern's dark red door stood unlatched. He shoved it open and entered warily.

The first thing he noticed was a large lit pantry, an *ad hoc* bottle shop, where a portly man stood at the shelf of a Dutch door, making change for a grizzled old man with a ragged coat collar raised up to his ears and a worn cap pulled down over his eyes. The large man who was making this sale had plump and ruddy cheeks, small eyes, glossy black hair parted almost in the middle of his head. As he shoved a flask of tawny fluid across the shelf to his customer, he took note of Kristian's arrival, made brief eye contact, and jerked his head to the left—indicating that Kristian should keep going.

He did, passing a darkened barroom with empty chairs and tables, then entered a dim hallway. This hall led to a restroom, then the door to a small kitchen, and next a stairwell, where Kristian encountered once more the odor of rich tobacco. Rolf sat atop the final tread of the stairs, puffing away on his pipe. He nodded at Kristian, stood, and beckoned.

He brought Kristian up into a spacious apartment that spread across the tavern's entire second floor. The main room held another small kitchen, table and chairs, a red plush couch, and a chiffonier with upper shelves populated by porcelain knick-knacks. Over by the window stood an easel that held a blank canvas. A tall stool lay on its side in front of the easel.

Two more doorways led elsewhere.

Rolf deftly tossed his Tyrolian hat up onto the nearest hook of a coat tree. His mouth widened to display heavily stained teeth. He tapped his temple with a forefinger.

"Brace yourself," he said. "I'm about to use my potent occult skills to access hidden knowledge about you, young Fiske. Ready? Here's how I read your aura. You're tired, you're hungry, and you very much need to take a rest."

~

Kristian opted for sleep first, with zero hesitation.

Rolf put him up on the couch. Went into a back room to get a pillow, and found Kristian already stretched out with his eyes closed. Rolf tossed a pair of knitted Afghans over him.

Hours later Kristian was lured back to wakefulness by the spicy aromas of a hunter's stew that Rolf had begun to heat on a gas burner. Kristian flung off his covers and sat up.

"Could you eat?" Rolf asked.

"Are you kidding?" Kristian held up the corner of an Afghan. "I could eat one of these blankets!"

Rolf chuckled. "Well, that certainly would be filling. But I imagine you'll find the flavor of Hermann's *hasenpfeffer* a bit more to your liking."

"If it's what I smell on the stove, then yes, absolutely. And by the way, who's Hermann?"

"Didn't you meet him when you came in?"

"The guy keeping shop? We saw each other. Didn't talk."

"That's Hermann. He keeps our bar running, he sings amateur opera, he cooks, he cleans our whole place up constantly. A perfect business partner for an untidy artist such as myself." Rolf sighed. "Hermann the German."

"German?" Kristian raised an eyebrow.

"Oh, he's not one of *those*!"

Rolf ladled rabbit stew into a bowl, atop a layer of boiled potatoes. He added a hunk of *rugbrød*—dark rye bread—on the side. He put the bowl on a round wooden table at the center of the room, waved a spoon at Kristian and set it down beside the bowl.

Kristian didn't need a second invitation. He quickly bent to put on his black tennis shoes, then saw that a pair of brown leather brogans had been placed beside them.

"Courtesy of Hermann, also," Rolf said. "I think you're about the same size."

"Yes," Kristian agreed, as he tried them on. "A little loose, not much."

"Here, toss me those dainty Brit ballet slippers of yours. The sooner we get rid of those clues to your highly suspicious past the better."

Kristian came to the table. The spicy fumes wafting off the bowl almost made him faint. He sat, grabbed the spoon and set to work. Rolf sat across from him, propped his chin on his fist and watched him eat.

"So, what are your plans?" Rolf asked him.

"For today?" Kristian mumbled through a mouthful of *rugbrød*.

"Today, and tomorrow. Or the rest of your life, if you feel an urge to truly expound."

Kristian swallowed. "First, I'll go to our apartment on Verksgata to see my mother."

"Ah, you're a local. You sound like one."

"And you. From Trøndheim, right?"

"Sure, I'm a Trønder. But I've traveled far and wide. Italy, Spain, Belgium. Then Germany. Hermann and I ran a dinner-theater in Munich. But we came up here three years ago, when it grew clear that Herr Hitler was about to run amok, without check or pause. Bought this building. Little dreaming that one day the Nazis might export themselves *en masse* way up here, too."

"So-o-o. Now you have chosen to resist. Instead of moving again. Brave."

Rolf gave a modest shrug. Kristian noted that he'd begun to tap lightly on the table with two fingers of his right hand.

"Have you picked up the radio I brought yet?"

Rolf shook his head. "We're just keeping an eye on it. We need to spend a day or so, see if anyone else is watching. Once we're sure that it's in the clear, we'll bring it straight up to our new place."

"New?"

"To get the best intelligence, we must be where the action is. That zone will be higher on the hill. We plan to open a tavern up there. Gives us a better view of the port, as well."

"You plan to run two places?"

"No, that would stretch Hermann a bit thin. We need to let out this one. Not that Hermann couldn't stand to be stretched thinner, mind you."

Kristian smiled.

"*Don't* repeat that joke," Rolf warned. "He's sensitive about his weight."

"All right, we'll label it 'top secret,'" Kristian said. "And since you wish to know my plans, well, when you get a radio link set up, you can ask the SIS what my plans are."

"They'll put you on a new assignment?"

"Maybe. Or ask me to come back, for more training. What lessons I received went by pretty quick. My instructors said it was a once-over-lightly."

Rolf nodded, scratched his cheek then tapped his lips. "And Fiske... You're a bit young for all this, aren't you?" he asked.

"Not at all," Kristian mumbled through a mouthful of stewed hare. "I'm twenty-one."

The truth was, he had barely turned eighteen during his training in Scotland.

"Sure, you are."

Kristian chose to change the subject. "You haven't asked me about the guy you told me to tail on our way here."

"You saw him?'

"Yes."

"Describe him."

"Short, thin. Slight limp. About forty years old. Round face. Brown hair. Who is he? From the state police? Or Gestapo?'

Rolf shook his head. "No. NKVD."

"What's that?"

"Sergei Sokolov is one of Stalin's agents in the NKVD, which is run by one of the filthiest assholes who's ever left a trail of blood and slime behind him, Lavrentiy Beria," Rolf said. He took in Kristian's look of confusion, then tapped on the table for a moment before he spoke. "I have to tell you the truth. You do worry me, young Fiske. Going back to England might very well be the smartest move for you."

"Why?"

"Espionage is tough work, highly hazardous, among monsters like these. Even covert resistance is no light chore! Trust me, things shall only grow more vicious, with no end of trouble in sight. You show talent, I'll admit, yet we both should also admit that you're a naif, not a knave." He tapped the table again. "You're a freshman in the College of Hard Knocks. You've been lucky thus far, but luck is far from all that's needed. Hate to say this, but I feel the Brits have taken advantage. You've been exploited. I'm pleased you got the radio here for us, but it's time to take leave of this crap. Go back to being a young man. Enjoy life for a while."

∾

Fists jammed in his jacket pockets, Kristian strode down the streets, heading for Verksgata and the Thorsen apartment. A storm of emotions churned inside him. He felt angry that Rolf had made him doubt his abilities. Most likely it was because Rolf regarded Kristian as a weak link, and he wanted to get him out of Stavanger before he upset their apple cart with a stupid mistake and thus jeopardized whatever operations Rolf and Hermann had underway.

Kristian not only hated feeling doubt, he also disliked a dawning realization that the idea of returning to England—and Greta!—*did* attract him. He didn't want it to feel that way. *What aspect of fleeing Norway again would mean I'm being strong, or being Norse, either one?*

Really, he should just bat that whole question aside. Wouldn't have to be answered until after the W/T was set up, and the SIS Section D had made clear its desires for Kristian or "Fiske." But leaving a decision on staying in Norway up to Cyclops and his cronies didn't please him, either. He wanted to be the author of this decision himself.

One thing Rolf was entirely right about. Cyclops wasn't above exploiting someone, if he thought it might give even a tiny boost to the British Empire's war effort. Which was exactly why the choice should be Kristian's. If he had to be a tool in somebody else's hand, at least he should be able to do so with his eyes open and a maximum degree of participation in choosing his fate.

The Thorsen home building stood before him, tan and blocky, with the bottom floor that held the print shop, and a short row of apartments on the next level up. Kristian's heart leapt in his chest. There was no light on or movement in those upper windows. Might Kari be there, right now? If she wasn't, he'd still get himself inside and wait there until she appeared, however long that might take. Days, if necessary!

The print shop on the lower level displayed a "Closed" sign on its front door. Kristian decided that was good. The staff inside might've recognized him on sight. He'd begun to think like a spy. Best if no one knew he'd returned to his hometown except for such individuals as he chose to inform. He turned up the collar of his jacket and tugged his cap down lower. *Old guy buying that booze at Scrimshaw Puben had the correct idea on keeping anonymous! Probably didn't want to be spotted by a minister when he came out carrying his sack of booze. Or by his wife, either.*

He jogged up the stairwell to the second floor, which held apartments A and B. The Thorsen front door stood behind the brass letter B. Kristian felt electrified with hope and anticipation as he neared it. Then he saw that the door had a new hasp and padlock screwed to it, right above the knob. Plus, a small poster stamped with a *Parteiadler*—the spread-winged eagle perched on a swastika—was pasted on the upper panel of the door. The poster stated this apartment had been sealed by order of the Gestapo. No entry was permitted.

Kristian gaped at it in shock.

His mind reeled. At an utter loss of what else to do, he knocked lightly on the door. No answer, of course. But he did hear a sound behind him. Another door being slowly opened, then swiftly shut. It came from apartment A. He went to its door and tapped. No answer. He waited patiently between two more bouts of knocking before he heard an old woman's voice quaver, "Who is it, please?"

"Mrs. Andersen, it's me. Kristian Thorsen. Your neighbor, Kristian!"

He heard something that might've been a gasp. Then, a bolt being drawn. The door cracked open and a bleary eye stared at him.

"Let me in, would you? I want to talk to you. I need to find out what's happened."

The old woman thrust her head out, looked quickly around the landing and down the stairwell, opened the door the rest of the way and beckoned for him to enter. Then she closed and bolted the door behind him.

"I shouldn't even be seen talking to you," she said.

She swiped at her nose with a hanky and returned it to the pocket of her housecoat.

"Why not?"

"They might arrest me too! They said they would come if I ever told anyone. They might throw me off the roof!"

"Who might?"

"You know, those ones who wear black, with those skull pins up on their hats."

"The Gestapo? The SS? For God's sake, tell me what happened! Where's Kari? Where's my mother?"

"Come. Sit. I will tell you. But after, please, for the love of Jesus, go away and never come back here again. For your safety. And for mine too."

They sat down by an oval table covered with a lace cloth, with a delicate tea service set on a wooden platter at the table's exact geographic center.

Mrs. Andersen held both hands, knobbed by arthritis, down in her lap and wrung them ceaselessly as she spoke of a day in Stavanger when the Gestapo chose to take over a new rest home built for the Norwegian elderly and turn it into their base. The state police sent word out that anyone with friends or relatives in the home had just a short period to clear them out. Most of its elderly residents managed to be rescued and were moved to other lodgings.

However, a few relatives lived in more distant towns and didn't get the word in time. An old friend of Mrs. Andersen, a woman up in Narvik had called her on the final night, well past the deadline, and frantic about missing it since her aunt was in the facility. She begged for help. Mrs. Andersen didn't think she could accomplish much on her own, and she knocked on Kari's door to ask her to come along. By the time they approached the rest home on Wesselsgata, the whole street was blockaded and German guards stood everywhere. Both women were barred from getting even a meter nearer.

"But you know your mother, when she puts her mind to something, no one can stand in her way. That's why I asked her to come with me." Mrs. Andersen wrung her hands. A tear ran from one of her rheumy eyes and tracked along the side of her nose. "And I knew she felt lonely, and at loose ends. She just had that one note from you, saying you and Ragnar were all right. But then she'd heard nothing, not for weeks and weeks."

"Yes. I'm well aware of that problem. Couldn't be helped. Then what happened? Tell me!"

"Kari knew a back route to the elder home. A narrow alley, just a tiny space between houses. It wasn't guarded. We went in through there. And then we saw... we saw what the Gestapo men were doing. They'd taken all the remaining old people, about a dozen of them, up to the top of the building. Five stories. And they threw them off. All the way down to the parking lot. To kill them! Where there was a dump truck. Some went in. Most didn't. The screaming! It was so high, thin, sad. Horrible! I can't forget it. I still hear it, all night sometimes."

Blood drained from Kristian's face. "What did Kari do?" He asked. He could already predict the answer but dreaded to hear his guess confirmed.

"She ran straight in. Tried to make them stop. Of course, then they arrested her. And I... I ran away. Well, hobbled. As fast as I could. I'm old. Just like those poor people."

Mrs. Andersen wept openly now. She picked up the hem of her apron with both knobby hands and mopped her whole face with it.

"I feel like such a coward!" she wailed.

Kristian had a fleeting impulse to comfort her but banished it instantly. This woman had knowingly put his mother in peril. And Kari felt like one of the last good things from his former life still clinging to existence in Norway. As for horror and dread at what the Nazis were capable of—well, he felt an incremental jolt, but not a complete shock. After the wanton sinking of the *Snekka*, no ugly incident involving the invaders could now surprise him. He figured that most Germans at their core were like that mocking *Luftwaffe* pilot who'd shot up their boat.

"Where did they take her?" His voice was low and urgent.

"I don't know. But the next day, they came here. Searched your apartment. Carried things away. Then they told me they'd been tipped off that I'd been seen at their new headquarters that night. I denied it. Well, they said if they ever heard that I said anything about it, or talked about your mother that I would be gone, too."

Kristian abruptly stood, almost knocking his chair over.

"You won't… you won't…"

"What!"

"Repeat anything about this to anyone else. Will you?"

His jaw clenched, Kristian turned and strode out of apartment "A," without uttering another word. Comforting this old woman now, he decided, would have to be someone else's business.

*"Opinion has swung in our favor in Sweden. It's the result of our victories, which are being greeted with the most enormous admiration, all over the world."*
—Josef Goebbels, *the Diaries*

## CHAPTER 14

Evening on Karl Johan Street. Helene strolled through a long summer twilight. Although it was 9 p.m., the entire dome of the sky remained tawny from an almost-sunset.

The scents of blossoms that she'd craved back in April were common features of evening air now, strata of aromatic magic that conferred delight.

But Helene's days in Oslo still felt blighted, due to the occupation's steadily tightening grip. Although the Germans still tried to waltz their way into Norwegian hearts, they did it wearing jackboots. A prime exhibit was that gigantic banner Goebbels and Lunde's minions had draped across the face of the Storting's building in downtown Oslo.

This traditional home of Norway's parliament, an architectural marvel of yellow brick, now sported on its stately façade a huge "V" for victory and a banner that proclaimed, *"Deutschland Siegt An Allen Fronten!"*— "Germany Wins On All Fronts!" The sign was an Axis attempt to pirate the Allies' spreading use of the V as a symbol of victory.

Helene hated seeing the thing on the Parliament building. It was like daubing a black beard on the face of the Madonna. But she couldn't refrain from glancing yet again at the banner as she passed it.

*Just as ugly as the last time. The Krauts would be far easier to take if they weren't so crude, so often, she thought. How can it be that they never perceive this? Lieutenant Ziegler does understand it. But that man's just one out of far too many who simply fail to see it at all. Bullying tactics seem to be the Nazi approach to just about everything!*

Across the street, the ornate façade of the Grand Hotel stood crowned by four lofty flagpoles, two on each side of the hotel's clock tower. Each pair of poles hoisted a red-and-gold St. Olav's Cross next to a red-and-black swastika.

*They keep cramming this idea down our throats that we should be united Nordic tribes. Natural allies. Brothers and sisters. Ha! I'm getting major indigestion from that.*

Just beyond the main entrance to the Grand stood glass-paneled doors to the street-level café, the Victorian-era hangout of the Kristiania Bohemians, a salon where Henrik Ibsen took his daily lunch or dinner, and where Edvard Munch had painted him taking it. Tonight, music and light spilled from the bistro's windows to wash and swirl around the crowded sidewalk tables outside.

Helene moved to open the door, but a *Wehrmacht* officer inside saw her approach through a glass panel, grabbed the knob on his side and beat her to it. He held the door open, stood respectfully aside and inclined his head as she entered. But he also scanned her up and down as if he could peel off her floral print dress with his gaze, then awarded her a grin that was primarily a leer bracketing a show of teeth.

Instead of thanking him, she ignored him. She stepped well inside the hustle and bustle of the room and scanned the crowded space for Ziegler.

The café was full of men in various styles of German uniforms, a few clad in civilian mufti, and all of them clustered around young Norwegian women who wore bright lipstick and their best summer frocks. The room was filled with guffaws and the hum of conversation, clinking glasses, a scrape of chairs on the floor. A small band bravely sought to pierce the din with a set of popular tunes—British, German, French or American, the origin of the songs didn't seem to matter much to anyone.

Waiters scurried through this whole throbbing maze with trays deftly upheld on their fingertips. Perched high over it all was the broad mural painted by Per Krogh, of the Bohemians of a previous century.

*Those old-timers all look dignified and respectable, compared to this bunch! Helene thought. Who might best render the scene we see here tonight? Goya, or Bosch?*

Ziegler was sitting at the far end of the café's bar. She made her way over to him.

"You look absolutely terrific," he said. He pulled his coat off the stool next to him and patted its seat.

"I made no effort," Helene said as she sat down, "to look any particular way."

"Well, you don't have to."

"Why did you wish to meet in such a noisy place?"

"It will do you good to be seen where Germans and Norwegians relax together. It's a theme we wish to stress. Also, noise can form a shield. People who matter will see us being sociable. That's a plus. And they won't be able to hear a word we're saying. That's another."

His fingers twirled the stem of an empty cocktail glass.

"May I order you a drink?"

"I don't touch alcohol."

"I must say, you're an exceptionally well-behaved young lady."

"I am," Helene conceded.

"Why is that?"

She shrugged. "Don't you have Lutherans in Germany?"

"Many. But only a few comport themselves with the discipline that you do."

She looked at him. "I have found, even if a person is careful, trouble can find you out none-the-less. I'm not the only person in Norway discovering that nowadays. Should one then go on the hunt for trouble? Sounds exciting, yet it's absolutely ridiculous. You could get double returns on your investment."

Ziegler sighed. "Helene, you are beautiful, smart, and strong-willed. You'll make some lucky man a fabulous wife, someday."

"Maybe," Helene said. "I'm in no rush to find out. What I *do* want to find is anything new about Kari Thorsen. That's why I'm here. Have you learned anything?"

Ziegler placed both hands palms down atop the bar and spread his fingers. "Not much. My best information is that she's not been shot. At least, not yet. I suppose you already know that she's been shipped off to a camp in Germany."

"I've heard it could be Sachsenhausen. Is that the one?"

He shook his head. "Perhaps," he said. "But if so, that may not be her final destination. Prisoners often get reassigned once their talents have been assessed. We need skilled labor in certain fields, and in various camps. Naturally, most inmates would much rather work than lounge about and get bored. Especially since, if they serve the Reich well, they can wind up winning an early release. '*Arbeit macht frei*,' as they say."

Helene looked puzzled. "Hans, you are an intelligence officer, correct?"

"Of the *Abwehr*, yes. We operate a foreign intelligence service for the *Wehrmacht*. I thought you knew that."

"How is it that you're not able to just snap your fingers and find everything out?"

"Well-l-l, that's simply not how it works. You see, our *Abwehr* is far from the only game in town. The Gestapo, I'm sure you're familiar with them. It's short for *Geheime Staatspolizei*, a national consolidation of police forces engineered by Goering. Then there's the SD, the *Siecherheitsdienst*, a security service for the SS, which is Himmler's creature. And there's the *Forschungsamt*, or "research office" of the Luftwaffe—a nice, bland name, right?—which we're not supposed to know about, yet somehow I do, and that agency eavesdrops on phone chats between people of any importance in Germany, then reports directly to Hitler and Goering. Each of those units has subunits, led by ambitious officials trying to score an edge on everyone else.

"Get the picture? Think of scorpions who fill a bucket, all fighting for a bit of space, light and air, which they can only win by stinging and pinching and wrestling their way up to the top. Borders between outfits are violated often, while everyone pretends to be looking the other way.

"Now, I'm *Abwehr*, and we're the original specialists in the intelligence game. We think of ourselves as the aristocrats. And in many ways, we are. We persuade, rather than compel. *In extremis*, we use the ice pick, not the cudgel.

"We must appear to adhere to all norms of the turf war. If I need info or an action from the Gestapo, or the SD, I try to offer them an equivalent in return, or consent to owe them some future favor. I've needed to make up a tale about why I'm curious about the fate of some particular Norwegian *frau*. I must take what I'm offered, and not raise eyebrows by pushing for more. Understand?"

Helene nodded soberly. "But you will find out more when and as you can, then let me know, right?"

"Well." He laced his fingers together on the bar rim. "Describe our transaction."

"What do you mean?"

"What can you offer me in exchange?"

Helene straightened up on her stool.

"What is it that you want?" Her tone was cool and clipped.

Ziegler smiled, and parried. "Do you dance? If you do, perhaps a twirl on the dance floor, at some point?"

Helene colored. "Folk dances, only. We were all taught them when I was younger."

"Very well. Let's defer that request. But your secretarial role at the *Reichskommissar's* headquarters intrigues me. It has distinct possibilities. You might overhear a hint of some big event about to occur. And personnel developments too, such as who's climbing up or who's being dragged down, and why."

"You make a rather vague request."

"You're sharp enough, Helene. As we visit and talk, which bits can be of use to me shall become more obvious to you, I think."

Helene thought this over. She gave a slight nod. Then she reached out and touched the back of Ziegler's left hand. She pointed at a band of pale skin that encircled his ring finger.

"What's that?" she asked softly.

It was Ziegler's turn to stiffen.

"I removed a ring," he said.

"Why?"

"I'm divorced. Well, truthfully, my wife and I are separated. A divorce is a tough procedure if you're high up in the Party. Our grand ideal, you see, is a solid German family, popping out litters of blond, blue-eyed Party members like pups, until our rapidly expanding nation is peopled by a whole swarm of them. Failure to live up to this goal is frowned on. Unless you're the Fuhrer. He can do what he likes. But Goebbels? He can't. For example, Hitler insists that he stay married to Magda. For the good of the Party."

Ziegler then seemed amused by a further thought, but he kept it to himself.

"If you had a wedding ring on your finger when we first met at the school, I don't recall," Helene said. "Yet since then, I've seen only this small, pale band of skin. Like the ghost of a ring."

"So?" Ziegler said, annoyed that he hadn't managed to shift the topic.

"It stays pale, week after week. Even now, in summer, when sunlight should tan it to match the rest of your hand. Which it *would* do if you kept your ring off. That means, on most days, you must wear it. When you're on duty, or around your office. Q.E.D., as we were taught to say in logic class. Do you only take it off for me?"

Ziegler's mouth bent. He wanted to offer a nonchalant grin by way of response but couldn't quite pull it off.

"See there, now? You *are* clever," he said. "And curious. Plus, you pinpoint the essence of intelligence work. One observes objectively, then one interprets. You might turn out to be rather good at it."

Helene slid off her stool. "I have to go," she murmured.

"Wait. Don't you want to dine…"

"I must get home. A good evening to you, *Oberleutnant* Ziegler."

Helene stalked toward the door of the Grand Café as the hotel band struck up *Lili Marlene*. Many in the crowd instantly stopped drinking, smoking, flirting and conversing in order to bounce to their feet, face the musicians and pour the blended slurry of their voices into the hit tune.

∼

Helene burst out into the night. The sun was finally below the horizon, stars had started to appear. Far fewer city streetlights competed now. Oslo's night sky had begun to look more like the skies out in the countryside.

She strode westward with vigor, heading to their flat. Not many streetcars would be running at this hour; it simply wasn't worth waiting around for one to trundle up.

Helene glimpsed a shadowy but somehow familiar shape moving up the street in front of her. Another person coming from the opposite direction muttered a greeting to that roly-poly shape, was handed something, then the recipient swiftly turned the corner. Helene observed the same type of exchange happen with someone new a bit further along the street.

This oddly familiar shape turned left and ambled along to the south on a side lane named Rosenkrantz. Helene glimpsed yet another shadowy figure walk past the shape, get handed an article of some sort, then turn aside.

*What seems so familiar?*

Intrigued, Helene chose to follow the round shape for one more block, down through the park, while she tried to figure it out. Doing that would not take her very far out of her way.

A single streetlight gleamed here. No one stood beneath it, or anywhere around it. And nothing moved ahead of her. Then the round shape stepped out from behind a bush and walked straight for her. A ball atop a sphere, a round head balanced on a dumpling body, it moved toward her quickly, with a basket dangling from one arm. A face framed by curly gray hair, a pair of sharp and beady dark eyes turned up to Helene as the shape walked by her.

Then a harsh voice came from behind her back. "Hey! What do you think you're doing?"

Helene turned around. The plump old woman stood there, both legs braced, glaring at her.

"What?"

"Following me! D'you think I'm stupid?"

"I just wanted to see who you were."

"Well, I know who *you* are. *Du er ei tyskertøse!*"—which meant, you're a whore who fucks Germans. The old woman spat on the ground, and at that instant Helene recognized her. She was that woman she'd first seen at the Solli Plass, the one whom Ziegler had threatened to arrest when she'd spat near them before, on that day they'd gone out to lunch.

"No." Helene answered calmly, but a deep cleft had appeared between her brows, and her eyes moistened. "That's not who I am."

"Then who are you?"

Helene paused. She grasped the collar of her dress and turned it up. A paper clip had been sewn to the underside.

The old woman saw it, nodded, but then set her jaw and continued to glare. Helene let her collar drop. Their eyes locked for a few seconds.

"All right," the woman said. "I'll take a chance. But you'll take one too! A much bigger one than you know. There are plenty of true patriots here who strive to protect me. And they'll stop at nothing to do so, understand? Here."

She reached into her basket and tugged out a loaf of bread, a narrow one, more like a French baguette than a proper Norwegian loaf. She handed it to Helene.

"Like what you read? Be here one week from tonight, at this same time. If you do not come, I warn you, your name will go onto a special list. We already know everything there is to know about you. And now, young lady, you turn around and get lost. Leave me alone to make my rounds."

Helene cradled the crispy loaf in both hands, feeling mystified and excited. The woman waddled away, grumbling to herself as she vanished into the park shadows. Helene squeezed the bread she'd been given, trying to evaluate it. The loaf felt hard, rather stale. She felt at a loss for what it all meant.

~

She didn't comprehend the true nature of that odd gift till she was back in her bedroom in Otto's apartment. A candle ablaze in a crystal holder on her dresser provided light. She observed a knife kerf that went entirely around the loaf. She deduced that one end of the loaf of bread had been sliced off, then glued back on. She tore the loaf open. A roll of papers was tucked in a hollow within. She plucked out this roll and unfurled it, inhaling the vapors of cheap mimeograph.

It was a crude newspaper, entitled, *Dette Er Vårt Land*, meaning, This Is Our Land. The first page held a feature about how to fill a washtub with dirt and use it to grow potatoes. That was not so exciting. The second page had excerpts from King Haakon's initial speech directed back to Norway via the BBC. It provided more of a thrill. The third page summarized the resistance plans of leading Norwegian trade unions. Helene found that utterly fascinating. Clearly, a movement was brewing in Oslo. Perhaps even a full-scale rebellion! Her pulse throbbed in her temples as she imagined what this might mean for her, for the city, even the nation.

*"Everyone imposes his own system as far as his army can reach."*
—Josef Stalin, *interview*

CHAPTER 15

Kristian lowered two fingers into his shirt pocket, began to pluck out the photo of his mother to look at it again. But he realized his knuckles still dripped blood from his punch through the apartment's window, which made him halt. He wiped the back of his hand on one leg of his pants, leaving red streaks.

The image of Kari in his pocket had been snapped on her day of graduation from high school, a fresh-faced, dark-haired farm girl. It was one of the few personal items left behind after the Gestapo had ransacked the Thorsen flat. Kristian had found it after he'd climbed up over a balcony railing and bashed his way into the apartment. It had infuriated him to discover how utterly their home had been vandalized, every stick of furniture knocked to slivers, dresser drawers dumped out, shelves pulled down, wardrobes tipped over, and the resulting mounds of Thorsen belongings picked through then booted up into drifts against the apartment walls.

Kari's student photo had rested in a small gilt frame placed on his mother's dresser. But that frame had been bashed apart in the search for something or other, and the print of his mom cast aside. He'd tenderly picked it up to tuck in his shirt pocket.

He brought his wounded hand up again to the outer fabric of his shirt. Kristian half-smiled, envisioned himself touching his mother's cheek and hugging her. *I send this touch to you, Mamma, wherever you might be!* It felt as though a living particle of his demolished past could accompany him once more. An isolated spark of brightness. Not much to weigh on the scales against the inky pall of everything tragically lost. Not much of an antidote to cure his dread of grander dispossessions to come. But something, a touchstone, an icon of hope. *Where have they taken Kari, what can they do to her? And what, if anything, shall I ever be able to do about it?*

This line of thought faded as he drew nearer to *Scrimshaw Puben.*

High time to be on his guard. Not dwell in the past, not speculate about a future, but inhabit in full this fraught present. And though it demanded his undivided attention, his approach to the bar still had to appear lazy and roundabout. The coast looked clear. He was surprised to find the front door locked. But he'd left by a rear entrance, so he slipped back there through an alley. He found a back-door key that Rolf had told him about, under a loose cobblestone, then let himself in. The place was dim and silent. He ascended the steps, opened the flat door.

And found Hermann standing there, with Kristian's rucksack turned inside-out and all of its contents sprawled across the table. This sight instantly reminded him of the messy search of his family's apartment and Kristian's fury ignited.

"What the hell are you up to?" he demanded.

"Performing a simply identity check, young Fiske," Hermann rumbled.

"Put everything back, exactly as you found it!"

"Sorry. I've not finished yet."

"Well, you should not have begun!"

"Fiske, you're a guest in someone else's house. Rules are not yours to make."

Kristian stalked up to him and thrust out his jaw. His impression of Hermann, when he'd first glimpsed him down in the bar, was of someone big yet soft. However, up close he could detect the bulk of muscle under all that padding. Still, anger outweighed caution.

He clenched both fists. "Just stop it. Now!" he commanded.

Hermann smirked as he continued to run his fingers along the seams of Kristian's spare clothing, pinching them in a search for hidden contents.

"Make me," he replied mildly.

Kristian jerked a hand back behind his neck to yank out his dagger. He drove it forcefully into the wood of the tabletop, while keeping his hand poised upon its hilt. Hermann quit smiling. Those small dark eyes drilled into Kristian's own.

"Fiske," Hermann said slowly. "I've been our bouncer at every club we've owned. You carry a blade? Bah! Doesn't worry me. I've dealt with such toys, many a time. If you put a grenade in your pocket, even that wouldn't bother me. Before you could pull its pin, you'd be bouncing down those stairs. After which, the next person to inspect your belongings would be a city coroner. All right?"

Kristian sucked in a deep breath, inadvertently taking in Hermann's odors of stale sweat, beer, spicy sausage, floral hair pomade and minty aftershave. He couldn't guess what his next move ought to be. Hermann didn't seem persuadable by any technique Kristian had acquired from Section D, or anywhere else for that matter. Attacking such an exceptionally large and extraordinarily composed individual, particularly after he'd been set on guard—well, that appeared to be a suicide mission.

Footsteps on the stairs saved him from a decision. The apartment door swung open, and a man appeared. Rolf no longer looked like a European gentleman of means, since he was clad in the dishabille of a waterfront bum. It took Kristian a full second to realize that he'd seen Rolf out on the street without being able to recognize him there.

Rolf studied the vivid tableau before him. And suddenly he was gripping a tiny automatic pistol and leveling its business end at Kristian.

"Take your paw off that knife, Fiske," Rolf said. "Then please, go sit down."

"But he's rooting through my gear!"

"I know. Because I asked him to."

"Why?!"

"Spies can have a good relationship," Rolf said. He rolled his shoulders and smiled. "Not compulsory, but they can. One way for them to get there is to know almost zero about each other. Another way is for them to know absolutely everything. The latter policy would be my preference. So, that's why I followed you around this afternoon."

Kristian eyed him.

"Sit and relax," Rolf encouraged. His tone had turned amiable, soothing. "Then, perhaps, I might take a swipe at bandaging up your hand." He pointed the barrel of his gun at Kristian's bloody fingers. "Here's another tip, Fiske. If a rock isn't available, there are two smart ways to break a window. One is, you pull your coat sleeve down to shield your fist before you strike. However, I recommend the superior method—just use your elbow. Assuming you have a good, stout coat on, of course. If you can manage find one with nice leather patches, like mine, before you go around breaking-and-entering, that would be best."

~

Hermann, oddly enough, had started to cry. His dark eyes gushed like tiny mountain springs. From them, silvery creeks trickled down the rounded hillocks of his cheeks.

Actually, they wept together. It began due to Kristian's rendition of the death of Ragnar. He told it simply, but the story was the more vivid and touching for that. And as he related all he'd just found out about his mother Kari's arrest by the Gestapo, finishing with his dread about her well-being now, the tear ducts on them all spurted into action.

Kristian then caught himself, bit his lips, and forced himself to harden. *Ridiculous!* he thought. *We appear to be weaklings and fools. You yourself despised Mrs. Andersen for all her sobbing. Are you a puny old woman, too? Plus, why should these men give themselves over to grief? They didn't even know my parents!*

Rolf tugged a big white cotton handkerchief out of a coat pocket to dab at his eyes, and simultaneously gave the back of Hermann's fat hand a few comforting pats. He exhaled heavily. Then he blew his honker of a nose.

"Well!" Rolf said. "You certainly have jolted our memories of the terror we sought to flee by coming here. We've lost persons near and dear too, a great many of them. Now, our beloved Norway has been forced to attend a *Hexennacht*. Germany's pagan Bacchanal. And thus comes your own chance to taste the gall in its Black Mass wine. The savagery Hermann and I've seen already predicts what will be experienced up here. It defies easy description. You'd need to see it to believe it. Even then you might not believe what you see! You've heard the idea of inmates taking over an asylum? Much the same. Next, stir in the notion of murderers running a prison. While turning your whole nation into one—a prison, I mean."

Hermann said, "Another part of the revelation comes as you learn what you must try to do to yank out that poisonous weed. It's a wretched struggle." He groped behind him on the kitchen sideboard for his rolled-up apron, unfurled it, wiped his face with it, then tossed it back onto the counter. "Let fascism establish itself, and look at the ridiculous measures one must take to try to uproot it." He slapped a meaty hand back onto the table as if to reset a balky meter or smack off an electric switch of some kind, then cleared his throat and gazed at Rolf.

Rolf nodded his agreement, his mouth set in in a flat line that was a pained attempt at a smile. He turned his attention to Kristian.

"So, young Fiske, you do check out properly," Rolf said. "Not that I greatly doubted you, yet we weren't quite sure of you either. One can't be, in this game. And that's why I spent my afternoon in a quest for fresh information."

"Yeah? What were your discoveries? My favorite color? The name of my childhood dog? Things I like to eat for lunch?"

"Confirmation of all of my earlier points. You're young, you're talented, and the British have used you in a cynical manner, without troubling themselves overly in seeking to grasp either your nature or your needs. Plus, I would add one more finding—that you are a quite dangerous young man. Some of which is intentional. And some I think, not."

"What is it you understand about me that the Brits don't?"

Rolf's basset-hound face arranged its creases into something that was more recognizable as a smile.

"When you told the English intelligence officers of your father's last words to you, did they ask you what it meant?"

"No."

"There. You see?" Rolf folded his arms.

"You didn't ask me about it, either," Kristian pointed out.

"Uh-huh. That's your big difference, right there."

"What?"

"I didn't need to."

Kristian shook his head. He looked down at the floor for a second. When he looked up his head was still shaking, yet he also wore a smile. "Rolf," he said. "I think you are perhaps the most arrogant person I've ever met."

"Thank you." Rolf beamed. "You can see why I had to get away from home for a while. Right? Norway's standards of humility or reticence, they're just not my style."

"Oh, no question about it," Hermann agreed. "If there was an Olympics in arrogance, Rolf would be out in front and pulling away. But I've grown used to it."

"I don't see how."

"You become infected with it. Or inoculated by it. One of those, I think."

"Well, how about hitting me with smaller doses. Please?"

"I should stop using my snow shovel, move on down to a spoon?" Rolf looked at Hermann.

"Why not, if you can manage it," Herman said.

"Well, we'll see," Rolf said.

"Won't we," Hermann said.

"Look," Kristian said. "I've told you about me, and you've also clearly done plenty of your own prying." He pointed indignantly at his emptied-out rucksack. "But I know next-to-nothing about you. That's not fair."

"Oh, it's fine," Rolf said. He flapped a dismissive hand.

"No, it isn't."

"Well, why not?" Hermann asked.

"You said yourself, spies should know everything or nothing about each other, right? Well, I don't need to know everything, but I already know something. Enough to compromise you, at any rate. You're at risk already. How about a little more? Why not gamble? As a sign of trust. Which you recently said, I believe, had increased for you."

"Perhaps you misinterpret my reluctance."

"Perhaps not."

Rolf sighed. "Well, at least part of it come from a different explanation. Our story's complex. Not very easy to summarize. And it goes back to a *much* earlier time inside Germany." He looked up at Hermann. "Should I?"

Hermann nodded.

"What do you call that illustrated column we see sometimes in large newspapers, or the film shorts in theaters? About things and people. The remarkable, the unbelievable." Rolf asked him.

Hermann frowned. "Ripley's?"

"Yes! 'Ripley's Believe It or Not.' Exactly." Rolf looked at Kristian. "You might find this hard to believe, youngster, but both I and Hermann helped to launch the Nazi Party."

Kristian's eyes widened.

"You see, in its early days, the word 'socialist,' well it represented a key plank in the National Socialist German Workers Party. You know, NSDAP, what we now shorten to Nazi. That socialism theme helped to keep labor engaged with the movement."

"Until we saw the truth, far too late," Hermann inserted.

"Hitler betrayed us when he let the capitalists retain the means of production, and the profits, as long as he and his cronies could manage and direct what they did. While a big chunk of their lucre went to fund his aims, of course."

"It was the first sign that our SA—the 'brownshirts,' we workingmen— were going to be fed to the dogs!" Hermann exclaimed.

"All the while, Hermann and I were activists loyal to the Strasser brothers, Hitler's main opponents within the party. We fought to keep the socialist themes out in the forefront. Hermann worked with Ernst Rohm and his staff, and I with the socialists and more *avant garde* artists of Munich."

"Don't fudge it," Hermann growled. "Tell him the truth."

"I am."

"Not enough of it. We have plenty on Fiske. Make it fair, like he says."

Rolf frowned, then smiled. "All right. Hermann was the socialist. But me, I went straight for the basic communist solution. I was a Trotskyite, if you want to know the truth."

"A bit more, please," Hermann insisted. "I *did* work for Rohm. Right at his side, in the early days. And whom did you work for?"

Rolf tapped two fingers on the table, then cleared his throat. "I was an agent for the GRU. I told you about the NKVD, Beria's outfit, which is the Soviet secret police. Russia's version of the Gestapo, if you will. In contrast, the GRU is the main intelligence arm of the Soviet armed forces."

"I have long known we have communists in Norway," Kristian said. "There are many on the waterfront, especially among the stevedores. Lars, who crewed on our *Snekka*, was a red."

"Right," Rolf nodded. "Norway's party is tough and feisty. And some units struggled to stay independent of the Soviets. Of which I now heartily approve. And I've come a good long way toward connecting with the cells up here."

"Meanwhile, former comrades have gotten irked at Rolf's departure," Hermann put in. "They'd much prefer him to stay in Stalin's harness."

"Is that why that NKVD guy is keeping an eye on you?" Kristian asked.

"Very good, young Fiske," Rolf said. "You *do* have talent. One might even say, an aptitude."

"Quit calling me Fiske. If you followed me? You know what my real name is."

"Sure. But I like Fiske."

"Is Rolf your real name?"

He shook his head.

"What is it?"

He shook his head once more. "Better if you do not know. Especially should you happen to wind up sitting in a Gestapo interrogation room, some day. But Hermann is indeed Hermann. How's that?"

"The goddamn hell you say!" Hermann exclaimed.

Rolf rolled his eyes. "Okay. He's actually Marlene Dietrich, in heavy disguise."

Hermann fat cheeks dimpled as his grin broadened.

"But in the interests of a complete survey of relevant issues, Fiske, there's an amazing rumor I heard today. I'd like to run it by you, see what you think. It seems there was a killing out at the Tungenes Fyr. A pair of slayings, really, and the Gestapo has gotten rather exercised about it. Do you happen to possess any additional information?"

Kristian smiled tightly. "Better for you if you do not know."

Rolf chortled, clapped hands. "See? Such a quick study this lad is!"

"I might not wear a deerstalker cap or a cape," Rolf continued. "Yet I *do* own a Meerschaum pipe! So, let me play Sherlock for a moment. Time of this killing is just before you paddled your boat into Stavanger. You did have to pass by Tungenes at night to get here. You mentioned to me when we first met that a bruise on your face came from a German whom you had annoyed, did you not? And just now, you and Hermann had a tense moment, and how did you propose to settle the disagreement? With this!" Rolf seized Kristian's dagger and wrenched it free from the tabletop, then rotated the blade slowly under the light as he studied it.

"Wilkinson's marque," he observed. "It's a Brit blade. You've had Brit commando training. Plus, you revealed that your hatred of Nazis is well founded. Thus, we now have stacked up means, motive and opportunity in one spot. A killer's unholy trinity. True?"

Kristian shrugged. "I don't just hate Germans in general," he admitted. "I hate the *Luftwaffe*, in particular. And since they took my mother away, I must lump in the Gestapo, too. Maybe they should be at the top of my list."

"Duly noted. Your list of enemies strongly begins to resemble our own. But, to return to events on Tungenes. Gestapo investigators were aghast at what they found there, since it looked like this killer truly enjoyed his work. That encroaches on their turf! They hate that. You see, the dead sentries were left in a macabre pose, suggesting they had a dispute and attacked each other. Positioning them like that was crude joke, really, since a forensic exam quickly demonstrated that their blades didn't match the death wounds. Have you anything to add?"

Kristian shrugged again but couldn't resist adding a slight smile.

Rolf steepled his fingers. "So much for the unfathomable past. Let me use my psychic skills to peer into the future. Clearly, we have a skilled assassin on hand. The Germans are beside themselves, trying to figure out who he is, who he works for, what his game might be. Is he a saboteur? A provocateur? A disgruntled local? Why kill two sentries, then vanish? And most importantly—who might his next victim be?

"Now, Hermann and I have special knowledge. We're also aware that this culprit is on the loose in Stavanger, but we understand that he might leave soon, to sneak back to Britain. We are even willing to ease his path, provide logistical support, a hide-out, plus access to Hermann's delicious cooking. Not every psychotic slasher gets a sweet deal like that, I'm telling you. And it occurs to me, perhaps our assassin might want to do us a favor in return, before he fades entirely from the scene."

"Such as?" Kristian asked. "If I happen to run across this mysterious assassin, perhaps I can tell him."

"Remember that NKVD tail that followed me, the morning you arrived? If this man could somehow be gotten rid of, well, that would absolutely be lovely for us."

"What reason do I have to attack a Russian? The Soviets have never done anything to hurt me."

"Ah. But they've dumped a massive amount of evil on others. Stalin's purges would've appalled even Lenin. Anyway, a certain birdie is tweeting to me that Sergei is now focused on gathering evidence that I might be a double agent, a two-timing culprit who's in bed with the Brits. Surely you can see, I cannot have this man reach any firm conclusion on the subject. Or after he's done so, share it with Moscow."

"Would not Beria's guys simply assign another agent, if he was killed?"

"Of course. But in our spooky business, *all* solutions are temporary. Any new agent would start off flat-footed. That buys us time, space and options. Plus, I can think of one more aspect to this job which you may find attractive."

"What's that?"

"After the Gestapo men find a Russian agent has been slain in Stavanger by the same blade that killed their sentries? Well, it will send them into an absolute tizzy! Fun to watch. It'll be like tossing a firecracker into a henhouse."

"Why don't *you* guys kill him? Why put me on it? Why try to get fancy? I can loan you my knife. Just remember to wipe it clean before you give it back."

"We can't. We'll be busy."

"Doing what?"

"Crafting air-tight alibis for ourselves. See, Fiske, you could evade a Gestapo dragnet simply by exiting from Stavanger. But we must stay. We've got a ton of additional work to accomplish. And we need to maintain a Caesar's wife type of reputation in town if we're to make our projects pay off."

Hermann crossed ham-like forearms. "*Jawohl,*" he agreed, as his shellacked boulder of a head tilted in agreement.

*"The Fuhrer says England must get a knock-out blow. Quite right! England's power is a myth. It must be destroyed, or there will be no peace."*
—Josef Goebbels, *the Diaries*

# CHAPTER 16

Otto sat brooding. He slumped in an armchair in front of a window that overlooked the urban street of Odinsgata, with its infrequent pedestrians and cyclists, the few cars spewing blue fumes from the crude gas generators mounted in their trunks. Street traffic had fallen off by half or more since the German invasion. Now the citizens of Oslo generally had fewer places to go, a lot less money to spend after they got there, and not much available to buy anyway. There had been a steady drain of products and foodstuffs and raw materials out of Norway so that these goods could be dumped pell-mell into the slavering, insatiable maw that was the German war effort. Shop shelves had emptied and storefronts been boarded up at an increasing rate. Display windows left exposed were frosted by dust—and became bulletin boards for any rogue with a mischievous finger.

Otto's basset-hound face sagged more than usual. At times he pinched his lower lip between thumb and forefinger while he puffed out a sigh. A pad of lined paper on his lap, ready to receive his notes recommending PR solutions for Quisling's administrative quandaries, held instead only wandering, looping, intersecting doodles.

Helene dreaded watching his swan dives into a sulk. Lately he'd performed many such plunges. Amid them, Otto managed to be both fretful and listless. He relied upon her to lure or coax him from his bad mood instead of taking any active measure of his own. Even then, she felt like she had to goad him almost continually before he deigned to manifest even a hint of movement.

*Like trying to dress a kid who refuses to go to school*, she thought. *And that really IS it, isn't it? Otto seems like a mopey child now. Hard to believe that he was his family's eldest son. Ragnar was younger than Otto by how many years, ten? Yet Ragnar had always seemed—what—more mature? Not that. He was really a big kid himself. But a steadier, more balanced one, on a somewhat even keel. Too bad such traits didn't run strong and true through the whole family! Well, Kristian had inherited Ragnar's sure and enthusiastic psyche—perhaps a bit too much of it. Hard to believe that both of those vital personalities were gone. Erased from the earth. It seems the darkness of these times can rub out almost any spark, no matter how bright or vivid.*

*The times have certainly put a damper on Otto. Three years ago, Otto became my guardian and protector. But it seems as if that arrangement is being stood on its head. So now, I get to be his mommy? A job I neither applied for, nor certainly ever wished for. Such a mystery is life. Where's the Lord's mighty hand to steer events, when you really need it? In fact, I'd settle for a little prod from His fingertip, at this point. It's hard to know what direction to go, which path to take…*

Helene brought him a hot mug of milky tea. Otto accepted the cup wanly, sniffed its vapors, set it on an end table without drinking.

"Sir, you've sat here for hours. It's a lovely summer day outdoors. Would you care to rise from chair and go for a walk? Get your blood flowing?"

"Can't. I've been tasked to write a piece for our *Acting Councillor.*" Otto pronounced the name of that office with an infuriated disdain. Couldn't bring himself to say the name of Gulbrand Lunde, that pompous official promoted over him at Quisling's whim. "He's assigned me an opinion column, praising the brilliance of Germany's air thrust against England."

Helene put her hands together and looked down at him.

"Why's that so difficult? The mere facts alone astonish."

"I know. What, fifteen hundred Luftwaffe planes flew over the Channel to rain bullets and drop bombs on the Brits the first day? But writing a description is not the problem. In fact, I turned in a celebratory draft of the story two full days before my deadline. But now we find, the *Councillor* objects to my *tone*. Demands that I please try again."

"Your tone? What does that mean?"

"Claims that I always sound like a stuffed shirt! Tells me to strive for a more common touch. Appeal to an ordinary man. All that rot."

Otto picked up his pencil. He pressed it to the pad at the spot where his last doodle had ended. He scowled. The lead snapped off. He flung the pencil to the floor.

"I don't need this aggravation. I should just quit Lunde's staff. There's other work I could do. And more valuable stuff at that. Our church needs leadership. The bishops, the ministers, act deaf, dumb and blind to the benefit of our uniting with the *Deutsche Christen* movement. The Book enjoins us to seek peace, true? Well, that's how we get there. Instead they all mutter of resisting, as if allying with the *Reich's* church didn't confer clear advantages. Resist Hitler? On that path lies more bloodshed and ruin, not less. Quisling and Terboven should quit pussyfooting around. Demand our clergy display loyalty and good sense, or flog them off the pulpits, I say!"

"Actually, they discussed doing something close to that very step at the *Reichskommissar's*. Only yesterday," Helene replied. "A campaign is soon to be launched. They'll start with schoolteachers. Demand that they all sign an oath of loyalty, then begin to teach Nazi principles in class. Bishops shall be next. After that, they want to replace professors at the University. Even though the Student Union has heard rumors and is already lodging complaints about it."

"Good. Had I myself been appointed *Councillor*, such measures would've been imposed already. And stronger ones, too." He looked up at her. "So, you now feel like the *Reichskommissar's* office is at the center of your cosmos, hmm? The place that our fate is declared? Makes you feel truly in the swim of things, does it?"

Helene's smiled faintly. Otto's sudden fit of envy for her menial job seemed entirely beneath him. "Oh, that building has its closed doors and locked drawers and whispered conversations, for certain," she said. "Yet, I still get to overhear some things. True enough."

"Well, if you hear of a high official who needs to be advised by an expert on Norway's history, culture and politics, say I'm available."

"Such a generous offer. I'll bear it in mind."

Otto moodily sipped from his mug. "You almost got the tea right," he said. "Put more milk in it next time, please."

"Milk has gotten expensive."

Otto sighed tragically, as if she'd reported a local outbreak of the plague.

Helene studied him for a moment. "I'm going out," she announced.

"Where to now?" Otto glared at her. "Some hoity-toity errand for the *Reichskommissar* himself, I suppose?"

"No. Just to gather us some wild herbs and greens. Around those ponds, east of town. We can still pick them for free. For now, at least."

Otto nodded. He leaned over and picked up his pencil. He examined its shattered point. He tugged a penknife from his waistcoat pocket, flipped open its blade and began to whittle.

"You know," she said, "your work might go a bit easier if you tried harder to look on the bright side of things." She paused.

Otto grunted.

"Bye," she said.

Otto kept on staring at his lopped pencil. He waved an irritated farewell to her with the hand that held the tiny knife.

~

Standing outside the apartment on the corner of Odinsgata and Torsgata, Helene sucked in a deep breath and savored a sense of relief. Air! Oxygen! Freedom!

*He's pitiful*, she thought, as she put her straw summer hat on, tying its black ribbon under her chin into a knot with a jerk. But another thought made her half-smile. *Kristian's really turning out to be dead right about Otto. Wonder why I didn't see it so clearly back then. I guess I'll be forced to admit that to him, the next time…* Then she stopped, remembering that Kristian and Ragnar and Lars had all gone down with the Snekka. *A horrible waste of three good Norwegian men. Well today's the day I finally get to do something about it!*

She lifted her round chin and stepped forward.

With the handle of a wicker basket nested in the crook of her elbow, Helene walked to a tram stop where she caught a ride across the city center to an address on Grønland. This was not the place where she hoped to harvest her greens. Before performing that chore, she had a much different sort of rendezvous to keep—an encounter set up by the old woman who handed out the underground papers.

Helene reached the small plaza on Grønland and scanned about for her contact. Her whereabouts were not apparent. Then the rotund old woman stepped out from behind a planter. *Her shortness*, Helene realized. *It's how she's able to hide well.*

"Are you ready?" she asked in her gravelly voice.

"Yes."

"You'll need to be blindfolded. I mean, before you meet them."

"All right."

"Follow me, then. Ten paces back."

She led Helene to what seemed to be a shuttered storefront. But the door was unlocked, and she swung it open and beckoned her within. They entered a dark foyer.

"Turn. Kneel."

Helene complied. A black scarf was wound twice around her head and knotted.

"Stand."

The woman took her by the hand and led her to a back room.

"I don't know your name," Helene said.

"So?"

"I don't know what to call you."

"Don't call me anything. Be quiet, now. Just answer our questions."

Dim light seeped in around the rim of her blindfold. Helene felt the hard edge of something behind her legs.

"Sit."

"Helene Berg!" a young male voice proclaimed.

"*Die Engel Rettungsschwimmer*," another voice said. "A most excellent friend of our German occupiers. The young lady whom they hold in most fond regard."

"You are making up a taunt," Helene replied evenly. "It's not a description of me."

"Quiet!" the old woman roared. "You're only here to answer their questions."

"Oh, for God's sake," Helene responded. "To blazes with the lot of you. If you only invited me here to waste my time, I'll find a way to resist all by myself."

The room went dead silent.

Finally, an older male voice asked, "Do we make you angry? Or nervous?"

"And if we do," another voice added. "Why?"

She didn't answer.

"Can't you even tell us that?"

"I'll wait for a more sensible question, if you please."

Another moment of silence followed, broken only when someone stifled a chuckle.

"Let me explain something to you, Helene," the older voice said. "Everyone in this room today does feel nervous. Including you, I'd bet! Since we're all just ordinary citizens. Among us are even young students, as you were. But we intend to stand up to one of the most rapacious and reckless war machines our world has ever seen. You understand, that's our aim?"

"Yes."

"Well, how does it make you feel?"

"All right, nervous," Helene admitted. "Yet determined, too."

"Why?"

"If we act as the Nazis wish us to, we won't own our country anymore. Oslo would end up a suburb of Berlin. Life won't be worth living. They intend to milk our country dry. In fact, that process is underway already. If we dare to object, they won't attempt to answer us with kindness or with generosity. They only use persuasion as a ruse. Nazis are bullies to the core. Whenever we try to stand up to them, it seems, they just mow us over. How should Norway make a stand, then? That's what I want to figure out. I mean, if we don't plan to just cower and submit."

"Helene Berg, you were an orphan, with your parents unknown. Yes, you happened to be born in Norway. But it could have been anywhere. I apologize, that may sound cruel, yet it's true. Do you consider yourself Norwegian, then? And if you do, why?"

Her brow stacked a few V's above the black horizon of her blindfold. "I've pondered this before, in private." She paused. "It's a worthwhile question, you needn't apologize for this one. Still, my answer is rather personal… I can say that being an orphan means you learn to cling to anything which you think might possibly be yours, I guess. A source of strength. Of meaning. Identity. Norway is something large that I can hold onto, that I can call my own. Like the hand of an absent father. And I embrace Christ too, certainly. Christ the Redeemer of all mankind."

There was a murmur.

"Yet, every day you go to work for the *Reichskommissar*. Explain this."

"We have explained it already. Is elaboration really needed? I am a girl who was cast out of the family she was born into. 'Orphanage' is a dull word. It may suggest to you a place of caring, but it basically means that I grew up on hand-outs. I hoped being a teacher would allow me to be kind to other children. It was clear to me how much that was needed back then, and it looks even more true now. After the Germans invaded, a career in education became doubtful. Not just because the Nazis had taken over most schools. But also due to what they want to have taught in the schools that are left. Simultaneously, I discovered they liked me at the *Reich's* headquarters. Not only because of that rescue I performed. My guardian also had connections. I was offered a secure job with more money than I'd make anyplace else, even if I could find another job. That was something to hold onto. My household needed an income. I chose not to be cold, and not to starve. Can you blame me?"

"Yet you see them all as bullies. Why aid them in doing harm to us, to all of Norway?"

"I did think to quit, when I saw up close what they were like, right on my first day. But then I realized that, if I did choose to fight back, I happened to hold a valuable position." She paused again. "A sentinel post, as it were. On high ground, right inside their camp."

"So it is," the mature voice agreed. "And so you do."

"You hold not just that advantage," someone added. "Your guardian whom you mentioned, Deacon Otto Thorsen. Can he grant you insights into plans of the NS and of Quisling himself?"

"Perhaps. But probably not as much as you imagine. Deacon Thorsen was an early member of the NS party, he boasts of a high rank there, true. Yet they still don't treat him very well."

"Why not?"

"Not sure. The group around Quisling feels quite jittery. They aren't confident about the level of support they have from Berlin, or even from Terboven. The Nazis taught them you can blow off steam by hectoring people and pushing them around, so that's what the NS brass like to do too. Imitate their masters. Unfortunately, Deacon Thorsen has become the type of person they enjoy giving a kick to. And he's not fighting back. It's as though he feels he deserves to be treated badly. Frankly, I don't understand it."

"We have a more important question. Our operatives have watched you keep company with a lieutenant in the *Abwehr*. He's a man you spend a great deal of time with."

"Yes. His name is Hans Ziegler."

"What's going on, between the pair of you?"

Helene felt the start of a blush. She curled her fists up and dug her fingernails into her palms in order to force herself to stop.

"He seems infatuated with me," she stated curtly.

"If true, then there may be certain things you could learn from Ziegler. I mean, items useful for us."

"Yes. But that depends…"

"On what?"

"Do I need to spell it out? Because I don't wish to."

"No. You don't."

"Enough." The mature male voice said the word forcefully, as if he held up a traffic sign to halt the proceeding.

"You've been forthcoming, Helene. We appreciate it. But words alone won't satisfy us. Deeds count. We'll judge you by those, and by the quality of intelligence you bring. There shall be items you find out on your own, there may well be things that we request. Be assured, we'll not only keep eyes on you, but observe you ever more closely. Betrayal has consequences. We're not tough guys, yet we do what we must. This is no game of cinema cowboys and fake red Indians, but a fight in earnest, with high stakes. And by the way, sorry for all this cloak-and-dagger stuff. We only seek to be as careful as we imagine we ought to be. Perhaps we overdo it, but I advise that you adopt a similar policy. An excess of caution is better than a disastrous lack of it."

"I understand."

"Your contact will be Addy, whom you've already met, of course. She's the one who brought you here."

A vertical crease appeared on Helene's forehead above the blindfold. "Aha, I finally am awarded her name. Does that mean I'm now somewhat trusted? But I should assume that name's still an alias, right?" Helene did not sound happy. "And why must she be my *sole* contact?"

"That's how we wish things to be at present. You and Addy will design a method by which you signal her that you've gathered material of interest.

What else can be done, well, we'll figure that out as we go along." The mature voice. Stern and final, this time. Pronouncing an unappealable verdict.

*That man sounds like he was once a judge,* Helene thought. *Definitely. Either that, or a school principal.*

****

Helene moved deep into a patch of greenery, shoving brush aside in the Klopptjern area so she could collect her wild produce. Her basket was now half-full of the tender curls of fern fiddleheads. On the far side of the Klopptjern pond, she hoped to find dandelions and young birch leaves. Enough to make a nourishing salad for tonight, and then add to a stew tomorrow.

*"Wir fahren gegen Engeland!"*

A sound of singing came to her. She lifted her head and stared across the flat water. She saw three German soldiers thrashing their way through the brush, stripping off their uniforms as they neared the pond. The man in front waved a bottle, keeping drunken time to the music, like the drum major for a shambling parade.

Helene decided that she already had enough greens. She spun around to retrace her steps. And found one more German soldier standing directly in front of her.

*"Guten tag, hübsche fraulein,"* he said, grinning. "Good afternoon, pretty lady. Wonderful to be outside, to sample the bounty of nature, is it not? Would you care to come over and join our group, and make some wonderful new friends?"

"No thanks." She tried to move around him.

He took a sideways step to block her path. "Not the most courteous answer!" he reproved. "Y'know, we've been ordered to try to get along better with all of our Norwegian brothers. We want to make a start by getting along with a Norwegian sister or two. You can help it turn into a lovely day for us all. It would be criminal to refuse."

Helene glared at him.

"Watch me," she said.

The soldier's smile faded. "Oh, all right," he said. "You have some important business you feel you must attend to elsewhere. Understood. And I shall indeed let you go on your way, at a tiny price." He grasped her just above the elbow. "A simple kiss is all that I require. Of course, if you enjoy it sufficiently, you may decide to adjust your posture. Then I would give you a second kiss for no additional charge."

He abruptly pulled her to him, pinned her arms to her sides by wrapping his own arms around her upper body. She was caught in a bear hug. He lowered his face. Helene let her basket fall, squirmed in his grasp, tried to stomp on his feet and kick him in the ankles. But he spread his legs apart and the thumps her kicks landed on shafts of his boots had zero effect.

She flicked her head from side to side as his mouth sought hers. Finally, the soldier gripped the back of her head with one powerful hand to immobilize her. Above and below her firmly closed lips she felt harsh stubble scrape like sandpaper against her skin. Felt his rolled-up tongue fight to thrust its way into her mouth.

For an instant, she imagined letting that slimy organ enter, then she'd bite down upon it as hard as she ever could. Wouldn't care if she made him bleed. Or even if she bit off the end of his tongue.

But someone shouted, "*Soldat, hör sofort auf damit! Lass sie los!*"—*it meant*, "Soldier, stop that immediately and release her! "

The soldier lifted his head and half turned. A man in civilian clothing hurried toward them.

"And who the hell do you think you are?"

"*Oberleutnant* Hans Ziegler of the *Abwehr! Beachtung!*"

The soldier let her go and stood ramrod straight, a shocked expression on his face.

Helene staggered, stabilized herself, and peered at the approaching man. It was indeed Ziegler, she recognized him now, in a loose linen shirt, a straw hat, tan cotton trousers. She'd never seen him out of a uniform before. And she'd never seen him with a look of consummate fury scrawled on his face, either.

"What the devil do you think you are doing? Were you assaulting her?"

"No sir," he said.

"Yes," Helene said at the same moment.

"Your name, rank and unit!" Ziegler snapped.

The soldier told him.

"Gather your fellow idiots across the pond," Ziegler told him. "All of you shall return to your barracks immediately. Expect a hearing. Then you shall be confined to quarters for quite a long time, if not to a worse place. Now go. *Schnell!*"

The soldier saluted Ziegler. From Helene's position, standing a bit behind him, she couldn't see the soldier also offer Ziegler a wink. Then he trotted away, moving at double-time through the underbrush.

"A shame," Ziegler said. "Let me say I'm sorry. Did he hurt you?"

Helene shook her head. "No. But I wanted to hurt *him*. I tried."

"The fool will be dealt with, believe me. But I ask you to find it in your heart to feel lenient, too. Our soldiers fight and work hard, are subject to heavy discipline. Yet they also are young. When they get time off, they can turn a bit wild."

Helene said nothing.

"Here, let me put your vegetables into the basket. Those that aren't squished, anyway." He knelt.

She glared down. "They assume they can take a Norwegian woman for the asking?" she said. "Not that your cad ever asked me anything, mind you."

"Please," Ziegler said, looking up and smiling. "We're not all like that. Let me be a gentleman. Permit me to make it up to you."

"How?"

"Your greenery will be collected again by me. Next you come to dinner at my hotel, The Federation."

"I must take my harvest home. I need to make Otto's supper."

"I'll bring you over to his apartment, after. And we can take along some restaurant food, then you won't need to cook. I just had my Mercedes coupe delivered here to Oslo. We can drive with the top down. It will be most pleasant."

Helene looked out over the brush, the rippling grass, and through a fringe of trees, and saw the distant glitter of an automobile windscreen on a road that curved nearest to the Klopptjern meadow.

"How fortunate I am that you found me," she said.

"I think that also," Ziegler said.

"Yet, how did you manage to even spot me?"

"I saw a disturbance," he said.

"You saw a soldier kissing a girl? As you drove your car, way over there?"

"Something about that picture seemed off."

"Okay. That's the explanation, then."

He stood up. Handed her the basket. Absorbed her skeptical look.

"All right. The actual reason I'm here at the ponds now is that, before, I went over to find you first at your apartment," he said. "Otto said where you'd gone. I came out looking for you, since I wanted to invite you to dinner, and to offer you a present."

She regarded him steadily.

"Saving you from a few drunken boors was a mere rescue of opportunity. Had those men not been out here, I still would've found you, and invited you to come and dine with me."

"Very well," Helene said. "I accept. Your present?"

"4711 Cologne," he said. "Just delivered from Paris. Along with a bottle of fine Cognac. We *Abwehr* officers ship such articles to one another using dispatch pouches. Of course, I know alcohol itself doesn't attract you. But its label is ornate, quite pretty. You can at least admire that, yes? I'll drain your snifter, right after mine. A genuine sacrifice on my part, yet one I'm perfectly willing to make."

*"News of Churchill. He's in a very depressed state, spending the entire day smoking and drinking. The kind of enemy we need!"*
—Josef Goebbels, from *The Goebbels Diaries*

## CHAPTER 17

Kristian was sound asleep and dreaming vividly about his single night of passion with Greta.

They lay at the center of a nest of tousled bedsheets and blankets, in that lodge by the Scottish burn. She straddled him, her hands braced on his shoulders. She lifted her hips up and moved them forward in a long, slow, gliding stroke. He felt her soft vulva open against his cock, felt her paint a glistening streak of moisture on it, all the way to the tip. She rotated her hips back, then slid them forward again. And again.

He shivered. He watched the tips of her small breasts sway above him. He reached for them, wanting to give those stiff, pink gumdrops of her nipples another randy pinch. She slid her hands down his arms.

"No, no-o-o," she whispered. "As I told you, this time, you aren't to move. Not a single hair. You are to only take what I give. Don't forget, the military has put me in charge of you, and you must do as I ask."

She lightly slid her slick labia up his cock again, painting one more streak of her slick and fragrant juices upon it. She paused for several tantalizing seconds at the tip, lifting herself off of him slightly. He groaned, tilted his own hips, tried to plunge into her. She rose higher.

"No, no." She laughed. "Will you force me to tie you down? Clap you in the darbies?"

"Wait…" he panted. "You brought handcuffs?"

"Maybe I did, and maybe I didn't. Now lie still, or I'll get up off of you. Leave this room. And fly on back home."

"Now there's a threat." He laughed. "All right."

Through a mighty act of will, he forced himself to stay immobile. As a reward, she put a streak of her sweet moisture on him again. And then over and over again, increasing her pressure and tempo with each stroke. Then she stopped, frozen, halfway up. He swore he could feel her labia stiffen like tiny wings and pulsate against him, felt his own cock almost vibrate in response.

"Ahhhhgh-h," he said.

"Is it good?" she cooed.

Then she lowered her hips all the way down and ground herself wantonly against him, hard. He felt the tight bud of her clitoris press down on his glans as if she were attempting to enter *him*. His cock no longer seemed like a fencepost, it was something longer, thicker, obscenely huge, a veritable telegraph pole! Then it exploded, a geyser of heat, a flash of light, a shower of sparks. And he cried out.

Kristian awoke, his own yelp echoing in his ears.

He found his lower belly almost entirely drenched in the hot, sticky lava of ejaculate. One spurt of it reached up his chest almost to the base of his neck. It took him a full second to remember where he was. On his back in a bed, in a room of Rolf and Hermann's apartment above the bar. Those partners were long gone, though, had moved into a new place high up on the hill.

Kristian arose, cupping his hand just above his thatch of blond pubic hair to catch the trickles of sperm as they dribbled down his body, and he went to the sink, where he washed and wiped himself off.

*Whew!* He thought. *That night we shared was indelible. And she was incredible.*

He'd never even fantasized he could learn this much about carnal love in a single night. Or indeed, that that one night itself could reveal how much more about love he needed to learn. And he had then and there vowed to let himself be taught all of it. If no additional lessons from Greta were forthcoming, well then, he'd try to learn from others.

Unbidden, an image of Helene popped up in his mind. He was startled by it. *And what's this, now?* It seemed as if this imagined Helene looked at him the same way she had at that moment when the *Snekka* pulled away from the pier in Drøbak, lovely, wistful, full of sadness and regret. *And untouchable, too,* he reminded himself. Helene now seemed like a girl coldly devoted to keeping an unassailable virginity. *I guess that is one more way in which our paths have split. That's now a larger issue than I ever imagined it could be. Plus, I should consider, she's in tight with Otto and the NS, which means she's also now in cahoots with Germans too—which makes her far less attractive to me. That morning the Snekka pulled away from the dock, it might well be the last time Helene and I ever look upon one another. I guess that when some human paths fork, they can never rejoin. And that perhaps is just how it ought to be.*

Kristian ran the water again, cupped both hands, dropped his face into the puddle of coolness he held and rubbed it into his face and eyes. The jolt of cold water refreshed him and awakened him entirely. The image of the beautiful Helene faded from his mind. He switched on the light, looked around for his clothes, got dressed.

He went over to the window to assess the progress of the sunrise. He almost made a mistake by pulling the drapes aside without switching the light off but stopped himself in time. Rolf had told him he could use the boarded-up *Scrimshaw Puben* as his personal lair for the present, but it absolutely had to appear as if no one was living there. A contract was being negotiated to lease the place out—a deal that should be signed in about a week or two. At which point he'd need to depart, too.

But this day looked to be off to a bright, clear start. Kristian went back to the sink to brush his teeth. He smiled when he saw a stranger looking back from the mirror. Two days earlier, Hermann had dyed Kristian's blond locks as well as the fuzz on his cheeks a dark brown. With his cap pulled down low and his collar turned up, he doubted if any acquaintances or even old school chums in his hometown would be able to recognize him.

≈

This was a Sunday, about an hour before the usual time of church services and the streets were mostly deserted. Kristian made his way along the waterfront, then turned uphill. He had almost reached the brick house on Klinkenberggata they intended to turn into their new club when he heard a harsh command come from behind.

"*Halt! Deutsche Sicherheits!*" It was the Gestapo's usual greeting.

Kristian stopped, and warily held his hands out from his sides. Two uniformed officers came around in front of him, both eyeing him keenly.

"Your papers," one said.

Kristian reached inside his coat, withdrew a long leather wallet. He flapped it open, took out his phony ID card and work permit, handed these over. The first inspected them, handed them off to the second.

"What are you doing up here?" the officer demanded.

"Washing dishes, mopping floors," Kristian muttered. "Cleaning glasses, polishing furniture. That sort of thing."

"So? Where?"

"The new café."

The officers exchanged a glance. Both smiled. They handed him back his papers.

"You may proceed," one said.

"Thank you. *Guten morgen euch beiden.*" Rolf and Hermann had both sought to educate him about stock phrases he could use to disarm suspicious Germans.

Kristian walked the short distance on to the two-story brick house that stood less than a block away from Stavanger's new Gestapo headquarters. *This must be close to where they arrested my mother.* As that thought overcame him, he took care to keep his face still and impassive. The brick building that he approached bore a freshly painted sign erected on wooden stakes out front that advertised the opening of *Café Heck vom Norden*. It also bore a portrait of a smaller, different building with high arched windows. Café Heck, Rolf had told him, down in the Hofgarten on the Odeonsplatz in Munich, had been one of Hitler's favored hangouts during his rise to power. And that was why he'd dubbed their new tavern Café Heck of the North—a moniker which should make it irresistible to the Germans.

He knocked on the door, and a beaming Hermann in a long white apron, his shirtsleeves rolled up on both meaty forearms, let him in.

Hermann pointed. "Go upstairs," he said. "I'll be there shortly. I'm making breakfast," he added.

"That's terrific news."

Rolf was sitting at a desk that held scattered papers and a small radio receiver that emitted strings of beeps mingled with bursts of static. Then Kristian realized he was hearing the rapid-fire operation of a telegraph key. Rolf, a dreamy expression on his face, was tapping his fingers on the desktop in time to the keystrokes.

"Hi," Kristian said. "What are you doing?"

"Trying to learn this man's 'fist,'" Rolf said.

"Excuse me?"

"The Gestapo's main W/T operator. I'm learning his touch, his rhythm on the key, his signatures. I do this in order that, eventually, I can mimic him."

"Oh. I can see where that might prove useful."

"Rather," Rolf assured him. "You know, I'm completely in love with both of those new radios you brought me in your boat. This type, in fact, we nickname a 'sweetheart.'" He placed a caressing hand on the radio. "Small and receives only. But it does that quite well."

"What about the other? The transmitter?"

"Splendid. Powerful. I have it on a friendly fishing boat in order to move it around. Makes it harder for German signal-trackers to locate. And I've already been in touch with our mutual friends. The Brits indeed want you back. However, first, they have one more task for you. They've sent over another 15-watt W/T unit. It must be taken to resistance partisans in Oslo."

"Huh. Well, all right. But how do I do that?"

Rolf laid a finger alongside his nose and smiled. "For that, Hermann and I have put our heads together and conjured up a completely implausible scheme."

They heard a clomp of heavy legs ascending the stairs. Their nostrils were soon teased by the mingled aromas of mushroom-and-cheese omelets and fresh-baked currant scones when Hermann came through the door. A pitcher of hot tea also stood upon Hermann's tray as he slid it onto the desk. By mute and swift agreement, they tabled all discussion of operating plans and fell to dealing with what lay right before them on the desk.

"This omelet is amazing," Kristian said through a gummy mouthful of it. "Thanks!"

Hermann grinned broadly. As his cheeks rose in merriment, his small eyes almost vanished. He held up a thick forefinger. "The secret to a good omelet is patience," he proclaimed. "Just as in much else, hmm? Slow cooking keeps your eggs fluffy, lets your filling rise in savor. The spices must cook too, see?"

Kristian washed down a crispy bite of scone with a gulp of hot tea, nodding enthused agreement.

"How's the new radio going to arrive here?" he asked Rolf. "Do I need to paddle out somewhere at night to pick it up?"

Rolf shook his head. "Clandestine boat runs between Scotland and Norway have been multiplying throughout the summer. Fishermen now convey all sorts of things. The radio was dropped off at Telavåg, then another boat brought it down here."

"Great. Then, what's your scheme for getting it into Oslo?"

"I plan to arrest you and take you to prison."

Kristian almost choked. Hermann chortled.

"We have obtained a *Statspolitiet* uniform," Rolf explained. "You know, outfits to dress up a new force the Germans and the NS have created. It's an umbrella group for organizing hand-picked members of Norway's local police forces. Modeled on the Gestapo, hence our wags have begun calling it Stapo. Hermann has tailored this Stapo gear to fit me perfectly."

"And I must say, he looks magnificent," Hermann interjected.

Rolf shot him a grin, then gave his attention back to Kristian.

"As for you, I'm having false warrant and transfer papers created. In a few days, you and I shall board a train to Oslo together, with you being clapped in chains. The radio we're to deliver is of the newest, most compact design. It will be in the suitcase that supposedly holds the items of evidence against you. Your crime is serious, but not grand—just some moves to counter Nazi propaganda. We are charging you as a distributor of an underground newspaper, and we'll be carrying genuine copies of *Stritt Folk*. Once we reach Oslo, we'll distribute them all, naturally. That's one benefit. And a side benefit is that all the 'evidence' against you goes poof."

Both of Kristian's eyebrows had gradually risen to form an expression of astonishment. He switched his gaze from one to the other, until he felt sure that they were not joking.

"That *is* bold," he said.

"An essential aspect of our plan is that Norway's Stapo is a brand-new force. Which means there shall be a short period when no one actually knows who's in it, who its senior officers might be, etcetera. Anyone who presents the ruse with a smattering of confidence should be able to sell it to just about anyone."

Hermann noted Kristian's appearance of lingering doubt and weighed in. "Theater!" he exclaimed. "It's the grandest of earthly powers. A skilled practitioner can summon up illusions like a wizard with a wand."

"I'm no actor," Kristian objected.

"We are *all* of us actors," Hermann insisted. "Throughout life. Read your Wordsworth and your Shakespeare and your Goethe. You must educate and enlarge your perspective, young Fiske. I can loan you the necessary books."

"Your part is not all that difficult," Rolf told him. "Do your best to appear downcast and woebegone. You're an apprehended scumbag, nothing more, doomed to face a reckoning at the central office of the Gestapo. Leave all the talking to me."

"He's good at it," Hermann affirmed. "Rolf could sell freezers to Eskimos. Or ovens to Hottentots."

"I've noticed. Yet, I am neither."

"I do have a sweetener for this job, something that may convince you. A creative, personal project that I've been contemplating. You despise the *Luftwaffe*, do you not?"

"Profoundly! And completely."

"Well, in Oslo, many top pilots and officers of the *Luftwaffe* live in a multi-story, downtown hotel named The Federation. Has incredibly old and lovely woodwork. A veritable carpenter's fantasy, that place."

"And?"

"Actually, the whole thing is built of wood."

"So?"

"Quite flammable."

Rolf and Hermann gave him a malicious grin simultaneously.

"One of our Oslo Cell operatives has just gotten himself hired as a relief chef for The Federation's kitchen," Rolf said. "Let's mix these ingredients together and see what our dessert might be: a torte of means and motive, thickly frosted with opportunity."

The slaying of NKVD agent Sergei Sokolov was attempted three days later. Hermann and Rolf had plotted this out as the first part of the overall operation. It was decided that Rolf, all spiffed out in his new Stapo uniform, would be the bait.

"What makes you think Sokolov will take it?" Kristian asked.

"That man has studied us for more than a month. Just now, he's been mesmerized by our move to Café Heck. In fact, he does not seem to have even slept for the past few days. He's always circling around, snapping photos with his little Minox, asking the neighbors questions. Why the Gestapo hasn't picked him up yet, I'll never know—unless he's bribed them to leave him alone.

"Anyway. After he sees me come out dressed like a freshly minted state cop, carrying a big case full of something or other, he'll be unable to resist. He'll feel compelled to see where I'm going, and likely snap pictures of me for his files.

"All right. There's a set of stairs just off Løkkeveien. They lead down to a narrow alley. *En route* to the station, where we intend to catch the earliest morning train. Very few passers-by at that hour. It's where you will lurk, young Fiske. Slumped in a corner, cradling an empty bottle, your head lolling, three sheets to the wind and almost comatose. I lead our target right past you. Whereupon you leap up, pounce, and work your magic."

They set their scheme in motion in exactly this manner. But despite the amount of thought put into it, the ploy did not go well.

Rolf indeed descended the stairs according to plan, observed Kristian crouched in a corner of the landing, disheveled, mouth open, eyes half-shut, cradling a whisky bottle a third-full of unsweetened brown tea.

"Get a grip on yourself, youngster," he said. "You're sliding down a road to perdition!"

A half-minute later, the NKVD man came down, following in Rolf's footsteps, walking lightly, peering about under the brim of his fedora, taking everything in. He studied Kristian, stepped to one side, maximizing space between them as he went on to the next flight.

What gave Kristian away? Perhaps a clue as simple as Sokolov noting a gleam of Kristian's eye whites beneath his half-closed lids, and a suspicion that those eyes might be tracking him. As Kristian leapt to his feet in order to attack, Sokolov instantly responded by leaning to one side, gripping the staircase railing with a hand, then delivering a side kick into the pit of Kristian's stomach.

Kristian thudded against the concrete wall of the landing, which knocked yet more breath from his lungs, and he fell heavily down onto hands and knees. That was bad. Much worse was seeing the dagger fly out of his grip and spin to a halt at the feet of Sokolov. Who quickly snatched it up. Kristian fought to suck in a breath. His mind raced. He couldn't battle his own keen blade—with nothing! He grabbed the bottle of fake whiskey by its neck.

Sokolov took his hat off, held it in one hand, the dagger in his other. Kristian could see lank brown hair framing the round face, and a look of supreme contempt on that face. The NKVD agent seemed certain that he had this fight in the bag. He stepped forward, faked a front kick with his left leg, faked a thrust with the knife, and then aimed a real kick at Kristian's head with his other leg.

Kristian's sole advantage at that moment came from his youthful reflexes. He leaned back and swung the bottle, managing to bash Sokolov's booted foot as it flew past his chin. The agent grunted, spun, landed awkwardly. Then he continued to spin. When he faced Kristian again, the hat was dropped, the dagger was out front, and he looked poised to use it.

The sneer had been wiped from his face by a look of resolve.

Despairing, Kristian did what he could to improve his odds. He bashed the bottle against the concrete wall. Now he was holding the neck—with its jagged crown of shattered glass—as he stood up.

They circled each other, wary, Sokolov taking a few exploratory swipes with the dagger to test Kristian's responses.

Then a gloved fist out of nowhere crashed against the back of Sokolov's skull. He pitched forward to reveal Rolf was standing behind him. Rolf had sprung back up the steps to come to Kristian's aid. Sokolov rolled forward, spun on his butt, lifted a leg and hooked it behind Rolf's knee, kicked up, flipped him over and sent Rolf tumbling back down the stairs.

Kristian saw Sokolov's hand that held the knife was down upon its knuckles, still gripping the hilt. The agent was propping himself up, preparing to shove himself back up onto his feet. Kristian dove. He plunged the sharp shards of his bottleneck into the back of the man's hand and wrist. Sokolov squawked and dropped the dagger. Kristian flung away his broken-glass shank and grabbed for the knife. Got it!

Sokolov rolled to sit up crookedly with his legs out, cradling his slashed hand, trying to stem the bleeding by gripping it in his good fist. His eyes were wide and white. He was shoving himself away from Kristian by kicking at the ground with his heels.

*Kicking, that's his main thing. I've got to close the distance, get inside the range of those damned legs!*

Kristian launched off the tips off his toes, flew over Sokolov's boots and jabbed the dagger straight up into the agent's groin. He screeched, dropped his wounded hand in order to grope frantically in his trouser pocket for something. *Probably a weapon.* Kristian rose to a knee, launched himself again and drove the tip of blade up under Sokolov's chin and deep into his neck, through the soft palate then bone and on into his brain. One of Kristian's hands gripped the hilt, the other shoved against the boss.

Sokolov's body jerked violently, shuddered, and went limp.

Kristian lay still atop the body of his antagonist for a second, catching his breath and gathering himself mentally.

Then he stood. Looked down the stairs to see how Rolf had fared after his fall. His companion had dragged himself to one side of the stairs, hauled himself upright, and was gesturing with both his hands. Kristian realized what Rolf was trying to tell him and signaled back, *All right, I get you.* He jerked his dagger free, wiped it off, and slid it back into its sheath. He grasped the body of Sokolov by both collar and belt, lifted him slightly, and slid him onto his own bumpy ride down the steps.

Kristian jogged downstairs after the body. It landed in a loose, disjointed heap. Rolf stood more erect now, and Kristian could see his face was bruised and he was breathing heavily. Gaps had been ripped in several seams of his new uniform.

"Are you all right?"

"Another joke? *No!* I'm fucking hurt. And on top of that, I'm embarrassed..."

"Why?"

"Had no idea he'd be that dangerous." Rolf panted. "Or that skilled. Had the reputation of being a clown, actually. But it looked to me like he was a real *tireur.*"

"A what?"

"A fighter, *savate du rue*. French gang stuff. Must've studied it. No idea where. Paris, probably. Anyway." Rolf shook himself, then jerked his chin toward a nearby manhole cover. "Get that sewer grate open. Roll the bastard down and in. But we need to search him first of course."

"Sure."

In the trouser pocket where Sokolov had been groping about during his final seconds of life, Kristian found a leather, lead-laden blackjack. In his other pocket, a fat roll of money that included high-denomination *Reichsmarks* and *Kroner*. There was also a small set of keys. Dangling from his neck, a small wallet with false ID papers. In a jacket pocket, a Minox sub-miniature spy camera. Kristian swiftly heaped these items to one side, gripped the square bars of the manhole cover, and with a burst of adrenalin-fueled power, yanked it open. After the NKVD agent had been consigned to his undignified place-of-rest, Kristian stood and held up his camera.

"Keep the negs? Want to see what he's been shooting?"

Rolf shook his head. "No. Too compromising. I mean, if they're ever found on us."

Kristian nodded, stripped the film out of the camera and flung its gleaming coil into the sewer.

"Toss his keys and IDs down there too."

Kristian complied, then wrestled the grate back into place, stomped it level with the pavement, and took the remaining items over to Rolf. He looked him up and down.

"Where are you hurt?"

"Pride, mostly. As I mentioned. Otherwise, yeah, I'm rather banged up. Luckily, I learned to fall downstairs when I was an actor. Unluckily, these particular stairs are faced with granite. I might limp, but I can walk. Give me that sap. It was stupid of me not to think to carry something like it. One big whack on his noggin, and we would've been free of trouble!

"Hmm. Oh my word, look at all this cash. That man was a walking bank. Here, you take it. Consider it a tip, awarded for creativity in the face of a threat, your ability to spring into amended action. As for that camera? We'll add it to our evidence case—as further proof of your perfidy, you damned agitator for the Resistance, you. Now let's grab up our suitcase and get moving."

"Get moving, to where? We should head back to the café. Get you fixed up and rested, mend that uniform. Then start over. Maybe tomorrow."

Rolf shook his head. "No. Throws off our timing. We need to be far, far away when Sokolov's body is found. *If* it is. Of course, we do want it found, just not very soon. Anyway, I've already concocted an explanation for our appearance. You became tough after I told you I was going to transfer you to the Gestapo main office in Oslo for deeper interrogation. You objected. Strenuously. As we trot along to the train station now, drag your knuckles along the walls, bloody them up a bit. To show that you've been fighting me."

Kristian shook his head in disbelief. "Can't I just bark my knuckles by popping you one on the jaw?" he said.

Rolf gave a lopsided smile as he shook his head.

"We have two ways to hide," he said. "One is to hide. The other is to act as if we have no need to hide. All right? It's what we must do now. Don't worry, practice makes perfect, as Hermann and I have amply demonstrated. Here now, while our case is open. Let me get this set of handcuffs out and snapped onto your wrists. Try to look hangdog! Not too cocky, hmm? Which is a lingering problem with you, Fiske, I have to say. All right, onward. Into the mouth of the wolf we go, heigh-ho."

*"The bold path is the path of safety."*
—Winston Churchill, *The Gathering Storm*

# CHAPTER 18

Rolf straightened his back and assumed an air of grim dominance as they descended steps to the train platform. They sailed nonchalantly through all the curious looks they drew from the small crowd of passengers. Kristian was impressed at Rolf's ability to brazen his way past hazard. It seemed to function with no impediment. Yet he was still flabbergasted when Rolf led them straight up to a Gestapo officer in front of a handful of SS troops—clad in the gray version of their uniforms.

"Good morning, gentlemen!" Rolf said. "I have here a rat dragged from his hole that I'm to transport to Møllergata 19 in Oslo. Would you care to examine the transfer papers?"

The Germans, won over by Rolf's correctly accented, fluent use of their language, demurred.

"What's he done?" the Gestapo officer inquired.

"He's a purveyor of lies and distortions," Rolf said. "And thus, an enemy of the *Reich*."

"A-n-d it appears that he might've tried to resist arrest?"

"Oh yes," Rolf confirmed. "But not for long. He threw a fit this morning, when he found out that if he refuses to name his collaborators, he'll be exposed to all the tender mercies that prevail at *De Victoria Terrasse*."

The Gestapo man answered with a mirthless smile. He eyed the suitcase—which dangled from Kristian's cuffed hands—and pointed.

"What's in there?"

"Evidence against the accused. A stack of those shitty rebel newspapers."

"*Ach! Ja, das ist alles Scheiße.* Make this swine all tote the evidence against himself, I like that very much. Why sprain your own wrist?" he said. "Listen, you should confine him in the first car, right behind the engine. It's the one we reserve for official use. If he offers you any more guff, just let me know. My method for subduing a troublemaker is quite effective. We need not wait on Oslo to bring him in line."

"*Wunderbar! Vielen Dank.*"

∼

They sat on a padded bench seat at the front of the coach as the train lurched out of the deep trough—a narrow, rocky valley—that cradled the Stavanger platform. Kristian could almost spot the green expanse of Lagård Gravlund off to the east as they passed it, but his only available line-of-sight was too acute. He knew where the cemetery lay, though, out beyond the embankment. Where it held a button buried in a tranquil patch of greenery that he now considered the grave of his father.

*I'm sorry. I hope you don't feel that I'm letting you down, Pappa, since I've managed to gut just two Nazi bastards so far.* He posted that astral thought through the ether to Ragnar. *I can't include the Russian agent I just wasted in our count. That is, if he was a Rusky and not some Frenchie who'd gone to work for Stalin under a Soviet code name, as Rolf now has me starting to believe. Rolf is kind of amazing, don't you think? His boldness, what he knows, the measures he's willing to take. How did he ever get so much… the way he is?*

Kristian glanced sidelong at Rolf. *He seems perfectly at home in a dark realm of spies and thugs and cops and soldiers. Easy to see the man was an actor. He's just now made himself look just like a cop, not only his manner of dress, but also in the way he talks, he sits, even how he holds his mouth. If I didn't know better, I'd buy into his act completely.*

Now the train had rolled far enough he could see back into the cemetery's upper end. Not all the way to the *menhir*—that flake of pre-Viking rock that Ragnar had called a *stående steiner*—but nearly. Kristian meditated upon the last object he'd buried in that special hidey-hole of his on another visit the previous day: that old student photo of his mom. Earlier, he'd studied it long enough that the image became imprinted on his nerves. Had he been an artist, he could've drawn it in exact detail from memory. He hated to let it go, but he knew where it belonged. *And it's not like I am even able to think of Mamma as, well, dead! I couldn't handle that. But if she is, I know she and Pappa would want to be together, close as can be.*

Out from the hidden stash, he'd taken rubber tubes of white phosphorus fuses, the key ingredient for incendiary grenades. Left behind again, on Rolf's advice, was the big-bore Webley revolver and the red-filtered flash.

"The phosphorus might well be sourced locally," he'd said. "The Minox camera was invented by a German and it's made on the Baltic. The new radio we're supposed to deliver is problematic, I grant you, but it's a German model, taken from a *panzer* with its power boosted and crystals modified. The SIS did their best to conceal those changes. But your Webley and your light scream British agent. Leave them. Why stack the deck against ourselves? I know you've got to carry your knife. By now, you probably feel naked without it. But stay ready to drop it or fling it away if it looks like it has to be shed, too."

The train chugged through the green meadows and farms of the Sola area, approached the bare crags and gulches that formed the spine of this broad Norwegian peninsula. From the vantage point of their rear-facing seat, Kristian could see four *Wehrmacht* soldiers sitting in the far back of the coach with their helmets off, playing a game of cards. Once the train got underway, two SS men left, sauntering back through the cars to demand and examine the papers of each passenger.

Kristian turned to Rolf. "All right," he said. "Out with it. What's the secret?"

The rheumy brown eyes suddenly looked both sad and amused. "Now, whatever can you mean?" he said quietly.

"How do you keep such composure, and calmly fool these Germans? We're in a Nazi staff carriage. We'll be stuck beside them for hours."

Rolf shifted his gaze away and shrugged.

"You've got us skating on some very thin ice, here."

Rolf looked back at him. "When ice holds you up? It's thick enough."

"You're not even nervous. Not that I can see. You must know something I don't."

"Oh, the secret of my *sangfroid*, that's what you're after? Think I give away the key to my special powers just like *that?*" Rolf snapped his fingers. Then he bared his stained teeth in a feral grin and reached in his coat pocket for his pipe. He tapped the stem on his teeth, chewed on it for moment, and laid the unlit pipe on the table.

"While I was fighting with the partisans in Spain, I met a man there named Asbjørn. He taught me that one excellent way for a man to stay brave—even in the middle of a gunfight—is to pretend you're already dead."

Kristian raised his eyebrows.

"That's what you're up to? And now you pretend it for us both? Are you joking?"

"It's what I must do for myself, just so I don't sit paralyzed in a corner, gibbering. And it's far from a joke. Hermann and I have friends who've died or been made to vanish in a horrid, despicable manner. Now I see that's a possibility for any of us at any moment. That forces me to stay calm and take care of business. Since it's clear that indulging in hysterics has the opposite effect. Fear tends to draw the feared thing in closer. Whereas confidence pushes it away. Have you noticed that? Allow me to make myself even clearer. Let's assume you're a Gestapo commander."

"Oh, certainly. Not a stretch."

"You must try to see the world through your enemy's eyes, young Fiske, if you're ever to have even a prayer of outsmarting him. So, let's say, you're an occupation force leader, but you find yourself stretched thin. Well, where do you assign your top guys? Not on a station platform or a train, for heaven's sake! Your stars need to deal with *much* more formidable tasks. Consequently, these Krauts assigned to this car? Third or fourth level personnel, at best. Here, I shall demonstrate."

Rolf stood, picked up his pipe and sauntered down the aisle to the card game, tugging out his tobacco pouch as he went. He interrupted the game of the *Wehrmacht* soldiers while filling his pipe and tamping it with his thumb. One corporal obliged Rolf's request by pulling a small metal box of matches from his tunic and lighting Rolf's pipe for him as he puffed away. Another soldier pointed a finger at Kristian, then made two fists with his hands and banged them together. Rolf threw back his head and laughed. He balled his own fist and struck out as if his hand itself were a sledgehammer and an empty spot in the air an anvil. He bugged his eyes out and clenched his jaw as he struck three times, showing how he'd beaten Kristian into submission. Now all the soldiers were laughing.

Next, Rolf pinched a substantial wad of tobacco out of his pouch, dropped it on their table. Another soldier immediately produced a pack of cigarette papers and each began rolling his own. They shook hands with Rolf, wished him farewell and resumed their game as they lit up and multiple wisps of blue smoke drifted up to entwine at the roof of the car.

Rolf returned to Kristian with a yellow-toothed grin on his face. The pipe projected from his mouth, wreathing his head with oracular fumes. Rolf turned his hands palms up, shrugged and sat.

"And you accuse *me* of being cocky?"

"Confidence and cockiness are far different things, Fiske."

"Oh, sure. Well, you'd be the expert."

~

Kristian dozed. At a stop outside of Kristiansand, where the direction of the railway began to shift around to the northeast and point toward Oslo, a young *Wehrmacht* orderly strolled into the car bearing a hamper that was crammed full of buns and sausages and pickles and bottles of beer for the Germans. Kristian roused himself. Rolf managed to finesse a handout for them both. As they contentedly munched away, they continued their conversation. The Germans didn't find it odd that Rolf chatted with his prisoner. Kristian was not such a repellent criminal; they considered him only a misguided patriot. The Gestapo would soon scare him straight.

Besides, Rolf had proven he was a good and trustworthy fellow, simply by sharing his tobacco.

"What on earth did you think you were doing, going off to fight that time in Spain?" Kristian asked Rolf.

"Well, I'd run out of luck in Germany," Rolf said. "I needed to be somewhere else."

"How did your luck turn bad?"

"My nemesis? Josef Goebbels. That chinless goblin! He decided I was one of the decadent artists whose works had to be mocked in a special gallery show. After that, I couldn't sell a painting to save my life. In fact, to stop my painting entirely seemed to be the safest move. So, I'd completely had it with the Nazis! The 'socialist' component of NDSAP was hogwash. A come-on, to suck up energy of the left, then toss it down an outhouse hole. After I'd been branded as a perverted artist, I heard that a legion of Nazi soldiers had been formed to fight on the side of the nationalists in Spain.

"If I joined the International Brigades, I saw I'd have a chance to go shoot some of those bastards. Did that in Spain for a year. Learned how to fight, but let me tell you, it's a miserable business. Learned I was better at fooling them and sneaking around than I was at sticking my chest out and going at it toe-to-toe and blow-for-blow. I returned to Munich disguised as somebody else and began to do something else."

"Is that when you met Hermann?"

"Already knew Hermann. He'd been a young, skinny, whip-smart university student in the arts. I'd been one of his professors. By the time I saw him again in Munich he'd already undergone his own grand disillusionment. 'Night of the Long Knives,' you've heard of it?"

Kristian shook his head.

"That's when Hitler showed himself as a consummate psycho. Part buffoon, part conman, and all ego. Empty bluster on an epic scale. No real loyalty to anything or anyone but himself. But vicious and horrid, all the same."

Kristian flicked a glance away from Rolf and down the aisle. He sensed this conversation veering rapidly into seditious territory. But the soldiers in the rear looked ready to nap after gobbling their lunch. They sought to find comfy lounging positions on the train car benches. Results appeared mixed, but they all stayed focused on solving this problem, which meant they paid no attention to him and Rolf.

"You see, to gain control over the *Wehrmacht*, Hitler needed to give up the SA, that brownshirt force of commoners that he'd used to nurse and protect his rise to power," Rolf continued. "Chose to betray the whole damn outfit. A bloodbath. Ungodly pagan sacrifice. Stretched into a three-day horror show. At the end, hundreds had been killed and all the rest co-opted. But a lucky few scattered. Hermann was one of those who got away. Fled to Munich, made a false identity, and disguised himself by rapidly putting on the kilos. Blow your body up like a zeppelin, and it changes the shape of your face, your posture, your gait, all sorts of things.

"One reason why Hermann hates the way he looks now is because it's not really him. Have you heard of an angel coming out of the marble, for a sculptor? Hermann is that same angel clambering back in, hiding in a giant blob of rock. He hates it. I hate it. But what can you do?"

Rolf chuckled. "I mean, Fiske, look at your own choices. It should amaze you, reacting logically to threats we face means performing... deeds such as this!" He swept his hand around, referring not only to their present spot in a Nazi staff car, but all they understood about the wilder aspects of each other's life. "Our madness is a pure testament to the insanity of our challenge, no?" His laugh became a cackle, then he cut himself off. He bent, cleared his throat and sat up, patting at his eyes with the end of a coat sleeve.

"Anyway. Hermann and I stayed in Munich to make a pile of money by helping men and women relax at all-night soirees. We ran off to Norway to get away from that, and everything else. Wound up in Stavanger a year ago. And the rest, you know."

~

Rolf and Kristian hustled off the train and away from the platform when it paused at the outlying town of Sandvika to take local commuters aboard. The pair moved with such speed and smooth confidence that no German had a chance to ask them why they wanted to debark before they had quite reached Oslo. A block away from the platform, they entered a waiting taxicab.

The cabbie was solemn-faced and surly. He and Rolf communicated in a few clipped syllables, and they drove off.

"Is everything ready?"

"All is in place," the driver muttered.

Kristian sitting on the front seat, assumed the taxi man was one of Rolf's local communist cadres, and that proper arrangements had been made—of whatever sort. He'd been briefed on all the essentials; he supposed that he'd discover the relevant details soon, but only when necessary. Rolf had explained that, in event of arrest, the less he knew about any operation the better it would be for Kristian as well as their covert accomplices.

Kristian only knew their next agenda item was delivering the highly modified *panzer* radio to a Resistance group in Oslo.

On the back seat lay an open satchel filled with rolled items of clothing. As they made their way to into the city, Rolf wrestled himself out of the Stapo uniform—which he bunched up and thrust under the seat—then dressed himself in clean but shabby workman's clothes from the satchel. Then he pulled out a pair of white chef's smocks and laid them to one side, winking at Kristian as he did so.

"Stop at that empty shop the gang uses on Grønland," Rolf informed their driver. "Here it comes. You see it?"

The cabbie grunted, then pulled up and braked to a halt. They were stopped in front of the exact same shuttered storefront where Helene met elements of the local Resistance a month earlier.

Rolf shoved the satchel of costumes aside and opened the suitcase they'd brought from Stavanger. He dug under the copies of *Stritt Folk* and to one side of the panzer radio, and removed the pyrotechnic fuses supplied to Kristian by the SIS. He snapped it closed again, then handed the case out the cab door to Kristian.

"Here's their goods," he said. "I'm told that members of this *Oslogjeng* are eager for it. All should go smoothly for you inside. They'll love a radio that can reach England on a reliable basis. And your Minox makes a spectacular bonus. While you visit them, I'll tour along the waterfront, come back in around twenty minutes. If I don't see you sitting out by yourself over in the plaza, we'll go 'round for another twenty."

"Don't you want to come in?"

Rolf shook his head. "Spies need to know either nothing or everything about one other. Remember?"

"Yes."

"I only reveal myself to strangers when I must. My general rule is, 'Less is best.' For spies, truth is your coin of the realm. Dole it out sparingly. My advice is, keep your most valuable stuff deep in a buttoned pocket. Someday, you could need to buy an item that's shockingly expensive. And if your pocket's empty, you'll be stark out of luck."

The driver turned his face toward them. He remained mute but nodded emphatically in agreement.

～

Kristian checked both ways on the sidewalk. The taxi made an effective visual block for anyone across the street. He slipped easily into the storefront along with the case. It was dim and musty within the foyer. He could make out the shadowy bulk of counters with tarps thrown over them. Then a human figure rose up behind one.

"Who are you? What do you want?"

"I am Fiske."

"And what brings you to Oslo, Fiske?"

"I've heard that your seafood is good, uh, at this time of year."

"It's exceptional."

"In that case, I think I'll have the salmon."

That human shape came out from behind the counter and approached Kristian. He wore dark clothing, his cap was pulled down low and his collar turned up, but Kristian could make out a young and handsome face, and bright pale hair.

"I am Karl. Karl Johan."

Kristian couldn't help but smile. "That code name is inspired," he said. They shook hands.

Kristian's peripheral vision alerted him to a new presence. Another young man stood and emerged from behind a counter. He had darker hair. He stopped and stood two meters away. Both his hands were stuffed into his jacket pockets, and the large, sagging bulges those pockets made suggested their contents included more than his own balled fists.

"And who's this gent?"

"Call me Torlieff." Voice of this new young man was deep. Assured. Not warm. "Let's see what you brought us, Fiske. Set that case down on the floor, please. Open it slowly. Then you rise, and back away from it."

"Sure."

Kristian complied.

Out of Torlieff's left pocket came a hand that held an electric torch. He flashed its bright beam down onto the open case. Karl came over, knelt beside it, and pulled out the wad of *Stritt Folk* newspapers.

"Wonderful!" he exclaimed. "We've heard about this issue but had not yet obtained copies." He craned his neck back. "Do you wish some copies of ours, *Dette Er Vårt Land*, to take back?"

"No. One trip across Norway, holding contraband? That was plenty for me."

"Understood."

Karl took out the Minox sub-miniature camera, held it up in the light and whistled. "What a beauty," he said, and put it down carefully. "Occupation plans and documents, here we come." He unlatched the wooden cover of the box that held the radio and opened it. He released a much longer wolf-whistle and aimed a grin at Torlieff. "Looks like we're in business for sure," he said. Karl put everything back in the case, latched it and stood.

"Can we offer you food? A place to stay?" he asked Kristian.

"Appreciate your offer. But don't need a thing. We have other plans."

"I see. But tell us, who do you work for?"

"SIS."

Torlieff's right hand stirred in its pocket. But Karl raised a palm. "Don't you mean, SOE?" he asked

"Not what they called it when I was there."

Both of the resistance operatives eyed him.

"It's new," Karl prompted.

"Oh, quite right," Kristian said. "Yes. That was in the message I got about bringing you guys this radio. I didn't receive the briefing, not directly. It was transferred to me. That one detail didn't stick out, when I was told. But now I remember it."

They still regarded him with suspicion.

"I wonder if The Cyclops made it over into the new outfit."

"Aha. You know The Cyclops?"

"Yeah. He's a real piece of work."

"As we've heard," Karl said. He shot a glance at Torlieff. Both of them began to appear more relaxed. "No, but what I was really asking about originally is, who are the people you work with *here*. Right now. In Oslo."

"Oh. No one you need to worry about."

"Let us be the judge of that," Torlieff said.

Kristian noted that his lips were bent into an expression that was not exactly a smile.

"It isn't mine to say," Kristian replied. "Their agent did not want to enter with me just now and meet you."

"Why not?"

"Well, why should he?"

They all stared at each other. Finally, Karl chuckled.

"Look, here's all you really need to know," Kristian said. "The man I came with is a good Norwegian. Quite talented. He belongs to a political movement that needs to step carefully just now. In *any* country. He's allied with your Resistance here, that's definite. However, I don't know where he gets his orders from. Or if he takes orders. Maybe he doesn't. I *can* say that he does seem to coordinate with people on the left end of the spectrum. But how far left? Which people?" Kristian shook his head. "Don't know."

"Fair enough," Karl said. "We call ourselves *Oslogjengen*—the Oslo Gang. We're an *ad hoc*, self-invented group. Students, ex-soldiers, you name it. We started within days after the invasion, blew up the bridge on the road from the airport to slow the Germans down. We've taken on much, much more since then."

"We got stung by some losses, in the beginning," Karl said. "We learn as we go. A few of us got snatched by the Gestapo and were taken to *Victoria Terrasse*, where they've set up their HQ. One friend threw himself out a top floor window and onto the sidewalk below. Because what was happening *inside* of that building was far worse than attempting such an escape."

"What happened to him?"

"He broke his neck. See what I mean? It straightened us all up. You too should take heed. What we're all doing is far from safe. No matter how many steps we take to increase security or secrecy."

"Our biggest job now is also the most nebulous," Torlieff said. "Finding out as much as possible about all that's going on with the occupation in Oslo. I mean, we'll never get there, we can't grasp everything. But we absolutely need to try."

"At the top of our list is hooking up with more Resistance groups," Karl added. "We've got to improve communication with them. But the main link we need to forge is with independent commando companies in England. We've heard one company will be composed entirely of Norwegians. So, this radio you've brought us is the key to both."

"Is that Norwegian company to be directed by the new SOE?" Kristian said. "Or, 'The Special Operations Executive,' I recall what those letters stand for now."

Both young men nodded. "Right," Karl said. "However, there's a desire instead to get it managed by King Haakon and the Norwegian government-in-exile. They're fighting to set it up that way."

"Much better," Kristian agreed.

"Back to Topic A. Please be clear, what happens to you now?" Torlieff asked. "Since you don't plan to stay with us. Have you any other tasks here in Oslo we should know about?"

"Oh, I'm heading back to Stavanger soon," Kristian said. "See what my SIS handlers want of me, if anything. Do they still exist? Or the SOE, if those guys consider themselves my current bosses. Whichever." He shrugged. "We'll see if I agree with their ideas."

Torlieff tilted his head. "Now you sound like that agent you described. The one who doesn't seem to take orders from anyone."

"I guess I do, don't I," Kristian admitted. He looked at them, smiled, and changed the subject. "What's the best way to get a message to you, when I happen to be in Oslo?"

Torlieff and Karl checked each other with a glance. Torlieff nodded.

"Go in the early morning to the Andersens' bakery. Number thirty, on this street," Karl said. "At the counter, when you place your order, say that you have a message for Karl Johan. Make it short, perhaps it's only a rendezvous time and place. Repeat it twice. Then pay, pick up your *kneipp* and a pat of butter, head out the door."

"Got it." Kristian raised a palm in farewell. "Till we meet again. All right?"

"Okay. Stay out of trouble," Torlieff said.

～

While Kristian had been visiting with leaders of the Oslo Gang, the taxi driver and Rolf had been parked on a side street, making petrol bombs. Pint glass bottles mostly full of gasoline were uncorked, rubber tubes of white phosphorus inserted and the bottles resealed. These bottles were placed in a wooden box in the cab's trunk and carefully padded with rags. Following his own "Less is Best Rule," Rolf hadn't told Kristian he would be doing this instead of driving around at random, because—in case Kristian was picked up by the Germans—it would be best for him not to know.

Their chore finished, Rolf poked his head around the corner. "He's out," he announced.

The taxi picked up Kristian at the plaza, and they went around the block and headed for the Federation Hotel.

A short distance away from the hotel, the cabbie pulled into a different side street and parked beside a small delivery van with a picture of a fresh-baked raspberry pie painted on its side. "*Herlig Bakeri*" a legend proclaimed above this mouth-watering picture. That was the logo of a non-existent baking shop. "*Du fortjener en godbit*," a line of script read at the bottom. "You deserve a treat!"

Rolf and Kristian, now clad in the white kitchen smocks, jumped out of the taxi. Kristian yanked open the van's rear doors, revealing a cart of pastries. The bottom tray on the cart held cakes. Kristian held up the bottom of each cake with a spatula, while Rolf shoveled a bottle of pyrotechnic gel beneath it, whereupon Kristian let the spongy confection drop back into place to conceal the bottle.

The tubes filled with phosphorus, made of a special rubber compound, had by then dissolved into a loose, sticky mass inside the bottles. The phosphorus then accumulated at the upper side of each bottle, the petrol at the lower side. These simple fire grenades, or SIP bombs, were now armed. They would need to be handled with the greatest of care.

"Ready?"

"Let's do it."

Rolf got into the driver's seat of the van, cranked it up, and headed for the Federation Hotel. At the round-about before the main entry, a German soldier checked their IDs and work permits, then directed them to a paved lane that went around to the back. Here they parked, and as soon as they exited the van, a man with a magnificent black mustache, a white chef's hat tilting atop his head, barged out through the door from the hotel kitchen and yelled at them.

"You're late!" he roared. "Get that dessert cart in here. Except for the tray of cakes. That goes to the parlor on the hotel's top floor. *Rask nå!*"

They lifted the cart out and rolled it into the kitchen. Kristian lifted out the tray of cakes, bearing it in both hands.

"I'll summon the elevator for us," Rolf said loudly. They moved toward the elevator, but as they passed the stairwell, they dodged into it.

"Four flights up, now," Rolf warned.

"I am ready," Kristian replied.

"It's not only about speed, Fiske."

"I know!"

Kristian gently turned the tray over onto the linoleum floor of the landing, plucked the glass SIP bottles out from the base of the cakes. He tore off his smock, tossed it on top of the cakes, and stuffed the pyrotechnic grenades into his pockets. Then he bounded smoothly up the stairs with Rolf right at his heels.

On the hotel's top floor, breathing hard, they emerged from the stairs into a hallway that stood empty except for a maid's cart. They peered in through the open door of a room as they passed and saw a woman in an apron making the bed. At the end of the hall, a metal ring at the end of a thin chain dangled from the ceiling. Rolf grasped it, tugged, and a long, counter-weighted door swung down, with a ladder attached to it.

"All right," Rolf said. "You are to throw one at each end of the attic, one at each end of the third floor, one at each side of the basement."

"I know."

"I'll spread the word to hotel staffers on every floor that a bomb's about to go off, and I'll yank every fire alarm that I pass. A few more of our guys are poised to do the same. At street level, I go out to the van. If you're not there, I drive four blocks away and wait."

"I remember."

"Good man!" Rolf clapped him on the shoulder. "Up you go, now. Rain some fire on these goddamned swine."

~

The first two bottles made a satisfying crash and exploded into flames. The hotel attic was stacked with old and unused furniture, which all looked like it could ignite quite easily. By the time Kristian slid back down the ladder, a fire alarm had begun ringing and the building already was vibrating with sounds of growing pandemonium.

Room doors crashed open and people in various states of dress began scurrying toward the stairwells. There were only a few on the top floor, but by the time Kristian reached the third, a tide of humanity was flowing against him as he tried to exit into the hall. He fought free, located two empty rooms, and set off another pair of incendiary grenades. Then he rode the flood of galloping, jostling bodies down to the ground floor, separated from the herd again, and got himself into the basement. *Smash! Smash!* Two bursts of white light and two instant, fat blossoms of orange flame, then gusts of noxious vapors.

He looked up. Sounds of uproar and tumult were radiating down from the entire hotel building over his head. He heard muffled shouts, stomping feet, clanging alarms. Kristian found himself grinning as he headed back up to the ground floor.

*Better not smile,* he thought. *Makes one stand out. Best to look sad, scared. Remember, this is the tragic loss of a historic building.*

The human flood burst out from the hotel doors, spread in hurtling rivulets and then thickening streams onto nearby sidewalks and roadways. This screwed things up for the fire trucks, as they roared in on the available approaches, weaving through stopped vehicles and clots of people, honking their horns and blaring sirens like mad. When they were finally able to park, men in helmets and turnout gear jumped off to wave people away from the hydrants and hook up their hoses.

Boxy trucks full of soldiers and sleek German staff cars were screeching onto the scene now too, and their personnel jogged out to form a long but ragged line as they tried to establish a security cordon.

*Soon they'll be checking everyone they've caught in the net*, Kristian thought. *I need to be outside of the line when it happens.*

But when he turned back to see how the fire was developing, he unexpectedly found himself entranced by its churning, dynamic beauty. The insanely rich colors, the mounting billows of dark smoke, the swirling glory of an unleashed, elemental force with a raging appetite for destruction. *We did it!* he thought proudly.

By igniting the blaze at far ends of the hotel, they'd planned to make the fire initially look much larger than it was, to inspire panic while also giving staff and occupants a realistic amount of time to flee. But since this old wood building was basically one large hunk of tinder, the whole structure was becoming involved by the conflagration at a stupendous rate.

*Christ, let nobody be caught inside!* Kristian suddenly found himself troubled by the thought. Then a more brutal idea intruded. *No one but Germans, that is! And I hope that Luftwaffe seaplane pilot is right smack in the center of it, terrified and screaming his lungs out as his tongue bakes in his mouth and blackened skin peels off of his face... Try to laugh then, you sack of shit.*

Nearly all the people he could see were seeking to get far away from the blaze, or at least far enough to gape at it from a safe distance. Meanwhile, the soldiers and officers struggled to herd all those still inside their cordon into a manageable clump. Kristian was already out on the perimeter. He saw a way to wriggle out of their round-up by going through a tall hedge, so he seized that chance in a heartbeat.

On its other side, he jogged along the hedge in a crouch for many meters. He finally stopped, straightened, and looked back at the hotel again. He was amazed to see some men apparently trying to find a way to enter the building. And they were neither dressed nor equipped as firemen.

*Must be lodgers, trying to retrieve their stuff. Their records, possessions, clothing, equipment. But such an effort seems futile. The whole place looks doomed.*

Then he perceived why the blaze seemed to score such a definitive victory. The Oslo fire crews weren't really trying to fight it. Not at all. Instead, they directed streams from their hoses onto adjacent buildings, onto nearby landscaping, even wasted it on the pavement... squirting it anywhere but on the hotel.

*They hope to see that Nazi den burn to the ground just as much as we do!* Kristian felt thrilled by this revelation of local support. *More good Norwegians, high and low, must be choosing a path of resistance. How welcoming, then, shall our country look to Nazis in a month? Or a year? All right, all right, I've seen enough. High time for me to go find Rolf and the van and get the hell out of here.*

He turned. He found that he could crouch a little and stay within the shadow of the hedge until he made it all the way out to that main urban artery, where Rolf and the bakery truck should be parked a few blocks away.

Kristian reached the street's curb just in time to see a Mercedes coupe roar up and jolt to a halt on its squeaking tires, drawing his attention. It parked about twenty meters past his spot and closer to the hotel. A man with an aquiline face leaped out from behind the wheel, slammed his car door shut. He shouted a few words to his female companion in the passenger seat. Then he launched into a sprint toward the blaze.

After a wait of a few seconds, the woman opened her own door and languidly stepped out. She moved to the coupe's front fender, leaned her hips against it. She draped a light blue sweater across her shoulders and knotted its sleeves loosely over her chest. She put both of her hands behind her on the car, shifted to sit more firmly against its fender and crossed her legs at the ankles. For a moment, Kristian thought she might produce a cigarette and light it up. Perhaps blow a smoke ring toward the mighty conflagration taking place perhaps a hundred meters away.

*How can she look this relaxed about what she's seeing?*

Kristian studied her. This woman appeared to be youthful, tan and lithe. She had coppery hair, a classic profile with a rounded chin. A shapely build.

She was Helene.

Kristian felt his mouth fall open. And through a long yet timeless moment, no one in the world existed but for her.

*"It is no use saying, 'We are doing our best.' You have got to succeed in doing what is necessary."*
—Winston Churchill, *speech 1916*

# CHAPTER 19

Opposing impulses warred inside of Kristian—to either run off yelling curses about how savagely depressing his day had suddenly turned, or to sprint for Helene and wrap her up in his arms. The response he managed split the difference. He retreated to the shadows at the end of the hedge and simply stared.

Finally, Helene felt someone's eyes on her.

Her head swiveled. She located a man who seemed to be peering at her between distant twigs and leaves. Then she saw that dim shape of a man back-pedal out of her line of sight.

*Hmm, odd behavior*, she thought. Then she frowned. *Someone who doesn't wish to be seen. Or recognized, perhaps. Is it a person whom I know? Or just someone who knows Ziegler and his car?* Hans had told her several times that *Abwehr* agents frequently found themselves spied upon by the other German intelligence services. Operators always hoped to steal each other's secrets. "It's no game of cat-and-mouse," Ziegler had said. "More like, cats-and-cats. Some big and as mean as leopards, others thin and sneaky, like feral cats from a dank alley."

Back among deeper shadow of the hedge, Kristian gripped branches with both hands and thought furiously. *Helene's long been Otto's ward and his devoted fan. That means she's long bought into the NS horseshit. And I just saw a guy who looks much like a German, driving Helene up here.*

This last observation ignited fury. *Is she going out with the Nazis? Spending nights with them?*

His burst of anger prompted a chaos of other ideas. *I should go hunt that guy down and stab him. I could run up there now and ask her what the hell she thinks she's doing. I ought to jump into that car and steal it. Just drive off with her…*

He breathed in deeply, tried to tug a scrap of sense out of his jumble of impulses. He looked around. A short way off, he spotted the bakery van parked by the side of the road. Rolf sat inside, waiting for him. *It's where you need to go. Now. Don't be stupid. Gestapo will swarm over this area too, in minutes. Haul your butt out of here.*

Kristian ran, bent over, back along the hedge. He had almost reached it the far end of it, a place where he planned to turn and make a run for the van. Then a man in dark clothing stepped out of a gap between the end of the hedge and the building. Then another man appeared. And another. Kristian skidded to a halt in front of them.

"*Ja, det er han!*" a voice said in Norwegian. It meant, "Yes, that's him."

Kristian heard running footsteps behind him. But before he could even react, something soft but taut swept around him, wrapped him up at the same moment that a man's hurtling body tackled him at the knees.

Kristian tried to fight back but found himself being overwhelmed by too many other bodies, faster than he could manage react. He sought to grab his dagger from its sheath between his shoulder blades, but instead he wound up immobilized with one arm raised above his head. *They're rolling me up in blankets! Who ARE they? They all sound Norwegian. But why do they want to grab me?*

～

He kept puzzling over this all the while he was being dragged into the rear of some sort of vehicle, and held firmly in place by having three men sit on top of him. Their weight plus the dense layers of fabric swaddling him made it hard for Kristian to breathe. He could hear people muttering as the vehicle lurched into motion but couldn't make out what they said.

A surprisingly long drive finished up with a series of rough jolts, and then the vehicle stopped. He was pulled out of it, carried up a flight of steps, and dumped unceremoniously on a hard plank floor. Hands reached up into the tube of blankets, found his feet, and wrapped a chain around one ankle. Then he was spun around until the blankets came loose and his arms could be grabbed and his wrists tied together behind his back. Kristian sought to make out the faces of his captors, but the room he'd been placed in was dark and their caps had been tugged low.

"Who are you? What do you want with me?" he demanded.

"Shut up. You can spill your guts soon enough. In fact, you'll have to!"

A padlock clicked, and Kristian saw his leg had been chained to an iron bedstead. Next, he found himself being frisked thoroughly. All belongings removed from him, including his knife. The men left. A door slammed.

Kristian levered himself up onto the lower tier of a double bunk bed, and sat crouched on its hard, thin mattress. The blankets used to shroud him had been tossed onto the end of the bed in a rumpled heap. He leaned his face down toward his knees, in the only comfortable posture he could achieve, and tried to think.

*Was Rolf close enough to see me get snatched? Did he follow me here—wherever here is—or did he simply take off? Am I on my own now?*

The door creaked open once more. Two men entered carrying a glowing kerosene lantern. He recognized them immediately: Torlieff and Karl Johan. They didn't look pleased to see him. Rather the opposite. Torlieff dragged up a stool and Karl a wooden box that he could upend. They hung the lantern on a peg and sat down in front of Kristian.

"What in God's name were you thinking, to pull such a crazy stunt?" Karl snarled. His formerly friendly face now was clenched in a scowl. "Or did you just not think?"

"Which stunt is that?" Kristian asked.

Torlieff flung out his hand to slap Kristian smartly across his cheek.

"Don't get cute! I asked if you had any more actions planned in Oslo.

Burning down the Federation Hotel, how did that slip your mind? One tiny scheme you forgot to mention?"

Playing innocent wouldn't wash with them, Kristian saw. Might as well speak the harsh truth. "You asked if there was something you *should* know about. In this case, my answer was 'no.'"

Torlieff backhanded him across his other cheek with a stronger blow.

"So, that's how you wish to discuss it?" Kristian said. "Untie me. Then I can make you a proper reply."

Torlieff shook his fist. "Oslo isn't some random, anonymous town. Not no-man's land, not an open battleground. It's *our* turf. Here, you play by *our* rules. We live here, we're the ones who suffer all consequences. You, you're only an intruder."

"I am every bit as Norwegian as you," Kristian replied evenly. "I have my reason for the actions I've taken. We both fight the Nazi occupation. Is this true or false?"

Torlieff looked as if he now aimed to punch Kristian in the mouth, but Karl batted his arm down.

"Let's hear Fiske explain himself," Karl said. "After that, we'll figure out what sanctions to apply."

"He can start by answering my questions. Why work with goddamned Bolsheviks? We saw that crew with you, and we know who they are! Can't you see they're utterly lawless? They answer only to Stalin."

"No, not all of them," Kristian said. "The one I came with? The Brits sent me to Stavanger with a radio for him. Next, they sent me and him here to Oslo with a radio for you. By the way, have you gotten that radio plugged in and switched on? If you do, don't fool around by grilling me. That man's a double agent. Ask the SIS and SOE about him, get it from the horse's mouth. Perhaps the concept of attacking the Federation Hotel even originated with those pooh-bahs over in Britain."

They both stared at him. "Do you have any real proof of that?" Karl asked, after a pause.

"No," Kristian admitted. "The seed, the root, of our plan is unknown to me. All its tactics, my partners concocted for themselves. I don't know if the initial order to make an attack came from somewhere else. But he didn't receive it from Stalin, and that's a lock. He hates Stalin as much as he hates Hitler. Maybe more."

"And his name? This Bolshy renegade of yours?" Torlieff demanded.

Kristian offered him only a faint smile, a slight head shake.

Torlieff responded with a grunt of frustration and a scowl.

"All right. So you don't know if your Brit bosses ordered the attack," Karl went on. "Not knowing, why did you agree to take part?"

Kristian glanced from one to the other. It was probably time to make a leap. *Spies need to know everything or nothing about each other.* It looked like the right time to pull some truth out of that buttoned pocket Rolf had spoken of. If he did not provide the Oslo Gang with reasons to trust him, who knew how long they'd keep him prisoner? Or what else they'd try to reduce their suspicions and doubts—like try to be rid of him altogether? He didn't doubt they were capable of it.

"I've an excellent reason for despising the *Luftwaffe*," he said quietly. "They killed my father. A few months ago."

"Oh really?" Karl lifted a skeptical eyebrow. "How?"

"A military seaplane. It sank our fishing boat, the *Snekka*, in the North Sea. We were trying to sail Norwegian officers to England. I was the only survivor."

"Indeed?" Torlieff asked. "How can it be that you alone survived?"

"Long story. The short version is that I went adrift in our dinghy. A British ship picked me up."

"So, what's your father's name?"

"Ragnar Thorsen. The *Snekka's* home port was Stavanger. My real first name? It's Kristian. And you might as well know the rest of it. My uncle's Otto Thorsen."

Karl's forehead wrinkled. "That's no ordinary name. You mean, Deacon Otto Thorsen, the one who ranks high in the NS?"

"Yes. And through him, I know Helene Berg, his ward, quite well. Since you seek to know all that's going on in Oslo, you should be aware that she's here in town too. And it looks to me like she's a collaborator with the Germans."

A look passed betwixt Torlieff and Karl which Kristian couldn't read. There followed an even lengthier pause. Torlieff ended it by clearing his throat.

"Let me explain to you why the attack on the Federation Hotel was such a crappy idea, Kristian. Quite apart from your superficial notion of scoring a blow against the *Luftwaffe*. Listen carefully. Almost the whole staff working in that hotel is Norwegian."

"We knew that. We took steps to make sure everyone got warned before the fire got too hot or spread very far."

"Does that mean you fantasize that there were no casualties?"

"Were there?"

"Yes. Two German men, and a woman in a room on an upper floor. That's all we know of thus far. Of course, there could be more. Easily."

Kristian paled. "Was that woman Norwegian?"

"Yes. And she *was* a collaborator. But, let's set the question of her death aside for the moment. The Germans would be mad enough if the *Luftwaffe* simply lost that whole structure, with all the documents and uniforms and equipment and personal effects that it contained. And the Abwehr and their files, gear and notes, by the way. They lodged there too. But killing a pair of *Luftwaffe* pilots on top of all that? The Germans are furious. They know the cause was arson. They now have descriptions of you and your red buddies as the perpetrators. And they identified members of our gang too."

Kristian looked puzzled. "How's that, again?"

Karl gave him an appraising look. "We sent a man to follow you on a motor scooter, after you'd visited us. Of course, we did. Because we had not found you particularly forthcoming, and we wished to gain a more complete understanding. Our man became amused when he saw you get into the bakery truck. He felt intrigued when he saw you go to the Federation. And he turned horrified when he saw the fire break out. He telephoned us immediately. We sent as many people in as we could spare, to make sure the place was evacuated. And we grabbed up blankets in order to smother the flames if we saw people on fire."

He pointed to the heap of blankets on the bunkbed mattress. Kristian finally became aware of the faint reek of smoke wafting off of them.

"Think you're the only one who enjoys whacking his enemies with a dose of vengeance?" Torlieff challenged. "Germans relish it. And none more than one Siegfried Fehmer. You've heard of him? He's the Gestapo chief in Oslo. He's young and brilliant and driven."

"And sadistic as hell," Karl put in, "once he has you in his grip, very bad things happen."

"Ought we to congratulate you? You've now become a special target for Siegfried. And your Bolshy pal as well. And at least a few of our boys were glimpsed by authorities at the site too, we're pretty sure. How could they not be? Their suspicions shall now also fall upon us."

"I must say, I am sorry about that," Kristian said slowly. "But please tell me one thing. Can you say if my Bolshy friend—as you put it—managed to get away from them?"

Torlieff and Karl glanced at each other. Torlieff nodded a permission to Karl.

"Your bakery van drove off. It wasn't intercepted. The sole clue the Gestapo found at the spot where it had been parked was a big black mustache, lying on the sidewalk. It came off the chef. Who I might guess was an accomplice?"

Kristian was unable to resist a grin. Torlieff and Karl remained somber.

"The van was later found at the edge of town, burnt to a cinder. Thus, the Gestapo extracted no usable fingerprints from it. Or any other clues."

"Thank God."

"Listen to us, Kristian. There's something we've learnt, which everyone in the Norwegian Resistance must come to understand. Since it's war, one might think there are no rules. And truly there aren't, not as such. Yet there is something else, a code you could call it, tit-for-tat, or give-and-take.

A tacit agreement that your struggle occurs on a certain steady level. No women and children to be hurt, for example. Civilian casualties minimized. But once that arrangement gets destroyed, if your battle plunges to a deeper and more desperate level, then all bets are off. Both sides compete to see how truly awful they can be. And to see who can be the most terrible first. That's what we hope to avoid in Oslo."

"Which you've now made far more difficult," Torlieff scolded. He abruptly stood. "All right, I'd say we've given this Bolshevik-lover enough stuff to think about. We should also award him time to think."

"Let's unbind Kristian's hands at least," Karl suggested. "Let him get some rest."

"No." Torlieff shook his head. "Let's be sure that thinking is actually what Fiske or Kristian or whoever he is actually does. He needs to grow far better at it, in my opinion. So, let's keep this shitbag tied up, to help him concentrate."

*"Terboven is taking a lot of pains and doing his part magnificently. He is the untrammeled master of Norway."*
—Josef Goebbels, from *The Goebbels Diaries*

# CHAPTER 20

For hours Kristian lay curled atop his thin mattress, occasionally flopping his body from side-to-side. Since his hands remained tied behind his back, it was his sole possible position for rest, and not a particularly good one. He dozed off occasionally. Most of his time was indeed spent thinking. A recurrent thought was that he didn't like Torlieff much.

He also tried to figure out the precise nature of his place of confinement. What with the long drive up here and various other clues, he figured he must be in the bunkhouse of a forest lodge somewhere in mountains northwest of Oslo. Given that his captors were young, only a few years older than Kristian, he'd lay odds they were current or recent university students. It meant they might belong to a Student Association. If that was true, then they had often undertaken treks to wilderness destinations, using this lodge as their staging area.

If so, that meant he was confined in a rural spot a seriously long walk from anywhere. Even if he managed to free himself from his bonds and escape the building, it still would take plenty of time to reach a major road, a town, or a train station. And that meant his captors would also score plenty of chances to track his path, nab him, and drag him back.

Finally, he mulled over what it meant if Torlieff was right, if Gestapo headmen had begun to identify him as a high-priority target. Showing up in or near Oslo could lead to big problems. What should his alternative be?

Drammen? Kristiansand? Or head east and hit Drøbak, then try to make it from there into Sweden?

*How worried must I be? The Gestapo can't have much more than a basic description. My hair's dyed, and they can't have many more details, like height and weight and age, since I was moving fast. I didn't see anyone in the hotel taking photographs. Anyone owning a camera had more important matters to focus on—like staying alive!*

*Even if the Gestapo connects me and Rolf to that odd pair who came to the Oslo region on the train, we used false papers to board. And I've got that whole other set I used up in Stavanger. That is, if the Oslo Gang gives them back to me! And my roll of stolen money. Plus, my dagger. But let's stay optimistic. Let's assume, even if they don't give my stuff back, that they ultimately let me go. They'll also want me to get as far away from them as possible. I could head for Stavanger or might try for Sweden. From either place I can return to England, on some sort of a boat or ship that's making a clandestine run. I mean, that's how the modified panzer radio arrived from Britain, as Rolf told me. So, there's got to be voyages back-and-forth. How often do they run?*

Karl eventually returned to the bunk room to free Kristian from the ropes that bound his wrists. But he left the ankle chain on him, and he didn't speak much. He did offer Kristian a wooden bowl of lukewarm chicken soup, a jug of water and a heel of rye bread. After eating, Kristian was able to stretch out on the bed, tug some of the blankets up over himself, and arrange his leg chain comfortably enough to fall asleep.

He snored his way into oblivion, began to dream. He envisioned himself lounging on a wooden bench near the waterfront in Oslo. And oddly, Helene was amusing herself by driving a big, black German convertible back and forth on the road in front of him. Each time she passed, she waved floridly and smiled beautifully, while musically singing out his name.

"Kristian. Kristian."

He realized abruptly that he was not dreaming. Some new person, clearly female, had entered the room and begun to call out to him, using a near imitation of Helene's voice. But why would anyone try to torment him in such a manner? Kristian's eyes snapped open and he saw a young woman who stood beside his bed. And the astonishing thing was that she physically resembled Helene, too. In fact, she looked like a perfect match.

Kristian sat up fast, clonked his skull hard against the iron frame of the bunk bed just above, then slumped back onto his mattress.

"Ow!" he yelped. He pressed a palm against what was sure to soon be a colorful lump.

"Hello, Kristian," Helene said. "Sorry I made you smack your head, there. But, well, are you all right? It's so good to see you."

He stared up at her, slack jawed. Yes, it was Helene in the very flesh. She wore a dark blue skirt, a brown wool coat. Her mane of chestnut hair was wound up in a coil, with a black beret pinned somewhat askew to the top of that heap. It looked like she'd entered the room by herself, without a single guide or guard from the Gang. She held a brass kerosene lamp up by its base. In its dim glow, he saw those eyes of warm amber lit by... something. Worry? Her ripe lips were bent in a smile. Yet there was also a sad and tentative aspect to her.

"Helene! What on earth are *you* doing here?!" Kristian blurted. Yet before she could answer, more questions—and much darker ones—leapt to mind. "Did you come on a raid by the Germans? To finger me for the Gestapo? Did the whole Oslo Gang get rolled up just now? Are you part of that?"

A cleft formed between her eyebrows as she shook her head. "Don't be silly," she said. Her tone was frosty. "You're not the only one who's struggled over whether or not to join the Resistance." She set her lamp down on the seat of a tall stool.

"Hm. Well, interesting comment. But I'm one who didn't struggle. Not in the least."

It was all he could manage to say, as he fought to get his mind around the fact that Helene actually stood before him. He also tried to fully absorb the notion she was trying to get across: *I'm not with the Germans, you idiot.* That made him feel relief. But on the other hand, he remained suspicious. There were no jackbooted stormtroopers at her side; clearly, a good sign.

Then he realized that all his responses to her thus far did not convey any signs of great intelligence.

He sat up on the bunk's mattress with more care, then swung his legs down to the floor, chain rattling, so that he could face her. And they stared at one another as as if they'd been separated for years, not just months.

"If they let you walk in here by yourself, the Gang must really trust you."

"They do now. Took a while. I had to show them proof."

"Of what?" He eyed her. "Doing what?"

"What do you think? Things that you might be able to imagine," she said, haughty now, her chin raised. "As well as plenty I'm sure you won't."

"I could surprise you. Most people wouldn't find my own tale at all believable. The Brits certainly didn't. Not at first." And he thought, *I bet you'd be really surprised if I told you I saw you in a German's auto outside the Federation Hotel.*

Her eyes moistened then, as she looked down at him.

"I do know all about *Snekka*."

"How?" he wondered.

"I'm a clerk in the *Reichkommissar's* office. I read about what happened to your boat on a part of a report."

"Terboven? You work at his HQ? You're right. That is difficult to imagine. Why on earth would you do that?"

She just stared at him.

"Oh. I see. That's an answer to my earlier question. Sorry. I'm just trying to get my bearings, here."

She extended a hand to him. When he took it, she wrapped it snugly in both of her own. He looked at their entwined fingers, scarcely daring to believe his own eyes. She was touching him! And quite voluntarily, at that.

"I'm very upset and saddened by what happened to your *Pappa*, and to Lars. And I must tell you, I felt completely... astounded... when the Oslo Gang informed me yesterday that you were alive, Kristian, and what you had to do to survive. I feel most grateful to God that he found a way to save you."

Kristian felt his head swim at the enveloping warmth of her touch, as well as her expressed care and concern. Her husky tone, the throb in her voice, let him know she was sincere. Her usual cool and remote air, for the moment, had vanished.

"Thank you," he whispered. "Me, too."

"There's more."

"What?"

"In that report I read. Having to do with your mother, Kari."

"I came back through Stavanger. I know already that the Gestapo came to our apartment and arrested my *Mamma*. And I know why. She protested and interfered with police work."

She sighed heavily and released his hand. He let it fall, still tingling from her touch, back onto his lap. "Good," she said. "I mean, I'm happy I don't have to tell you about that part."

He blinked. His eyes flicked from side to side as he sought to guess her imminent message before she could voice it. "Well, say *this* first! Is Kari alive?" His voice quivered as he asked.

"Oh, yes. She is, as far as we know. But she's been sent off into Germany, to a concentration camp. Sorry. We think it might be Sachsenhausen, near Berlin. I've been trying to get some confirmation of that. But no luck, so far."

"We have to get her out of that shithole! And back home!"

Helene didn't reply, just watched him. Kristian yanked angrily at his ankle chain. Then he groaned, leaned forward, propped his elbows on his knees and dropped his head into his hands.

"If we can ever figure out a way to do that, we'll certainly make an attempt," Helene said. "But our far more immediate problem is how to get you out of Oslo."

He looked up, grasping at a straw of hope. "Well, how much sway do you have with the Gang? Must be some. I mean, they let you come visit me by yourself."

"That's because I told them I had some highly sensitive information to share with you about your *Mamma*. They seemed sympathetic." Helene took the lamp off the stool, set it on the floor. She pushed the stool closer to him, sat on it. "I also told them you were highly unstable and impetuous, Kristian and the best way to keep you from causing them any more trouble in Norway was to get you shipped back off to England."

"What if I don't wish to go?"

"You *do* wish to go." She lowered her voice. "First, because the Gang really hopes to see the last of you, and that's the safest way for you to make it happen. Other solutions might not be nearly so pleasant. Second, going to England is the only way for you to complete a special mission."

"A special mission, for who?"

"Me."

*"I have a visit with the Norwegian propaganda chief,
State Counsellor Lunde. Clever man, for a Norwegian.
Says that Quisling's movement is growing."*
—Josef Goebbels, from *The Goebbels Diaries*

# CHAPTER 21

"Clarify, please. What mission is this?"

"Take something over to the Brits."

"All right. What?"

"Information."

"You're being tiresome, Helene. Just tell me, okay?"

"I can't, not yet."

"German info, or Norwegian info?"

She shook her head.

"I'll make it easier. Stuff from that German boyfriend you go on long drives with, in his great big Mercedes, or from somebody else?"

Her amber eyes widened. "How do you know about that?"

"Never mind. Consider this point. How can I possibly agree to something I know absolutely nothing about?"

"What if you got captured, interrogated? It's far better if you knew nothing you could tell them."

Kristian rolled his eyes. "Rolf used that very same excuse for keeping me in the dark. I didn't like it the first time I heard it, and I've grown to hate hearing it now."

"Give up, Kristian. I'm not going to tell you."

"Okay, let's not talk about the mission itself, then. Not yet! Instead, please answer a different but related question. Why pick me for it?"

"Because I trust you."

"*You* trust *me*?"

She looked exasperated. "Kristian! I've known you for years. I know you're brave. And you've proven to me that you can stubbornly persist. Plus, I know you'll do anything to strike at those monsters who killed Ragnar and Lars and kidnapped your mother."

"Well, that last part is certainly true enough. But, consider your other options. You trust me more than you do Torlieff or Karl?"

"Right now, yes. There are fine people in the Oslo Gang. But they're all just starting up the path of Resistance. They don't yet grasp the depth and scale of this growing evil we face. However, because of the mayhem inflicted on you and your family, you *do* get it. I do as well, since I'm around the Nazis day in and out. I know how they speak, and act, and the sort of jokes they make when they think no one else can overhear them. It's horrible."

"Now there, Helene, you put your finger on something. Torlieff told me that we shouldn't race the Nazis to the bottom of the barrel. However, I'd say, no matter how bad we seek to be, those bastards have already shot past us to burst *through* the bottom of the barrel. Like it was tissue! They're now lost in a kind of black abyss beyond."

Helene nodded. "Exactly," she said.

"But what about you?" Kristian asked. "Since it sounds like you'd call Torlieff and Karl beginners. How would you describe yourself?"

"I can tell you that growing up in an orphanage gave me a type of training that one might not suspect," Helene responded. "Perhaps you think it was one big, cheerful family in that crowded institute. But it was more like, every girl for herself. I grew to understand how violence festers right below a thin varnish of respectability. I learned what one must do to rise to the top, to avoid suspicion of those in charge, to cultivate allies and to sabotage rivals. And that of course was among…" she cleared her throat "… all these beautiful and innocent children. Who none-the-less managed somehow to give me an excellent primer on how to deal with the not-so-innocent."

"All right. I see a bigger story there. I also get that you work *with* this Oslo Gang, but not *for* them. Is there any kind of spy-boss at all for you?"

"My boss? No one."

"My, my, does that ever sound like you."

Helene's grin created a fetching dimple at both corners of her mouth. "But there are plenty of people that I do work *with*. All of Norway I suppose. Root and cheer for the home team. God has put me in a place where I can uncover aspects of German plans almost before anybody else. Some things that I hear would really shock you." Her smile faded. "Anyway, I've stumbled into something that could save thousands upon thousands of lives. But to do so, it must reach the British fast. Very fast. I'll tell you this much—it has to do with London, Manchester, Coventry and all the other cities that get flattened by bombs and set on fire every night."

"Really?" Kristian gnawed on his lower lip. "Okay, I'll consider it. Give you my final answer after I learn a little more. How do you wish to proceed, here? Can you get me out?"

"In about a minute, Karl and Torlieff will come into this room to inform you that you must return to England. I told them that after I talked to you about your Mamma, I'd soften you up on the idea of leaving town. But when they come in, I want you to insist on staying here in Norway. Tell them you even plan to move into Oslo for good."

"Okay. But why?"

"So that all three of us can work you over, and argue, and gradually convince you, Britain's where you need to be."

"And you need to make it complicated, why?"

"They'll feel so glad about winning a victory, they won't care much about how or why or when you go."

"And that matters, because?"

"Because of psychology. They'll feel so relieved, so happy to wash their hands of you and leave any specific arrangements in my hands. I don't want them to try to help me. Or interfere otherwise. And that, I think, will make our chances of success go way up."

"Hmph. I guess perhaps you may have learned a thing or two."

~

His negotiation with the Oslo Gang proceeded much as Helene had foreseen. Kristian played the foot-dragging, obstinate, unwelcome guest. He proposed remaining in Oslo to join up with the Gang. Even volunteered to assist them on their operations. Torlieff and Karl flatly refused to take him up on that offer.

Instead they praised the virtues of jolly old England, the security and relaxation he could enjoy there, his fresh chance to learn more about the new SOE, get in synch with the big picture. He might even pick up more specialized training and become a mightier force in his crusade against Nazis. He could then take his new powers practically anywhere in the European Theater. Czechoslovakia, say. Or Poland. Perhaps help the French Resistance in exotic North Africa, if not Paris itself.

Helene would occasionally toss in a useful bit by reminding Kristian that staying near Oslo would be dangerous, not only for him, but for anyone around him. The Gestapo had launched an all-out manhunt for that despicable Federation Hotel arsonist.

Kristian responded to their every entreaty with obstinacy and reluctance. For a final display, he insulted the clumsy fishing boats they wanted to use to smuggle him back to Britain. "Way too slow. They're all sitting ducks. I've had one boat shot out from under me. I'm *not* eager to have that happen again. Surely, you can understand why."

He preferred to be picked up by a British airplane at night, perhaps one landing in a farm field nearby, he told them. Preferably, a Lysander. In fact, he refused to depart by any other means.

"That could take a long time to arrange," they objected.

"I don't care," he replied stoutly.

Fishing boats were far safer these days, the trio sought to persuade him. Experienced skippers were making repeat nocturnal runs, enough that their route had won its own nickname, *Shetlandsbussen*—The Shetlands Bus. There was special radio equipment aboard each vessel to keep in touch with England and the British navy, as well as expertly forged sailing documents in case they were ever stopped and inspected. Good, stout, Norwegian crews manned these boats too, the sort of lads with whom he'd have a grand time sailing, since he'd once been one of them.

Gradually, Kristian allowed himself to be convinced. "All right," he told them. "I guess I'll go that way, then."

The relief that Karl and dour Torlieff then displayed made them appear almost giddy.

Helene suggested that a boat from Kristiansand could pick him up in Drøbak. It would approach no closer. Nazi water patrols multiplied in strength and frequency the nearer one sailed up the fjord toward Oslo—since Norway's capitol was now also headquarters for the German occupation.

The easiest way to get him out of Oslo and down there to Drøbak, she said, was to pose Kristian as an invalid, being sent away to recuperate in the countryside. Germans were uniformly repelled by infirmity and disease, a mental tic born of their relentless boosterism of Aryan purity. If Kristian appeared to be sick, they'd likely offer to speed him on his way out of town. And with his dyed brown hair cropped down to its blonde roots and his fuzzy beard shaved off as well, the odds of anyone identifying him as looking anything like that infamous Federation arsonist should be quite low.

Kristian asked if he could have his possessions returned: the fake IDs, his big roll of *Reichsmarks* and Kroner, as well as his Wilkinson dagger. Torlieff informed him that he could have it all excepting the knife. "Last thing we need right now is any more German bodies scattered about, to mark your trail," he said.

Kristian decided it wasn't the best moment for him to mention the array of corpses he'd left behind him up in Stavanger. It wouldn't improve his chances of retrieving his dagger. Best to let the weapon go, anyway. It could pose a problem if he were stopped and searched. A new knife could always be found. Meanwhile, he'd take quiet comfort in knowing that he'd drawn nearer to paying off the bill for the *Snekka*. Adding in those incinerated pilots from the Federation, he was now just three Nazis shy of a long-sought reckoning.

He didn't bring that up, either.

Helene told Karl and Torlieff that she had a weekend off from her job at the *Reichskommissar's* office scheduled. And she could deal with Otto by telling him that, due to overwork there, she desperately needed to take a short respite by herself out in the country. Otto wouldn't mind, since he'd buried himself in a project of trying to persuade Norway's Lutheran church to ally more fully with the German *Reich's* church.

She said that she'd dress herself up in a nursing outfit and then wrap Kristian up in bandages, so their day of travel down to Drøbak should go off with nary a hitch.

But first, Helene felt compelled to add a wrinkle or two. Kristian was swaddled up in a bit more than bandages. Thanks to a doctor friend of Helene's—also in the Resistance—both his left forearm and his lower right leg were immobilized in plaster casts. And inside his arm cast the physician had tucked a clutch of purloined documents. These secret papers had been tightly folded, sealed in a narrow sleeve of green oilcloth, then buried within plaster and fabric layers of the cast.

When the time came for Kristian to stump up on his crutches to a bus and board it at Oslo Central station, Helene also handed him a pair of tart wild raspberries and a spotless white handkerchief.

"Just before the Germans check our papers, chew up those berries, and shove the pulp into a corner of your mouth with your tongue. Then, as I talk to them, pull out your hanky and cough into it. Be sure you put a nice, fat stain in the middle."

"Wow," Kristian said.

"I'll tell them you sustained some internal bruising in a recent automobile crash. Your lung problems could stem from that, or it could perhaps be an onset of tuberculosis. That disease runs in your family. You're dairy farmers."

"Where'd you pick up that trick?"

"Originally? Created it at my orphanage. In order to give myself a string of days in the infirmary. Gain some peace and quiet. As well as a lot more time to read."

Horror crept over the faces of the German guards as they observed red blotches oozing through the handkerchief with every wet, hacking cough that Kristian spewed.

Helene's venerable ruse still worked like a charm.

∼

After they had been encouraged—strongly—to board the bus first and sit far toward the back, Kristian and Helene went to the rear bench seat, where he could position himself with his supposedly broken leg stretched out. They settled down next to each other. Then Helene scooted herself sideways to put an inch or two of space between their respective thighs and hips.

The rest of the passengers began to board. It looked if those passengers preferred to fill in all the seats up front, as far from Kristian as possible. It gave him and Helene a private moment.

"How did you find out about my mother?" Kristian asked.

That amber gaze of hers turned, and it warmed him. He reminded himself that such a look did not indicate the presence of any given emotion in her. It was simply an aspect of Helene's physical appearance. Due to genetics, a person's eyes might acquire a certain coloring; that's all there was to it.

"Well, I told you," she murmured. "It was in a Gestapo file."

"Right. But how on earth did you ever get to read it?"

"Every day, I'm at the *Reichskommissar's* office. The headquarters for *Festung Norwegen*. Know where they installed themselves? Smack in the former *Handelsgymnasium*. That new high school built downtown. The place where Otto was supposed to become vice-principal."

Kristian did know of the school—every newspaper in the country had boasted about it while it had been under construction, calling it the most modern, the most progressive, the best-built, a giant step forward for Norway, and so on and so forth. Of course the Nazis had seized it for themselves.

And lately, he'd begun to hear the phrase, *Festung Norwegen*. Meaning "Fortress Norway" in German. Now all things solid, valuable or useful in the country, were being perverted to serve that concept. Hitler aimed to transform the whole nation into a bulwark that might protect his northern flank. From the British, at first. Or Stalin's Reds driving across Finland, then down the peninsula. And later perhaps, the Americans.

"So, you work directly for Terboven? Our Nazi overlord?"

"Shhhh." Helene flicked a look up the aisle but saw no one yet sitting near enough to overhear him. "No," she whispered. "For his secretary."

"She had a file on Kari? His secretary? She knew it interested you?"

"No. Found it on my own. I'd been worried over what happened to you and the *Snekka* since that day the *Merhlicht* sank. Otto said he'd heard nothing. I told him we ought to telephone your mother. We tried, and he also sent some NS party personnel from Stavanger to visit her. But she was never home—or so they said."

"Then what?"

"At the *Reichskommisar's*, I saw her name pop up on a list. She was an agenda item for a judicial hearing in *Det Hyggerommet*."

"You call a place in that Nazi headquarters 'The Cozy Room'?!" Kristian looked puzzled.

"About a half-dozen of us Norwegian women work in the headquarters. That's just our nickname for a chamber Terboven uses with his top officials. They gather to judge the fate of people grabbed in the most important arrests. Some also call it, *Døds Ventestue*."

"Death's waiting-room," Kristian drawled. "Even catchier."

"I heard Kari's name mentioned, she was up for review. And I got my hands on the indictment files they use in the chamber. I hid in a stall of the women's bathroom and read Kari's entry before I went on and gave her paperwork to Terboven's crew."

Kristian whistled and raised an eyebrow. "Wow. That's a risk."

She nodded, then shrugged. "Sure, but I had to know. I saw Kari had been arrested for interfering with an *Aktion Gnadentod*. A mercy-killing? But her indictment didn't say what sort…"

"Well, I've got the inside report, there. In Stavanger, the Gestapo took over an old folks' home. Wanted to use as their HQ. So they cleared the place out, *sehr schnell*. But a few elders failed to be picked up by friends or relatives or anyone else. So late one night, those Nazi pigs just threw them off the roof and into a dump truck."

Helene shuddered. "I'd say no, that couldn't happen, they'd never do such a thing. And yet, I've already heard of far, far worse."

"Kari tried to make them stop. So, they grabbed her."

"That day I read Kari's file? There in Terboven's cozy room his crew had to decide whether to put her in prison or just shoot her," Helene said. "They chose a concentration camp. As I said, we think it might be Sachsenhausen."

Kristian said nothing. Helene glanced at him, saw the sad and stricken look on his face. She reached out to give his hand a furtive squeeze.

His expression was doleful. "Mamma in Sachsenhausen. That sounds more dreadful every time one hears it," he muttered. He swallowed hard.

She gave a wince of sympathy. "A bad moment for me, too. I mean, I'd begun to think of Kari as my aunty. Then, I got shocked even more by a footnote I glimpsed under the indictment, about *Snekka's* fate. A very cold and curt summary. Said Kari was married to a skipper who'd been caught trying to smuggle Norwegian officers over to England. And so your boat was promptly and efficiently sunk by a Luftwaffe patrol plane, an action that left no survivors."

The brilliant gaze lingered on him. "So, I was stunned. Thrilled, when the Gang let me know you were truly alive, and well, and back in Norway."

"But your Oslo Gang—not thrilled by me quite so much."

"No. They see you as a serious problem."

"Which you seem to have solved."

"Somewhat." She offered a rueful smile. "So. What was that like?"

"Being caught by the Gang? Altogether confusing, at first."

"I meant, *Snekka*."

"Ah."

Kristian looked out the bus window. He rubbed both of his thighs vigorously with his palms. He snapped a brief glance back at her, and she saw his face had reddened and his eyes were watering.

"You know the core of it right?" His voice sounded husky. "I don't feel able to give you more details. I mean, why?"

"All right. I understand."

"Good." He paused. "But, well, maybe there's one thing about it that you can help *me* to understand. Since you've been around Germans now for quite a while. Still can't figure out why the *Luftwaffe* came after our boat. I guess some informer must have been at the beach near Sola, on that day when Lars and I rowed some army officers away. We did want to help them flee the Nazis, and they saw that, and reported it. But *Snekka* was far offshore at that point, at an inlet near our boathouse. Even if someone saw her in the distance, she would've just looked like another boat."

"I don't know." Helene shook her head. "The footnote I saw in the report didn't give me that many details. Sorry."

"And the seaplane that attacked us? It circled around *Snekka* at first, flying low and slow, as if it *was* trying to identify us. Like they had good info to work on, exact details, our ID number or the boat's name or the colors of her paint. You know, it's just strange. Why would the *Luftwaffe* be sent out to hunt for us, in particular? We shouldn't have been a big deal. Not during an invasion, with so much else going on!"

Helene sucked in her lower lip as she started to ponder it. At first, her face stayed blank. Then she began to frown.

A suitcase thumped as it was flung into the upper rack. They looked up, saw the bus was filling in. A passenger had picked a seat just three rows ahead. Kristian plucked out his berry-stained handkerchief and coughed vigorously into it. The passenger glanced at Kristian and his eyes widened when he spotted the reddened rag in his hand. He spun around to select a seat that was one row nearer the front.

The bus rumbled to life and swung out onto the road south to Drøbak. Kristian settled into his seat and shut his eyes, seizing a chance to rest—or perhaps to be alone for a moment with his thoughts. Helene glanced at him, reached her hand out to touch his, as if she had suddenly thought of an important item to tell him. Then she stopped, reconsidered, pulled her arm back to her side and let her hand drop. Frowning, she turned her head to gaze out the bus window. Beyond the glass, the suburbs of Oslo began to shift toward a sylvan landscape, with infrequent glimpses of the blue waters of the fjord that lay just beyond.

~

As their bus swayed along the final approach to Drøbak, Kristian roused himself and looked around. He saw that most of the passengers had gotten off at earlier stops.

"Hey there, welcome back," Helene said. "Get a nice rest?"

Kristian waggled a hand. "So-so."

"You can't quite see it, but the Germans put up a new monument over there," Helene said, pointing out the window.

"Yeah?"

"Dedicated to soldiers and sailors that died on the *Mehrlicht*. Josef Goebbels came here to Drøbak to stick a wreath on it personally."

"Well, if he had any guts, the bastard should've been on the *Mehrlicht* himself," Kristian groused. "Which would have made it a lot more fun to watch the damn thing sink. Then we'd put up a memorial to him, the Grand Master of Horseshit." He brooded for a moment. "Know what a friend of mine calls him? The Chinless Goblin."

"Fits!" Helene exclaimed.

"He says Goebbels is the real Nazi. Hitler's only his creature, his golem. Goebbels puts out a myth of the peerless leader, Hitler struggles to live up to it."

"Well, it's one theory." Helene sounded dubious. "Or, how about this? Hitler's an organ grinder, and Goebbels, that's his prancing monkey. Which is how all that seems to me."

"Hmm. Both couldn't be true at the same time, could they?"

"Sure. Demons feed off each other all the time. I see it at Terboven's office. They labor all day, and every day, to make the horrid seem normal. It's difficult to keep from retching when I'm anywhere near them."

"I'll bet."

"I've gotten to be a fairly decent actress. But pretense is a skill I'm not the least bit proud of."

~

The bus rattled into town on Osloveien and screeched to a halt at the main stop on Torggata. Helene hustled them around a block of shops and into a small apartment on a building's back side. Here they were met by an older woman with a stern, professional manner who wore a white linen coat. Kristian speculated that she was an actual nurse. She efficiently deployed a small surgical handsaw to take the cast off his lower leg. Meanwhile, Helene went into another room, and shed her own nurse's outfit for drab civilian dress.

"All ready?" she said when she returned.

"Yes," Kristian said. "Look! Your friend has healed me. A real miracle worker. My leg feels just like new."

The woman permitted her stiff face to crack a slight smile.

"Keep the crutches," Kristian said grandly.

"Good. I can sell them," she replied evenly. "Probably for enough for a week's worth of stew vegetables."

"Kristian? Please wait inside here for, oh, twenty minutes," Helene instructed him. "Then go up to Otto's house and enter by the garden gate.

I'll leave it unlatched. And, of course, don't do anything to call attention to yourself."

"You bet. No dancing about. No screaming out loud or cursing. No stripping myself naked, no smashing of windows, no setting of fires. In addition, on my way over, I intend to perform no killings or robberies. Absolutely not. You have my word."

Helene rolled her eyes. The traumatized and sad Kristian—someone she could let herself pity and try to comfort—had apparently receded, to be replaced by the more familiar sardonic and teasing Kristian. She was not sure, really, which lad she preferred.

～

After making sure no one on the side street could observe him, Kristian slipped in through the garden gate. He walked over flagstones and up a short flight of steps to a side door of the house to find Helene had left that portal unlocked and open as well. He located Helene herself in the kitchen. She had pinned her bright chestnut hair up in a coil, put on an apron, and was preparing to make them dinner.

"Your menu choice is limited," she told him. "Not much to work with. In the pantry, I found some moose meat put up in jars and berry preserves. There's that, and we have potatoes and onions from the cellar."

"I can't complain."

"Can't, or won't?"

"Neither one. The soup the Gang fed me at the lodge was swill. Your stuff sounds better."

"All right. I shouldn't complain either, since you've set such a low bar."

He sat on a stool at the kitchen's butcher block table and watched her begin by starting a fire in the stove. Plenty of kindling and fuel jutted up from the wood box, he saw no immediate need to perform any chores himself. But then he thought of one useful task. He got up, took the narrow stairs down to the root cellar and came back up with a dusty bottle of plum wine.

Helene eyed it. "Where'd you find that?"

"When I stayed here, I made it my hobby to discover the places where Otto conceals his goodies," he said. "Ragnar put me up to it. Just a game. But today? A quite useful one." He blew dust away from the neck and cork. Then he rooted around in a drawer for an opener. The cork was dry and broke off. He pushed the rest of it down into bottle, then poured reddish-beige wine and bobbing cork crumbs into a pair of glass tumblers.

"I don't want any," Helene said.

"You must take some. Refusing a gift from Otto makes you look seriously ungrateful."

Helene grimaced.

"And you shouldn't make me drink a whole bottle by myself. I'd go mad. Or die of indigestion."

She shook her head.

"I'm grieved, madam," Kristian declaimed. "Yet, far be it from me to storm your virtue's lofty ramparts." With a fingertip, he shoved most of the floating crumbs to the rim of his glass, then lifted them out with a fingernail. He raised his glass and looked her in the eyes. "Skål!" He saluted her with his glass and took a hefty gulp.

"Not all that bad," he said. "At least I am one who appreciates your generosity, my dear Uncle Otto."

Helene silently put a cast iron pan on the stove with a puddle of cooking oil on the bottom, added sliced potatoes and onions and covered it. She sat down across the table from him.

Kristian swallowed another gulp. He tapped the bottom of his glass against his arm cast, where the thin green envelope lay concealed in the many plaster-soaked windings. "Tell me. What deep, dark secrets do we have here, strapped to your carrier pigeon?"

"Can't say."

"Oh, come on. It's not like you lose anything if you tell me. I get caught by the Germans? Inside this cast is the first place they'll look. I mean, right after they check my shoes and my underpants."

"It's still best if you don't know."

"Can't imagine why. And what's to stop me from opening this cast up myself, once I'm out on the boat?"

"You shouldn't do that!"

"Why not?"

"The British might think the documents have been altered."

"By me? To what end? Helene, please, can you loosen up a bit here? If I can learn what I'm carrying, it will heighten my resolve to complete our mission. Isn't that what both of us want?"

She glared at him with her full lips crimped. She shook her head. "You are so completely relentless," she said. "Stubborn as hell. Like most Norwegian men!"

"And you're not? Hah."

Kristian took the second glass, cleaned it of cork crumbs the way he had the first, then slid it over the table to her. Helene regarded the glass as if it held poison. He pushed it a bit closer. Her shoulders sagged. She curled her fingers around the base of the glass. A moment later, she lifted it and took a tiny sip.

"There," she said. "Satisfied?"

"Almost."

"You're right. It *is* good."

~

Helene dumped a clump of fried onions and potatoes onto the broad red bowl in front of Kristian, topped it with warm slices of moose meat, then followed that with a heaping spoonful of pickled bilberries.

"Stir it up with your fork if you want," she said.

"Thanks. The very finest in rural cabin cuisine."

She filled her own bowl and sat across from him again. They ate in silence for a moment, devouring the simple grub and chasing it with sips of wine.

"Well, all right. It's radio beams," she said.

Kristian wasn't sure he'd heard her correctly. "Beg pardon?"

She pointed her fork at his cast. "A new German technology. In the documents you have." She took another sip of wine.

"Oho, our mysterious sphinx tells a secret! Could any more miracles be in store?" Kristian stuffed a hunk of moose meat into his mouth and chewed it thoughtfully. "Radio beams, huh? Beams that do what, pray tell?" he asked, after swallowing.

"Guide bombing runs."

"Interesting. So how's that work, exactly?"

"You might say it began as a way to cope with bad weather days at German airports—which they have plenty of, I guess. They devised a new method to help pilots aim their planes down to runways, so they could land during storms, or even at night. The pilots would track a tight kind of radio beam that I think is called a Lorenz. Well, next they adapted that system for war. Instead of just using one beam to land, they now use several at once to direct missions while the planes fly out. They trace a route along one radio beam as they go from bases in Europe. After it intersects with a different radio beam over an English city, they know that's the right place for them to drop their bombs."

Kristian's fork stopped and hung in midair. "Brilliant," he said.

"And devastating. Now, they can mount precision raids even at midnight. Makes it much harder for the Spitfires to find them and shoot back. The whole scheme is code-named, *Knickebein*, which means 'bent leg.' I guess because the angle where the beams intersect must be a big part of it."

"All right!" he said. "Thank you. I am now fully motivated." He took a celebratory gulp of wine. "If I know the Brits, they'll be over the moon when they lay their hands on your stuff. 'Gob-smacked,' as they say. What, specifically, shall we give them?"

"Two lists, mainly. Frequencies the Germans will use for their system. They plan to change those weekly, in case the English try to jam them. And locations of an array of broadcast towers that send out the intersecting beams. They're being erected at camouflaged sites all along the Atlantic, from southern France to Norway. One is even planned for Stavanger."

"Most likely, they'll stick it out at the Sola airfield, I bet." Kristian tapped his fork on the table, then pointed it at her. "And you! Sneaky Norwegian spy-girl. How'd you discover this? I don't suppose a spastic Nazi general happened to drop a nice, fat envelope in your lap at the *Reichskommisar's*?"

She shook her head. "No. That's not the only place I can gather intelligence. I've also spent time at the Federation Hotel. Where the *Luftwaffe* and *Abwehr* stayed? The place that burned to the ground. Have you ever heard of it? I think you might've gone by there. At least one time that I've heard something about, anyway." She tossed her head and grinned. She'd just discovered that she enjoyed teasing him back. "At the Federation bar I overheard some pilots boasting about a new system. Not directly, but I could tell they were ecstatic about a new trick that would make their night raids far easier. That was my first clue."

"Sure, I can see a good eavesdropper picking up a rumor that way. But finding secret documents to back the gossip up? How did you pull that off?"

She stared at him. "There are Norwegian girls who date Germans," she said flatly.

"I know. And are you one of them?"

"No. Not exactly. Not in the way those girls do it."

"I see."

"One night, a *Luftwaffe* officer wearing civilian clothes came into the Federation holding a leather documents case. Others deferred to him in a way that told me he was a man of no small importance. Anyway, after a few drinks, he got quite friendly with one girl and decided to go to a room and, um, relax a bit further."

"And?" Kristian prompted.

"While that was happening, I snuck into their room and stole his case." Kristian slapped his hand on the table. "No!"

Helene nodded. She put her fingers to her lips to stifle a tipsy giggle.

"Yes. I scarcely can believe it myself! Once I got the case open and saw all the goodies inside, I realized I needed to take fast notes and cram everything back into place as soon as possible. If that case had gone missing, all of Oslo would've been turned upside down. That girl would've been in bad, bad trouble. Plus, the Germans could then alter what they were doing and shift the places where they're doing it. That would make my stolen info worth much less, or even nothing. It's why I didn't try to send it out via the new radio that you brought to the Oslo Gang, by the way. What if Germans intercepted that message?"

"You dared to *reenter* that room, to return the case, then? Fantastic!"

"Actually..." Helene blushed.

"What?"

"Well, that was the easy part! You see, by then the officer was, um, fully distracted."

Kristian chuckled. "Helene, give me your hand, please," he said. "I wish to shake it. I've known since the day we first met that you were one remarkable lady. But you exceed even the high estimate I had. You richly deserve a medal. Like, the 'Norwegian Order of Absolutely Amazing Resistance Heroines,' or something. If I happened to have one on me, I'd hand it over instantly. Maybe the king will give you a medal someday. Maybe two kings will. Both England's and Norway's."

"I don't give a tinker's dam about that." Helene tossed her head, and a few tendrils of coppery hair fell loose to dangle about her face. "First things first. We need to get this stuff over to England. That's your job. Earn a medal doing it, if you want. My aim is just to stop people from getting killed."

Kristian slid a hand across the table, palm upturned. Helene gazed at it, tapped her fingers on his as if simultaneously acknowledging and dismissing his gesture, then snatched her hand back before he could grab onto it.

"You ought to go get some rest," she told him. "You need to awaken before dawn to meet the fishing boat that'll transport you. I'll clean up here."

"Wait. We've not finished our wine. That's bad luck."

"You do it," she said primly. "I've had plenty."

She jumped up, took their plates to the sink.

Kristian followed her. She sensed him moving up behind her and spun. But he was too close. He ducked under one swinging plate and got both of his arms around her before she was able to stop him. And before she could emit a bleat of protest, he dropped his face to plant his mouth on hers. Both plates that she held dropped from her hands to clatter on the floor.

Kristian's head spun. Helene's lips were plump and soft and seemed far more yielding than he ever imagined they would be. One of his hands was at the small of her back, pressing her hips into his, one in the middle of her back, pushing her firm breasts close to his chest. He felt intoxicated with joy, finally able to feel her shape completely fitting itself to him. His nostrils filled with her scent, a rosy cologne, soap, a slight tang of old female sweat caught in her clothing, and something else, a faint musk.

She slumped against him as he continued to kiss her. He had never thought she would surrender to him this easily. Then he realized that something altogether different was occurring. Helene's knees were buckling, her entire body was limp, she'd turned as slippery as an eel, and he had to use all of his strength just to hold her upright.

Helene had fainted.

*"In general Norway is still pro-English. This will change after our victory."*
—Josef Goebbels, from *The Goebbels Diaries*

## CHAPTER 22

Kristian managed to put an arm behind Helene's knees just before she toppled over entirely, and he swept her up. He glanced with chagrin at her closed eyes and lolling head, then hustled her into the home's tiny front parlor and over to an old horsehide couch.

He laid her on its worn cushions and tried to conjure what to do next. He loosened her shoelaces and the sash on her dress, propped a pillow behind her neck. He went into the kitchen to grab a clean dish towel and soaked it with cold water. When he went back to the couch, he saw Helene with her eyelids fluttering, trying to sit up.

"Might be best if you just let yourself lie there for a second," he said.

She flopped back down, blinked a few times, looked up at him. Her expression wasn't a scowl, he thought, but something close. Confusion, perhaps. He attempted to drape the wet cloth over her forehead, but she snatched it away and scrubbed vigorously at her own face. All over it. Including, he noticed, her mouth.

"I'm sorry," he said.

"Truly?" Her eyes were hard to read in the dim light. "I don't think so."

"Okay. Maybe just a little. But it's for real."

She sat up. "Kristian," she told him sternly. "It's late. You and I ought to be in bed by now."

He stared, not believing his ears.

Her cheeks flared with color. "I mean… we… are in different rooms! You must take Otto's."

She planted her feet on the floor and stood. "I'll put on an alarm clock. I'll get you up an hour before we need to go down to the waterfront."

He stood. "All right," he said.

"And I intend to lock the door to my room. My window, too. Don't bother to try anything. You'll only be wasting your time."

"*Greit,*" he said. "Okay."

He couldn't really decide if Helene was joking or teasing him or not. But he figured that at this juncture, it would be smart of him to err greatly on the side of caution. A thought of Greta then crossed his mind. She and Helene were wildly different creatures. To blend their female qualities in a single being would likely be far beyond even the powers of God—assuming one existed. If he had to choose one of them, whom would he pick? The idea irritated him.

"*God natt,*" he said. "Good night."

"Yes. See you tomorrow."

～

She walked into his bedroom carrying a lit candle.

"Wake up," she said.

"I am awake. Heard you coming."

She was already dressed for a hike in the morning chill.

"I've made a porridge, with cinnamon and sugar. I found coffee too. It's waiting for you downstairs."

She stood in the fuzzy globe of yellow light. He saw pearly droplets from the fat wax taper had spattered her wrist. He wondered why she hadn't bothered to put it in a candlestick before she carried it up here.

"Don't take too long," she warned. "It'll get cold." She stuck the lit candle into a ceramic holder on the bureau and left it behind.

He arose, dressed. Checked his money and IDs. Studied the cast on his arm. Realized that being stuck with such a readily identifiable item wasn't such a great idea. Tried to pull it off. Couldn't.

On his way out of Otto's bedroom he saw a longer telephone cord had been plugged into the service jack. That fat black cord ran up the wall, where tape secured it in place, then went through a hole in the ceiling. Kristian gazed up at it, puzzled. He recalled that the home's top floor consisted of an attic room with a dormer window that looked out on the fjord. In fact, that attic had once been Kristian's favorite place to hide and play with tin soldiers when he had visited the house as a much younger lad. Otto must've recently converted that upper space into an office or a den or something.

He went down to the kitchen. Helene had found two new, unbroken bowls. One sat empty, holding just a residue of breakfast. But his bowl had a pale glacier of steaming grains heaped in it, puddled with butter and sugar. A spoon stuck up in the center of the pale mound as though ready for a diminutive Arctic explorer to attach a flag.

Kristian sat and fell to. After he got halfway down through the food, his nose finally became able to deliver a message to his brain: it had been beckoned by the aroma of coffee long enough! Next to the stovetop he spotted a speckled enamel pot sitting with two cups beside it. After arising to pour himself one, he glimpsed a bobbing light through the kitchen window. Helene was coming up through the garden.

She came inside and switched off her electric torch. Her cheeks, the end of her nose and her chin had been stung pink by the cold. Especially at such a predawn hour, more than a hint of autumn chilled the air.

"I just did a scout-about, nearly all the way down to the water. Nobody else is up or around except for a few fishermen."

He swilled some coffee. "All right," he said. "Good for you. Thanks."

"The boat should be arriving in forty minutes or thereabouts. It's the *Heldig*. She'll bring you to Farsund, where you'll transfer to a boat that's headed for Scotland."

"Perfect." He looked at her. "So, are you mad at me?"

She shook her head. "No."

*Excellent, he thought. In fact, that's a damn sight better than it might have been. Maybe she and Greta aren't so different, after all. Helene's just a little behind in her, ah, development. Or, a lot.*

~

They departed via the garden gate and made their way down a side street, slick with dew, and then the glistening Husvikveien main road. They headed for a private dock not far from the pier where the *Snekka* had tied up. This dock had a plank walkway that circled around a small boathouse. On the shed's open side, Kristian could see a rowboat lying keel-up across a pair of sawhorses.

Kristian and Helene stood together on a narrow platform that thrust on joists out above the water.

"See anything?"

"No. As the *Heldig* approaches, we're supposed to exchange flashes." She brandished her torch. "Four from them, one from me, two from them and then three from me."

But she never got a chance to raise her torch again and use it, since the waters of the fjord remained bare of new, incoming boats. Only a handful of small fishing craft, dories and the like, circled about slowly, dragging lines and nets. A pair of hours crawled by. They kept themselves warm by walking up and down the dock. Helene seemed be brooding over something, and uneager to talk. Kristian decided not to bother her. They made their circuits in silence.

The tidal prism shifted to ebb, and the fjord's patchwork of slick surfaces, seamed by current, began to reflect pastels from sunrise.

They walked back to the house.

"Maybe it shall come tomorrow," Helene said. "I'll find out."

A figure paced at the entrance to the side street. Kristian saw it was the older woman, the one he thought might be a nurse, who had skillfully cut the cast off his leg. She spotted them and hustled briskly over.

"I just got a phone call from the captain's wife," she said. "The *Heldig* was stopped and boarded by German sailors outside of Filtvet," she told them. "They've been accused of sailing without the right papers or permissions. That's all I know."

Helene bit her lip.

"Shit!" Kristian exclaimed.

Helene thanked the woman and told her she'd talk to her later. They went in the house.

"What do we do?" Kristian asked.

"What, indeed. Let's finish off the coffee, while we consider that. I'll heat it up."

"Don't bother. Let's just drink it."

They sat on opposite sides of the butcher block table, sipping the tepid brew from blue enamel cups.

"What do you imagine will happen to the men on the *Heldig?*" she asked.

"Hard to say. They can claim ignorance. Or make excuses. They can offer a bribe. Or beg for mercy. But here's a part that's certain. No matter what, the Germans won't rest until they find out where the crew planned to go and what they hoped to do once they got there."

"Meaning, German investigators will come to Drøbak. How much time do you think we have?"

"Smart to act as if we don't have much, that's for sure," Kristian said. He looked at the cast on his left arm. "I need to loosen this."

"Why?

"Then I can get it off."

Helene's eyes widened. Her jaw clenched and that round little chin of hers thrust out.

"Oh, relax! Not in order to get rid of it. I just need to vary the way I appear. This thing is a big identifier. People will remember it. So sometimes, it will need to be off. Don't look at me like that! And don't worry. I'm committed to making your delivery. No matter what trouble or hazard that might entail. Understand me? No matter what!"

He stomped down to the cellar, where he tried to force himself to calm down. *How could she doubt me? After I practically swore that I'd get her damn packet over to the Brits? Doesn't she realize I'd do anything for her? Well, almost anything...* He rooted through Otto's sparse tool collection and came up with a ballpeen hammer and a cold chisel. He realized he couldn't use them by himself. He'd need her help. So, he went back upstairs to ask for it.

She didn't answer right away. When she did speak, her tone was cool. "I do understand your point. I'm not stupid, you know."

While she cracked the plaster right around his wrist—which was the cast's main choke point—Kristian pondered the issue of the seized boat. He hoped its crew had indeed found a way to get out of their trouble. But even if they had managed to wriggle free, it still left him with no method for getting out of Drøbak, much less all the way over to the British Isles. He turned the conundrum over in his mind, trying to locate a shred of revelation that could be coaxed into an actual solution. The big unknown was how much the Gestapo and undercover NS operatives had penetrated the Resistance. That affected how much he could trust strangers, even if they were Norwegians. He obviously would need help from people. *How far can one man get, relying only on himself? Perhaps, all you have to do is start*, Kristian told himself, *and then you'll find the answers to your questions as you go. You can't figure them out in advance, because you can't know what all those questions are.* That thought was logical, but still not comforting.

He found himself able to rotate his cast and pull it past his wrist, he told Helene to stop tapping on it with the hammer and chisel. He asked her to conceal the damage to the plaster as much as she could by filling the cracks and smearing them with a paste made of flour and water.

She was proceeding to do that just when Kristian finally hit his eureka moment. He plunged his right hand into his trouser pocket and hauled out the wad of NKVD cash. He slapped it down on the table.

"I've got it! Our plan." He snapped his fingers. "The first part, anyway. As soon as the sun sets today, I'll go back down to the dock and steal the rowboat we saw. That one inside the boathouse." He picked up the roll, peeled off a few large denomination bills. "Only, it must not be reported to any authorities as stolen, since then police will be on the lookout for it. Therefore, I want you to take a nice chunk of this cash, find out who the owner is, and give him half. Show him the other half. But tell him he only gets it if, two weeks from now, his boat still isn't reported as missing."

"Oh my gosh," She said, staring. "How did you ever get your hands on so much money?"

"Would you believe... I pulled all of it from the pockets of a dead Soviet agent?"

"I might." She eyed him. "But tell me. How did this man die?"

He hesitated.

"You didn't kill him, did you?"

"Well, yes," he said finally. "I did."

"Why?"

"It's not easy to explain."

"Did you have to?"

"That's one way to put it."

"How does it feel, then, to have blood on your hands?"

She drew the question out, hesitantly. He realized she actually was curious, not blaming him.

"Well. I'd say... it doesn't make me happy. Yet somehow, it does. And I'd say I'm not proud of what I've done. However, that's not quite true, either."

"Oh-h, Kristian," Helene said. Her tone was doleful. She sagged in her chair and looked down at the table. She picked up the chisel and turned it from side-to-side, studying the tool as if she needed to perform a simple, physical movement to distract or ground herself.

"Surviving," Kristian observed, "might not be all it's cracked up to be. When the Snekka sank, my *Pappa* and all the others died, my own survival was not so joyous for me. I mean, sure, I'm glad I'm alive. But I've also found that remaining among the living these days arrives with some very serious obligations. Perhaps I'm even cursed by them. I feel compelled to take measures to make those Nazi bastards answer. And rather terrible measures at that, I must admit."

Helene tapped the chisel on the table, still staring at it. "Yes," she said at length. "I see, that's how it is." She paused again. "And not only with you." She looked up, her eyes brimming with tears.

Kristian reached across the table, removed the chisel from her hand then gripped her fingers with his own. She did not resist his touch.

"Look. It can't be helped. It's the times. They're transforming me into someone I didn't foresee or ever wish myself to be. Getting hard now to recall how I used to think and feel about things before last April. Maybe that's why it was such a blessing to see you walk into that room back at the lodge, and why it's such a relief to be near you right now. It reminds me of how I once was. Now I can draw a deep breath, take some measure. Adjust course. Recall how things once were. Perhaps that means I can get back there someday, when all of this is over. That is, if it does end! At present, it seems as if our world will just get worse and worse for all time."

She scanned him up and down, eyes narrowed, as if seeking to evaluate how much she should invest in what he'd said.

"Yes, the Nazis are fiends," she said. "But Kristian, we can't let ourselves turn into monsters too, just to stop them. Can we?" She shook her head wearily. "And yet, I don't see any way to avoid it."

"If I happen to think up a method, I'll let you know."

Helene briefly squeezed his hand, then extracted her fingers.

"What's happening to you, it might not be happening only to you," she said. She glanced at him, then looked down at the cast on his arm. She shook herself like a swimmer who emerges from a cold lake, just prior to reaching for a towel.

"Let's focus on the topic at hand," she said. "Be practical." She knuckled the moisture from her eyes. "If you take that boat, how do you intend to use it? Please don't tell me you're going to do something ridiculous, like try to row yourself to Scotland again."

He straightened, cleared his throat, half-smiled.

"One attempt like that on the North Sea was plenty. No, my idea is just to use it to cross the fjord. Find a rural train platform on the other side, one without a lot of personnel. Probably, I'll do that at Nykirke. Then buy a ticket to Stavanger."

"And once there?"

He smiled. "In Stavanger there will be more choices and some excellent help. There's a certain pianist—did you know that's what the Brits call a good W/T operator? I'm sure by now he's got a solid link up with the SIS. Or the SOE or whichever. Anyhow, with his radio I bet I can request English help in getting across the Channel. By plane, submarine, fishing boat, I don't care. Whatever they can do that's the quickest."

"But what if they can do nothing?" Those amber eyes were locked on him again, probing, challenging—her moment of tender vulnerability had vanished as if it had never happened. "The Nazis have clamped down on travel, all up and down the coast. Along the Swedish border, too. They stopped the *Heldig* for no obvious reason. They'll grab anyone at any time, then force you to account for yourself. They've been pouring soldiers into new bases at every port."

"Ultimately, yes, that's right, I could be prevented. In which case, we'll have to send your info over to England by radio, even if we don't wish to. But my man's a genius with a telegraph key. Maybe he can either create a way to code it or bury it in an innocuous transmission. Whatever the safest method might be, he'll find it."

Her eyes narrowed and that little round chin poked out again. "But you won't let him in on our secrets? Except as a last resort?"

"Correct. The man himself generally operates on a 'Less is Best Rule.' Spies must know only a small amount of necessary information, he believes, in case they get caught. So, at first, I'll explain only a few basics. He will see your documents themselves only in the event that all else fails. After that, I might offer him a roundabout way to contact you. Through the Gang, say. If you get a message from a man who calls himself Rolf, answer. He could have a question for you from the Brits. Something they need explained or confirmed."

"I see."

"All right." Kristian levelled his blue eyes at her. Even though their conversation had turned impersonal, he still felt a spark of excitement at any chance to gaze into her eyes. "Tell me. Do you fully approve of this plan, or would you change anything?" This was, after all, Helene's mission. She'd originated it.

She frowned as she thought. "Well!" She tossed her head, and her hair threatened to fully escape the grasp of its pins. "What other choice do we have?"

"Pretty much my point."

"Also, there's a huge time factor. For each day this information isn't in the hands of the English, they win another night of German bombs raining down on them. So, delay equals death."

~

Kristian tried to imagine a look that would let him board a train while facing the fewest questions from any cop or official who happened to be present. He decided to be a Norwegian laborer, a man who hoped to head north to find work helping the Germans build pillboxes and gun batteries—to further their fantasy of a *Festung Norwegen*.

He dug out a canvas duffle he'd seen down in the cellar. This bag was large, stout, with heavy straps and metal grommets. Looked as if it had been made according to some old unit's military specs. How Otto had wound up with it, he had no idea. Into the duffle he dropped a few tools and all the clothes he could find that looked like they might belong to a blue-collar worker. Lastly, he shoved in a coil of rope just to round the bag out.

While rummaging around, he recalled that a certain footlocker in the cellar had been used for personal storage by Ragnar. He hauled it out and opened it. Right at the top, he discovered a fillet knife. He took it from its sheath, raised it in the dim light. Its thin blade was freckled with corrosion, yet still keen. He grinned. He sheathed it, then shoved the greasy leather sheath down his sock and into his boot. He tied the knife's hilt off to his calf with a length of twine. After he dropped his pantleg back over the hidden weapon he felt oddly satisfied. *I'm naked without a blade now*, he realized.

After his gear had been prepared, Helene fed him again, he slept again, and then it was sunset.

"I'm ready," he told her.

"I'll come down to the dock," she said. "See you off."

"Want to row over the fjord with me?" His suggestion was frivolous. But now that their moment of separation was approaching, he wanted to put it off.

"No. It's better if I'm in Drøbak. That's what Otto and everyone else expects. I'll stay here and polish up my act of innocence."

"But… you excel at that already," he teased.

She pursed her lips. Her eyes sparkled. For a second, it looked as if she wanted to stick her tongue out at him.

~

They walked through thickening twilight down to the shoreline boathouse. Inside, he made a closer inspection of the rowboat. The craft looked seaworthy enough, clinker-built, with a high prow, narrow transom and plenty of rocker along the keel. And it proved useful that Helene had come along, for when he sought to lift it, the boat also turned out to be stout and heavy.

Working together, they wrestled the craft into the water. He dropped its ash oars between the hardwood tholes, then tossed his duffle into the stern.

Helene stood facing him on the dock. "Goodbye," she said. "I hope to see you again. One of these days. Do try to send me a postcard to tell me you've reached England, with a picture of a palace or the queen, please. Then you can just write some anonymous words on it, like the price of milk or something."

*So, she wants to make jokes, now?* he thought. *That is dismaying.* In their final seconds together, that didn't seem like an ideal tone for her to take. But with her next words, he realized Helene was in earnest.

"I shall pray my most heartfelt prayers for you and your safety," she said. "Every bit as hard as I pray for the success of our mission."

He gazed down at her and held himself stock-still, feeling awkward and at a sudden loss for the correct thing to say back. But as it turned out, he didn't need to say anything.

She took him by the hand, drew him closer, stood on her toes, and kissed Kristian on the cheek.

On impulse he seized her by the waist. She leaned back in his arms so that she could look him in the eyes. He didn't see any fear. He didn't see any desire. He did see, however, an unblinking acceptance. Whereupon it was all he could do to keep his own eyes from watering. He had long fantasized that she would look upon him in this manner. At last, and at the very least, they'd made a connection. But of what sort of link it might be, he did not know. It didn't feel romantic. Oddly enough, it felt different and deeper.

She took his face in both her hands, raised herself up and kissed him warmly upon the lips. This time, the contact was made fully by her kissing him. He dared not move his own lips, for fear of making her stop. Or perhaps inducing her to pass out again. He felt the end of her tongue flutter gently against his lips, a quick brush of a feather. And then she did stop.

"Now. You, fisherman. Get out there and do your job," she said, pointing to the dark waters of the fjord.

She dropped her eyes, spun, and strolled away with no backward glance. He saw her lift a hand. He thought for a moment she was about to turn and wave to him. Instead she just used that hand to brush something off her cheek.

Then Helene did stop and turn, and she resolutely strode back up to him.

"I know your opinion of Otto is not high," she said. The statement sounded blunt and bleak, coming as it did without preamble or preparation. "But I have to say, we are all of us sinners. And Otto has struggled to be a loyal follower of Christ, in his own way. He wants to feel saved much more than he wants anything else. But his politics make him confused over how he ought to go about it. He's torn in different directions. Even steady reading of the Bible does not solve this for him."

Kristian stared at her, befuddled. *Otto's not the only one confused*, he thought. *But why lay this guff on me? And right now? She knows I'm no one's idea of a believer. And whatever Otto may be up to now has got to be the least of our worries!*

Helene gazed back, assessing him, wondering if she'd said too much or too little. She plunged onward. "On that day the *Mehrlicht* sank, Otto had to phone in reports to Oslo. That was his assignment from the NS. He repents of doing it now. I imagine, to a great degree, seeing what's happened. Consequently, he's on a path to seek forgiveness and redemption. I think that explains all his sad behavior in recent days."

The amber eyes stared up at him fiercely, as if she sought to bring him into full understanding by the power of her gaze. But she saw that her message hadn't gotten through. Not yet, anyway. She gave him a wan smile and shook her head.

"And so, let God's grace descend upon us all," she murmured. "But you may just call it luck, if that sounds better to you."

She turned and walked off, this time for real. She stepped around a corner of the boathouse and was gone.

*How utterly Helene baffles me*, Kristian thought. *Of course, I find her beautiful and bewitching. As ever. Yet also incomprehensible, confounding! And never more so than at this moment.*

～

His reckoning of the boat's seaworthiness proved correct. Despite its heft, the hand-built craft did float and steer well. The steady rhythm of leaning forward, planting the blades, leaning back and hauling on oars came easily to Kristian. But this act of rowing also brought up memories of his night alone on the North Sea. The horrendous cold that had deepened and drifted into him.

*Some things, parts of my heart, my innocence, my very youth, froze deep inside of me on that night, he realized. Yet, being around Helene over these last few days has warmed a bit of it back up. As confusing and strange as Helene can be, at least she also produces that sort of good effect.*

He looked away to port, where he saw a searchlight from the Oscarsborg sweep its shimmering track across the water. It didn't bother him; he was too far away and his boat too tiny to be picked up in its beam. From the spot where he floated, those lofty battlements looked much as they had months earlier, when it had been a Norwegian fortress. But every command uttered over there now would be spoken in German.

*A dark tide works on us,* Kristian thought. *A swelling flood of this sewage of Nazism. Helene says I should do my job! No small task. We fight to keep that tide from sweeping completely over Norway. And Britain. It wins there, and it goes where next? Across our entire earth, I suppose. To halt their attack, my weapons are now this rowboat, a wee packet of information and a rusty fillet knife. Well, God—if we do indeed have a deity who arranges all things, as Helene likes to think—must have a completely bizarre sense of humor.*

Thinking about a metaphoric tide led him to reconsider the real one. He'd hoped to use the shifting currents of the fjord. Any decent fisherman always did so. He'd laid his plan to hit a slack, just before start of the ebb that would take him down the fjord. The timing looked good, but he had only a rough idea of the course that would take him to the proper inlet at Nykirke. If he hoped to arrive there before a flood tide shoved him back up, he ought to quicken his pace. He bent to his rowing with a will.

As he worked the oars, his mind drifted to what Helene had said about Otto. It was no surprise to hear that Otto had phoned in reports about the *Mehrlicht's* doomed cruise into the Oslo Fjord. *Otto likely thought the invasion would go off without a hitch. Such an ardent admirer of German ways. A shock for him then, to watch those brilliant Nazi plans fall completely apart. And if he was calling in steady reports to the NS offices...* well, that would explain the phone cord Kristian had seen running up through the ceiling of Otto's bedroom. He'd likely set up the attic dormer as his observation post and made his reports from there. A smart choice—that window offered fine overviews of the strait. Otto likely had equipped himself with field glasses too, or a telescope, so that he could scoop up the interesting details. *Too bad he had to report on the* Mehrlicht *getting shot up, torpedoed, burning, capsizing and sinking. But what else of any importance was going on?*

Kristian suddenly quit rowing. He felt as though he himself had just been socked by a torpedo as understanding finally hit him. Helene had tried to tell him something important, without coming right out and saying it.

*Otto! Damn that bastard! HE was the one who turned in the* Snekka *to the Germans!!*

Kristian could visualize it now as clearly as if he had been standing at that window himself.

*Otto saw me bring Stein Larsen and the other soldiers aboard. He watched that German officer try to commandeer the boat, Lars bash him with that boathook, and saw us fling the man back over the side. Then that traitorous brother Otto told the NS, who told the Nazis. Maybe people on the beach at Sola gave an additional report, that we'd picked up more Norwegian soldiers. That seaplane didn't come upon us by accident. It was sent out on a hunt. They already had the boat's name and number. Otto. That fucker slew his own brother. Damn near killed me too, in his devil's bargain.*

Kristian's hands began to tremble on the oars. A wave of heat swept through his body. Passion soared beyond rage—a primal irruption. Without even deciding to do it, he spun the bow around and pointed it back at Drøbak. The stout ash oar shafts bent into slight arcs as he poured the full power of his back and arms into his next few strokes.

Then he paused. He stared down at the cast on his forearm. Inside folds of plaster and cloth lay that green packet of documents, holding data that could save lives in England and thwart the German air war. If he stayed in Norway to smack Otto with his just desserts, thousands of innocent lives would be the forfeit. Could personal vengeance, no matter how well-justified it might seem, outweigh *that?*

*Helene! She understood this moment would come. That I'd be already on the mission before I figured out what she'd been saying. That's why she made it the last thing. Even then, she almost didn't do it... I had to be told. Yet she did it in a way that would only sink in after I was way out here, in the middle of the fjord.*

Kristian brought the hafts of the oars together, lifted the blades. The boat spun like the needle of a busted compass. He bent forward and leaned his forehead onto the backs of his joined hands.

*Too clever by half. Calls herself a Christian, yet she's diabolically sneaky! 'You must be as wise as serpents?' Well that's Helene.* Kristian raised his head. *She calls Otto a follower of Christ too, but if he is, no wonder Ragnar never wanted to join him. Any idea that Otto ever repents is total hooey. What he really wants is to not be found out! But you are indicted now. You'll get what's coming to you, Otto, I swear it. Yet unfortunately. there's something else I must do first.*

Kristian lowered an oar and cranked with it until his bow pointed southwest, to Nykirke. Then he dropped the other blade and began to sweep both oars back and forth in a steady, determined rhythm.

*"Good flying weather. Total hell is being dropped on London. I would not like to be an Englishman at this moment."*
—Josef Goebbels, *the Diaries*

# Chapter 23

Over his shoulder, Kristian glimpsed a shadowy line of trees that rose up to blot out the stars. That ragged band of black had drawn steadily closer as he rowed. Now he could see forest on both sides as well. He'd made it into a cove of some sort. But he'd have to wait till dawn to find out which inlet it was.

Gravel and sand grated under the keel. He shipped his oars, grabbed the painter, sat on the gunwale and slid his legs down into the shallows. Cold water seeped into his brogans. Throwing the painter over his shoulder, he hauled the skiff up as far as he could.

He tied the boat off to a large, half-rotted log at the water's edge. A falling tide would keep the boat secure. He intended to be on his feet and fully awake by the next high tide. He grabbed his duffle and hiked through reeds and brush up to the tree line. He kicked dead leaves into a pile, opened the duffle and put on another layer of clothes. He threw his coil of rope down onto the leaf heap and pulled it into a rough ellipse, laid his body in its center and tugged his cap down over his eyes.

~

He was awakened by a train whistle. He sat up abruptly.

"O, *Faen!* Hell!"

Why had he slept so long? This was *not* how he'd planned it.

He stood and looked for the boat, but it couldn't be seen down on the cove beach where he'd left it. All he saw was bright, gently rippling water. He felt another stab of disappointment, followed by a burst of anger at himself.

He'd miscalculated. This present high tide was at least a meter higher than the previous one. Without a tide chart, such an event was not easy to predict. He shaded his eyes with a palm and looked across the fjord, then up it. He saw a distant brown dot that might have been the boat. *It must've floated free, then pulled my rope off one end of the log.*

Well, there was no way for him to retreat across the fjord now. Or row anywhere else, for that matter. No way to find a different inlet. He'd be forced to just head inland and deal with whatever he happened to encounter next. That prospect made him feel uneasy. His options had narrowed to one.

He frowned, repacked his duffle, slung its strap over his left shoulder. Then he hiked toward the place where he'd heard a train.

The track ran along the southwest border of Nykirke, a rural town even smaller than Drøbak. As he neared its modest cluster of buildings, he thought how unlikely a train stop here would be. Even so, he saw it had a platform. Not much, a wood deck built on pilings that stood perhaps two meters in height. This platform's big feature was a metal pole with a hook on it for mailbags. A fat green canvas mailbag hung from it, awaiting pick-up.

And a guard was on site, an old man clad in a new Stapo uniform. He leaned against the pole that held up the mailbag while he smoked a cigarette. At present, he faced away from Kristian.

Kristian paused to mentally rehearse his tale. *I am a workman. I am a country bumpkin. I'm heading to Stavanger to try to find a job, any job. If I don't succeed there, I'll continue by sailing on a ferry further north. I and this cop are both Norwegians. He'll want to help me get work. If he's Stapo, he won't mind if it's with the Germans. All right, that should play.*

He squared his shoulders, walked over the tracks, stomped up the steps to the platform.

"Good morning," he said. "Can you tell me, when does the next train come through, westbound?"

The cop squinted at him. "You some kind of idiot?" he rasped. "Do I look like a station master?"

"Sorry. Where's the station master?"

"Tiny outhouse of a town like this? Doesn't have one."

"Oh."

Up close, Kristian could see the man had red-rimmed eyes, moisture dripping off the end of a long nose, a face etched into an expression of habitual joylessness.

"Where is it you plan to go?" the old cop gruffed.

"Any place the Germans hire men to build things. Thought I'd try back home in Stavanger first."

"Work? With a cast on your arm?"

"It's due to come off soon. And I can still wiggle my fingers."

The cop flicked his cigarette butt out onto the railroad tracks. "Show me your papers," he growled.

Kristian pulled out his leather ID wallet to hand them over. But the cop fell into a paroxysm of coughing. Then he swatted the wallet back into Kristian's hands after barely taking a glance at the contents.

He pulled out a handkerchief and wiped his lips. "There are trains, and there are trains," the Stapo man said.

"Yes?" Kristian waited for him to clarify.

"A passenger train for laborers like you only goes west in the morning, after the morning eastbound passes through. And you've missed it. One comes back midday, another by evening. Both head east to Oslo. That's it."

"Ah. You're saying, I need to wait for tomorrow morning's train."

The cop tapped his temple with a forefinger and winked. "Real quick on the uptake, aren't you," he said.

"Thanks," Kristian said.

"Hell, why don't you just go work in Oslo?" the cop grumped. "It's closer. Plenty of construction is underway there. Germans want to fix up the port to suit themselves."

"Oslo's too big. I grew up in small towns, and I prefer them."

"Yeah? Well I don't! I'm from Oslo. On the city police. I was just a year off from retirement. Then, these Nazi bastards swarm in to knock it all upside down. Inform me I've been drafted into a new national police force. Be glorious for me, they say. Next thing I know, they've got me marooned out here in the fucking boondocks."

He plucked open the lapels of his tunic with both hands as if he was offering to take it off and hand it over. "You want a job? Here, take mine! I'd love to quit."

"Why don't you, then?"

"Orders. Apparently, it's not up to me. They want a trained policeman out here, I'm one, and that's that."

"Doesn't seem there'd be much crime here to investigate."

"Even *less* than that." The cop snorted. "Me and my partner are supposed to catch criminals on the lam from Oslo. They wire us with bulletins and descriptions. Like the arsonist who burnt the Federation Hotel. Ask me? A spy like that? Gone! Smarter than them, or he wouldn't have been able to sneak his bombs into that place. Had a savvy escape plan ready to go."

"I see. Well, you said there won't be another train for hours. What are you doing, then? You must stand out here just to guard the mail?"

The cop's face hardened. "What's it to you?" He groped in his tunic pocket for another cigarette.

"Nothing. Only making conversation."

"Morning train failed to snatch the bag. Missed by a full meter. Some drunken bastard on the hook, probably. Now grabbing it will be up to the night train west."

"Thought you said there wasn't one."

"All night trains are *freights* now. No passengers. Military. Every single one. Just crew and guards on board. They make freight runs in total darkness, to keep the Tommies from flying over and shooting 'em up." He eyed Kristian. "And there's no way any German on a military freight is ever going to let a bum like you jump on, so don't even ask."

"I get it. All right. Tomorrow morning's westbound is the only chance for me. I'll need to find a place to stay today and tonight, then."

The cop tapped his skull once more. "Such a brain you have," he said. "I'm so impressed."

~

Kristian walked off the platform and went a block into town. At the crossroad in its center, he could gaze down almost every street. The place was a cluster of scattered houses. No sign of a hotel, tavern or inn. To spend a night, his sole option might be to knock on the door of a home and beg permission to sleep in a barn or toolshed.

He shot a swift look back to the train platform. The Stapo man again leaned against his pole. His face remained turned in Kristian's direction as he puffed on a fresh cigarette.

*Curious to see what I'll do next,* Kristian realized. *Besides watching the morning train completely blow grabbing the mail sack, my visit might be the most interesting thing that happens to him today. I must uninterest him. Bore him even more. The best information for me to provide now is zero information. Don't even try to leave a false trail. Leave no trail.*

He saw a way to angle down a street that would let him disappear from the cop's view for a bit. During that moment of invisibility, if he crossed the street, hopped a low fence, went around a house, the cop would have no idea where he'd gone. And no easy way to figure it out, either.

He made the move. Next, he bushwhacked a route—hopping fences, cutting through meadows and gardens and rolling farm fields. While up on the platform, he'd spotted a trestle arching above the railroad tracks. It stood about a hundred meters out of town, on the westbound route toward Kristiansand and Stavanger—the direction he wanted to go.

He reached the trestle and scouted it out. Looked at from one end, he saw it had a trapezoidal profile. Dark timbers gathered at its summit to support a narrow crossing above the tracks. Distance from the trestle's lowest beam to the top of a freight car passing below, he estimated, would be about two meters. In other words, a do-able drop, but only if a train chugged along slowly. Trying to jump atop one that was blowing through town could end up mangling him, or worse.

He backtracked, found a tall thatch of brush in the corner of a fallow field. He wormed his way into the center of the clump, dragging his duffle behind him. He rolled over onto his back, laced his fingers together behind his head, plopped his shoulders and head on top of the duffle to use it as a pillow, relaxed, and began to think. At first his thoughts wandered back to Helene and Otto, but he wrenched them on a different course through an act of will. *I already thought enough about that bastard! Leave it alone.*

*Trains. That's what I must ponder. Any military freight would likely roar down this track. An engineer won't haul his throttle back for a one-horse burg like this. Except the crew will likely have orders to grab that mailbag. Can't be missed. They need to go slow past the platform, take care to hook the sack properly. Good, then!*

*And... I'm hungry.*

He sat up, hauled the duffle around, opened its neck and felt around inside for the bag of food Helene had given him. He'd packed it near the top. The bag held a sausage, a heel of bread, a lump of hard cheese and a glass jar full of water wrapped in a dish towel.

As he ate, he thought about the types of cars he might see in a military freight train. *Engine, oiler. Then a guard car of some kind. Open thing like a flatbed, holding sentries, AA guns on top. Boxcars. More flatbeds with panzers on them? Or halftracks at least, maybe something like that. Tanker cars that will be brimming with fuel for aircraft and trucks and everything else. More boxcars. A barracks car for the soldiers? Probably a final guard car, anyway.*

*And I guess I like those tanker cars the best.* He mentally visualized one, a long black tube, a metal walkway on top that spanned the length of it. *That's my pick for a landing. But why do I like it? What do I base my opinion on? What strikes me as right about it?* Upon request, a reason bobbed up into his consciousness to explain his intuition. *If German soldiers need to worry about air attack, they won't put their open guard cars near the fuel tankers. Those things are rolling bombs. In fact, they'll be as far off as possible, won't they? And so, a tanker car in the middle would end up as their blindest spot.*

He looked down into the duffle. He turned it over and let its contents slide onto the ground. *All right, what do I really need, and what can I leave behind? No tools, I think. What must I deal with? Cold, for sure. Bad, smoky air, deep in tunnels. Difficulty in holding on for the whole trip. Number one is that I must stay hidden. Even if this train doesn't stop before Stavanger, it might roll through some place with lights. Can't risk being seen. And caught. How should I manage that?* He snapped his fingers. *The rope! Deciding to tote it along was a stroke of fortune. The rope might be the key to making all of this work.*

~

The first train whistle he heard that evening constituted a false alarm. Its shrill blast came from the direction of Kristiansand. That meant it was a worker-and-commuter train heading eastward to Oslo.

Even so, for a moment, the sound filled Kristian with panic.

*Am I ready for this?*

But the next whistle came to him from the east, the Oslo side. Emitted by a westbound freight. Now there was no time to fret about it; he had to perform. Kristian slid his body out from the trestle's lowest beam, ducked his head down, and took in an upside-down view of a military freight pulling up to the platform. Its whistle was followed by a shriek of brakes. He saw tiny showers of sparks shooting out to the sides of the tracks.

Then the chug of the locomotive began to increase in tempo. Kristian stared at what he could see of the train moving through the puffs of steam and greasy smoke released by the engine. A slight bend in the tracks helped. Yes, this train had a tanker car in the middle. More than one.

He pulled his head up and got ready to jump. He rehearsed his movements. *Land on your boots but leaning ahead. Fall forward onto your left arm with the cast and the bunched-up duffle. Keep legs relaxed, don't let your knees hit too hard.*

Another whistle, louder, closer. Then a reeking cloud of fumes welled up around him as the engine whisked by below. Next the oil bunker, then a flatbed that bristled with raised gun barrels. Each AA gun had a clot of helmeted *Wehrmacht* men lounging around it. Whisk, whisk. The cars rattled on by under him. The first tanker! He had to leap onto the next. He had seen at least two. He doubted that there were three.

*Bang!*

His boots hit the catwalk, he pitched forward and landed hard, felt the plaster cast on his arm crack on impact, felt the duffle's rough fabric catch and drag on the metal grid, felt the knees on his pants rip and the steel teeth of the walkway gouge into his kneecaps.

A painful landing. Definitely. He'd not anticipated being jerked ahead so roughly. His body in a split-second had been forced to match the train's speed. Still, he'd made it on board. He raised his head cautiously and looked to the front of the train, then the rear. Okay, there had been three tankers, not two. Then behind them a box car, and a passenger car, and a final guard car. And no soldiers at the front or rear of the train seemed to be raising any sort of alarm.

Time to secure a hiding spot. First, Kristian checked on the condition of the cast on his left arm and its precious cargo. The hard landing had shattered most of the remaining plaster on one side. Chunks of plaster were falling off. Underlying fabric was coming loose. And just by touching it with the tips of his fingers he could make the packet of documents wiggle.

*Not good!*

He worked it loose entirely, then shoved the packet down the front of his pants.

*Well, I suppose that means I won't need this cast anymore.*

He shoved if off over his hand, then flung the cast away, watched it spin off into the night.

*No, that was an error. A swirling, pale thing for the guards to see. Should've just dropped it, let it bounce down the side of the car. All right. That's over and done with. But no more mistakes… all right?*

Clawing with his hands, pushing with his toes, he moved along the walkway until he got to the front of the car. He'd prepared by tying two lengths of rope through the metal grommets at the mouth of his duffle. He secured one in a loop to the underside of the catwalk, tying it with a square knot. Then he gingerly lowered his feet and legs into the duffle. Once he was standing in the heavy canvas bag and felt sure it would support his weight, he threaded the other rope up around a walkway support, then through the last grommet. Pulling his upper body up tighter under the walkway, he gradually hauled the duffle higher with his lower body inside, until the bag would rise no more. Then he tied it off.

*All right. I've hidden as best I can. Now I must slow my brain and my body down. No care about comfort or discomfort. I need to put myself into a state where I can endure. Because everything about this ride will be awful.*

He'd already put an extra layer of clothes back on, in part to pad his landing, in part to guard against the cold. He'd also sliced a flannel shirt into rags and stuffed them in his pockets to use as smoke filters for his nose and mouth whenever the train went through a tunnel. He pulled out one of these rags now, folded it, and laid it between the vibrating steel of the tank car and his cheek. Then he laid his head down and spread his arms out underneath the catwalk. Kristian already knew that slumber was unlikely. He just hoped to drift off into a kind of trance that would help the hours float by.

~

The train slowed for Kristiansand. Then it groaned to a complete halt. He heard German voices, the rhythmic bong and scrape of hobnail boots climbing up a steel ladder. A beam of light played along the catwalk. He dared not move; he barely even breathed. The light vanished. More chatter in German accents. A couple of shouts. The locomotive huffed, car couplings clanked, and the train began to lurch ahead.

~

He was numb, weary, hypothermic and groggy. For these reasons, he almost missed the approach to Stavanger. Buildings around Sola, to the south of the city, were blacked out to shield the airfield from British air raids. In his addled condition, even that homey place was tough to recognize. But a blast from the train's whistle jolted Kristian back to awareness. *The engineer's warning vehicles at the road crossings. Must be nearing the city. I've got to hurry.*

He kicked his legs inside the duffle, squirmed around and managed to get a hand down far enough to snatch out his fillet knife. *Don't drop it, now.* He sawed through the loop of rope with the square knot. Then he put the knife's hilt between his teeth and loosened the half-hitches that secured the cinch rope.

*Go fast but stay smooth. Success depends on whether the guards look ahead of the train to arrival in the city and the end of their shift. Also, whether I can stop moving when I hit the ground.*

He let the rope pay out through the grommets as the duffle slid down the side of the tank car. When he reached the widest part of the car's long black barrel, he spat out the knife, released the rope entirely and took the drop. He put his hands in front of his face, told himself to stay limp. Then he hit, bounced, fell, rolled and thumped to a stop. He found himself wedged between a mound of the track's gravel ballast and a ragged line of brush.

Kristian took inventory. His knees still hurt from the impact of his initial landing on the catwalk. He felt stiff, cold, and bruised. *But otherwise, you are tip-top, he informed himself. Fabulous, really! And are there any other lies you can tell yourself so you can feel better about this?*

He wriggled out of the duffle bag and sat up. The train, all its brakes groaning, slid around a curve to enter the Stavanger rail yard. Nobody on the last guard car was looking backward or toward Kristian. *Already those soldiers are thinking about steins of beer, lit cigarettes, cuddling with women and belting out the choruses of drinking songs. Maybe not in that order...*

He waited until the train disappeared into the station house, then stood. He tried to dust himself off, but realized it was hopeless. His clothes were ripped, stained, coated with soot and dust. *That Stapo cop back in Nykirke is more right about me now than yesterday. I do look like a bum. When I go into town, I guess I should act like one, too.*

Leaving the bag behind, he shuffled back down the track, from the spot he had landed, in search of the fillet knife. But that too was hopeless. It was too dark to see much and his blade had likely bounced off into the weeds. Then he stiffened in shock. Something else was missing. He patted himself on the groin. *Helene's packet! Of documents!* He'd put it in the front of his pants, but where was it now?

*Fantastic. You launch this hellish trip, and then you lose the whole reason for it? Such a genius. Maybe that cop was right about your brain power as well.*

He retraced his steps, scanning the dark ground with consummate care. He didn't remember feeling anything slide from his crotch or slither down his pant leg. He eventually found the duffle and groped inside. Whew! There the thin green packet was. It had slid down his trousers and into the bottom of the bag upon landing. And he should now put it where... well, into the empty knife sheath, still strapped to his calf? He pulled up the leg of his pants. Sure. The thin packet fit into the sheath. He jammed it down as far as it would go.

*Don't know if I'll have a use for the duffle bag, but I might as well drag it along with me, as a prop. Keep that bum appearance going on.*

The track was lined and bordered by tall fences on both sides. He didn't feel quite up to scaling it. Should he try to exit the track by going through Stavanger station? Even at this early hour, there'd be guards and officials. At least, they wouldn't think he'd come on the military freight, since he hadn't been detected climbing off it. That would've been impossible to explain, and he'd have been arrested as a potential saboteur, a spy, or both.

He'd have a much easier time explaining why he walked along the tracks. He could spice that excuse with a dose of pure stupidity—an act he already knew he could pull off. *As though I have a natural gift there, or something.* Maybe he should try to look like a drunk, also.

But just prior to reaching the station, he saw he didn't need to enter it.

Some other wanderer had created an arrangement of his own, perhaps for jumping on trains, or maybe walking the tracks. Behind a pile of dead brush, a hole had been chopped in the fence. Kristian moved the brush, ducked through the hole, then tugged the brush back into place behind him.

On the far side, he found himself by an outside corner of the station. The streets in front of him were dark and quiet. The only sounds—trucks pulling up, derricks creaking, an occasional shouted command—wafted over from the other side of the station.

He took a deep breath, then walked forward into the night. He had just gone a few steps when he heard the dread words ring from the shadows, *"Halt! Deutsche Sicherheits!"*

He stopped, turned slowly. A clapboard guard shack had been erected against the station wall. Obviously, a new security measure; it hadn't been set up when Rolf and he had departed a week or so before. Two men emerged from the shack, both in greatcoats and gloves. One had a helmet on, the other a peaked officer's cap. The helmeted soldier was carrying a rifle.

"What have we here?" The soldier said. "Curfew violator, at minimum."

He set the rifle butt down on the pavement, gripping its barrel with his right hand. With his left, he produced an electric torch from his coat pocket, switched it on and sent its beam up and down Kristian's body, then let the light linger on his streaked and smudged face.

"There's a curfew?" Kristian asked. "Truly?"

"Started yesterday," the officer said. "Where are you from?"

"Sola."

"What are you up to, skulking around in the dark?"

"I walk the tracks, all the time. Back and forth. I find things, stuff people drop. Or throw out. Things that fall off."

"Fall off? From trains? Aha, you're a thief." The officer smiled thinly.

"No, no, no. I was taught not to steal. That is against God's command. Now, my grandma just lets me walk around and look for dropped things. I find them, sometimes."

"Your sack looks awfully empty. What did you pick up tonight?"

"Nothing." Kristian released the duffle, let it plop to the ground.

The soldier tilted his flashlight from Kristian's face back to his knees and sniggered. "See that?" he said. The pantlegs over Kristian's knees were torn open and drooping. Frayed edges of the rips were stained with blood. "I say, this guy is lying to us. Bet he makes his living by kneeling by the tracks, giving blowjobs to railroad men."

The officer emitted a bray of laughter. Then he held out a gloved palm. "Your papers," he said casually.

"Sure."

Kristian reached into the inside pocket of his coat. But he felt nothing there. He remembered that he wore another layer below. He confidently reached into the coat beneath the first one. Also nothing. He clapped both hands against his waistline, as if searching for an object that had slid out of either of those pockets. But, nothing. Maybe he'd kept the packet of *Luftwaffe* documents, but it was clear he'd lost his ID wallet, and everything inside it. His face turned pale. And in achieving that effect, he did not need to act. His adrenalin level, already high, surged powerfully.

"S—s—sorry," he stuttered. "I must have dropped them. S—somewhere."

"Oho!" the officer said. "Now, here's a man who violates curfew, who lacks any ID, and tries to hoodwink us with a ridiculous tale. An excellent candidate for a more robust interrogation. Let's give the Gestapo a crack at him."

"Wait, wait, wait. I have to admit it. I've been lying to you," Kristian said.

His words brought them up short. They straightened. And while they stared at him, Kristian's mind raced.

"In truth, I did not find much of anything along the tracks. But I did pick up one carton of wonderful, beautiful cigarettes. Turkish! Do you wish to see?"

He snatched up and overturned the duffle. Nothing fell out. But both Germans were now looking down at the ground.

Kristian threw the mouth of his bag over the head of the soldier and kicked him in the balls as hard as he could. As the soldier groaned, reeled and toppled, Kristian swung his eyes to the officer. That man had yanked his coat open, was clawing at a holster on the right side of his belt. Kristian hurled himself at him, ramming a shoulder into his chest while snatching with both of his own hands for the officer's pistol.

They fell to the ground together, Kristian on top, and his body's weight knocked much of the breath out of the officer. Nevertheless, the German retained enough strength to continue to grapple with Kristian for control of the gun. He fought to aim it at Kristian's face. Kristian managed to shove it aside and at the same time deliver a blow with his elbow to the officer's chin.

The gun went off next to Kristian's head, emitting a blinding flash and a deafening bang. The soldier he had kicked was now back up on his feet and staggering toward them. And the hurtling bullet center-punched the soldier in his belly.

The officer was nearly as surprised by this as the soldier. In his shock he fumbled the gun and Kristian managed to snatch full possession. He rose to a knee and pumped three rounds straight into the officer's lower chest. Then he spun. The soldier was sitting on the ground, legs outstretched, both gloved hands clasped to his bleeding gut. Kristian aimed carefully and put four bullets into him. He flopped heavily over onto his back and spasmed. Kristian checked on the officer. Still breathing, but in shallow gasps, he stared at Kristian with distended, glistening eyes. Kristian aimed at his head.

"*Nein… nein…*" the officer gurgled.

Kristian pulled the trigger. *Click.* The pistol's magazine was empty.

Kristian thought frantically. *He'll be dead soon. Maybe not. But he needs to be dead. If he's alive, he can describe, identify me.* He saw a knife sheath on the other side of the man's belt. He dropped the pistol and snatched out a dagger with a shapely black hilt. *This is how to finish him.* He leaned forward and rammed the blade up through the man's throat and into the back of his brain. Then he wrenched the knife free and stood.

Whistles were blowing. There was a hubbub of guttural shouting. A motorcycle started up.

*They've heard my shots. They'll be coming over here. Fast!*

Kristian launched himself into a frenzied sprint, running as hard as he could for a band of deeper shadow across the street.

*"War is mainly a catalogue of blunders."*
—Winston Churchill, *The Grand Alliance*

## CHAPTER 24

Kristian pounded down the sidewalk, raw panic spurring his pace. After many blocks he finally dared to pause and leaned on one hand against a brick wall, panting and quivering as his heart continued to pound. He fought to regain both his breath and his wits. *Don't spring around aimlessly, idiot. Get yourself someplace! But where?*

His original plan had been to head for Café Heck and connect with Rolf and Hermann. And via them and their radio, with the Brits. Back at Nykirke, he'd visualized this as easy to accomplish, a calm sequel to the train journey. Well, that plan had just gotten kicked to smithereens. All right. What should he do instead?

Noises of turmoil came indistinctly from behind. He heard the sounds of an accelerating motorcycle, then others. More vehicles, like army trucks. *They'll circle the blocks, make expanding rings... Wait. I've got it! Head for the graveyard. They can't ride down those long stairs.*

He resumed running, but now with a goal in mind. He peeled off his outer coat, jogged a short distance and tossed the garment onto the pavement. It had some blood spatters on its sleeves, which he figured would entertain his pursuers. Then he reversed course and went straight for the Lagård Gravlund. At the end of Kortegata he found a flight of shadowy brick steps and raced down them, ignoring bolts of pain that shot out of his knees. His first thought was to run the path that spanned the length of the cemetery, then head back onto the streets. *But then what? They'll still be coming after me!*

His next thought made him slow to a walk. He glanced up at the head of the valley that cradled the cemetery. He saw the standing stone that marked his buried cache—and what he considered Ragnar's final resting place. *I'll be damned if I let them ever take me alive, to beat me to a pulp in some airless room. I should dig up my Webley and its ammo, then take as many Nazis down with me as I can tonight! Fall down fighting in the open air like a man, just as Pappa did.* He took a step toward the standing stone. *No, you can't. You might win a final blaze of glory, a last measure of vengeance. But next, how many English civilians shall die under German bombs? Instead, you must use everything you've got to deliver Helene's papers. Leap for any window of opportunity, no matter how narrow, no matter how slim your chance of getting through. She expects nothing less of you.*

He ran on. At Paradisveien he left the cemetery to continue down Frue Terrasse. He heard no sounds of accelerating engines now. Not yet. Time to turn and head for the waterfront. But how could he stay ahead of the Germans?

He saw a brick house with a wooden balcony. And gleaming slightly as it leaned over the balcony's upper rail, a bicycle's handlebar. He promptly scurried over. He drove the German's knife into a seam of mortar between bricks of the wall, jamming it in as high up as he could reach. Then using it as a handhold and scrambling with his boots, he pulled himself up. He got a hand between the balusters, hauled himself up, placed a hand atop of the rail, then he was over.

It was a woman's bike, with a curvy frame, fat tires and a basket behind the seat. He threw it over the railing, then clambered back down. On the ground, reaching up, he yanked the knife out and stuck its blade under his belt.

Over his head, a window of the house lit up, and a female voice said, "*Hva er det?*"

Kristian picked up the bike, sat on its low seat, wrenched its handlebars into place and shoved off. Soon he was accelerating down Figgjogata, then Nylundgata, aiming for the waterfront. *Take a left soon*, he reminded himself.

As he sped downhill, his thoughts leaped ahead to his destination. *I know—I'll ditch this bike, toss it into the water and climb under the pier, get my English kayak launched, and paddle the hell away from Stavanger.* Then he realized, *No, that's dumb. Paddle away from here, and then do what? I can't paddle Helene's packet over to England! She and I were both right about that. One ordeal on the North Sea was plenty.*

He backpedaled, started to apply the bike's coaster brake. *There's no good way to escape and also deliver her packet. Not if I fail to arrange a stronger means of transport. Has to be something the Brits provide, sooner or later. Preferably sooner. Means I need to contact them. And that means I must indeed get to Rolf and Hermann so they can light up their radio. But... no way I can approach Café Heck now. The Gestapo's HQ is likely buzzing like a hornet's nest. They'd grab me and put me under arrest without even knowing I'm the one who killed their soldiers. Just because they're mad and they want to catch somebody, anybody. Later, they might figure out the connection, whereupon my tail would truly be in a jam. But how can I ever reach my friends?*

He realized he was careening down the exact same block that had hosted Rolf's *Scrimshaw Puben*. Not only that, he'd almost gone past the building that hosted the tavern. Well, the hand-painted sign with its whale tooth design was gone. He released the brake, heeled the bicycle over, pedaled hard around the next corner and shot into the alley behind the bar. The tavern's back windows, just like its front ones, were dark. Kristian dismounted, and with desperate hope he plucked up the loose cobblestone that had hid the backdoor key. And it was there!

With trembling fingers, he unlocked the door, brought the bike inside, shut and locked it once more.

He pricked up his ears. No sounds. "Hallo?" he called out. No answer. He flicked an electric light switch, but the power was off. Would there still be running water? Suddenly, he felt desperately thirsty. Shuffling through the shadows, he located the stairs and went up to them. In the apartment faint light bled in through the curtained windows from outside. The main living area looked empty, except for the couch and table.

Kristian went to the sink, twisted the tap. Water dribbled out. He instantly pressed his lips to the faucet. But the trickle turned into droplets, then ceased. He groaned. He trudged to the table, tugged the dusty cloth off it. He pulled the knife from his belt and rammed the tip into the tabletop. It would make the weapon much easier to grab in an emergency. He went to the couch, flopped down, draped the tablecloth on himself like a blanket, then sank into oblivion.

∼

Clear light seeped into the room. Traffic sounds. Indistinct human speech.

Kristian awoke, blinked, stretched. It took a moment to orient himself. *I'm in Rolf's apartment, above the old bar.* He felt still felt exhausted. Also, desiccated and cold. His head hurt, and his knees too. He swung his legs off the couch and sat up. He saw he hadn't managed to remove his boots before falling asleep. He bent over stiffly, unlaced them and tugged them off. Then seeing the sheath on his leg and remembered what he'd stashed there, he dug into it with two fingers and tugged out Helene's packet.

He stood up, walked to the table and tossed the narrow green envelope onto it. "You were meant to be a blessing. But now you're my curse," he told the packet. He looked more closely at the German knife he'd left sticking out of the splintered wood. The weapon had a vase-shaped black hilt with a pronounced metal boss and guard. Its blade had an etched motto on it: *"Meine Ehre Heist Treue"*—meaning, My Honor is Loyalty.

He shifted his gaze to the sink. Was it likely that more water might have come into the pipes? No. But a fresh inspiration came to him. He rummaged around the kitchen. In a cabinet, he found a battered tin cup that Hermann used to measure flour.

He took the cup into the bathroom. By standing on the toilet's lid, he was able to reach over his head, raise the top of the water storage tank and dip the cup into it. He filled that cup, slurped the water from it down greedily, and repeated this operation a half-dozen times. With a tiny sigh, he stepped down, sat on the toilet lid and leaned back. *What next?* During his search for a cup, he'd seen there wasn't a scrap of food. *But that's not my biggest need. Got to get a message to Rolf and Hermann. How?*

He shuffled back out to the living room. Bright sunlight now slashed in around the curtain edges. He tugged a drape askew to peek out. Work trucks and cars fuming with woodchip gas generators on the back and even a horse-drawn cart trundled about on the waterfront. Hard to believe this calm, quotidian scene was occurring on a continent at war. But if people were still moving about, unhindered…

*I might be able to select a messenger from among them. Maybe an old friend from school, or a fisherman I know. Summoned to the back of the tavern. Hand them my message. But, but, but! If the Nazis nab a person like that, they'd squeeze him till they learned of my hiding place. So, anyone I send can't know where I'm staying.* He smiled. *Okay then! She's perfect. But will that old biddy do it? She does owe us something. Quite a lot, actually.*

He returned to the bathroom, dragging the tablecloth along with him. He dabbed it into the toilet tank, then stood in front of the mirror, wiping his face methodically with the wet end, and patting it dry with the other portion. After he was finished, his face was mostly clean, but streaks of oily soot from the train ride emphasized his eyebrows, and the stubble around his chin. He looked like he sported a goatee.

"Hey," he murmured at his reflection. "If Rolf and Hermann are correct about the power of theater, this should work." Funny, though, how much this *ad hoc* make-up made him resemble characters played by Charlie Chaplin and Groucho Marx.

~

Kristian knocked on her apartment door at midday. As before, it took Mrs. Andersen a long time to answer.

"Who is it?" her voice quavered through the door.

"Charlie Marx," he said.

"Karl Marx?" If that's what she thought she heard, she was right to sound suspicious.

"No, Charlie."

"That's a very odd name…"

"Yes, I know. My parents seem to have played a bad joke on me."

"What do you want?"

"Special ration cards are now being printed up for the elderly. I've been sent around to pass them out. Don't you want any?"

"Oh."

A bolt was drawn and the door creaked open.

"Hello, Mrs. Andersen," Kristian said, as he shoved the door further open then gently but firmly pushed past her into the room, while she sought in vain to block his passage with her scrawny body.

"You… you! You lied to me!" she protested. She gathered the collar of her housecoat around her neck with one hand, as if shielding herself from his gaze, or armoring herself against a possible sex-fiend attack.

"Relax. That was just me saying stuff in order to get inside. And see? It worked."

"What did you do to your face? You look strange."

"Right. That's the idea."

She stiffened. "Get out. Leave! If you don't, I shall telephone the police."

She tried to hold her bent spine erect and look fierce. She succeeded in adding a centimeter to her height and looking scared.

"I don't think you will."

"Why not?"

"A lot of reasons. First, because I'd physically stop you. Both of us know that I can, easily. Second, the last thing you should want is to alert Norwegian or German police to the fact that you know the son of Kari and Ragnar Thorsen and you've just seen me alive and kicking. How many hours do you wish to spend being grilled by them? Third, no, I don't have ration cards. But I do have a ton of cash, and you can use some of it to buy another person's ration cards. Or score food on the black market, whatever you want. Fourth, I wish to offer you a chance to redeem yourself."

"Re*deem* myself?" She scoffed. "You should know that I am a good Christian woman," she said haughtily. "I certainly don't need…"

"Mrs. Andersen." Kristian stepped up to her, put his hands on her bony shoulders, and tilted his head down so his eyes could bore straight into hers. "Because of you, my mother Kari was grabbed by the Gestapo. You remember that? No matter how much you'd rather forget it. Well, she's now being held in a German concentration camp. Sachsenhausen, near Berlin."

Her rheumy eyes widened and moistened. She raised both hands to her withered lips. Her spark of rebellion was quenched, and she seemed to shrink in his hands.

"Sorry. I'm sorry to hear that," she murmured.

∾

Kristian sat at her lace-draped table while Mrs. Andersen made tea. He was also able to coax her out of a slice of bread and a precious pat of butter, which disappeared into his growling stomach in an instant. Next, they made plans. She needed a good reason to visit Café Heck, and they decided that reason could be bringing the place some supplies. Kristian's cash would allow her to purchase a basket of pastries at a bakery, then hire a taxi to help her deliver them.

"Once you get there, just give the big man, named Hermann, or the older, thin one, named Rolf, this bill," Kristian said. He peeled a *Reichsmark* off his roll, plucked a pencil from a mug holding a cluster of them at the end of her table, and wrote down two words on the margin of the bill: *hval tann*. This meant, whale tooth. He folded the bill several times and handed it to her. "You won't have to say anything else or give them anything else. In fact, I don't want you to even try." He then also extracted a small wad of *Kroner* and put them on the table.

"Do this one small favor for me, and then I promise you, I'll never darken your door again," Kristian said.

She looked at him dubiously. He peeled off a few more *Kroner* and held them up. She nodded.

"All right." She took them, placing them on top of the other bills. She tidied the stack with her fingertips, folded it in half, and then stuffed it into the pocket of her housecoat. "Afterward... You must agree that you'll never come around here and bother me anymore. At least, not until long after this war is over," she said.

Kristian nodded. "Sure. If there *is* an 'after,'" he said, "or an 'over.' And that both of us are lucky enough so that we live long enough to see it."

$$\sim$$

Light that had formerly bullied its way in around the curtain hems had shifted to a gentle blue glow. Kristian, lounging again on the couch in the pub's apartment, heard a distant metallic click. The tavern's back door creaked. He jumped up, wrenched the German dagger out of the table and rushed to conceal himself behind the open door. But when he heard a slow, ponderous thump of the feet on the stairs, he grinned.

"Hallo, Hermann!" he called out.

"Hallo, Fiske," Hermann said, as he stepped through the doorway. He glanced around the living area in puzzlement, then stepped sideways and swung the door closed to reveal Kristian's hiding place. He only raised a single eyebrow when he spotted the dagger poised in Kristian's hand.

"Aim to add poor Hermann to your bloody trail, hey?" he said. "Well, you ought to show mercy instead. After all, I've brought you food." He raised the wicker hamper in his hand.

"Fabulous. You've not only purchased your life. You've also won my undying esteem."

"Undying. Ah, marvelous," Hermann said. "And you'll demonstrate your immortality, how? The Gestapo, the *Wehrmacht*, the SS, the Stapo, and even the *Luftwaffe* all hope to nail your hide to a wall."

"Well, they don't know that I am me," Kristian said, as he tried to snatch the hamper. "Or do they?"

Hermann swung it out of reach while he shook a thick finger at him.

"Manners, young Fiske. In my cafes, customers await service. Tut-tut! No boardinghouse reach, if you please."

Kristian paused, looked abashed. Hermann set the hamper on the table and unlatched its lid. He looked for the tablecloth, saw it was a wrinkled heap on the couch, and frowned. He took a pair of red checked napkins from the hamper and spread them in its place. Kristian came demurely to the table. He drove the tip of the knife into the tabletop and sat.

Hermann rolled his eyes. "You know, once upon a time, this was a fairly nice piece of furniture," he said. "Till you started jabbing blades into it."

"Got to keep your weapon close to hand," Kristian said. "A spy can never tell what he might have to do next."

"Oooh, you want to seem dangerous?" Hermann sighed. "This is maybe intended to make me bring the food out faster?"

"That works! Glad you thought of it."

"Hmph."

On the napkins Hermann laid thick curved bars of *rostbratwurst* sausages, baked potatoes, slices of black bread, hard-boiled eggs and apples. Between the napkins, he set down a pot of mustard and another of sauerkraut. Then he put a beeswax taper in a candlestick and lit it. Finally, from the basket's bottom he produced two bottles of dark beer and uncapped them with a flourish.

"Now?" Kristian begged.

Hermann nodded grandly and swept a hand above the table in mute invitation.

Kristian fell to. He grabbed a sausage, jammed it into his mouth and bit off a third. Hermann sipped from the neck of his beer bottle. It gave him no small degree of amusement to see Kristian gobble up his repast at such a frenzied pace.

"So," he rumbled after a while. "You ask if the Nazis know that you are

you. In the main, your answer is no. Word hasn't spread that a fisherman's
son might've survived the sinking of a certain boat, and now has a very
big ax to grind. Even idle rumor hasn't linked you yet to infamous deeds,
cropping up in Oslo a few months after that day."

He smiled at Kristian. Then he pinned his own attention on the food
and proceeded to construct his lunch. He tugged the SS dagger loose from
the table, gazed at its blade for a second, then brought it down to cut a
*rostbratwurst* lengthwise. He used it to slather coarse ground mustard
on black bread, laid the sausage halves athwart a slice, topped that with a
dome of sauerkraut, then laid the final slice. After pressing it down with a
palm to flatten it, he contemplated his sandwich, chomped off a bite and
chewed with delight.

After swallowing part of his first mouthful, he continued. "They *do* have
their eyes on the outline of a shadowy somebody. Guy who uses a certain
favored killing trick." He swallowed again. "What they've not figured out
is a rationale for his attacks. Targets scattered all over, no pattern to these
deaths. But they're impressed enough to award this ghost a nickname."

"Yeah?"

"*Der Schattenmann,*" Hermann said. "Shadow Man."

"Like it," Kristian replied with a grin. "Almost, well, romantic."

"Go on, laugh," Hermann said. "Not the right way to see it. Means
nabbing you has turned into a special project." He poked a finger at the
blade of the German knife. "SS dagger, right. You slew both a solder *and*
an SS officer. In less than a minute, using their own weapons! Lovely job.
Later, you must say how you managed it. But clapping you in irons and
having their way with you is now a high priority for the SS. Nothing to
celebrate."

"But as you said, they still don't know who I am."

"Yet!" Hermann gulped some beer. "However, on the SS officer's pistol?
Are your fingerprints. As I understand it, nice, dark, visible ones."

"Oops." Kristian mulled this over. He inwardly berated himself for
leaving the gun at the scene. "I was in a hurry," he said. "No time to wipe."

"As I can well imagine."

Hermann picked up the dagger, turned it over in the candlelight, read the inscription on its blade. "*Meine Ehre Heist Treue*," he said. "That's a blood oath of the SS. Which they do take seriously."

"Yeah? So?"

Hermann saw an opening to pontificate.

"Loyalty's the currency of any one-party system, young Fiske. Doesn't matter if your system is Soviet communism, or Italian fascism, or Germany's peculiar Nazism. The more numerous your political parties, the more your nation can debate policy, compare results. Sheer merit can then win. But if one party holds dominion, none of that is true. The one party must be correct, no matter what. Loyalty and cohesion become most important. Deviance must be punished. So when those wolves come after you, they come as a pack."

"Um, Hermann, your lesson is fascinating. I'll treasure it always. But I must tell you that I *remain* in a hurry. A great hurry, to be honest. I do need to rest. But I also need to get underway again as soon as possible."

The black eyes studied him. "How so?"

"I possess incredibly valuable intelligence, on certain stolen documents, that must get to England quickly."

"Intelligence? What sort?"

Kristian shook his head. "Promised the person who stole it I'd not tell anyone, even friends. If the Nazis find out that their secrets have been compromised, they'll swiftly render all the information useless."

"I see. Without compromising the material, can you indicate its value?"

Kristian thought it over. "May sound melodramatic," he warned.

"My theater experience is broad." Ends of Hermann's grin disappeared into creases in his plump cheeks. "Melodrama creates quite amusing scripts. So, try me."

"Thousands of civilian lives could be at stake."

"You're not kidding!"

"No. Nub of it is, with information I carry, the English can take measures to cancel out German advantages in the air war."

"But we can't transmit this material via radio? Even in code? Rolf does have the W/T you brought us fully up and humming. He's in regular contact."

"Can anyone guarantee such a transmission won't be picked up? And its code broken?"

Hermann stroked a few of his chins. "Always a possibility," he conceded.

"Then we need to use Rolf's 'Less is Best' rule. I wish to take my packet to England and stick it right into the hands of the Cyclops."

Hermann's tiny eyes twinkled, and he nodded. "All right. As soon as we heard you were back around, and the depth of the trouble you'd gotten into, we thought we should ship you back to England, *tout de suite*. Anyway, Rolf's already dreamed up a plan."

"Delighted to hear that."

"I'll even request that he speed it up."

"Perfect. Thanks. Meanwhile, I'll figure out a way for you to acquire the same information, after I leave. So, it can be available to send in a different way, if I don't happen to make it."

"Always a possibility as well. Wise of you to admit it."

Hermann shoved back his chair and stood. "As for me, the wisdom now would be to head back to the café. I can't run afoul of the curfew. Presently, my reputation with my countrymen remains pure as the driven slush. I aim to keep it that way."

He swung a broad hand over the remains of their meal. "Keep this, feed on it as you wish. But before I go, please show me your knees."

"Ah. You noticed my wounds."

"Of course. Due to rips in your clothing, bloodstains, obscure clues such as those."

He stood, put his foot up on his chair. Hermann bent and poked at the tear in the leg of Kristian's pants.

"Deep cuts, considerable swelling." He hummed to himself. "Could be infected, too. How's your other?"

"The same."

"I'll send Rolf down in the morning with salve and bandages. He probably also will have polished up your extraction plan by then. Most likely, it will have to do with boats." Hermann snapped his fingers. "And he'll bring you drinking water, too. Sorry, I'd forgotten that's been turned off in here."

"It's okay. I did find some. Up in the toilet tank."

"Not down in the toilet bowl itself."

"No."

"You display a fine judgment there, young Fiske."

*"Churchill makes a speech on the radio. Packed with lies and distortions. He has aged a lot. But he remains a cunning old fox."*
—Josef Goebbels, from *The Goebbels Diaries*

# CHAPTER 25

Rolf arrived at the shuttered tavern as beams of yellow sunrise light began to slip under and around the front curtains.

Kristian was awake already. When he heard the grind of the backdoor's bolt being drawn, he jumped down the stairs to greet his new visitor. However, he did not forget to carry his knife.

The door creaked open and they saw each other. Rolf reacted to Kristian's lethal-looking blade in about the same way as Hermann. He thrust both arms above his head in mock surrender. He was wearing his gray tweed coat with its leather buttons and trim. A military canteen hung from one shoulder by a canvas strap; a hunter's game pouch was suspended from the other.

"Not in a Stapo uniform, as any fool can plainly see," he told Kristian. "Therefore you, *Schattenmann*, should make no error that might prove irreversible."

"And you, no sudden moves, or else!" Kristian said.

"I paid eighty *Kroner* for this tweed coat. Best Irish quality. Think I want to get any slashes in it?"

Kristian smiled and shook his head. He dropped the SS dagger point-first and its tip embedded in the rough planks of the hallway floor.

"Cuts could be vents. Make it a better summer coat," he said. "You could wear it all year."

"No advantage, there. I do so already."

Kristian looked into Rolf's wrinkle-ringed eyes, cuffed him under his bristly chin and assaulted him with a too-vigorous hug.

"So, I gather you're still alive," Rolf said. He put his hands up on Kristian's ribs and pushed him away. "And still making more trouble than anyone has a right to."

"Sorry. Won't happen again."

"Speaking just for myself, I'm sad to hear that."

Rolf's face rearranged all its basset-hound creases into something like a smile.

"By the devil's forked tongue!" Kristian exclaimed. "Like that line? One of my father's favorite oaths. 'Hell's afire!' That's another. Rolf, last time we saw each other, we were at the top of the Federation Hotel, and you were telling me to roast the *Luftwaffe*."

"We did inconvenience them a tad, I think."

"To be accurate, I did see you one more time. Parked in that bakery van, waiting for me to run up to you."

"I searched for you in the mirrors. Saw you get jumped." Rolf shook his head. "I thought the balloon had really gone up, and we might all get grabbed! Then I and Filip..."

"The chef?"

"Yes." Rolf nodded. "We had to take off. I was relieved to find out it was the Oslo Gang who snatched you and not the Gestapo. But I only found myself able to draw a deep breath after I'd heard that the Gang had finally let you go."

"Well, 'let me go' doesn't quite describe it. I was sent out on a mission. Well, two. My first mission was to get myself the heck off their turf in Oslo. Go as far away as possible. The second was to take crucial information over to the Brits. Fortunately, these aims coincided. A pair of birds with a single stone, as they say. So, here I am."

"Details to come, I hope. All Hermann did was tease me." Rolf swung a hand to point up the staircase. "Shall we?"

Kristian grabbed his knife, and they ascended the steps.

Inside the apartment, Rolf set aside the pouch and canteen, then emptied the lower pockets of his coat onto the cherry wood table. From one pocket came a rubber-stoppered bottle of wood alcohol, a packet of cotton balls, a roll of gauze, a lead tube of ointment. From the other pocket emerged a battered silver flask with a metal crest soldered to it that said "Schultz" above and *"Cedo Nulli"* below. Between these words, a snarling lion stood embossed.

"Who are the Schultzes?" Kristian asked.

Rolf shook his head. "You'd need to ask my burglar. I'm only the fence." He eyed Kristian. "But first, I have a question for you. Alcohol inside, or outside, as we start?" He raised the flask.

"Tough question," Kristian said. "Inside, I guess."

"Good choice," Rolf approved. He uncapped the flask, took a vigorous swig, and held the container out to Kristian. *"Skål,"* he said. He wiped his lips with the cuff of a coat sleeve.

"Wait a minute. I take it, you're going to try to fix my knees. Can't we do that last?"

"No," Rolf said. "Best to get it out of the way."

"Well, *faen,*" Kristian said. "Okay. Let me have that." He took the flask and sniffed its opening. He wrinkled his nose. "What is this stuff?"

"Akevitt. Take care. But you only need be careful when you start. After five swallows, you'll lose all ability to care."

Kristian took three gulps. Then one more, just to be safe.

"Okay. Knees up."

"Where?"

"Sit. Swing your feet up onto the table."

"Dirty boots on the table? Hermann wouldn't like that."

"Hermann isn't here."

Kristian sighed and complied. Rolf peered down at the gouges on the kneecaps he could see exposed through the pantleg tears, and *tsk—tsked* a few times.

"This might sting a little," Rolf said.

He uncapped the wood alcohol and briskly poured a liberal amount over the puss-filled cuts. Kristian tilted his head back to shriek, then crammed a closed fist into his mouth. When he finally felt able to take his hand away, it was printed with toothmarks.

"Mother of God," he said weakly. "Swear words. Curse words. A great number of truly awful words."

Rolf looked at him curiously. "Why not just say them?"

"Don't know any that're bad enough."

Rolf chuckled. "Well, now the worst is over."

"All praise to a merciful God, amen."

"I think it's over. Perhaps. Well, I mean, possibly."

Rolf began to dab at the wounds with the cotton swabs. He looked up. "Now, don't take this the wrong way," he said. "But I'll need you to remove your pants."

Kristian looked at him warily. He mutely put his legs down and removed his boots. Then he stood, dropped his trousers and stepped out of them. He snatched a checkered napkin off the table, and sat once more, while draping the napkin over his loins.

"Proceed," he said.

Rolf did. He shoved his used cotton balls into a small pile and picked up the tube of salve. He cleared his throat.

"Well, here's my verdict. I can't see whether or not you've fractured your kneecaps, but I don't think you did them any favors, either." He held up the salve. "This is a silver ointment. Great stuff. And not cheap, either. I'll put this on and bandage you as well. Leave you with this gauze and this goo. Change your dressings at least once per day if you can. It's best you're going back to England, since you'll need much more care than I can give you."

"Okay, getting me to England is the important part. What's the plan?"

Rolf pushed clear beads of ointment out of the nozzle of the tube and into Kristian's cuts. That action hurt, while the salve itself then felt soothing.

"Tonight, a while before midnight, you start off. You'll go back to the pier down on the waterfront. You know that dock where you hid the kayak? I had our boys check on it. Luckily, it's still there. Get it lowered and launched, then paddle north out of the harbor. At midnight sharp, a fishing boat will come up behind you. The *Ombo*. She has a brown hull, a white pilothouse. Her skipper's name is Mathias Hagen. When he sees you, he'll hit you once with a spotlight, then slow down. Bring you aboard, take you out beyond the Tungenes Fyr. Finally, he'll let you paddle off. Whereupon you take yourself off to that rendezvous point where you were originally dropped off by the British. Be in position by sunset tomorrow. And keep appearing at that spot at sunset on subsequent days until you get picked up."

Rolf swathed Kristian's knees in layers of gauze and tied them off with knots both above and below each knee.

"Did the Brits inform you of the location?"

Rolf shook his head. "*You* need to know. It's better if I don't, for the usual reason. You can remember the place, right?"

"Sure. Can I put my pants back on now?"

"Please."

As he carefully slid his bandaged legs back down into his trousers, Kristian mulled the plan over and thought he spotted a hitch.

"How will I know when midnight is?"

"Good point." Rolf slid back his jacket sleeve and popped open the metal clasp on a Swiss Rolex. "Here. Take this."

Awestruck, Kristian cradled the weighty timepiece in his palm. He'd heard rumors about these pricey chronometers but had never laid his eyes on one. He'd imagined Rolexes to be the sort of waterproof whirligigs that only ranking admirals wore on their arms.

"Are you sure?"

Rolf shrugged. "I know where I can get another."

"Well, I bet you do. Thanks." Kristian strapped it on his wrist. "One more thing. I suppose Hermann told you I must keep the intelligence I'm carrying under wraps. But you guys should have a way to discover it for yourselves, in case I'm caught or killed."

"Or if you just fall asleep under a bridge somewhere. Or stop at a dairy and fall in love with the farmer's daughter. Or... "

"Right, right. Be quiet for a second, Okay? Here it is. On the ocean shore, somewhere around Stavanger—I'd bet it's at the German-held airfield at Sola—a new type of radio antenna and transmitter is being built. If you can find out where that is, what it is, and how it's to be used, that should lead you straight into the story."

"Oh, a spy story!" Rolf rubbed his hands together. "I love those."

"For key details, there's a certain young lady, well-known to the Oslo Gang. Her initials are HB. Try to get in touch with her. For your bona fides, explain how you met me. She knows all the essentials. In fact, she's the one who put me on this crazy mission."

~

Kristian shoved his thin packet of documents into the fillet knife sheath, tucked the tip down into his sock and boot. This time, instead of string, he secured it to his calf with windings of the gauze that Rolf had brought. The SS dagger posed more of a problem; he had no fast or easy way to create a good sheath for it. He decided to slice a strip of thick fabric off the bottom of one of the curtains and wrap it around the blade before thrusting it under his belt.

Making it down to the pier at the right moment was a larger riddle. Kristian decided to wait until after sunset but before the onset of curfew. He thrust himself out onto the streets—his cap tugged down and his collar turned up—amid the general hubbub of laborers plodding home at a workday's end. Just because that chaotic parade was commonplace didn't mean some men wouldn't get stopped at checkpoints. Still, the Germans had no way to deal with the whole human flood. The key for Kristian would be to keep well-away from any checkpoint without looking in the least like he sought to avoid it.

By the time Kristian reached the head of the pier, that part of the waterfront was largely deserted. He sat on a massive steel bollard and rested until he felt sure no one was looking his way, then ducked down beneath the pier and descended the mossy stonework of the seawall, finding his way by feel. The scummy beach he'd landed his kayak on months before was now almost completely awash. Light was fading fast, and the cold of night was sure to descend soon. He didn't want to get his feet wet, but it was unavoidable. Besides, his gumboots, foul-weather gear and woolens awaited, stashed in bags within the boat.

One absent item that he ardently wished he possessed was that red-filtered light from the Brits. It still was in his stash up in the Lagård cemetery; he'd not wanted to expose himself in public during the time it would take to dig it up. However, Rolf had given him a waterproof tin of matches, and he struck one now. In its flare, he saw the kayak still hanging from its berth up between the dock joists. He freed the lines from the cleats, let the kayak splash down, then drew it up parallel to the stonework.

It was complicated to get his old clothes off and the fresh clothes on while wading about in the low wave-wash. But he accomplished it, then stowed the canteen and the pouch with his food and medical supplies. He unclipped the stern line, sat down in the cockpit and tried to warm himself up again, mainly by shivering. He let himself drowse by leaning forward, folding his arms on the cockpit rim, and resting his forehead upon them. Periodically, he'd rouse himself and strike a match to check the time on his new watch.

A half-hour before midnight, he pushed off and let the bowline ravel through the pulley overhead. After it dropped free, he paddled ahead and gathered the line, coiling then lashing it to the deck beside his compass. He fastened the spraydeck over the cockpit then slid the boat out through the pier's long, dark corridor to emerge into the night.

He lifted the paddle from the water and took in his surroundings. Wind gusted from the northwest, not strongly, but it did hold a scent of rain. A loud *clang* vibrated briefly in the air as if a big thing had tipped over, perhaps a hoist of some kind. A man shouted. Next came a mysterious, continuous pounding that faded behind him as he made his way north. Working ports made lots of odd noises at all hours, he reminded himself. Nothing to be concerned about.

Kristian stroked ahead at a slow and measured pace. He assumed the *Ombo* planned to pick him up before he passed the string of tiny islands marking the outbound side of the shipping channel. He'd be harder for the *Ombo* to find if he was out in the broad and inky fjord waters beyond that point. Before he went completely by the last islet, he should stop and wait.

But he didn't need to. As the metallic pounding sound faded behind him, it was replaced by the *tonka-tonk* of a fishing boat's single-cylinder diesel. Kristian decided to take a risk. He dipped a hand inside his rubberized mackinaw, took out his matches and struck a bunch of four of them simultaneously. This improvised torch flared briefly, blew out. A white beam shot out from the bridge of the approaching vessel, scratched across the channel, lingered on him for a second, then went dark.

Kristian aligned himself with the vessel's course, paddling along at what he felt would be a proper match for its speed. His unladen kayak floated like a feather and felt easy to maneuver. The boat slowed as it came alongside. Kristian felt the kayak surf briefly on its bow wave, then slew and bump against the hull.

A crewman in a pea coat and a watch cap leaned over the rail. "Tell me your name," he said.

"Fiske," Kristian replied.

"We like that," the crewman said.

"Permission to come aboard?"

"Why not..."

Kristian opened the spraydeck, unlashed the bowline and flung the coil up to the man, who caught it, walked forward and took up slack before wrapping the line around a deck cleat. Kristian tossed his paddle over the rail, levered himself up, stood in the cockpit, grasped the boat's gunwale and drew himself up and over and onto the deck.

"Use the line to pull the bow of my kayak straight up, please," he told the crewman.

When he obliged, Kristian leaned over the rail on his stomach, grasped the cockpit rim in both hands, and together they wrestled the thing on board.

⌒

Up in the pilothouse, Kristian spoke with Mathias Hagen, the skipper. He was a short, bulky man with a bald head, a white beard and a calm, grave manner. The *Ombo* and Hagen were a vessel and a captain Kristian had not heard of before; he guessed they'd come down from an island, port or village further north.

"Perhaps not the best night we might have picked," Hagen said softly.

"How so?"

"Weather coming in."

"I did smell rain."

"Is your nose so keen? Can you sniff hail and sleet, then? I'd say, those would be most likely."

Kristian shrugged.

"We're told we're to drop you off beyond the Tungenes Fyr. After that, what's next for you?"

"I paddle away to a certain location."

"Your destination best not be a far one, then."

"Far enough."

"What if we lay to, somewhere in the fjord, and let this storm blow over?"

"How long?"

"Only a day or two."

Kristian shook his head. "Can't. My mission won't wait. Not to mention, my rendezvous."

"You're taking a big chance."

"I've taken them before."

Hagen looked at Kristian, lifted his eyebrows. He looked back at his lit binnacle and adjusted the wheel by a spoke.

"I spoke with a captain who made harbor an hour ago," he said. "The seas outside are rough and getting rougher."

Kristian said nothing.

"It makes me worry a bit, even about how we can launch you again."

"I've got an idea on that," Kristian said. "Just now, I found my kayak rides very easy beside the hull of your boat. What if you put me back in the water inside the fjord, where it's still calm. Run the bowline through my front grab loop, back to me in the cockpit. When the time comes, maybe even before Tungenes, I just drop the rope and I'm on my way. And then you are on yours."

Hagen shook his head slowly. "My way might be to just turn around and go back to the dock."

"Well, I can't do that."

Hagen looked at him again, and his gaze lingered. "Is there any other sort of help that we can offer you?"

"I don't think so."

"Food?"

"What've you got?"

"That shall keep? Easy for you to carry? Smoked cod. Even have tins of smoked salmon roe."

"I'll take it." Kristian smacked his lips. "Been far too long since I've tasted any of that good stuff."

"All right."

"And please, Mathias, don't worry about me. I grew up fishing around here. I know every rock and nook offshore. I can find a lee cove where I can rest if I need to."

"The son of Ragnar Thorsen? I'd guess that you might."

"Ah. You knew him."

"Mostly heard of him."

"Then you also know what happened? With the Germans?"

"Yes."

"How?"

"I was told. While I was being persuaded to do this. Otherwise, I would not have taken you on."

"I see." Kristian peered at him. "But you do understand, don't you, the fewer people who know any of this stuff, the better."

"I do."

⁓

The sweeping beam of the Tungenes Fyr came in view. Kristian and the *Ombo's* crew re-launched his kayak in the manner he'd devised. Kristian held the end of the rope in his fist as he sat back down in the cockpit. The hull of the *Ombo*, with the kayak coursing right alongside, had just begun to porpoise over deep-water swells rolling into the fjord, when a crewman leaned over the rail.

"The Germans! They're coming," he said.

Kristian looked up at him. "Where are they now?"

"Off to our port side. It's an E-boat. Heading out from Tungevika."

"All right," Kristian said. "Goodbye, then."

*"Må Herren og hans engler beskytte deg!"* the man cried. It meant, "May the Lord and His angels protect you."

"And for all of you aboard the *Ombo*, I offer that same blessing," Kristian said. Like his father Ragnar, Kristian didn't invest in what he saw as spiritual balderdash. Still, it felt like the proper reply. He released the line and it raveled out from the bow loop. He tilted the kayak away from the boat hull and pushed off with his paddle. A moment later, Hagen swung his wheel and turned the *Ombo* to port, widening the gap between them.

Kristian heard a siren's blare. Next, a searchlight blinked on, illuminating the fishing boat as a stark silhouette. He heard the *Ombo* throttle back and the white lines of its wake vanished. Hagen was showing the Germans he was ready to be stopped and searched, while also shielding Kristian and his kayak from their view.

Kristian couldn't predict how the torpedo boat might approach the *Ombo*, or how it might behave once it came alongside. He did know that he had to make full use of any second of grace. The paddle shaft bent in his hands as he drove his kayak further out into the night's borderless shadow.

A spatter of fat raindrops rattled against the black hood of his mac and the kayak's canvas deck. Kristian welcomed the sound. Now would be an excellent time for an approaching squall to drop a scrim of rain between him and the other boats. But the storm held off from performing this favor.

The E-boat swung out around the *Ombo*. Glancing back over one shoulder as he paddled away, Kristian could see it clearly: a low and sinister gray shape, more than thirty meters long, bristling with guns and helmeted sailors. Searchlights on the E-boat combed the waters all around the fishing boat. He guessed that during their approach the Germans wanted to first look for any contraband the *Ombo's* crew might've heaved overboard.

At this moment, his kayak was out past the area they were sweeping. But it might not remain so. He dropped into a trough between swells, then realized incoming seas also could work as a screen—if only intermittently. At the top of the next wave he took another glance back and saw that Hagen had taken a huge risk by turning on his own spotlight and focusing its beam on the bridge of the E-boat. The German skipper did not take kindly to this and ordered a gun to fire. There was a flash of orange, a sharp *bang*, a splash of white on waters abeam of the *Ombo*. Only a warning shot—for now. Hagen promptly switched off his own light. He'd already accomplished his purpose by distracting the Germans and granting Kristian more time to get away.

Glancing back over his shoulder one last time, Kristian saw the E-boat grapple itself to the *Ombo*. He hoped the vessel carried no item that would arouse suspicion, and that her captain and crew bore up well under German questioning. Most likely, they would. Norway's fishermen were notoriously recalcitrant in the face of any authority. An interrogator would have to be remarkably patient to extract anything beyond monosyllables and grunts.

~

Both inbound and outbound shipping tended to maintain tight routes past the Tungenes Fyr. Kristian swung wider to the north before pointing the kayak's bow out to the open sea.

Now he faced directly into winds from the incoming storm and felt their chill nibble on the bare skin of his face and hands. He cinched the hood of his mac tighter and leaned forward. In the flash of the lighthouse beam, he acquired a reading from the compass on his deck and took note of his angle against the incoming swell. The storm's overcast had blanketed all the stars. He'd have to make his way out to Alstein Rock by maintaining a steady angle of attack on the approaching waves.

As each dark mass rose to tower before him, the wind lessened. But as he crested each wave, the blast shot up in strength and lashed his face with spume. Then he slid forward into the blest lull of a trough again.

A spate of thick raindrops crashed down, this time with an impact that stung the backs of his hands. In the next flash of the lighthouse beam, he saw white pellets bounce off the deck of the kayak and pock the black surface of the sea. He realized it was hail. Mathias Hagen had predicted the weather correctly. Of course, an old skipper could easily do so. Kristian wondered if Hagen also could be right about the wisdom of turning around and postponing his voyage.

Within the hour, he found Hagen was right on that score, too.

*"Hitler knows that he will have to break us in this island or lose the war."*
—Winston Churchill, *speech to Parliament*

# CHAPTER 26

Alstein Rock offered no refuge.

Incoming seas, shoved and shredded by the rising gale, crashed against the weather side of the islet and exploded into geysers of epic size. Pale cascades of spume flooded over the dome of rock to run in boiling creeks off its lee side. Here, surging black waters leapt up to gather the run-off and then fell away, making steep troughs more than three meters deep.

Landing anywhere on Alstein's lee or even trying to shelter there would be impossible now without smashing the frame of his kayak to kindling.

It meant Kristian had no choice but to paddle onward. But onward, where? Back to port? Or should he go the other way, try to struggle south to Ragnar's boathouse on Ukjent Øy? Landing there might also be tough, though odds were better that the island's height and girth meant it would provide a safer shore. The big problem with getting to Ukjent was bad visibility. After the deluge of hail, a frigid rain had begun to fall. Strobing beams of the Tungenes Fyr were stifled by these thick-threaded curtains. He could no longer read his compass. Striking a match now to try to score even a brief glimpse was such a ludicrous thought that it made him grin.

Kristian would have to dead-reckon his course by relying only on maintaining a certain angle to the prevailing swell. The size and power of the storm meant that swell direction should stay constant, even if waves increased in size. But if they grew so tall that they began to break out in the open sea, the end would come for him quickly.

And if the rain became mushy sleet, as Hagen had predicted, he'd succumb to hypothermia. Then the end would arrive slowly. But either way, an end might easily come.

*What if I turn about this instant? I should be able to ride the wind and swells straight back into the mouth of the fjord. But then what? Can't stop at Tungenes, it's overrun with Germans. I might find another rock to bivouac on, but I'd be just as cold as I am right now. Colder, even, since I wouldn't gain any warmth from paddling. If I go all the way back to Stavanger, I'll land in a city where Gestapo men want to hunt me down like wolves chasing a moose calf!*

He continued to paddle as he deliberated. His kayak felt far more stable when he at least had one paddle blade thrust below the surface. Then he noticed he'd had already turned his craft, aiming it in a southerly direction. As if his decision had just been made by a power beyond his control... one that had not even consulted him.

*Oh well. Looks like I'm going for it. If I reach Ukjent Øy to make my rendezvous, the Brits get Helene's packet that much sooner. If I don't, they might get something like it eventually, thanks to Rolf's net of informants and his radio. Yet think of all the deaths, meanwhile. Think of the rage the Germans will feel if Brits do manage to frustrate their bombing runs. All I'm gambling on tonight is myself. And I believe I can make it. Only a dozen kilometers of open sea. How bad could it be?*

Much worse than he ever imagined.

Selecting a proper course meant that the swell and the wind should both be quartering on his stern. And this meant his actual course was subject to constant adjustments, as he slid down the wave faces at an angle, wallowed in the troughs, then shot up again onto each towering summit. At the wave crests, potent gusts batted his light kayak around like a shuttlecock. To arrive anywhere near his goal, he had to mentally add up each writhing plunge his kayak performed, then calculate a route that averaged the squiggles—all of them varying in angle, length and speed.

A wildly gyrating compass couldn't help, even if he'd been able to see it. He'd need to trust fully to intuition. Meanwhile, the waves jacked ever higher as the wind's pitch rose to a banshee shriek.

The most terrifying moment of Kristian's voyage came as a big wave went under him and he slid back down into an abysmal trough. He heard or felt a shift in the overall tumult that made him look back over his shoulder and up at a pale wave crest already beginning to fling a parapet of wind-torn spray out over his head. Spurred by fear and by instinct, he paddled furiously, as if he could somehow claw his way back again onto the rear of the wave he saw disappear into misty darkness ahead of him. But it was the wave behind that now took control of his fate. His kayak rose relentlessly up the black wall of the swell face and the fearsome drop before him steepened. He swung the paddle shaft vigorously back and forth, chopping away at the water as though his life depended on it—which he believed it did. It seemed certain the bow would plunge into the black water and the stern be tossed around over his head by the curl at the top of the wave, making him cartwheel to his doom. But at the last instant, his kayak's entire hull seemed to bounce up and break free of the wave, skittering down its face at an astonishing velocity. Then foam from the tumbling crest bunched around the stern and the cockpit, almost swallowing his body up within its churning mass.

Next the kayak floated up into the cloud of roiling pile like a bubble, and the bulk of the wave swept on beneath him. He dropped down into the next trough, looked with terror at the next oncoming swell, but realized it was smaller than the one he'd just survived. He released a breath in a gasp of relief, almost like the exhale of a breaching whale. After that sea swept past, he began stroking once more along on a southerly course.

*A teacher once told us a quote from a philosopher, he said it was his favorite one. 'That which does not kill you, lets you live.' From some German guy. Well, I guess it went something like that…*

A tiny spark of light flashed off his port bow. It pulsated. Slowly. Like the heart of an angel, wrapped in clouds, dozing away in the very center of the storm, as only an unearthly sprite could.

But then he realized it was a thing altogether earthly, another lighthouse—Flatholmen Fyr. Never in his life had he felt more relief. *My thanks to those who've kept that lighthouse working. Even if—and all the devils in Hell can smite me for this—they happen to be Germans.*

He knew now that he'd make it to Ukjent Øy. There'd be a huge amount of surge at the entry to the inlet where the boathouse stood. He'd have to get his timing exactly right to make it through the chaos of currents. But it wasn't a problem on the scale of surviving the giant comber or his other puzzle on this stormy night: simply finding the blasted place!

He paused just off the rumpled lee shore of Ukjent Øy, watching waves sweep around the island and collide in fans of spray at the inlet's mouth. He waited until these collisions subsided in a brief lull, then stroked furiously toward the rocky slot, heaving a sigh when he passed its entrance. Once within the cove, black water bounced the kayak up and down while refracting wavelets slapped at it from both sides. But now Kristian could see that he was safe. For the moment, anyway.

Near the glistening, wet stone heap of the boathouse, he heeled the kayak over, braced his paddle against the sloping shore, and clambered out. He pinned the kayak to shore by inserting his paddle blade back into the cockpit and pulling hard against its rim. Then, he was able to take a deep breath as he watched gusts of rain, pallid with swatches of ocean spray, whisk overhead like covens of flying specters.

A burst of icy sleet whipped through the air. It sent a wave of cold through his rubberized weather gear, jabbed through his already damp woolens. Kristian saw then that danger was far from over. He had to take shelter, and quick. He pulled out his paddle, gripped the cockpit rim, dragged his kayak out of the water and hauled it up the rocky slope.

He found the key under the slab of slate, unlocked the oaken door and shoved it open against the wind. He dragged the kayak inside and found it was a half-meter too long for the space. *All right. Who cares if that door stays open? I'm still far better off in here than being out in the gale.*

He took the tin of matches from an inside pocket of his mac. He struck one and in its brief, sputtering light, saw a flat place on the highest stacks of boxes and barrels. He went there, stretched himself out as best he could, thrust his folded hands under one cheek and plunged into nearly comatose slumber.

~

He awoke in a world gone gray. Through the open door, he watched a leaden sky drop fusillades of sleet into a leaden sea. Gale-force winds ripped the crests off swells and sent spray swirling off into the gloaming. The end of his kayak bounced and jittered against the door of the boathouse. He realized it was this banging that had awakened him—not the wind's treble shriek.

He was not as cold as he'd been on that April morning, months ago, when a British corvette had plucked him from a sinking rowboat out on the North Sea. But it felt close. His oilskins had stiffened as if they'd been dipped in iron. His brain seemed turgid and his muscles barely twitched in response to commands.

*I need to do something—and it must be done immediately.*

He rolled himself off his impromptu sleeping ledge and found himself only able to stand in an apelike crouch. He swept his gaze over the gear in the shack and struggled to devise a plan. Then it came to him: he picked up a bucket and stumbled with it to the upper end of the boathouse, where the floor narrowed to a wedge of sand between a pair of rock outcrops. As he'd hoped, the sand here was still dry. He scooped it into the bucket until it was half full, then went back to a drum of diesel fuel that had been set up with a hand pump. He squirted fuel into his bucket of sand, then set it down on the floor. He plucked a match out of the tin and scratched it on the striker patch inside the cover. When it flared, he dropped it into the bucket.

Yellow flames and stinking fumes danced up from the top of the sand. He put his pale, wrinkled hands out over the heat. When the stiffness had melted out of his fingers and he could flex them, he opened the front of his rubber slicker and sighed as he felt vital warmth seep in through his layers of damp wool.

*"There is no bad weather, only bad clothing."* One of Ragnar's beloved adages came to him, making him grin. It had been one of Kari's favorite sayings, too. She cited it when she presented them with a cozy item she'd made—a knitted scarf or a cap, or a hand-loomed wadmal shirt. This Brit gear wasn't bad. It had seen him through a hazardous voyage and a freezing night. Of course, his wool fishing sweater was of Norwegian design and Kari's making, which had certainly helped. It was the garment that helped him survive the North Sea.

The diesel fuel in the boathouse might last him a week. Food and water? Enough for a few days. Come to think of it, he was ravenous. He fetched Rolf's canteen from the boat's stowage compartment. He chose to munch on the smoked cod Hagen had given him. The fish bestowed a true taste of home and of far happier days, a time when his boyhood realm had felt safe, predictable and secure.

The face of Kari, broad and open and hearty, seemed to arise before him. He recalled a day when Ragnar had goaded her, quoting from a Lutheran manual for a holy married life that Otto had bestowed as an anniversary gift.

"Can you believe it? We can have an even more joyous home!" Ragnar proclaimed. "A wondrous method, revealed by men with knowledge of the ways of heaven."

He quoted from Paul's epistle, 'Wives should be subordinate to their husbands as to the Lord. For the husband is head of his wife just as Christ is head of the church.'"

Kari reddened. She shook her fist in Ragnar's face. "The Good Lord never meant that to apply to Norwegian women!"

Ragnar guffawed and the three of them collapsed in laughter. The idea of Kari ever gently submitting to anyone else's commands, at any time for any reason, well, the very idea was preposterous.

Kristian heard a harsh, strangled cry. A seabird must have been hurled by the storm against a wall of the boathouse. Then he realized it had come from him. Another sob wrenched itself loose, convulsing his chest and tearing at his throat. He buried his face in his hands and gave himself over to grief. Once unleashed, it seemed it would never stop.

When the fury of his weeping subsided on its own—not due to any check he'd been able to apply—the fire in the bucket had gone out and he was surrounded by frigid air once more. Then the only sounds were the winds that tore at the rock walls and a slap of rain against the slate roof.

"No," Kristian croaked. "No."

No to the death and disappearance of what had been the invulnerable Ragnar. No to Otto for his weakness and willingness to place ideology above family and blood. No to the Nazis tightening their malignant fist around Kari. No to their haughty subjugation of Norway and their attempt to vanquish and silence the king. No to their attack on the innocent and their assault upon all of Europe and their massive effort to impose a maniac's will upon an entire world. Just, NO!

He raised his head, got to his feet and staggered to the door.

*I can't let myself feel so much. It's debilitating. It's dangerous. Maybe when you push things down hard for a long while, this is how they burst free. Is that it? A man must either dam up his feelings entirely, or drown in them?*

He expected to see ice and snow heaped around the rocky inlet, but the tempest had warmed and now seemed to be in retreat. All the rime ice on the ground was trickling into the sea. The ocean still humped and seethed against the shore, but with far less violence than when Kristian had arrived. He pulled back his sleeve to peer at the Rolex. Seven hours to go until sunset.

*No vessel will show for a rendezvous, he decided. Not today. Not even a sub. If there's a submarine out there, for safety's sake it will lurk as deep as it can go. Maybe tomorrow. Okay, make a plan. Be methodical. Prepare for both what might happen and what might not. What would Ragnar advise?* He turned around. *Load up your spare Webley and the Sten gun, to be ready for unwanted guests. Make a new fire in your diesel stove. After you're warm, take off your gum boots and lower layers, check and make sure you still have Helene's packet, redo those bandages on your knees. Eat more food, maybe the leftovers from that lunch Hermann brought you.*

*Was that only three days ago? It feels more like a month!*

*"This is a strange Christmas Eve. Almost the whole world is locked in deadly struggle, and with the most terrible weapons which science can devise the nations advance upon each other."*
—Winston Churchill, *speech in the United States.*

# CHAPTER 27

Kristian's next day on Ukjent Øy was also cold and overcast. But the winds had dropped to a fitful breeze, and cloud cover was only a net of cirrus veiling a sapphire sky.

Steady use of the improvised stove meant he'd been able to dry all his clothing. He slept in relative comfort and awoke refreshed. After creating a meal from his cache of leftovers, he sorted through his gear—and made an annoying discovery. The banging of the kayak against the door had a consequence worse than the noise. All that jostling had scrubbed a hole through the canvas fabric where it stretched over the boat's frame.

*Should've considered that,* he berated himself, *as he gazed at the long tear. Should've done something to prevent it.* To come up with a fix now was a real head-scratcher.

Eventually he used the SS dagger to cut away the cuff of his mac and use it for a patch. A tube of bearing grease supplied a tacky substance to make it adhere over the hole. *So far, so good.* But the sole solution he could devise to hold it in place was to use the last of Rolf's gauze to wrap a belt about the whole hull. His knees would have to go without a changed dressing. The next problem was keeping that gauze in place. He sought to address it by wrapping several loops of rope atop the gauze and cinching it as tight as he could.

*Ugly job,* he thought, as he assessed his handiwork. *And drag from that rope will scrub off speed. But at least I won't have to bob around on the water for very long when my transportation arrives. I hope.*

He decided to leave the boathouse and hike around the island. He didn't know if it would be good or bad for his achy knees, but he had to get his blood moving. He brought the revolver and the Sten gun. Ukjent Øy looked much as he remembered it, a heap of eroded rock garlanded with mangled brush in those spots where—against long odds—a few inches of soil had managed to accumulate. Those bushes in turn had accumulated driftwood, bits of lumber, glass net floats and other litter. Kristian saw not one item of interest.

Until he looked out to sea.

The sky's milky hue bleached the surface of the water and the horizon had grown difficult to discern. But out in the pale distance, a dark speck seemed to be afloat. And moving. Toward the island.

Kristian sat down in the lee of a rocky ridge and watched the dot. No doubt about it, something was heading his way. *German patrol boat? Or... what?* He had to watch and wait. Identification had to happen before he could respond. Meanwhile, he should not move or otherwise draw any attention to himself. He crossed his legs and leaned back against the rock.

He saw the vessel was a fishing boat. It had outriggers deployed and multiple lines trailing. Its hull colors were pure white and pearl gray, blending with the day's major shades. Its course suggested that the skipper intended to pass close by the island, perhaps circle it. That would be standard fishing procedure. Islets like Ukjent Øy often hosted schools of game fish near their shores.

He still detected something odd about the vessel. Then it registered: the boat's engine emitted a steady hum rather than the resonant *"tonk"* noise of a typical fishing boat.

The boat passed from his sight, moving around the west shore of the island.

A sudden thought jolted him. *If they do circle, if they have binoculars, if they know where to look or are just damned lucky, they might see the boathouse. With its door open! They won't identify the kayak, only see its stern. But they might be curious about why that structure looks unlocked. Perhaps they'll even guess someone is here.*

Kristian jumped up and—ignoring pain in his knees—jogged as well as he could back toward the boathouse. He intended to drag out his kayak, hide it next to a wall and slam the door shut.

He was too late. The boat lay hove to off the mouth of the inlet, rocking gently in the low swells. He could see crewmen moving about on its decks, facing in his direction.

*Might be friendly to me. Might not. Could be a boatload of collaborators though, right? Quislings.* The answer to this question could be crucial.

He fingered the Sten gun. The thing could throw a lot of lead quite fast, but its accuracy was terrible past twenty meters.

Out on the vessel, now drifting a bit abeam to the inlet's entry, he saw a crewman unfurl a roll of fabric and let it drape off the side of the hull. It displayed a pattern, a blue cross rimmed by white on a red field—the Norwegian battle ensign. Next to it the crewman unrolled another oblong of patterned cloth. Which revealed the Brits' Union Jack.

Kristian's lips split in a grin. Elation lit every nerve between the soles of his feet and the crown of his head. He drew his Webley, pointed it at the sky and fired three jubilant rounds to reply.

****

*"Gwynn."*

As Kristian paddled his kayak up to the fishing vessel, he saw the boat's name painted in blocky gray letters on her flank. A handful of men stood on the rear deck, bundled up in peacoats, hands thrust into their pockets. He paused mid-stroke, let the kayak glide nearer.

"Ahoy, *Gwynn!*" he called out. "What brings you out to Ukjent Øy? What sort of luck have you had?"

"Not so much," a crewman responded. "With fish, anyway."

"What else would you want?"

"A certain person," said a man leaning against the deckhouse.

"Oh well, I happen to be a person. My name is Fiske."

"Sounds about right," the man said, as he came forward. He wore an ordinary wool coat, like the others, but his pale gray eyes gleamed under the visor of an officer's cap.

"May I catch a ride to England with you?" Kristian asked.

"I suppose. Get your tail over here so we can haul that odd little craft of yours aboard. Then we'll scoot off."

"So, you're in a hurry? Good, because I might be too."

"We're eight kilometers from the Nazi airfield at Sola. The weather's turning good enough for *Luftwaffe* planes to fly. What do you think?"

"I'd prefer not to see them."

"Well, I agree."

Kristian slid up beside the *Gwynn's* hull. Crewmen climbed the gunwale, put their boots on the splash rail, bent to reave ropes through the grab loops. Kristian loosened his spraydeck, stood up in his cockpit, then clambered aboard. The boat was hauled up behind him.

"Thanks," Kristian said. "Delighted to meet you all."

The man wearing the officer's cap said, "You're Fiske, hm? A distant relation of Ragnar Thorsen. Or so I hear."

"Not very distant," Kristian said.

"Before we set out, I got told a few stories about you. I am Andreas Johannessen." He shook Kristian's hand. His calloused fingers offered a firm grip.

"You're the skipper?"

"Only until these mutinous bastards throw me out of the wheelhouse and elect someone more capable."

The men around him grinned.

"Hey, shall we go? Or just drift here till we can make positive ID on approaching German aircraft?"

Everyone on deck shook their heads. The crewmen scattered to attend to chores. Kristian applied himself to removing bags from the kayak, then yanking pins and taking the frame down until the boat's canvas covering sagged to the point that it looked like a big, limp sack. As he worked, the vessel's engine noise rose to a vigorous hum. Tarred deck planks began to vibrate under his feet. He glanced at the water and the boat's wake and realized they were moving about twice as fast as a typical fishing boat.

He carried his packs up to the wheelhouse and piled them in a corner.

"Not there," Andreas said. "Take a berth ahead of the forward hold."

"All right," Kristian responded. "Thanks."

"We don't charge much for a bed, not for a single crossing. Plus, we'll give you a Resistance fighter's discount."

Kristian smiled. He looked the skipper over, trying to read the man from his appearance. Johannessen was of average height and build. He dressed like a crewman, except for that cap. But far from conferring status, that shabby article appeared to have been dragged behind a horse cart for about a week. Johannessen's pelt of hair was thick and glossy and black. He had weathered facial skin, a strong jaw, a wide mouth with a lower lip seamed by scar tissue, and a broken nose with a flattened bridge. He seemed to be mild enough in manner, yet he looked like a barroom brawler. Kristian reckoned him to be in his early thirties.

"Surprised to see you this morning. Since the plan was to make a rendezvous at sunset," Kristian said.

"I chose to sail over last night, chasing hard on the storm's heels," Andreas explained. "A calculated risk. Yet it had certain advantages."

"Which you calculated, how? Just curious."

Andreas eyed him. "I'd been informed, Fiske, you bear crucial intelligence that must reach the Brits as soon as possible. One factor. Also, some important gents had concerns about your well-being. Now that I've met you, can't imagine why."

"Me either," Kristian said. He shrugged. "No accounting for taste, right?"

"Right."

They grinned at each other.

"Please excuse me for a moment," Kristian said.

He stepped out of the wheelhouse, shaded his eyes with one hand, and carefully scanned the skies astern. But nothing seemed to be flying anywhere along the indistinct horizon, not even a seabird. He glanced down at the boat's churning, elongating V of wake. He came back in and stood beside Andreas.

"What's *Gwynn's* power?" Kristian asked.

"A new kind of six-cylinder diesel," Andreas said. "She can do eleven knots, if I coax her. Gives us an extra bit of safety from air and sea patrols, since we can make ourselves scarce at a brisker pace. And we have another trick." He poked his chin toward the bow. "See those fuel barrels on deck? When you go forward, ask a crew member to show you what's in them."

Kristian wondered what the barrels might contain that offered protection of any sort from the *Luftwaffe*. He came up empty.

"My calculation also touched on Sola." Andreas glanced at him. "The *Luftwaffe* had to prepare for the storm by getting planes into hangars or lashed down. Now they'd probably like some big puddles on their landing strip to dry. But they'll put patrol planes up just as soon as they can."

Kristian nodded.

"And speaking of that storm," Andreas asked, "when did you get to Ukjent Øy? Did you paddle through the shit?"

"Yes."

"How was it?"

"Cold. Dark."

His response won a slight nod. Andreas seemed to be a fan of understatement.

"And it was a bit rough."

"Must not have been your first voyage."

"No. Nor my second. That helped."

"And you used such an itty-bitty boat."

"Yes. But a well-made one."

"*Gwynn* must seem almost like the Queen Mary, by comparison."

"No, the Titanic! Wait, scratch that. Let's go with the Mary."

The conversation paused for a second of mutual amusement.

"Who sent you to get me? SIS, in the form of Section D? Or this other group I've heard of, the SOE?"

"Both," Andreas said. "Either. Neither. We're new. Just up on our wobbly legs like a foal. We call ourselves, 'Norwegian Independent Company Number One.' Based in Scotland. And yes, we get some direction from Special Operations Executive. Might take on a task or two for the SIS. But only if they ask politely. As they did in your case."

"Huh."

*Norisén*, that's what we want to call ourselves. Shorthand for NOR-I-C-1."

"Is this the group I've heard rumors of? You hope to put it under control of our king, Norway's government-in-exile?"

Andreas' scarred lips curved. "More the other way 'round. The King's navy brass would love to slap us into harness. We object. See, that means taking orders from prigs who demand triplicate reports and other rigmarole. We'd prefer not! Whereas, SOE chiefs are complete rogues. No saluting, if you catch my drift. A man's got elbow room to manage his affairs. That's more our style. We're mostly fishermen, you see."

"Yes. That sounds right," Kristian said. "Guess I'll go get myself settled, then."

Andreas nodded, checked his course on the binnacle, and nudged the throttle ahead.

~

Kristian made his way forward, went down the companionway. He located an unused bunk up in the very eyes of the *Gwynn*, unrolled its thin mattress, spread out blankets and arranged his dunnage. On his way out, he met a crewman.

"Hey, what's in those barrels?" He pointed to the deck over his head.

"Come on, I'll show you."

They went back on deck. The large metal barrels looked in every way like they could be used for fuel storage—except for welded flanges that bolted them down to the deck, and a strange pedal that projected from one side. At the first barrel, the crewman unlatched a ring that attached the top cover, pulled it off and handed it to Kristian.

"Hold this," he said.

Then he stomped on the pedal. Kristian heard the click of a release lever, and then was impressed when he saw a pair of light machine guns swing up out of the barrel on a spring-loaded chassis. The guns ended up pointing into the sky at an excellent angle to respond to an aerial attack.

"Wow!"

"Lewis guns," the crewman said. "Each pan magazine holds nearly a hundred rounds of British .303 caliber. Each gun can fire at a rate of five hundred rounds a minute. Of course, you need to change out the ammunition pans, which slows that down."

"I *like* these!" Kristian exclaimed. He vented a sigh. "Wish my old boat could've had 'em." He paused. "Can you show me how they work, please?"

∼

Day wore into dusk as the *Gwynn* steadily pared away at the span of nautical miles between Norway and Scotland. Kristian hung out with the crew in the boat's galley. A question of what to make for dinner came up. Eager to contribute, Kristian told them a fresh tin of smoked salmon roe was in his packs. A wave of enthusiasm greeted his announcement. Whereupon, omelets garnished with salmon roe were chosen as their supper's centerpiece.

"We've a basket of eggs from beautiful, speckled Scottish hens," one crewman crowed. "Perfect way to use them up!"

The feast grew more boisterous after Andreas entered to brandish a bottle of *Seksti*—sixty-percent grain alcohol. Most fishing boats stashed a bottle of firewater to provide the crew with a rewarding tipple after a hard day. This potent distillate was usually locked in a cupboard to which only the captain held the key. To buffer its effect and improve palatability, it would be mixed with other potables, from water to syrup drained from cans of fruit.

But on this night the bottle was left alone out on the table, and its level dropped fast. Kristian was encouraged to sample its strengths undiluted. The third time they challenged him, he succumbed. It felt like swallowing liquid fire. The clear hooch scorched its way down his throat, sizzled a moment in his stomach, then seemed to thrust vapors into his arteries that snaked up to fog his brain.

Woozy, Kristian begged off another round and headed forward to his bunk. He pulled off his weather gear and gumboots, kept his woolens on, stretched out, tugged a blanket over himself and slept the sleep of the dead.

He awoke early to a morning gauzed by low mist. Without bothering to pull on his boots, Kristian padded up to the wheelhouse to query the crewman standing watch about how to operate the hot shower in the deckhouse bathroom. Satisfied that he grasped the procedure, he entered the white steel cubicle, stripped, and hung his clothes on the available hooks. He unwrapped the SS dagger and used it to cut away the bandages around his knees. The gauze was soggy, brown with old blood and suppurating fluids. His knees hadn't improved after a day without care, if anything, they looked much worse. *Well, I guess there'll be a doctor in England willing to entertain himself by taking a look at me.*

The final item to drape on a hook was the sheath, holding its precious green packet of documents. Kristian stroked it once with his fingertips.

"Soon, you'll go where you need to be," he told the packet, "and do what you're supposed to do. Your mission of mercy is nearly done." He heaved a sigh of satisfaction. Bringing Helene's intelligence this far had been an ordeal. Now both he and it were nearly home free.

He got the hot water to stream—well, dribble was a better verb—out of the nozzle and exposed himself to its insufficient caress. After wetting himself all over, he reached for a cake of soap on a tin holder.

That was when he heard a roar of aircraft engines as a plane flew low overhead to buzz the *Gwynn*. Kristian did not mull over what he ought to do about that. Zero thinking was involved. No time was wasted, either. He banged open the door to the cubicle, sprinted from the deckhouse and ran naked across the boat's foredeck to the barrels concealing the machine guns. He yanked the locking ring open, tossed the cover aside and stomped on the release lever.

The long black Lewis guns slid smoothly up and tilted into firing position. He snapped back charging handles to fill both their chambers with an initial round then clasped his hands around the grips. He was about to stuff his fingers in the trigger guards and put his eyes to the sights when he got tackled by a crewman.

"*Nei! Nei!*" he shouted, "*Det er Engelsk!*" Meaning, no, no, it's English.

A second crewman appeared, drawn by the commotion. He knelt and pushed Kristian's shoulders down to make sure he remained prone on the deck. Then Andreas arrived, still buttoning his coat, a hard look on his face.

"Turn him over," Andreas said.

Kristian found himself staring up at a trio of faces that held expressions of consternation, fear, and worry. They were trying to assess exactly how crazed he might be at this moment, and what they ought to do about it. He sucked a breath down to the bottom of his lungs and struggled for composure. He had to calm his pounding heart and whirling brain, then reassure his shipmates.

Meanwhile, the aircraft circled low to make another pass.

"Stow those guns away," Andreas ordered. "And be snappy about it."

A crewman jumped to comply.

Andreas looked out at the plane, pointed a finger at it. "It's a Spitfire," he said. "From Coastal Command."

"Ah yes, a friendly," Kristian said. "I see that now."

"We're near to making port at Peterhead," Andreas told him. "He's only checking us out. Still, if you'd shot, he would've fired back at us. It would not have ended well, I think."

"Sorry," Kristian said. He hesitated. "I…"

"I know." Andreas cut him off. The gray eyes drilled into his. Andreas extended a hand. "Let's get you back on your feet."

The skipper and the first crewman helped him up.

"Must say, I've been warned that you could be a bit of a hothead, Fiske," Andreas said. "Are you a hothead?"

"Sometimes," Kristian admitted. He put a hand on his face, above his eyebrows. "But I seem to be cooling off now."

"Good. Let's get you back inside and dressed. And… what's happened to your knees, there?"

"Oh, nothing. Too much praying, maybe."

"Uh-huh. Well, let us know the next time you do it. Perhaps we can join you. We did get a little practice, a couple of seconds ago."

*"To establish necessary conditions for a final conquest of England,
I intend to intensify both air and sea warfare against the English homeland."*
—Hitler, *Directive #17*

# CHAPTER 28

White bodies lay atop mounds of ash and debris that almost filled the urban street from curb to curb.

The sight filled Kristian with revulsion. Although these bodies weren't human, they greatly resembled humans. The naked shapes, some missing heads, others limbs, many with their torsos ripped in half, were mannequins that had been flung out through the lower floor windows of a large department store.

Its roof had been pierced by a *Sprengbombe-Cylindrisch*—a 250 kilogram bomb designed to penetrate deeply into structures before detonation.

Flying high above a road between Portsmouth and London, the crew on a *Luftwaffe* DO-17 mistook the broad roof of Booker Mercantile Emporium for a British military warehouse. Nettled by antiaircraft fire from below and harassed by Hurricanes and Spitfires above, starting to feel a strong urge to flee back across the Channel, the German crew had rushed the job and dropped their cargo of death before really identifying the recipient.

Precision bombing was a chimera, anyhow. Early on in this war, both Axis powers and the Allies piously boasted that they'd avoid civilian casualties by focusing all raids on military targets. The noble strategy did not endure beyond a spate of self-congratulatory newsreels. It soon grew obvious on rubble-strewn streets of British and European cities that the policy would be honored mainly in the breach.

A *Guteklasse* 1 SC-250 bomb, designed to penetrate targets deeply before exploding, had smashed through the roof of Booker Mercantile, plummeted through a floor of men's suits, accessories, shoes and toiletries, then shot past a floor of dresses, blouses, skirts and lacy unmentionables and penetrated a floor crowded with Christmas decorations and suggested gifts to finally slam into a basement where it detonated. The blast hurled a huge bolus of materials up and out that included all the mannequins in the display windows on the first floor, as well as retired older mannequins that had been stacked up in a storage closet between the windows.

The ensuing spectacle was made especially disquieting by the odd paleness of the stiffened bodies, and the heedless way victims of a false massacre had been flung so casually onto moraines of rubble.

But the Home Guard crews and Auxiliary firemen with their shovels didn't have much time to spare between raids, nowadays. Roads had to be cleared fast so real citizen casualties could be borne on stretchers, packed into ambulances, whisked off to hospital.

So the mannequins had been cast aside in a way that would initially shock any observer who happened upon them. Then might come a moment of relaxation, upon realizing they were only facsimiles. Still, for the prescient, a moment of dread might well tread on the heels of relief. In a way, those pale stiff forms foretold the grotesques heaps of real human bodies that this war would soon harvest and discard as it roared along on its wanton way. Such a sight would grow much more common than most people could imagine in the autumn of 1940. Except, of course, for aging veterans who'd emerged from the trenches a score of years earlier. It was the sort of scene they'd struggled to forget. Something they'd hoped to never see again. However, it was growing clearer by the day that their prior "War to End All Wars" actually had not achieved anything resembling such a result.

"Gives a bloke a bit of a start, yeah?" said the redcap driving Kristian to a meeting with Cyclops in London. "That creep-show sure is a jolt. When I first came through here on my way to collect you, I mean."

He sharply twisted the wheel of their sedan to swing it around a bomb crater in the center of the pavement, their car's tires complaining loudly. An air warden just emerging from the intact bottom floor of a largely flattened apartment building heard the screech, pushed his white helmet back with a thumb and gave them a severe look. Were these lads being playful? At such a doleful time? At minimum, they wasted the rubber on their auto's tires, an extravagance in wartime.

"Makes a man think, 'cor, that's how it is when your number comes up?" the redcap driver said. "Right, then! Out with you, bugger. Onto the tosh pile.'"

Kristian appraised him. The soldier, a strapping, freckled, strawberry redhead, might well have been older than Kristian, yet he seemed in many respects a great deal younger. To reply, Kristian offered just a nod of agreement.

"Almost every night, the Jerries have been at us. Since August!" The driver shook his head. "When shall it ever bloody end, mate?"

"In truth? It's something I'm here to see about," Kristian said.

"Brilliant. Well, I'm chuffed to give you a leg up, then."

∼

Kristian stared out the car window at bomb-gnawed suburbs of London.

He thought back to his arrival in Scotland. By the time he'd limped ashore in Peterhead, his shipmates had put considerable effort into helping him get cleaned up and have his appearance and gear sorted out. They popped open their medical kit to put fresh bandages on both of his festering knees. Unfortunately, they'd initiated the treatment with a tooth-grinding application of alcohol from the bottle of *Seksti*. They smeared on the last of Rolf's silver gel, then tied everything up nice and tidy with strips torn out of a boiled bedsheet. Their bandaging looked good, but Kristian could see that his medical condition wasn't on the upswing.

The SIS officer who called himself "Tom" met Kristian on the quay where the Gwynn had tied up. He was the short, plump, affable, sandy-haired gent Kristian had met during his imprisonment in London at Latchmere House. The same man who'd tried to jolly Kristian up and put him off his guard before taking him up to a parlor to face his final test from Greta.

Kristian shook his head, grinned. Not because he felt happy to see Tom, but because Tom reminded him of her, and his memories of Greta always made him smile.

Still, he felt disappointed that the Brits had managed to muster only a one-person welcoming party. He thought the intelligence he carried would be seen as having a much grander import. He'd imagined being met by a red-capped crew of military police, then whisked off from the waterfront in a convoy, led by a motorcycle equipped with a siren.

Tom took him on a brief walk. He massaged Kristian with a few pleasantries, mystified him with empty chitchat as he led him up Jamaica Street from Harbor to Rose. Tom guided him into the private back room of a pub called The Boar & Thistle. They sat on benches to either side of a plank table and put in an order for fish-and-chips and pints of draft ale.

He finally assumed a businesslike air. "Very well then, Fiske," Tom said. "What've you got for us?"

Kristian cleared his throat. He said, "I wish to give my material directly to the Cyclops."

"Oh, bother. Unnecessary! Lay it out for me, man, and I'll pass the findings on. Through proper channels. Don't worry, I'll see you get full credit."

Incautiously, Tom over-emphasized the last two words. That gave Kristian greater pause, while he puzzled out the man's game. He decided that Tom's performance did underscore the value of the packet he carried. Tom wanted to be the clever operative who handled that intelligence, edited and interpreted it. So that he could give it to the SIS brass with a flourish. Boost his own status.

"No." Kristian shook his head. "The Cyclops. To him, only."

Tom narrowed his eyes, even while he continued to grin.

"Thought you didn't care much for the Cyclops," he said.

"I don't. However, I trust him."

"What now, you don't trust *me*?" Tom spread his hands palms up, and chuckled. He sought to come across as an effusive, charming, guileless 'Tommy'—everyone's pal.

"No," Kristian said gravely. "Not a single bit."

He watched Tom's cheeks flare with what could've been embarrassment but was most likely anger.

"Besides," Kristian continued. "You must admit I have a right to choose, to do it in my own way. Something I've earned."

"Dear me!" Tom raised his eyebrows. "Now, what's that mean?"

Kristian thought, *I just told him what I meant.* He guessed he had to make his point more forcefully. He'd swaddled the SS dagger in cloth again, including its hilt, before thrusting it under his belt. He pulled the dagger out, held an end of the cloth and let the wrapping unwind until the knife fell free and thumped on the table. It spun for a moment, glittered in the dim light. And it produced the desired effect. Tom's eyes bugged out as he took in the silver eagle clutching a swastika on its ebony grip, the German inscription on its blade.

"I took this dagger from an SS officer, then I killed him with it," Kristian said. "So, that's what I mean. About earning. See?"

Tom leaned back, drummed fingers of both hands on the tabletop. His eyelids fluttered while he contemplated the situation. Clearly, Kristian was not persuadable. Any attempt to dominate him and harvest the intelligence would backfire. A struggle over the packet—even if Tom used proxies— would first be tasty gossip and next depressingly common knowledge within Britain's clandestine services. Which might ruin his reputation and his career.

The pub lunch was delivered to the table and both men consumed it in a hostile silence.

The upshot of the debate was that Kristian and his packet got bundled aboard a twin-engine Airspeed AS.10 Oxford ambulance unit, scheduled to fly south and land at an airfield near Portsmouth before noon.

~

Now, Kristian was being chauffeured onward through city blocks that grew more and more horrifically damaged as the car neared the heart of London. There stood an apartment building with a wall gone as if a giant dollhouse had been whacked open with an ax. Its bedsteads, wardrobes, cupboards, mirrors and family photos still clung to such walls and floors as remained intact. Here was a blast crater with the hulk of a double-decker bus protruding from it like a swizzle-stick thrust into a giant's cocktail glass.

An old man who looked like he might be wearing three sets of clothes piled on top of each other slowly picked through debris, adding items to an improvised pack made from a blanket with its corners knotted together. A dejected woman sat on a mound of rubble drinking something from a china cup. Two air wardens in white helmets and blue coveralls emerged from a basement carrying a blanket-draped body on a stretcher.

The air seeping into the car reeked of smoke, petrol fumes, cordite and rot. Kristian did not wish to speculate on precisely what might be rotting. He began to breathe through his mouth.

"Grand that you landed when you did, mate," the soldier said. "We've a few hours left before today's first wave. Jerries prefer to drop by late afternoon-ish y'know, get some fires going. Then your next waves have those bright spots to aim at as they fly on through the night."

His driver brought him in past Wandsworth Common—a sprawling green where it appeared some Londoners had elected to camp out, rather than risk staying in buildings. They took a right on a small street called Fitzhugh Grove and then were obliged to halt at a control point in front of the Royal Victoria Patriotic Building—an ornate edifice built eighty years earlier as a school for girls orphaned by the Crimean War.

They stopped at a pipe gate. A soldier approached the car to demand the driver's military ID. He scanned it with care, handed it back, and pointed at Kristian. "Who's he?"

"I'm Fiske," Kristian said.

"Who?!" the soldier demanded. "Let's see your paper."

"Don't have any."

The soldier's forehead creased.

"Check your list," the driver advised. "Most recent permissions."

The soldier reentered the guard shack to flip through sheets on a clipboard. He came back out and saluted. "Right, then. In you go." He gestured to another soldier, who shoved down on a counterweight. The striped pole lifted. The driver let out his clutch and the car rolled ahead.

The building had three stories of brick and stone, or four if you included its lofty towers. Above the main entry was the statue of a royal figure in armor, driving a lance down the throat of a writhing dragon. Beneath this lyrical rendering of St. George, the driver let him out. Here Kristian picked up another redcap, who stood ready to guide him into a restricted part of the glorious old heap.

The building's basement had been redesigned and reinforced to serve as a bunker and air raid shelter. The Cyclops sequestered himself regularly down in a guarded portion of this basement like a troll in his cave. Here he maintained a private office he used to deal with highly sensitive, your-eyes-only issues.

~

Kristian was led past more barred gates and finally ushered into a spartan waiting room. It held only four metal chairs upholstered in baize, and he was deposited on one to twiddle thumbs while awaiting a summons from the gray eminence.

That summons was delivered by a hulking personal guard clad in khaki woolens with no insignia. He also wore the black tennis shoes Kristian had grown to expect on personnel in this outfit. He missed the ones Rolf had made him get rid of in Norway. They'd been wonderfully comfortable. *Perhaps the SIS will issue him another pair. Not that great for November weather, but fantastic otherwise…*

The bodyguard had a stern face garnished with black seven-o'clock shadow, a big Colt .45 automatic holstered on the right side of his Sam Browne belt and a rattan baton in a ring on its left side. He opened a door from an inner hall, looked Kristian over, then beckoned with a finger. Kristian arose, went to him, and entered a box of concrete with a gray metal desk at its center. Shaded bulbs suspended on long cords dropped circles of light on the desk and a man who sat on a metal chair behind it.

The Cyclops did not look up. He slid the tip of a freshly sharpened pencil along the margin of a document as he peered at it through his thick monocle.

The guard pointed at a steel chair in front of the desk. Kristian went to stand beside the chair. He'd found that sitting now had begun to bother his knees. He surveyed the room. In the shadows along the walls he could see black filing cabinets. In one corner stood a tall safe with a combination lock on its door. In an opposite corner was an army field cot with blankets neatly folded at one end, two pillows stacked at the other.

Cyclops looked up. A frosty gray eye behind the glass disc of his monocle regarded Kristian impassively.

"What did you bring me?" Cyclops' raspy, uninflected voice sounded like gravel rattling down a chute.

Kristian put his boot on the seat of the chair and lifted his pant leg, revealing the knife sheath strapped to his calf. The guard took a keen interest in this procedure and Kristian made sure to move slowly. He tugged the green packet out with two fingers and tossed it on the desk. He smiled at the guard.

"What's in it?" Cyclops said.

"Information about a radio-beam system the Germans invented to boost the accuracy of their bombers," Kristian told him. "As I understand it, the *Luftwaffe* sends out their planes along one radio beam, and when the pilots detect another beam, they know they're over a target. So, the destruction can be made most precise, even at night."

Cyclops poked at the packet with a fingertip.

"We know about that already," he rasped. "So much so, we've been able to initiate our counter-measures. Brought down a bomber, quite intact, y'see. Did a close study of its navigation gear. Including all its latest equipment."

Kristian felt the blood drain from his face. Had Helene taken her risk, had he undergone this ordeal of getting her packet to England, for nothing? Dismay burned inside him. Then he realized that he should be thrilled the Brits detected the Germans' technologic trick some other way—since that meant they were already saving lives. And, possibly, some scrap of fresh intelligence lay hidden in the documents Helene had secured, a tip that might still aid the war effort.

Cyclops leaned back in his wooden swivel chair and laced his fingers over a tan cummerbund that was part of his Gurkha uniform.

"But I thank you," he said, as if reading Kristian's thoughts. "We'll have people from Bletchley Park look over your material. Discover any usable bits."

Cyclops flicked a look at his bodyguard. Kristian sensed that his interaction time with the eminence had almost expired. Soon, he'd be escorted out. If he had a point to make, now was the time.

"My papers show locations where the radio towers that broadcast the beams shall be built," Kristian said. "There's a list of frequencies they'll use. As well as the *Luftwaffe's* schedule for shifting them."

Cyclops was already reaching for a fresh folder from a pile of them that loomed atop his desk. But his hand froze in midair. The glass disc clenched in his right eye socket tilted up toward Kristian.

"Really!"

Kristian heard notes of wonder and enthusiasm in the man's voice for the first time.

"Yes." Kristian glanced at the guard, who'd already taken a few steps toward him, seemingly with an intent of grasping his elbow to usher him out. Kristian tapped a finger on the cloth-wrapped dagger under his belt. "May I?"

The guard narrowed his eyes but nodded. He also put his own hand on the haft of his baton.

Kristian drew the knife out, unrolled the fabric, then leaned over the desk. He used the tip of the dagger to slice open Helene's packet. He pulled out the thin sheets of tightly folded paper covered in Helene's tiny scrawl. He slid this onionskin stationery from the Federation Hotel over to Cyclops, who duly spread the sheets out and bent his head over them. After a moment of scrutiny—during which Kristian realized he'd been holding his breath—the Cyclops looked up at him. That somber gray eye behind the lens now appeared to be twinkling.

"I say!" the Cyclops exclaimed. "Nice job. Calls for a spot of celebration, I should think."

He reached down to a lower desk drawer and hauled it open. His hand came back up holding a bottle of Caol Ila—a single malt whisky.

"Quinn?" he said to the guard. "Glasses, if you please. Top drawer, last filing cabinet on the right."

*"Yellow gun flashes are lighting the sky, splinters are rattling on the housetops, and London Bridge is falling down..."*
—George Orwell, *The Lion and the Unicorn*

# CHAPTER 29

"Won't you sit?" the Cyclops inquired. He poured neat doses of the single malt into glass tumblers his bodyguard had placed upon his desk. "The way you keep standing makes me nervous. Relax! Grab a pew too, Quinn. Let's call it teatime. Or, a 'take five,' as the bloody Yanks say."

Kristian sat. He started to cross his legs but a spasm pain in his knees forbade that, so he sat with his legs outstretched. The bodyguard dragged in a chair from the outer office and sat close by. He passed a tumbler to Kristian, who took a sip and decided on the instant that he had a new favorite tipple. He took a larger sip, then another. It made the *Gwynn's Seksti* seem like turpentine. It also made him feel bold, even somewhat suave. He decided to take a chance.

"I didn't believe you for one second," Kristian told the Cyclops.

"Eh? What d'you mean?"

"I make *you* nervous? Isn't your job making everyone else nervous?"

"Quite right," Cyclops said. He chuckled. He raised his tumbler as though it were a chalice, inspected the tawny scotch beneath the light, and thumped it back down. "That is my job. When I question someone, my aim is to see that man end up perched in a puddle of his own sweat."

"Or piss," Quinn put in.

"Only in extreme cases." Cyclops picked up his glass again. "Here's how," he said, then he tossed its whole contents down his throat in a single vigorous move. Kristian was impressed. He doubted he'd ever be able to drink like that. However, the flavor of the Caol Ila certainly gave him ambition. Perhaps his skill would improve with more training.

"When a man proves himself in my employ, I tend to ease up," Cyclops said. He flicked a few stray droplets of whisky off the bottom of his mustache with a forefinger.

"Not invariably," the bodyguard opined.

Quinn had a sly quality, an Irish lilt in his voice. Kristian found himself liking him. He heartily approved of both of these men now, actually. The pervading warmth of the scotch perhaps had something to do with that.

"Blast. I forgot to make a toast. Oh well." Cyclops grasped the Caol Ila and poured himself another healthy dollop. "Altogether fixable. Gentlemen?"

Kristian and Quinn both held out their glasses and were rewarded with another dose.

"To you, young Fiske," Cyclops said. "You may be a mere prat, but you've acquitted yourself well."

"Thank you."

Quinn and Cyclops drained their glasses with one swallow. Cyclops drove the stopper back into the neck of the bottle with the heel of his fist. Kristian felt glad he hadn't tried to toss his own portion down. He hoped to make the tasty stuff last a bit longer. He detected wisdom in pacing himself.

"Does our celebration mean there's more to that green packet than you had first thought?"

"Indeed, it does." Cyclops leaned back and laced his fingers over his cummerbund. "I'd cite the woeful conditions in Coventry, for example. Our radar can say when German bombers are coming and in what force, but not really tell us where they're headed. One month past, Coventry got some bad news delivered via air freight. Five hundred bombers in a single night. *Monscheinsonate—Moonlight Sonata*—the Luftwaffe called this operation. I must tell you, Quinn, those Huns have jolly well scuppered Beethoven for me!"

"Another thing to hate 'em for," Quinn said.

"I don't have the room to put any more reasons on *my* list," Kristian said.

"Thus for us all," Cyclops agreed. "And yes, they used the radio system you described to guide that mission, Fiske. Amazing accuracy. Town center was obliterated. Hundreds of civilians killed, a thousand injured. A third of all factories gone, many homes flattened. And a new threat, the Krauts didn't just drop HE and incendiaries. They floated giant naval mines down on parachutes. As soon as their triggers touched, they detonated at ground level. Like blockbusters."

"Well," Quinn said. "Can't fault them for a lack of creativity."

"No," Cyclops said. "But I chide them for gloating. The bastard Goebbels has coined a new term, '*Conventriert*.' It means, 'We'll do a Coventry on you.' It's now the Nazi plan for London, Plymouth, Manchester, Liverpool, and every other major English town within bomber range."

Cyclops unlaced his fingers and thumped a fist on his desk. "As I said, we did learn of their radio beam system earlier, took steps to disrupt it. Not enough, but some." He pointed a finger at Kristian. "Now, with what you've brought us, we can do much more. Jam their signals, create false beams. Knowing their frequency shifts in advance? Well! Priceless."

"What if we launched commando raids, or targeted bombing runs, against those sending towers?" Quinn suggested. "Since now we know where they are."

"I warrant such measures will be discussed," Cyclops said. "But that first option rather tips our hand, doesn't it? More effective would be a bombing run that seems to go astray. Say, a Hampden with a faulty engine forced to turn out of its squadron. The pilot chooses to dump munitions on some anonymous stretch of shore, before sprinting for home across the Channel. Just happens to hit a radio tower. To the Huns, looks like an accident."

"Devious," Quinn said.

"My specialty, hey?" Cyclops said. "Anyhow! Not so bright of us to have a spy sit right here listening to us jaw about covert tactics."

"No," Quinn agreed. "Were you to reveal anything more, I'd have to kill him."

"Quite right. But what should we do with our lad, short of that? Any place we could send him for a lovely bout of R & R?"

"Uh, well, in truth, I should probably go to hospital. I need to see a doctor."

They both swung their eyes to Kristian.

"What? How's that? What on earth's wrong? You look to be in the pink. Other than being a tad weather-beaten. Which is a commonplace for field agents."

"I cut up my knees a few days ago. They've gone infected."

"Oh. Well. We do possess a medical sanitarium of our own. State-of-the-art, as they say. For those who come back rather the worse for wear. Facility's put well out of harm's way, up near Ruislip Wood. Good place for a debrief, too. Quinn, what do you think? Can we arrange to have someone run him over there?"

"We can always arrange to have someone run over, sir."

"You know that's not what I meant."

"Yes sir, I do. I shall see to it. Straightaway."

"Good. I thank you both." Kristian stood and set his empty tumbler back on the desk. He reached for his knife, then thought better of it. He spun it around, aiming the hilt toward Cyclops, and slid it toward him. "Here. I won't need anything like this for a while. Would you care to have it?"

"Would I?" Cyclops emitted a hoarse laugh. He grasped the knife, looked it over and held it up. "See here, Quinn. Fiske wants me to own a genuine SS letter-opener."

"Very good, sir. I don't think anyone else in the building happens to have a souvenir of like pedigree. Not yet, at any rate."

"Likely correct. I'll use it to point at things on maps in conference. That should help people remember what I say."

"But sir. Can it be that Fiske wishes to ply you with a sort of a bribe, here?"

"To get on my good side? Thought we'd established that I have not got one."

"An attempt to exert undue influence. Perhaps best not to risk it."

"Ah. See what you're saying, there. You want this dagger for yourself."

"Wouldn't turn it down, sir. But only if my taking it off your hands serves to gird up your professional integrity."

"Well, forget it. Fiske bestowed the blade on *me*. And don't for a second dream about trying to pinch it while my back is turned. Just so you can use it to impress that lot of loose women you cavort with while on leave. Oh yes, I know all about your sordid habits, Quinn."

"Of course, sir. And may I say, it delights me to hear that you take such a keen interest in my holidays. Everyone should have a hobby."

A three-story brick house on Breakspear Road appeared in most respects to be a tranquil country home. Its interior looked like a surgery ward. On its ground floor were whitewashed inspection and treatment spaces. The top two floors were divided into small rooms equipped with hospital beds. Kristian was brought up to one via a wheelchair pushed onto an electric lift by an orderly.

The lift ride followed his inspection, diagnosis and treatment by a doctor who did nothing to conceal his dismay at the deteriorated condition of Kristian's knees. He *clucked* and frowned a great deal while he looked Kristian over. The verdict he delivered held few surprises, but they were big ones.

"Had you treated this promptly and properly, you wouldn't be in such dreadful shape," the doctor scolded.

"Had to keep moving. I was on a mission," Kristian said.

"Oh, now there's a novel excuse," the doctor said.

"I'd bet not."

"Medical humor," the doctor said. "Indulge me."

The physician was middle-aged, with crow's feet that fanned out from the corners of his eyes to his ears, and an omega of gray hair that only served to emphasize the gleaming pate it bracketed.

"I've done the best I could with what little I had," Kristian told him. "Alcohol disinfectant. Silver gel. But I couldn't change the dressings often, and I couldn't stop getting wet. One person said my kneecaps were not broken. Are they?"

"They are not. And that's your sole bit of good news. But it's damn near overwhelmed by the bad. The kneecaps are likely merely chipped or cracked. The tendons may be torn somewhat—how badly, I can't tell without surgery. I'll get clues after we snip away some of the damage. The big issue here is your infection. It's ugly and it's deep. If it can't be curtailed, you're looking at a serious operation."

"How serious?"

"The first would be to remove the kneecaps."

"After that, would I be all right?"

The doctor folded one arm across his chest, perched his other elbow on it, and pinched his chin between thumb and forefinger. "Well, it would reduce your chances of dying from sepsis. But you'd never walk again."

Kristian was lying face-up on an examination table. At this, he sat bolt upright. The doctor put a hand on his chest and gently pushed him back down. Kristian's eyes watered as they rolled from side-to-side. He began to pant. Then he sucked in a deep breath and cleared his throat.

"You said, my 'first' operation, doctor. Does it mean there'd be another?"

"Depends."

"On what?"

"Your infection. And your choices. A complete amputation might be something that you'd prefer. I know I would. Both of your legs would then be fitted with prosthetics. You'd be able to walk—after a fashion. Rather stiffly. Moving from the hips, like Mr. Roosevelt, the current American president. Have you ever seen him go up to a podium in newsreels? Yes, he's stiff and slow and he staggers a bit, but he can still move."

Kristian swallowed hard several times. *Vær sterk. Vær nordisk,* he thought. He repeated the phrase until he could feel the essence of the motto start to calm him.

"All right," he said, and blinked. "You said, the operations happen if this infection isn't stopped. So, how can we stop it?"

The doctor smiled. A thin smile, not hearty, yet sincere.

"Good man," he said. He reached down to pat Kristian on the shoulder. "I like to trot out worst-case scenarios straight off with you tough blokes. Once you confront the ugliest prospects, the balance of your prognosis might not sound so bad.

"Here's what we'll do first. I'm going to dig out all the bad tissue I can reach, right now. I must warn you, that will hurt like a bastard. Then we wrap your knees in salt packs that we change twice a day. Your job will be to lie flat on your back with these things on you for a week, while hoping for the best. Those packs will sting, all the damn time, a level of pain that will be constant, boring, and unescapable. During that time, perhaps I can scavenge up a drop or two of morphine to keep you comfy.

"Next, should we find your infection isn't responding, well, there's one more measure we might try—maggots."

"No! Seriously?"

The doctor nodded. "Sounds medieval, I know. But thanks to research by Dr. Baer at Johns Hopkins in the U.S., we know it's one of the most precise forms of debridement we can apply. If salt packs don't turn the trick, it's a further technique to try."

"I..." Kristian felt himself at an utter loss for words. Then he recovered. "No maggots. No amputations. I promise you! I'll make those salt packs to do the job."

"Are you a praying man?"

"No. But I do know of a good young lady who claims that she prays for me."

"Excellent. Let's hope she has the ear of the Almighty. Now, I want you to lay back and concentrate on holding yourself still. I'll summon a nurse to assist me. Then both of us shall make you suffer for a while. After that, you win a long bout of rest. Sleep as much and as often as you want. Mentally, I want you to only focus on that—a period of stupor and sloth isn't far from your reach. You'll get there soon."

~

Like howls from a far-flung pack of metallic wolves, air-raid sirens went off at sites across London to announce a fresh approach by a wave of German bombers. After several long minutes of this eerie screech, the night sky was filled by a grinding sound. It was the blended rumble of scores of aircraft engines, wafting down from on high.

Scattered, echoing *bangs* from distant anti-aircraft artillery began, then came a full chorus of those guns as their rounds rocketed upward to counter the invaders. Next was heard a *crump! Crump! CRUMP!* of exploding bombs. It sounded as if a wrathful Titan had begun to march across the city, gleefully stomping flat whatever happened to lie in his path.

Kristian aroused himself from the highly medicated stupor in which he'd lounged for three days. He groped around the head of the bed for his cane, raised it and used its tip to push apart the blackout curtains that shrouded his window. Only a dim nightlight bulb shone in his room, so he did not compromise the facility's safety. His hospital bed was tilted just enough to allow him to peer out.

The sanitarium's location, on a ridge on the city's western outskirts, and his room's position on an upper floor, afforded him an overview of London under siege. A cherry-red glow had begun to saturate the cityscape, a result of spreading fires. He could see miniscule black outlines of buildings and the feeble spikes of church steeples silhouetted against this hellish light like the peaky cutouts a child might scissor from paper.

A sudden roar of an airplane diving low somewhere nearby, the fevered clatter of machine guns and another aircraft's racing engine dominated briefly before blending back into the overall din.

Kristian puffed his cheeks and blew out a breath, frowning. Had the intelligence he'd brought done the British any real good?

Outside, the ruby glow on the ground began to broaden and swell, inflating into a dome of surreal light that soon threatened to occlude the entire heavens. The clouds above took on a sickly pink cast, and where no clouds were present, the red incandescence first shifted toward yellow, then a noisome green, before fading into the absolute stygian black of night. On the glow's vague periphery, Kristian thought he could detect a few white pinpricks of stars.

He tried to imagine what it would be like to be an AA gunner, an air raid warden, or an Auxiliary fireman out there in the rampaging inferno, battling to remain alive while also performing terrifying chores, even attempting desperate acts of mercy.

He lowered his cane, let the drapes close, sank back upon the mattress, utterly drained. He'd succumbed to Doctor Thompson's invitation to use morphine, less as an effort to control pain—though it certainly proved miraculous at that task—and more as a way to burrow into a torpor that let time pass without feeling riven with impatience over its dragging pace. Healing demanded he remain inactive and passive, a policy utterly at odds with his basic nature. He yearned to find some path back into the war, then sprint down it. Yet he had to admit, many days would have to lapse before he could seriously contemplate doing so.

That is, if he ever could return.

That last notion was one he loathed, one he found wearying to fight off. It repeated in his brain like the gong of a grandfather clock, inflecting the plodding pace of all his waking hours. He refused to admit that he might've already shot his bolt. But he also realized a day might come when he'd need to accept it. And on the other side of that day stretched a drab future he didn't care to visualize.

The door to his room creaked open. A nurse entered.

"So! How are we, tonight?" she inquired brightly.

Her voice was familiar, but Kristian's brain was too befogged to apply any name or identity to it. A quartet of nurses had rotated through shifts to take care of him, including the one who had helped Doctor Thompson work on his knees. Jane, he thought her name was.

"*Båtlaus mann er bunden til land,*" he muttered. It was one more of Ragnar's aphorisms.

"How's that, again?"

"A boat-less man is shackled to the land," he translated.

"Well then, we must see if there's a way for us to get you afloat again, yes?" she replied. "I hear there's nothing more worth doing than messing about with boats. Which would sort of make me Rat to your Mole now, right?"

Kristian's brow furrowed as he struggled to make sense of this odd clump of verbiage. Didn't sound like anything a nurse might say. Or anyone else, for that matter.

She came over to the bed and leaned over him. She unpinned and removed her winged cap. She was a short-haired blond. Then she unbuttoned her starchy white dress and let it fall to the floor. Kristian was startled. His eyes widened. He saw the woman now wore just a peachy taffeta slip that showed off a slim body with small, firm breasts. He shot up to full wakefulness like a diver accelerating from the sea's depths to its glittering surface.

"Hello, Kris," Greta murmured. "Thought I might drop by for a short visit. Heard you'd wandered back to us, all drenched in glory. I aim to see if I can add a wee dose of joy to this otherwise too gloomy Yule. D'you mind if I finish unwrapping your present?"

"No! Not hardly," he said. "Greta, I can't tell you how amazing it is for me to see you in this dreary place. For days and days, I've only been able to look at either my bandaged knees or that grotesque rumpus going on every night outside."

As he said this, he realized the uproar from the latest German bombing run had lessened somewhat. The current wave seemed to be ending. Of course, it would likely repeat. Perhaps within a few hours.

"Ah, looking at you now rests me so much. You bring me joy. It makes me think that perhaps all things could still work out for the best."

Greta smirked. "Don't want to rest *too* much, do you Kris? Might lose your edge." She drew back the covers. "Perhaps a bit of light, therapeutic exercise could be the ticket. Now, don't worry," she said. "I'll be brilliant. Gentle and careful. Just lean back and let me apply your therapy."

"I must ask. Did my doctor approve of this treatment of yours?"

"No. He might've, if he only knew. However, I made sure that he won't. See, I'm for your eyes only."

She brought her face before his, stared and smiled at him for a moment. Then her eyes closed and she moved her parted lips down to a point just above his, where they paused, hovered. He shut his own eyes then and just lay there, basking in her warm breath, the aroma of tobacco, her perfume, whatever was in her hair... And finally he could stand the suspense no longer, he lifted his head off the pillow a fraction of an inch to kiss her first.

Greta's hands were on his shoulders, pushing him back into the mattress. Her mouth was on his, pushing Kristian's head back onto the pillow. And her slip was hiked up past her hips as she swung a leg over him and pressed his whole torso down into the bed.

Her tongue was fast, pointed, darting. Her lips loose and yielding, then tight and hard. Her teeth took his lower lip in between them.

A vision of Helene drifted through his mind. He shooed it away. And he felt guilty about that right afterward. But then in the minutes that followed, he didn't.

~

The next morning, a man in a bowler hat had himself driven across a still-smoldering London, to an address on Howletts Lane. The chauffer, a Sikh in a dark suit and a turban, steered a sleek Humber Pullman sedan to the curb before a two-story home with shrouded bay windows, where he braked to a stop.

A curtain was pulled back on a downstairs window by the house's front door. A square-jawed man wearing a khaki uniform without insignia peered out. He studied the car for a long second. A moment later, the front door swung open and the man waved to them. Then he disappeared, leaving the door ajar.

"Should I wait here, sir?" the Sikh asked.

"Do, Guneet, if you please," Stewart Menzies said. "I shan't be long."

Menzies—head of the Secret Intelligence Service—clapped the rear door of the car shut, then jogged nimbly up the front steps of the home. The door swung wide open and the Cyclops himself stood in the opening to greet him. He was still clad in his bedchamber attire: a velveteen smoking jacket, pajama bottoms and shabby leather slippers that looked as if they'd been gnawed by a litter of pups.

"Hullo, Stu," he said.

"Robbie," Menzies responded.

"You're just past time for second breakfast. Care to partake? I'm sure we've got assorted bits left. Some, certainly."

"No thanks. But I'll take tea, if you've got it."

"Darjeeling all right? Oolong."

"Always!"

"Come in, then."

The square-jawed man, who'd watched this exchange, went back to the front parlor. He set himself down on a hassock by the window and picked up a newspaper.

Robbie led Stu into a sitting room and tugged a chair away from a highly polished walnut table garlanded with doilies and lace placemats. He gestured that his visitor should take a chair. He then leaned through a swinging door and called out. "Henrietta? More tea. And cakes, if you please."

He slid out his own chair.

"Good to see you let yourself relish a day or so of rest at least every other month, Robbie," Menzies said drily.

"The horse collar does tend to rub one's hide raw in a few spots, and that's a fact," the Cyclops responded.

"Y'know, it's rumored that even our Deity takes off one in seven. Sets a sterling example for us all. You should think it over. I mean, if it's good enough for Him…"

"Well, I'd bolt for that option like a shot, but the Huns won't ever let me do it. What a lot of bloody persistent, highly, highly annoying buggers they are to be sure, I must say."

A set of double doors burst open. A stout woman in a frilly apron backed into the room bearing a tray.

"Ah! Here's some balm for the soul. It's from Bengal, not Gilead. But it just might turn the trick," Robbie said.

She poured them each tea, and Robbie brusquely nodded a thanks to her before she turned around and left. He picked up a pair of silver tongs and poised them over the sugar bowl. "One lump? Two?" he asked.

"I've already had all the lumps a man could ever wish for," Menzies said.

"Suppose that's true. Milk, then?"

"Certainly. A dollop. I'll add it. Pass it here, if you would."

"You'll like the cakes. Lemon custard. Henrietta excels at them."

"Aces." Menzies gave a thumbs up.

They sipped their tea in silence for a moment. The Cyclops removed his monocle, polished its glass with his napkin and screwed it back into his eye socket. He peered at Menzies. "How did the 'Knickebein' dossier play out?"

"Oh, what we call 'Headache' y'mean? Splendid," Menzies said. "We applied 'Aspirin.' Made a Liverpool raid go all wrong. Hugh Dowding tells me there should be more successes like that in weeks to come. That lead your man Fiske gave us on frequency shifts was pivotal. Once Goering has a chance to pore over his recon photos, he's likely to soil his silken drawers. Many a bomb wasted on rural hayricks. All their planes and pilots put at risk for bloody naught! Cheery news for us. For him and the *Luftwaffe*, not so much."

"Aha. But shall Field Marshal Der Blimpo Goering redouble his air war, or slacken it now, d'ye think?"

"Pivotal question. Only time will tell. He doubtless must recalibrate, though."

"Blimpo and those other tossers have already made a pair of huge errors. One might well hope for more."

"Indeed. How would you reckon it?"

Robbie raised an index finger. "First was in September. They quit bombing radar stations, RAF fields, hangars, and aircraft production. Back then, our losses had begun to exceed our replacement ability by a nasty margin. But they switched over to terror bombing London. Even as our RAF lads had been shoved back onto their heels. Quite a boneheaded move on the part of the Hun. Wonder whose decision it was."

"Could've been Goering, could've been Kesselring, or both." Menzies tapped the table with a finger. "Ask me, my money's on Hitler. He's the shot-caller. And you shouldn't underestimate the crappy judgment potential of a megalomaniac in a snot-flinging rage."

"Believe you me, I don't. Anyhow. Once they started thumping London, if those bastards really knew what they were about, they should've dumped all their ordnance on our east side. The working poor would've seen that as clear evidence of connivance between their upper crust and our posh set over here. Oswald Mosley—or perhaps some rampaging populist over on the left wing—could've scored a flood of fresh recruits. Maybe both wings would've won. Anyway, between the Reds and Mosley's brownshirts, our ruling class would end up out on their bums. And who can say what sort of confusion might reign, after?"

Menzies smiled. "You must appreciate then the Queen Mother's comment after Buckingham itself got whacked. 'Well, I'm glad we've been bombed. Now I feel we can look the East End in the face.'"

"Truly. Rather astute of the old girl." Robbie said.

"What's the word now, on our agent who brought us the goods?"

Robbie thrust out his hand palm-down and waggled it slightly. "Ah yes, Fiske. His condition isn't the best, sorry to say. Legs damaged badly. Future hangs in the balance, that sort of thing."

"Might a medal cheer him up?"

"Doubt it. Norwegians don't seem to lust for such. Officers in their regular navy, maybe. But these fishermen, no. They'd probably heave it over the side, dangle it for a lure."

"Shall we keep Fiske attached to the Service, then? Or engineer some sort of honorable retirement? Assuming he survives, I mean. Surely the man's condition is not as dire as all that. Or is it?"

"Well, the medicos say it all has to be watch-and-wait. Greta's keeping an eye on him."

"Only an eye?"

"A very good eye."

"Ah. His morale should improve somewhat."

"No question. Mine would."

The Cyclops propped his elbows atop the table and steepled his fingers. He tapped them against each other. "Fiske has proven himself, beyond all doubt. Yet hiring him was purely a matter of timing. That was simply us making hay of circumstance. Opportunistic, yes, but there it is. Ordinarily, he wouldn't have been such a great fit for us. And he still may not be. An agent must have initiative, an ability to carve space for independent action. Fiske's got those things, but his talents are in wild excess. He's a natural rogue, a soloist if you will. A colt who holds the bit in his teeth and shakes his head at a mere touch of the reins."

"Agreed, that he's a thruster. More ways than one. Just read his debrief. Rather stupefied by it, actually. One reason I wished to visit. You buy that whole bloody narrative?"

Robbie spread his hands. "Fiske's no braggart. All other reports dovetail with his."

"And yet you still don't want to use him?"

"Our SIS is like an orchestra, Stu. One we've put a great lot of trouble into assembling. All elements are designed to act in concert. Not always in harmony, mind you, but consistently. We've rehearsed. We have a score. And we follow a conductor. Of course, you."

"Yes," Menzies responded vaguely. He sipped tea, replaced his cup in the saucer. "Does that mean you're ready to ship him off to the infant SOE, then? And you wish me to sign off."

Robbie smiled. "Stu, were you a lady, I think we'd be able to waltz through the entire ball without you ever treading on a toe. Right! And since Winnie's appointed Dalton to chief of the SOE, I'd say he and Fiske would make a brilliant match."

Menzies answered the Cyclop's grin with his own. "Dalton *did* see our need to face the fascist threat, early on. He's keen for the work, and highly creative. On the other hand, the man oft does put the 'prick' back in 'prickly.' Won't suffer fools gladly, and will shuffle as many staffers as he can into that category."

"One difficult bastard deserves another. Matter settled. More tea?"

"Thanks. And there's that new outfit inside of the SOE. Norwegian Special Independent Company or whatnot, right?"

"Right. More fishermen. Fiske was our first, but it seems he'll be far from the last. These men are independent and willful. They even dislike having their king order them around, so they especially hate having Germans hold sway in their homeland. They've begun to move commandos, radios and munitions into Norway, while toting refugees from the Gestapo back out. Using only their fishing smacks! Have a secret naval base a'building for them in the Shetlands, even as we speak."

Menzies groped in his jacket pocket for his pipe. Without bothering to fill or light it, he popped its stem into a corner of his mouth. "Consider the Norwegian nation, as a whole," he said. "What, a full fleet of merchant ships plus the crews on 'em that've defected? Near a thousand? And trade unions, school teachers, even ministers—for heaven's sake!—have joined their Resistance. Compare that to France. Somehow, I doubt there shall ever be a Vichy Norway."

"Yes. Occupying Norway is a formidable problem for der Führer. Like trying to corral a wild lynx with your bare hands, I think. Hitler's scheme to turn the country into a fort to protect his flank shall prove doomed in toto, I believe. We're about to discover who can be more stubborn—Norwegians or Nazis. I know how I'd bet. My wager's success will be cinched by men like Fiske."

"Cast our hound out for another run then, hey? Over the fences and through the hedges we go." Menzies said. "Tally ho! If any rider hoists a mask in Berlin, we do humbly implore heaven that it bears a toothbrush mustache." He took a nibble of a lemon bar. "Spectacular," he said. "Relay my compliments to Henrietta."

"Definitely. She'll be tickled."

ALSO BY PAUL McHUGH

CAME A HORSEMAN

THE BLIND POOL

DEADLINES